Die For You

A
Zanne Sweeney
Stand-alone
Romantic Suspense

Dedicated to all members of our Armed Forces, past and present.
Partial proceeds from this book will go to the Semper Fi Fund.

1

1998 Belle

I was five years old. My momma and gram were standing beside me. My great grandmother, Gigi, stood across from us. A rectangular hole in the ground separated us. Pastor John, with his black robe and starchy white collar, stood at one end of the earthy pit. Across from him was a mound of freshly dug dirt that beckoned me. I wanted to climb on top of that pile of dirt and slide down it. I smiled imagining how filthy I would get, and how that would then warrant a visit to the swimming hole to clean off all that dirt. That would be awesome!

As Pastor John spoke I continued to daydream about swimming. My momma kept a clean house, so I would first have to swim with my clothes on, to get all that loose dirt off me. Then I would strip down and skinny dip. There was just something so exciting about swimming naked. The stream was very secluded and no one except my family ever saw me. Yet, somehow I knew, even at my young age, that skinny- dipping was something other people did not partake in on a regular basis as we did.

The sun was brilliant and blinding and I held my hand over my brow to shield my eyes. Gram tapped my hand gently urging it down. There was a slight breeze rustling the tops of the pointy tall pine trees nearby, but unfortunately the breeze did not reach us. I could smell the musky pine scent though. I loved that smell and often made little sachets with the fragrant pine needles. Large black birds sailed through the cloudless sky above us. My momma nudged me gently with her hip bringing my attention back to my great - grand father's funeral.

A man I'd never seen before stood behind us during the service. I wanted to peek at him, but I knew I would be reprimanded if I did, so I stared straight ahead. The man had been standing as still as a statue near the open grave when we had arrived. I had been captivated with his blue jacket with shiny buttons. I noticed his white belt too. I wondered if he had borrowed the belt from my momma because she had one that looked just like it.

Pastor John read from a worn Bible, and Gigi dabbed the corners of her eyes where her skin was lightly creased with fan-shaped lines. I knew she referred to those lines as crow's feet and that thought made me look up to the sky again at the birds above. I refocused back to my Gigi and saw that she was wiping away tears. That scared me because my Gigi never cried. I hated that she was sad and I wanted to hug her. She said my hugs were the best.

Pastor John began to recite a prayer that I knew by heart, and when I heard my Momma, Gigi, and Gram saying it with him, I joined them. I didn't hear the man behind me saying the Our Father prayer; I guess he didn't know it.

After the prayer ended my mom and gram escorted me to the edge of the grave. They threw in the flowers that they had been holding. I peered over the edge before throwing in my one flower. A long knotty pine box sat in the bottom of the hole. I had thought I might see my great-grandfather lying in there. I'd never met him, but I did know what he looked like because my Gigi kept a picture of her and him on her nightstand that was taken on their wedding day. I realized he must be inside the box and a tremendous amount of relief surged through my little body because I didn't want to see a dead person, even if it was my great-grandfather.

My daisy was resting on top of the wooden box, as were the black eye Susan's that my Momma had tossed in. Grams honeysuckle bouquet had missed the box and lay between the box and the dirt wall. I guess it didn't matter though because no one jumped into the hole to resituate them.

We backed up from the grave and I watched as the man in the pretty outfit come forward with a folded American flag and handed it to Gigi. Gigi took it and I heard her whisper a thank you to him. The Pastor said a few more words and then my momma and gram took my hands. We walked away from our family cemetery that was up on the hill in the East Meadow. I glanced behind me and saw the Pastor talking with the man in the fancy outfit, and I saw Gigi sorrowfully looking down into the hole. She tossed her flowers into the grave and blew a kiss before following behind us.

Later that night when we were sitting out back watching the fireflies and listening to the sounds of the night Gigi started talking about her Maxwell, my great grandfather. Gigi wasn't the talkative type, so when she started reminiscing I kept my mouth shut and listened.

She said he had been a tough, but kind man. They had married and then the very next day he left to fight in the Korean War. I watched as my Gigi smiled gently and patted my Gram's hand. She said that God blessed her that first night they had been together as husband and wife, because God knew what was going to happen to my great-grandfather. I sat on the cool flagstone patio leaning against my Momma's legs listening to my Gigi speak. My great- grandfather had been a Marine. Two things I learned that evening was; Once a Marine, always a Marine, and that a Marine never leaves anyone behind. My Momma explained what that last statement meant, and I was instantly so proud of my great-grandfather for being a Marine. Then Gigi told me that the fancy dressed man who had handed her the flag was a Marine. He had stayed up on the hill with my Great-Grandfather the entire night before the funeral. I figured he didn't want my Great Grandfather to be scared up there, all alone. When I said that to Gigi she smiled and said I was correct. I instantly fell in love with those Marines.

Gigi continued talking with a day dreamy look in her eyes. Her voice got a little wobbly as she talked. My great-grandfather proudly served his country,

but when he came home from the war he was
never of the right mind again. Then he got real
sick, and he went to live in a hospital just for brave
men like him who also fought in wars. Gigi visited
him twice a month. I knew that already because I
would sometimes make extra get-well cards, so she
could give them to the men that were there that
didn't have any family.

2

2009

Eleven years later, I was once again standing between my momma and gram at the family cemetery on the hill near our home. I was sixteen years old. Doc Ellersby and Mr. Bee were standing behind us. The aromatic scent of the nearby pine trees triggered the memory of the last time I had attended a funeral; when we had buried my Gigi's husband.

This time was to bury my Gigi. I tried very hard not to cry, but tears clouded my vision and escaped to slip down my cheeks. Gram handed me a handkerchief, and I remembered how Gigi had used one at her husband's funeral. That memory made my tears fall faster. I was trying to be brave, but I was so, so sad. I was sixteen and fully grown as my Gigi had said. Gram was stoic as she listened to Pastor John, out of all of us, she was the least emotional. My momma, who was the most emotional of us four, covered her face with her hands, but I knew she was crying because her shoulders were moving up and down.

I had been living with Gigi, Gram, and Momma in our farmhouse since I was born. They were my family, my everything. The three women had homeschooled me and taught me everything I knew.

I hadn't even known schools existed until I was ten. While on a trip into town my momma and I were walking to the market and a girl about my size passed by us. Even though her Momma tried to hush her I heard her say, "Is that the poor girl who can't go to school?"

I immediately asked my momma what school was. I wanted to know why I couldn't go to school. She gave me quick explanation. It sounded fun, and I liked that there were other kids there to play with. I yearned to play with someone other than my Gigi, Gram, Momma, and the animals.

My momma said she wouldn't answer any more questions about school until we got home. That night the three of them explained why I didn't go to school. Momma told me it was too far to travel to every day. We lived a good twenty minutes by car out of town, and the school was even further away in the next town over. My gram said that everything I needed to learn I could learn from them. My Gigi explained that I was too smart for school, and she didn't want me to have to hide how intelligent I was like she had done.

My Gigi had been very smart. Gram had told me she was considered a genius. I didn't even know what that had meant at the time. Gigi explained to me, in a very matter-of-fact manner, that men didn't like it when women were smarter than them, so she learned to dummy down her intellect. I still didn't understand why she needed to do that, but it had something to do with finding a husband.

My Gigi had been the one to teach me about math and science. She also knew a lot about healing people and animals, so she taught me about medicine too. Gigi had been a nurse and had graduated from a local college with a degree. She had wanted to be a doctor, but she had been dating my great grandfather at the time, and he said it would be embarrassing if she became a doctor, because it would appear that his wife was smarter than he was. Gigi's parents had also squelched her dreams saying that when she, my Gigi, had children she could easily quit being a nurse and be a stay at home mom. At that time that was what women were supposed to do. Gigi told me she accepted her situation, and she did marry, and was, of course, blessed with Gram, so I never heard her complain about her not becoming a doctor. I did know she kept up on her learning. Neighbors often called upon her when they had a medical emergency, and Doc Ellersby could not be reached. My Gram was amazingly smart too. She taught me how to read and write, and she knew all about history. Not just American history, but even other countries history. She said it was important to learn history so that we don't repeat bad mistakes made by our predecessors. My Gram had also been married. I never knew him either. He was a truck driver and had traveled a lot. I learned that they had only been married a month before he was killed in an accident during a snowstorm. The day my grandfather was killed was also the day my Gram realized she was pregnant with my Momma.

She never even had the opportunity to tell him he was going to be a father. Gram told me he would have been a wonderful father.

Now, my Momma, she was not as book smart as my Gigi or Gram, but she could do plenty around our little farm. Important stuff too. She taught me all the practical things, for instance, I could sew, fix things around the house, plant a garden, milk a cow, kill, pluck and cook chicken. I seriously hated the killing part, so after I had shown my Momma that I could do it, just that one time, she never made me do it again.

We all had jobs to do to keep our farm running. My Gigi had taken care of the house and helped with the doctoring when someone got sick or hurt or when Doc Ellersby couldn't be reached. My Gram took care of the outside of the house, including the farm. She mowed the lawn and kept the barn in order, and the farm machines running. My Momma told me that when she had been a little girl, Gram had used Henny, our horse, to pull the old wooden scraper down our long drive to clear the snow from it. Now Gram used a plow that we attached to our truck. I remembered one time when we had a small leak in our homes tin roof. Gram had climbed up there while it was still raining, with a welding torch and a sheet of metal, and fixed it.

When I was younger, Gram was the one who would go into town for supplies, but when I learned to read that job fell to my Momma and me. We loved visiting Lansing, the small town near us.

We would stop at the public library, and I would pick out books. The library was my third favorite place to be; our stone patio behind our home and the old swimming hole were a tie for my first favorite places.

My Momma did all the cooking and the laundry. She cooked every meal and often cooked extra for less fortunate people that Pastor John occasionally mentioned. Momma sewed most of our clothes and could make a dress in a day. She would patch up our jeans when they got worn, and she could knit and quilt too. Every bedroom in our home had a quilt laying on the bed and curtains hanging in the windows that she had made. My Momma's most favorite job was taking care of our garden. It was big and surrounded by a very tall, sturdy fence that also ran a foot underground. My Gram had built it before I was born. She'd been determined that no rabbits, deer or any other animals were getting into Momma's precious garden. My Momma grew all kinds of vegetables and fruits. We had rows of strawberries, blueberries, pumpkins, and even two apple trees, and one cherry tree. Each spring Momma started the vegetables in a small greenhouse that was next to the garden and then she would transplant them into the garden when the weather warmed. It was a big production transplanting all those fragile seedlings, and we all had to help Momma on the day she declared planting day.

I looked just like my Momma; everyone said so.
Well, everyone meaning the five or six people I
knew. When I was younger, I thought that meant I
was also supposed to be like her too. I tried to like
sewing and quilting, but I didn't; it was boring.
After a while, my Momma finally conceded that I
was never going to enjoy the things that she did.
Thankfully, she was satisfied that although I was
proficient in sewing, cooking, even knitting, I was
much happier being outside.
I had daily chores just like Gigi, Gram, and my
Momma. I baked the bread every morning and
took care of the animals. I also helped with the
canning. I liked picking the fruit the best, and I
helped in the garden in the summer and fall. I
didn't enjoy weeding, but I liked eating, so that was
a trade-off. When I finished with those daily
chores, I had to do my schoolwork, then any
remaining time was mine to use as I pleased. My
favorite pastimes were swimming in the summer
and reading in the winter.

My Momma nudged my shoulder with hers,
bringing me back to the present, and sadly Gigi's
funeral. Pastor John recited The Lord's Prayer and
my Momma, Gram, and I spoke it with him. When
the Pastor finished the prayer, he walked over to
two men, who were standing off to the side and
spoke with them. Then he walked to Doc Ellersby
and Mr. Bee. Mr. Bee was a lawyer and a family
friend who handled our finances. They had been
standing behind us during the service. The three

men left our little family plot and waited quietly outside of the iron enclosure.

I asked who the two men were that Pastor John had spoken too, pointing at the two men remaining and Momma said that they were church helpers that would fill in the grave. I gently rubbed my red palms together and silently wondered why they had not dug the grave too. I didn't remember if they had been at my great-grandfather's funeral. We had spent the better part of yesterday digging Gigi's grave. We climbed the hill with shovel's and a string and as Gram marked off the grave dimensions with the string she said digging the graves of our family members was a family tradition. I knew better than to question her or worse to even think about complaining, so we quietly spent the day digging my Gigi's final resting place. I told momma that I didn't remember digging my great-grandfather's grave. She said I was too young, and they had done it when I'd gone to bed.

After we each said a tearful good-bye to my Gigi we walked down the hill to our home. We served Pastor John, Doc Ellerby and Mr. Bee a meal. The grown-ups chatted while I played outside with Josh, our hound dog. After the men left, we had a family meeting and divided up my Gigi's jobs. We still had a house and a farm to run.

With Gigi gone. I became the chief medic for our family and our animals. I continued to read Gigi's medical books and made Momma get a subscription to a quarterly Veterinarian magazine. I was also going to help Momma with the family's laundry too. Gram would clean the bathrooms, and my Momma would clean the rest of the house. Even with all my chores, I kept up with my homeschooling. I was already two years ahead of where I would be if I attended a regular school. My Gram and Momma were very proud of me.

When my Momma and I would drive into town we had a routine. First, we would stop at Mr. Bee's office, I would wait in the outer office area, and after a few minutes, my Momma would return with an envelope of money. Then we would go to the post office where we would mail my completed lessons to the school I was registered at, and pick up an envelope containing new lessons.

After we left the post office, we would head to the hardware store, which had a grain and feed section. There we would purchase feed for the animals, and anything else Gram needed for the house or barn. Then, best of all, we would visit the library. At the library, I would check out books to read just for fun. According to the library rules, a person was only allowed to take five books at a time, but Mrs. Bee, who was Mr. Bee's wife, was the head Librarian and we were allowed to take as many books as we wanted. My Momma loved going to the library too, because before we left Mrs. Bee always handed my Momma a paper bag full of month-old magazines. My Momma loved those magazines. She'd read through every one of them and sometimes, at night if Gram approved, she would read articles to us out loud. Gram had to deem them educational or newsworthy. My Gram would not allow me to look through the magazines on my own, even as I got older. My Momma had to keep them in her bedroom, because Gram said they were filled with garbage, and she didn't want what was in them to clutter my mind with useless thoughts. I secretly wondered why it was okay that Momma was allowed to 'clutter her thoughts,' but again I wisely kept my uncluttered thoughts to myself.

The last place we would go to in town was the market. We always went to the market last so we could get the cold food home before it spoiled. The market sat directly across the street from the town's diner, and I always liked to watch the people that were sitting inside at the booths near the large windows. There were picnic tables that were placed outside the diner during the warmer months, where we would often see people eating. My Momma said it had always been a local hang out. I loved to watch people, and so did my Momma, it was our little secret that we had shared.

I always looked forward to those trips into town, but as I grew older, I began to notice things; like how people stared at us when we walked past them. I began to realize that my clothes were different than most girls. Except for the jeans I wore, all my clothes were handed down from my momma or hand sewn by her. The library not only had books and magazines they also had computers. I listened to the radio every morning, and I knew those computers were how people connected to the Internet. I took out a book about technology so that I could understand what the internet was. It was fascinating, but I didn't understand many of the technical terms, so it was a difficult read. I gleaned enough to grasp the concept of what the Internet was. I wanted to learn more about televisions too, even though we didn't have one. There was a small television set on the wall behind the cash register at the hardware store. It was always tuned to a news station. I wished we could have a television, so did Momma, but Gram wouldn't even consider it. When we got a washer and dryer my Momma baked my Gigi and Gram special dinners for a month to show them how much she appreciated those two machines.

I learned about cell phones too. I often saw people talking into the little handheld objects; even kids that were my age had phones. I didn't even bother wanting one of those; whom would I talk too? We didn't even have a landline in our house. My family didn't talk to anyone other than a few people, and Gram said if someone wanted to talk to us they could come to the house. I knew that I was being brought up differently than most other teenagers, but except for wishing I had someone my own age to talk and play with, I was pretty content.

I remembered one time when I was fourteen, I had accompanied my Gram to the hardware store. Mr. Greeter's son, who was about my age, had tried to talk to me. Before I knew what was happening, my Gram dragged me out of the store and made me sit in the truck. She then went back inside the store, and I could see her waving her finger at Mr. Greeter and then pointing at his son. After that, whenever I went into the store, if the boy was there, he went into the back room. I don't know why my family was keeping me so sheltered, but I was brought up to respect my elders. I knew if I started asking questions they would not be happy.

That night, after we had buried my Gigi, I felt such sorrow that my insides hurt. I knew Gram, and my Momma were sad too because even though they tried to hide it, I saw their eyes were red and watery. Gram was more ornery than usual, and my Momma who always smiled just couldn't seem to muster one.

3

2015

I was twenty-one and Gram was sick, really sick. I
had tried everything to ease her pain. She was
coughing like crazy and had been running a fever
for five days straight. Nothing I did seemed to
help. Her shallow breaths were horrifying to listen
too; gurgles and desperate wheezes. I knew she
would soon suffocate from lack of oxygen, so I
made Momma drive to town to get Doc Ellersby.
Gram's eyes bugged out when she saw him. She
didn't like men in general and she sure as heck did
not like the doctor. My Gigi had liked him, but not
Gram, not at all. Unfortunately for Gram she was
too weak to protest.
I helplessly looked on as Doc Ellersby placed his
stethoscope on Gram's chest and tapped her back.
He looked into her eyes and down her throat, and
he even looked at her fingernails. I knew he was
looking at what color they were. When they
changed color, it meant the body wasn't getting
enough oxygen. I had done all those things too, but
I still felt better that the Doc was there. When he
finished his examination, he confirmed what I had
figured; that Gram had a lung infection and needed
to be hospitalized. Gram was weak and slipping in
and out of consciousness, but she forbade us to
take her to the hospital. Doc Ellersby even pleaded
with her, but Gram was stubborn. She said if it was

her time she wanted to die in her home with her family.

Doc Ellersby finally gave up trying to persuade her, so before he left; he gave me medicine to help ease her coughing.

After the Doc left, I asked my Momma why Gram didn't like him. She told me that the good doctor had tried to convince my Gram to give her up for adoption when she had been born. He even had a nice family picked out.

I already knew that my Momma's father had been killed before he even knew Gram was pregnant. Momma explained that the Doc had delivered my Momma, even though Gigi had been planning on doing that since she was a certified midwife.

Anyway, Gram had gone into town that day, and my Momma decided to come four weeks early, so Gram ended up delivering my Momma in Doc Ellersby's office. After delivering my Momma, my Gram, who was not an emotional person, cried so hard that the Doc thought my Gram didn't want my Momma. But that was the furthest thing from my Grams mind. She was crying because her husband was not alive to see their beautiful baby daughter.

The Doc thought he would help my Gram by arranging for a quick adoption with a family from a nearby town. The Doc had the couple in his office an hour after my Momma was born. He showed them into the room where Gram lay, holding Momma. When Doc told her that they were there to take her baby home Gram climbed out of that bed, with my Momma, and even though she was weak as a kitten, she drove herself and my Momma home. Gram never forgave him for suggesting she give up her baby for adoption. Momma said the Doc had tried to apologize numerous times, but Gram was stubborn.

One very long and challenging week later we were back up at the family cemetery, this time burying Gram. For as hard a week she'd had physically, she passed away almost peaceful-like in her sleep. My Momma and I were right next to her when she slipped away. We held her hand and whispered to her that we loved her and for her to tell Gigi that we missed her. Momma and I sobbed for a long time after she was gone. The next day we dug her grave.
And just like that, there were two of us left; my Momma and me.

At first, my Momma and I continued living the way we had been living when Gigi and Gram had been alive. We still kept to ourselves and only ventured into town once or twice a month. I asked about our finances and my Momma assured me that we were fiscally fine. We ran a tab at the market and the hardware store. We bartered for our meat with the butcher, so we always had meat. Whenever Momma needed something that we couldn't buy in town she just told Mr. Bee and he got it for us. Mr. Bee paid all our bills from an account that I knew existed, but had no idea why it existed, or even how much money was in it. I asked Momma about it, but she told me not to fret about it.

Our simple life began changing after our truck broke down. It was done, kaput; Gram probably could have got it to run, but nothing that Momma and I tried worked. A week later when we didn't show up in town, Mr. Bee drove out to make sure we were okay. When he found out about the truck dying, he told Momma she needed to buy a new one.

 Mr. Bee put Momma in his car right then and there to buy a new one. He said he was taking her to the big town of Springfield. It was an hour away. I had never been there, and I wasn't sure if my Momma had been there either because she seemed pretty excited to be going. I wished I could have gone with them, but I had too many chores to do, plus I needed to take care of the animals.

Momma came home that night driving a shiny new pick up. It was a pretty red color and had a cover on the back bed to keep stuff dry. There was a hitch and a working radio too. I asked why it had taken so long and Momma explained that after she had bought the truck, she had a meeting with Mr. Bee in his office. I wanted to ask what the meeting was about, but Momma was all giddy and had rushed me into the new truck for a drive.

I knew right away something had happened while she had been away that day. She couldn't stop smiling, and she was even more talkative than usual. I got goose bumps on my arms feeling that there was a change coming, and for the first time ever; I was worried.

4

2016

The first big change was that we got a phone.
Momma wanted a cell phone, but we didn't get any
service on the farm, so she settled for a regular
phone. Three days later Momma got in her new
truck and returned with a television. We had to
wait to use our new TV because a company had to
come out and install a special line. We couldn't get
reception without it.

My Momma was so excited when the cable man
finished. The television was much bigger than the
one in the hardware store. It had a large flat screen
and came with a remote control. The first two
weeks we had it I swear Momma was glued to it.
She could see it from her usual spot in the kitchen
while she cooked and baked. Momma watched
celebrity news shows, cooking shows, and at night
she loved watching reality television shows. I was
very curious to watch TV too. However, I wanted
to watch shows, like the ones I found on the
Discovery Channel. I had to wait until Momma
went to bed before I could watch my shows
though, but I didn't mind. I still preferred listening
to the radio and reading.

My favorite time to listen to the radio was when I
was making the bread in the morning. That had
been my job since I was big enough to lift the
heavy ceramic bowl we used. I enjoyed the
morning news; it made me feel connected to life

outside of my farm. After the news, I changed to a station that played music. I loved country music. My Momma loved listening to music too, especially the oldies station. I discovered that certain songs made her eyes glassy. One time a slow tune was playing, and I saw her swaying to the music. I giggled and teased her, and that's when she told me that she and my dad had danced to that song. I immediately felt bad that I had teased her, but she quickly shushed my apology and said that it was a good memory. It would have been the perfect opportunity to ask her about my dad, but I didn't want to ruin her happy moment.

I had no idea who my dad was. I knew that my Momma had been married to him though because my Momma's and my last name was Janson. My Grams last name had been Rollings, and my Gigi's had been Green. The mountain we owned half of was called Green Mountain, which I thought was perfect because Vermont was called the Green Mountain State. I once asked if it was called the Green Mountain State because of my relatives, but Gigi laughed and said there was no connection. Watching the television shows made me realize how sheltered and irregular my life was. I loved my Gigi, Gram, and Momma. However, a tiny hole began tearing into my heart when I realized I had missed out on a great many things that normal people experience. I now understood why people stared at us when we went to town. I was an oddball.

The hand sewed, practical clothes I wore were not what girls my age wore. I did wear store-bought jeans, but I soon discovered my jeans were work jeans, more like what boys wore. The girls on television wore skintight pants that sat well below their belly buttons. I thought that they looked uncomfortable, but they did make them appear very feminine.

My Momma began to buy clothes from stores about two days after the television was installed. She even bought me a few things; a pretty skirt that stopped above my knees, and a top that had beautiful embroidery on the front. I wasn't sure when I would ever wear my new outfit, but I was happy that she had thought of me. She also bought me a pair of flannel pants with barn animals on them. I adored the soft pants, and I wore them every night when I read or watched television.

I loved my life on our small farm, but I did regret that I had missed out on going to school. I was twenty-two and had never spoken with anyone my age. I played with the sheep in the barn, and I loved old Josh, my hound dog. He was my constant companion.

Before we had the television, I was intrigued while listening to the radio hearing the hosts interact with each other. I remember hearing a female host talking to her male co-host, and I couldn't imagine joking and laughing with a man, the way she was; it seemed so personal. Now, I was able to watch the different relationship dynamics play out on the television screen. It was interesting to see, but it was also a bit intimidating. The only people I had ever interacted with, besides my family, were Doc Ellersby, who had died a few months ago, Pastor John, Mr. Greeter at the Grain and Feed/Hardware store, Mr. and Mrs. Bee, and now, just recently, Mr. Bee's new secretary Miss Donna. Miss Donna was near to my age, but she seemed much older. She had just started working for Mr. Bee. When I would go to Mr. Bee's office, I would take note of the clothes that she wore, how her nails were painted brightly, and how her hair was always perfect. If she was representative of how most women dressed I was glaringly different.

While I spent most my evenings reading or listening to the radio, my Momma was spending hers watching television or talking on the phone. I had no idea who she was talking to; I did know it was a man. When I asked her, she said it was a friend that Mr. Bee had introduced her too. I reasoned that if Mr. Bee introduced him to Momma, then he had to be a good man. Momma would talk to him every night and speak in hushed tones. I even heard her giggle.

A couple of weeks later Momma started going out at night. She'd take off in the truck wearing a store-bought dress, and she would come home late at night.

She never told me where she was going. When I asked she simply said that she was running errands, but I knew she was lying; we didn't run errands at night.

I was pretty annoyed with my Momma, but I held
my tongue because she was happier than I'd ever
seen her before. Momma started spending more
and more time off the farm, which left me with
more and more to do. I didn't mind the extra work
though. I loved the farm. I kept up with the
garden, my baking, the animals, and I even
managed to mow the lawn. I was so exhausted by
the end of the day that I'd fall asleep before
Momma even made it home.

The only problem was that there were little things
around the farm that needed doing and I didn't
have the time to get to them all. I decided that I
was going to have to have a serious talk with my
Momma.

So that night I lay on the couch, reading a book,
waiting for Momma to come home so we could
have a talk. I heard a car coming down our drive.
Old Josh started howling, and like him, I too knew
it wasn't our truck. I went to the window, and Old
Josh followed me. I was surprised to see the
Sheriff's car come to a stop outside in our front
loop. I opened the door before he had a chance to
knock. My stomach was pinched tight. I knew
something was wrong.

"Are you Eliza Janson's daughter?" He asked right
away.

I nodded.

"I'm Sheriff McDaniel's. Can I come in?"

It was after 10:00 PM, but I opened the door for
him to enter. I'd never, in my entire life, been
alone with anyone, other than my family, and that

weird random thought made my insides squeeze
uncomfortably.

The Sheriff walked inside and immediately took his
hat off. He had dark hair that was starting to gray
at the temples. His green eyes appeared sad, and his
lips were pressed tightly together. He immediately
knelt down and rubbed Josh behind his big ears.
For some reason, the mannerly gesture of taking
off his hat and the friendly petting of Josh put me
at ease. He then stood up, and I saw him take a
deep breath.

"Ma'am, you better have a seat." His hand
motioned me to the chair my Momma always sat
in, but she wasn't here, so I sat there. He took a
seat opposite of me in the chair that Gram had
always sat in.

"I have some bad news," he said, as he turned his
hat in his hands. I could tell he was nervous. Gigi
had once given me an entire lesson regarding
verbal and physical cues of human beings.

I didn't respond, and the Sheriff cocked his head
slightly to the side, so I knew he was going to ask a
question.

"Do you understand me?" He asked.

I realized that I had not spoken a single word since
his arrival, prompting his question, so I answered
yes, but my voice was barely audible since for some
reason my mouth had gone dry.

"Okay, you're Miss Belle Janson? Your mother is
Eliza Janson, birthdate December 22, 1978?"

"Yes," I answered quietly. Somehow I knew what he was going to say next was going to be bad, very, very bad.

"Miss Janson, I'm so sorry to have to tell you this, but your mother was killed in a traffic accident tonight."

I looked into his green eyes and could see that he hated delivering that news to me. He waited for me to speak, but I didn't. I couldn't. I was barely breathing. My muscles tensed up, and I thought I might vomit, so I slammed my hand over my mouth.

The Sheriff quickly stood from the chair and got me a glass of water. He sat back down on the ottoman in front of my chair. Tears ran down my face as the news took hold. My body trembled as my mind clawed for sanity. A small whimper escaped from my throat. Breath I needed to breath. I couldn't draw air and dots swam in front of my eyes. Finally, I drew in a breath. I heard the Sheriff whispering for me to focus on my breathing. He handed me the glass of water and I awkwardly gulped it and started choking. My hands were shaking so badly that the Sheriff took the glass back from me and held it. I was looking everywhere but at the Sheriff. I didn't want to look at him; it would make it all real. I was praying that I was dreaming.

That's when I noticed a few of my Momma's magazines on the table. She had stopped hiding them in her bedroom about a month after Gram had passed. A sob broke free from behind my hand as I broke down.

"My Momma's running errands." I finally choked out, refusing to believe what I knew, deep down was true.

The Sheriff didn't say anything, just looked at me sadly.

I covered my face with my hands and cried. The Sheriff waited patiently. His hand patted my shoulder a few times, and I heard him gently say, "let it out."

Josh knew something was wrong because he instinctively placed his head on my lap as I wept. I absentmindedly ran my hands over his soft fur.

I don't know how long it took me to compose myself; the Sheriff was patiently waiting for me to do so. My first question was if he was sure it was my Momma. He nodded his head yes. Then I asked how it happened and where was she now?

The Sheriff explained that my Momma had been driving on the highway that leads to Springfield. Her truck had veered off the road and hit a tree. He divulged that there was an ongoing investigation. He said that she had died on the scene. The Sheriff explained that they knew who she was because of her driver's license, which they found in her wallet. Also, in her wallet was a card listing me, Belle Janson, her daughter, as next of kin. The Sheriff informed me that Momma's body was at the morgue in Springfield.

"Miss Janson, we need you or a family member to come to Springfield to identify the body."

So many things were whirling through my head that I was not processing some of the information that the Sheriff was giving me.

"Do you understand what I'm saying, Miss Janson?" The Sheriffs voice was low, soft, but strained.

"Yes." My voice was clogged with emotion. "My Momma's dead. A car crash."

"Yes, and we need someone to come identify her tomorrow."

I didn't understand why she had to be identified if they had found her ID, and I asked the Sheriff that. He said it was procedure.

"Is there someone else that can go to Springfield or will you be able to?"

"I'm the only one left." I whispered. That awful realization brought forth more sobs.

The Sheriff once again patiently waited for me to collect myself.

"I'm so sorry. You will need to go to the morgue in Springfield. You'll need to tell the Medical Examiner if the person they have is your mother."

"Who else would it be if it wasn't my Momma?" I whispered.

The Sheriff blew out an exasperated breath. I really didn't understand, and I felt my heart rate accelerate, and my breathing became slightly erratic. I knew I was starting to have a panic attack; I was experiencing all were telltale signs.

I prevented the debilitating attack by drawing air in through my nose and exhaling out through my mouth. That was another one of Gigi's medical practices I had learned. Tears continued to cascade down my face, and I hiccupped uncontrollably. I helplessly thought that this had to be a dream; no way would God take Momma from me. Through the tears I managed to convey to the Sheriff that I had no way to get to the morgue.

He kindly offered to come back in the morning and drive me to Springfield, if I wanted. I said I would. He then asked if he could call anyone for me. I murmured for him to call Pastor John. Then added not to wake him tonight, he could be called in the morning.

The Sheriff paused and then nodded. Again, I knew he wanted to ask a question, but he must have decided against it because he stood from the chair and headed towards the front door. Once again he asked if there was someone he could call, this time adding, to stay with me. I shook my head no.

I followed numbly behind him. Josh followed behind us. I thanked the Sheriff for coming, and then I wondered if it was appropriate for me to thank him for delivering horrible news. He smiled gently, placed his hat on his shortly cropped hair, and said he would see me tomorrow morning at 11:00 AM. I shut the door after watching him walk to his car and drive away.

I wasn't sure what I should do. I knew I was going to cry some more. My Momma had been the closest to me in age, and her smile and laughter had been infectious. She had been the fun one. My Gigi had been cerebral and good-natured but in a reserved way. Gram had been very matter of fact, a realist, and a serious soul. My Momma though, she had been a little whimsical, sometimes even silly. She had taught me my first joke, and we had annually pranked Gigi and Gram on April Fool's Day. She was a dreamer, and so kind and gentle. The past few weeks she had been happier than ever.

This couldn't be happening.

Momma had been the one who made sure that birthdays were celebrated, and she had been so clever when it came to decorating the house for any holiday. My heart splintered as I remembered her smiling brightly as she had said goodbye to me tonight.

5

And Then There Was One. Me

I sat down on the couch and closed my book,
which I had left open. My movements were rote
and stiff. I drew the afghan from the back of the
sofa and choked as tears streamed down my face
unchecked. My Momma had knitted the afghan as
a Christmas gift for me.
She couldn't be gone.
I lay down wrapped in the familiar soft blanket. My
head was pounding, and my heart felt as if it was
being squeezed with a clamp.
I knew that going to my bedroom would undo me.
I just couldn't go upstairs to bed. I was still holding
out hope that Momma would walk through the
door.
I cried hysterically after saying my prayers. I prayed
that there had been a horrible mistake, but my Gigi
had explained the stages people go through when
they are grieving, and I was well aware that denial
was one of those stages.
 I had so many images racing through my mind. I
pictured Momma flitting around the house, and
then, of course, that triggered thoughts of Gram
and my Gigi, prompting me to cry even harder. It
was unfathomable that I was facing a future
without them.
I slept fitfully throughout the night. I couldn't stop
crying; even in my dreams I must have cried. I'd
wake with a jerk; my cheeks wet with tears, feeling

confused. Then I'd remember that Momma was gone and I was alone, so very alone. I wasn't sure what time it was, but I knew I wasn't going to get any rest. I decided to get up and start what I knew would be a horrible day.

It was still dark outside, but waking up before the sun rose was normal for me. Despite how I was feeling the animals still needed to be taken care of. When I saw the time on the clock, I sighed seeing that it was only 4:30 in the morning.

After leaving the warmth of the couch I used the bathroom. I let Josh outside and then sat at the kitchen table to make a list of what I needed to do. I was a list maker; it focused me, and I prided myself on always completing my to-do list. Gram and Gigi had made lists too, not Momma though. A lump formed in my throat and I swallowed it down angrily while wiping a stubborn tear from my eye.

I had to be strong.

I began writing my list:

feed animals

shower

~~bake bread~~

I then drew a line through bake bread because there was still a whole loaf from when I had baked yesterday, and now it would only be me eating it. That thought wretched a solid sob from me, and I felt my resolution to be strong beginning to crumble. I slammed my fist on the table and told myself to focus.

feed animals

shower
~~bake bread~~
call Mr. Bee
call Pastor John
go with Sheriff McDaniel
dig grave

I realized I'd probably not be able to dig the grave
today, but I left it on my to do list. I made coffee,
not a full pot like I usually made. I cut a piece of
whole wheat bread and smoothed on a layer of
strawberry preserves that Momma and I had put up
last summer. My stomach rolled remembering how
we had laughed when a blob of jam had fallen on
Josh's nose and how comical it was watching him
try to lick it off.
I looked at my bread and pushed my small plate
away. If I ate, I'd only throw it up. I hated throwing
up. I contemplated adding more items to my list
but decided against it. My hand unconsciously
moved to my forehead; it was pounding painfully,
and I knew I needed to take some aspirin, or I'd get
a migraine. My eyes ached from crying, and I was
sore from sleeping, well lying on the couch. I
swallowed two aspirin with the last sip of my
coffee and wiped down the table before pulling on
my boots and heading outside. I didn't even have
the energy to change out of my comfy pants.
Josh followed me as I worked through my morning
chores. Usually, he would meet me when I walked
outside, wait for a quick head rub, and then find a
shady, or depending on the weather, a warm spot

to lay in. Today he remained alongside me. It always amazed me how animals were so in tune with their caregivers. I sighed wearily; at least I still had old Josh.

I emptied the almost empty bucket of table scraps into the pig's trough and added a corn and grain mixture. I fed Bessie, the cow and after she ate I led her outside to the larger corral. She didn't give us milk anymore, but that was fine because we just bought it from the store now. Gram had wanted to barter Bessie off to the butcher, but my Momma, and I had raised such a fuss that she relented. I cleaned Bessie's stall then returned to the corral, where Henny was waiting for me. Depending on the weather, if it were warm enough, Henny would spend the night outside in her corral. She nuzzled my neck, and I hugged my old friend. I had no idea how old the sweet mare was. We no longer worked her. I don't even remember the last time we had harnessed her into the small carriage we had. I had learned to ride on Henny; she had always been gentle. I gave her a final squeeze and then fished out a sugar cube from my coat pocket for her. Henny and Josh followed me around the corral where I emptied a tin of grain into Henny's food bucket.

Next, I moved to the smaller corral that ran along the one side of the barn nearest the forest. This corral was for our sheep. There was a lean-to shelter that Gram and I had built for them, and we had also cut a small hatch into the side of the barn.

When we left it open the sheep could access a smaller enclosed area inside the barn.

I shooed the sheep that were in the barn into the outside corral; it was going to be a nice day, no sense wasting it inside. Gigi had said that all the time. I guess I did too, now. As I fed them, I noticed that Mimi was keeping herself separated from the small herd. She was going to give birth soon. It made me think of traveling to Springfield with the Sheriff; I couldn't be away from the farm for too long. I made my way to the chicken coop next and let them out of their nesting house so they could strut around their large wire enclosure. I tossed feed out to them and watched as they scurried about pecking at the seed. Next, I needed to give all the animals fresh water. I unraveled the heavy hose that was kept along the side of the barn and walked it to the four troughs. I meticulously rolled the hose back up and then walked back to the chicken enclosure to collect the eggs from the coop before heading back inside.

I stopped on the back porch and turned back around to look at the barn, the garden, the thick woods that lay beyond our grassy yard and Green Mountain. I smiled thinking of Gigi and Gram. They loved how beautiful the mountain was during all the Vermont seasons. A fresh wave of pain assaulted me as I thought about Momma. She mostly liked the summers so she could garden.

I liked all the seasons in Vermont. The fall brought colorful foliage. It was vibrant and never failed to take my breath away. I remembered, when I was younger, how I would collect the bright leaves, and Momma would place them between two pieces of wax paper and then iron the paper, affixing the colorful leaves permanently between the waxy squares. My grandmas would make such a fuss over how beautiful they were. We would use them for placemats and even made smaller ones that we used as coasters in our living room.

I always felt that the beauty of fall was a gift from God to us for taking such good care of our property. My theory was that he wanted us to remember the magnificence of that season while we endured the harsh, bitter winter months.

Winters in Vermont were long and hard. I did love how the snow, especially when it first fell, was pristine and how the ground looked like it was covered with a fluffy white blanket. It sparkled in the sunlight, and the crisp air felt cleansing when I breathed it in. The hard part of winter was that the days were short of sunlight and the cold temperatures made being outside problematic. Tending the animals when the temperature dipped below freezing was laborious. I often had to use a hatchet to break through the water in the troughs for the animals. The chickens and sheep remained inside for the winter. The pigs were sold to a local meatpacking business in the fall, so I didn't have to care for them. If it were a sunny day, I would let the animals outside for a little while so that I could tend to their stalls. I would first have to shovel a path in the corrals to the water and food bucket if the snow was too high. Bessie refused to go out when it got cold. Henny went out all the time, but I was careful to not leave her out for too long. The sheep didn't care either way as long as I fed them. Spring, or mud season, was the season of rebirth. The trees grew back their lush green leaves, and the wildflowers sprang up in fields and along the side of the road, but what I loved most especially was seeing the baby animals. The spotted fawns, the tiny foxes, even the baby moose that would venture into our back hay field. They were so ugly that they were cute. The lambs and piglets were adorable, and I loved holding them. Spring was when I helped Momma prepare the garden for planting. Momma started our plants from seed in a small greenhouse that Gram had ordered from a catalog. She and my Momma had put it together in one afternoon. In the spring the barn animals loved being able to go outside regularly, and Gram had loved being able to fix all the things around the farm that the heavy snow and ice storms had destroyed.

Summer was lush pastures, golden hay fields, blue skies, fireflies, and my personal favorite, the old swimming hole. It was a short walk through the backfield and down a woodsy trail. That's where I swam and sometimes even bathed. There was a grassy bank, just above the water where I would spread my towel and read or even nap. Summer nights were beautiful. The temperature cooled, and the stars were so bright and magnificent that you swear you could reach up and touch them. The fireflies lite up the night skies. When I was little, I'd catch some every night, put them in a mason jar, and then set them free in the morning. My Gigi said it was natural night-light.

My family loved to cook outside in the summer too. My Momma was a master grill person. We had a great big pit right out behind our house on the stone patio. Over the years we had expanded it so that we could roast a pig on a spit, grill meat, and even smoke meat or fish. We got all our meat from the place that we sold our pigs too. Gram had explained to me that we gave them our pigs, and in return, we got meat and sometimes cash too, depending on the pigs. That was bartering, she had said. I loved that back stone patio. My Gram had built a wooden picnic table where we ate many of our summer meals. There were four Adirondack chairs on the patio too, all facing the woods and Green Mountain.

I sighed thinking of my lost family, and the tears fell again as I made my way back inside.

I had a few more hours before I needed to go with the Sheriff, so I headed to the garden. Momma had said just the morning before that she wanted to weed the squash area and check that the tomatoes were properly staked. I was tired and emotional so I spent two hours in momma's garden doing a job that should have only taken an hour.

When I finished I trudged inside and checked the clock; the Sheriff would be arriving in an hour. I sluggishly walked upstairs and was thankful the door to Momma's bedroom was closed; I still hurried past it. I peeled out of my tee shirt and comfy pants and went into the bathroom. The bathroom was between our two rooms. I brushed my teeth before stepping into the shower. The reflection looking back at me in the mirror was one I barely recognized. I was sad, exhausted and under duress. I'd been sad before and even tired, but I couldn't remember ever feeling this stressed.

I cried in the shower; I couldn't help it. I had been holding the tears back while I was with the animals because I knew animals could sense when people are distressed, and I didn't want to upset them, especially Mimi who was going to give birth soon. As the shower teemed with steam from the hot water my Momma's scent filled the glass stall. She used rose body soap. She loved the smell of roses. I didn't care for it. I was happy with the white bar of Ivory soap that my Gigi and Gram had insisted on using.

Memories pummeled me, and I once again had to focus on regulating my breathing. While holding the bar of Ivory soap in my hand, I thought of my Gigi. When I was younger, during the summer, the four of us would bath in the swimming hole. My Gigi praised the makers of Ivory Soap because Ivory soap didn't have a smelly floral fragrance or any added chemicals in it. I just loved that it floated. I would chase it down the stream thinking it was great fun. Momma had started buying rose scented soap even before Gram had passed. She received a sample in the mail one day, and she loved it. After that, she always purchased that fragrant soap. She claimed it was her one indulgence. After Gram passed, she bought herself rose scented shampoo and conditioner too.

I sank to the floor of the shower as sobs wracked my body. On my knees, with my hands holding up my small frame I was now even closer to the bath products, and the sweet smell of my mother overwhelmed me. I gathered my Momma's shower items and angrily threw them out of the shower, praying the rose smell would follow.

Anger coupled with agonizing grief ripped through me, and I began to vomit uncontrollably. I wretched loudly until nothing but saliva hung from my open mouth. I couldn't stop crying. I could barely catch a breath, and I screamed and yelled banging my fists on the tiled floor until I had worked through the first three stages of grief; denial, anger, and bargaining.

I lay exhausted on the shower floor until the water turned so cold that it stung my skin. I refused to leave the icy shower, and that's when I realized I was now in the depression phase of grieving.

I lay on the frigid shower floor as the water slaked down my shivering body. My body was freezing, and my teeth chattered uncontrollably. I had to move, I had to go to Springfield. I uncoiled from the fetal position I'd folded into. Forcing myself off of the icy cold floor I stood up slowly. My legs felt like Jell-O, the frigid water had me quaking uncontrollably, but I refused to leave the shower until I had washed. Quickly I washed using my shampoo, conditioner, and Ivory soap. When I finished, I exited the shower feeling drained, depressed, but slightly more in control of my emotions. I was not going to be a mopey Mattie, as my Gigi called it. I needed to accept the situation that God had handed to me. I may not have my Gigi, Gram, or my Momma with me anymore, but, I would always carry them with me in my heart. I was them. They each had contributed to who I was. I said a prayer and asked God and my family to help me survive this horrible ordeal. I would be strong for them. I would make them proud of me.

I changed into what I hoped was an appropriate outfit to go to Springfield. I had no idea what one wore to the city. I put on a dress that my Momma had made for me last spring. She had seen one similar to the one she made me in a magazine, so she made us both one.

I then called Mr. Bee. His number was written on a piece of paper next to the phone. There were only a few phone numbers on the paper, and I realized I had never even used the phone before. My Momma had always used it.

I pressed the buttons that corresponded with Mr. Bee's number, and when a woman answered the phone, I was so unnerved that I almost dropped the phone. Her cheery voice sounded through the phones speaker, "Hello. Hello?"

I gripped the phone and asked to speak to Mr. Bee. The woman asked who was calling and I realized it was Mr. Bee's pretty new secretary, Miss Donna. I told her who I was and she then told me to hold.

'Hold what?' I thought. I made sure I had a firm grasp on the phone; maybe she knew I had almost dropped it. Then I heard Mr. Bee.

"Hello, Belle? Is everything all right?" I never called him, so he knew something was wrong.

I whimpered softly thinking that' no nothing was right.'

"Belle, are you there?"

"Yes, Mr. Bee I'm here," I said finding my voice.

"Honey, what's wrong? Where's your Momma?"

"She's dead. The Sheriff came here last night and said she was killed in an accident. He's coming to take me to identify her this morning."

There was a slight pause before he answered me.

"Belle, I'm so sorry. Are you okay? Do you want me to come out there?"

"No thank you, Mr. Bee. I'm leaving around 11:00 with the Sheriff."

"Do you want me to go with you?"

"I can do this Mr. Bee. The Sheriff said it had to be family."

"Yes, of course, please have the Sheriff drop you at my office afterward, okay?"

"Yes, Mr. Bee."

"And Belle, I am so, so sorry."

"Thank you, Mr. Bee I'll see you later."

Next, I called Pastor John. He had received a call from the Sheriff earlier that morning, and he told me he had just been about to call me. He said he was sorry for my loss and that if I wanted him to come to the farm that he would. I told him I was heading to Springfield with the Sheriff. I was hurting and tired, but I had the presence of mind to ask Pastor John to be ready to perform the funeral when Momma was brought back home. He said that he would be honored.

The Sheriff arrived right at 11:00 AM and escorted me to his car. In the enclosed space of the car, a clean spicy scent wafted over me, and I realized it was the Sheriff that smelled so nice. He offered me a stick of gum, but I had been forbidden to chew it when my Gram had been alive, and I decided I wasn't going to start now, so I politely declined. The Sheriff asked me how old I was, and I told him that I would be 23 in seven days. I could see the revelation that I would be having a birthday so soon after losing my Momma weighed on him. I couldn't guess his age. The nameplate above his pocket said, W. McDaniel. He wore a silver wedding band, and his shortly cropped hair reminded me of the Marine from great granddads funeral so long ago.
"Are you a Marine?" I asked.
He seemed startled by my question, and he glanced nervously at me.
"I was," he answered. I could tell my question had surprised him.
"My great-grandfather was a Marine. I saw a Marine when he was buried. He gave my Gigi a flag. Your hair is short like that Marine's was. I guess I just made a presumption."

The Sheriff chuckled. "I guess most Marines do wear their hair like mine, but other men do too."
The Sheriff peered over at me.

"You really have led an insulated life haven't you?"
I didn't know what to say to that, so I didn't say anything. I knew what insulated meant. I had led a life that was different than most, but I didn't think I'd been cloistered.

"Oh, boy," the Sheriff said after seeing my face. "Let me explain."
I turned towards him and waited.

"I know that you and your family are private people?"

"We go to town." I argued.

"Yes, but you don't socialize. You keep to yourself, live off mostly off of what your farm provides you, correct?"

"We do live on a farm and it's a bit away from town," I said thoughtfully.

The Sheriff smiled nervously. "Do you socialize?"
I didn't even have to think about my answer. "No, we keep to ourselves. I guess we are pretty private. I don't think my Gram even liked people." I said jokingly making the Sheriff chuckled.

"I think my Momma was starting to socialize, though. She had been going out more."

"For the record," the Sheriff said softly. "I didn't mean to embarrass you. I like that you say what you are thinking. It's refreshing."

We rode in silence for a while, and as we drove further away from my home, I stared sullenly, but curiously out the window. We drove through a small town, and I saw people who appeared to be my age sitting around a picnic table near a small building with lots of glass. A large sign that read Dairy Queen was above the glass. All the people that were there were eating ice creams that twisted upwards out of their cones.

"Have you ever had a DQ ice cream cone?" The Sheriff asked.

"DQ?"

"Dairy Queen."

"Oh. No, I don't eat ice cream very often. I do love it though. Once in a while, my Momma would buy me one at the market in town, but I had to eat it right away because it wouldn't make it home without melting. We would make it sometimes, especially around the 4th of July, but Gigi had been the one to make it, and she always made chocolate. I don't care for chocolate. We haven't made it lately." I finished softly.

"So, you've never had a Twist?"

"Is that what those people were eating?"

"Yes, its soft ice cream"

"No, I have never had one."

We rode in silence a bit longer, and I saw a sign indicating that we were Now Entering Springfield. Large buildings and so, so many stores selling everything and anything, were clustered together. There were traffic lights at every corner, and I loved it when the car had to stop because then I could get a better look at what was around me. People were everywhere; I had never seen so many people. I saw a group of women walking together and laughing, a couple, who appeared to be my age, walking hand in hand, and a mother pushing a stroller while the father held the hand of a toddler, as they maneuvered down the sidewalk. I wish I could sit somewhere and watch everyone without them seeing me. It was amazing. My heart ached thinking that my Momma would have loved watching all the people.

The Sheriff chuckled, and I glanced at him. "Pretty different than what you're used to isn't it?"

"There are so many stores and people," I answered; awe evident in my voice.

I thought about my Momma driving here and wished she had taken me with her. I knew she would have loved all the stores. I was flabbergasted when we passed a storefront that had very lifelike mannequins dressed only in unmentionables, right out in the open for everyone to see. My Gram would have had a fit. I stared at the small bra and underwear the mannequin was wearing. They were pale blue with lacey edges, and they matched. The underwear didn't come over the belly button as mine did. I knew my Momma would have loved to wear those. She liked pretty things. Sadness shrouded me knowing I would never share any new memories with her.

The Sheriff put on the car's blinker, and we turned off of the busy street into a parking lot next to a large brick building.

We exited the car, and he guided me to a side door that had a doorbell next to it, which he rang. A buzzing sound emanated from a small square plastic box near the door, and the Sheriff opened the heavy door. We walked down a dimly lit gray hall and then through another door until we reached an office. The Sheriff knocked on the window next to the open door, and a woman in a white coat and glasses stood up from behind the desk and exited the office to meet us.

"Hi, William." She said shaking the Sheriff's hand. I realized the W. on the Sheriff's nameplate stood for William.

"Hi, Katarina. This is Belle Janson. Belle, this is the Medical Examiner, Doctor Larson."

We shook hands, and I murmured a hello. My chest was beginning to tighten. I realized that I would be seeing my dead Momma soon, and I wasn't sure what to expect, but I prayed I wouldn't see too much blood. I could handle blood if I were doing the doctoring, but knowing that my Momma was dead, and seeing her covered in blood might be more than I could handle.

We walked down a hallway and through a door that opened into a room with square silver doors on one wall. Surgical instruments lined another wall, and two rectangular shaped metal tables were in the middle of the sterile, cold room. A domed shaped silver light and an oversized magnifying glass hung suspended from the ceiling over each table. I shuddered knowing what the doctor did on the tables.

Had my Momma been on one of them? Nauseous rolled in my stomach.

The Sheriff guided me towards the wall with the small silver doors, and I watched apprehensively as the Doctor opened one that was chest high. She slid out a flat metal bed. My heart was beating so loudly it was pulsing in my ears, and I hoped I wouldn't pass out. A white sheet was covering what I knew was a person; a dead person. Irrationally, I pleaded with God for it not to be my momma. I attempted to steady my emotions by taking a few deep breaths. My hands were clutched together over my chest. The sheriff put his hand on my back and asked if I was okay. I took a second before nodding yes. He then nodded at Dr. Larson. The doctor peeled the sheet back, and I saw my Momma's face. She was so pale like Gram had looked when she died. I could see Momma had bruising around her forehead and a gash had been sewn up underneath her eye, which was also bruised. She wasn't smiling, but she wasn't frowning either. Her hair was brushed back off of her face, and thankfully I did not see any blood. "Belle, is this your Mom?" The doctor asked gently. "Yes, that's my Momma."
Tears blurred my vision even though I kept swiping them away. I attempted to be brave, to act strong, but a whimper escaped as I stared down at her. She was eerily still, a stark contrast from her usual self. Momma had been so animated and full of joy. The last few months she had been having fun doing goodness knows what. She had been happier than I'd ever seen her. I tentatively touched

her cheek, and it was so unnaturally cool that I quickly drew my fingers back.

"Do you want a few moments alone with her?" The doctor asked.

I nodded, and the Sheriff and the Doctor stepped away from the pull out bed, but they did not leave the room.

I bent down and kissed my Momma on her forehead and then her cheek. I whispered in her ear that I loved her and that set off a surge of tears. I was aching with grief. I spoke softly to her as tears barreled down my face. I told her I already missed her, and that I would make her proud by being a good woman. I whispered that I hoped she was happy, and that she had found Gigi and Gram. My body started to tremble with the anguish I felt. I was afraid if I gave into the intense sadness I felt, I would blubber uncontrollably, so I decided I'd talk to her more after she was buried, when I could talk to her privately and let my emotions go.

It was important to me that I hold my emotions in check. I did not want to appear weak. Gigi, Gram, and my Momma had drilled that lesson into me. I had already cried in front of the Sheriff once, and now again in front of the Medical Examiner. I had to keep myself collected.

I kissed Momma one more time and took a small step back from her body. The doctor and the Sheriff stepped next to me again, and I saw the Sheriff look at the doctor. The doctor pulled the sheet back over my Momma's face and pushed her metal bed back into the rectangular drawer before shutting the door. It banged shut with a hard click I jumped at the sound and fought the urge to reopen it. Momma hated to be closed spaces.

"Are you okay?" The Sheriff asked gently.

"I'm as alright as I can be I guess," I answered honestly.

We walked back to the doctor's office because I had to sign a paper. I was screaming on the inside. My thoughts ran together; I had so many of them. I had never been in such awful physical and emotional distress before. The Sheriff asked what I wanted to do with my Momma's body and I asked if they could put her in a box and deliver her to the farm.

They both gave me a funny look, but the Sheriff said he would handle it.

After I signed the paper stating that I had identified the body as Eliza Rollings Janson, the doctor unlocked a drawer in her office and handed me a large clear plastic bag, which contained my mother's purse. I looked at the doctor, and she anticipated my question.

"I can give you her clothes, but they're not in good condition."

I understood what she was implying, so I nodded telling her that she could keep them, and then I thanked her.

The Sheriff and I walked back to his car, and I appreciated that he wasn't trying to make small talk. As we drove back through the city, I wasn't as enamored with it as I'd been while driving in. The

truth was I was starting to feel a little off-kilter.
Last night was the first night I had ever spent
alone, and tonight I would be alone again, and the
next night, and the next. I was feeling afraid, and it
was a foreign feeling.

We drove out of Springfield, and when we got to
the Dairy Queen, the Sheriff pulled in. I looked at
him nervously, my eyes wide.

"Do you mind if we stop for a cone?"

"You want ice cream?" I asked slightly confused.

"Yes, is that all right?"

"Of course," I answered. The man had been so
kind to me. If he wanted ice cream, I thought it
would have been rude to say no.

He got out of the car, and when I remained inside,
he came around and opened my door. I think he
was letting the people that were staring at his
Sheriff's car know that I wasn't a prisoner. I
remained sitting in the passenger seat.

"I'll be right back." He said giving me a little grin.

I looked at the people; some gathered around the
tables, others waiting in line. Some openly stared at
us. Did the Sheriff recognize how out of my
element I was?

He had left me sitting in the car, with the door
open. I thought it was so no one would think that I
was a criminal. I turned in my seat so that my feet
rested on the pavement, but I remained sitting in
the car. People continued to look at me, but I was
looking at them too, so I decided we were even.

The Sheriff returned and handed me a small cone
that held a twisty pile of soft vanilla ice cream

covered in colorful little bits of sprinkles. My momma sometimes decorated her cakes with sprinkles. A lump formed in my throat that I pushed down. The Sheriff handed me a napkin, and I thanked him politely.

"That's my wife's favorite, vanilla with sprinkles. I hope you like it."

I took the delicate cone in my hand; it smelled as wonderful as it looked.

My first lick of DQ ice cream was incredible.

"Oh, my!" I exclaimed as a tiny smile spread across my face. I licked my cone enjoying the sweet little candies that were coating the most delicious vanilla ice cream I'd ever tasted.

The Sheriff peered at me from behind his cone, and I saw him smile. We finished our cones at the same time, and I wiped my mouth and hands with the napkin he had given me. He took the napkin from me and walked it to the trashcan nearby. Then we got back in his car and headed back to Lansing.

The ride back was quiet. I was thinking about all the things I had to do, including digging Momma's grave. Digging a grave was hard work. My Momma and I had dug Gram's grave, and it had taken us an entire day. I also needed to go to the market and the Feed and Grain store too. The problem was that I had no car. In fact, even though I knew how to drive, I didn't have a license. I wondered if Henny could pull the old wagon again.

"Sheriff, my Momma's truck. Can I get it back?"

He looked over at me then his eyes returned to the road.

"Belle, it's in pretty bad shape. You won't be able to use it."

"Oh, it was brand new."

"It's been towed to a garage in Springfield. I could have them tow it to your farm, or you could just sell it for parts. That way you will get a little money for it. You're Mom probably had insurance on it. You should check that out."

"Okay, I will. I guess I probably wouldn't like seeing it anyways."

"No, you wouldn't, no one would," he paused.

"I'm so sorry Belle; I know this must be awful for you; you are being unbelievably strong."

"I have been crying." I pointed out.

The Sheriff chuckled, "Well, Honey I think you're entitled to cry."

I smiled sadly; he was a nice man.

"Sheriff would you be so kind as to take me to Mr. Bee's office, please."

"Mr. Bee?"

I looked at the Sheriff and thought he must not know him. "Mr. Bee is my family's lawyer. He has an office near the hardware store in town."

The Sheriff nodded. "Yes, I know him. Does he know you are coming?"

"Yes, we spoke this morning."

I could tell he wanted to ask me a question and I looked at him waiting for it. When he saw that I was looking at him, he chuckled. "You're a smart young lady aren't you?"

"My Gigi and Gram told me that I am very smart,"
I answered honestly, without conceit.

That made the Sheriff chuckle again although I
wasn't sure why.

"Belle, are you going to be all right out on your
farm, you know, without your Mom?"

I sighed, "I will admit it is unnerving to be alone.
I've never been alone for any length of time."

"You don't have a car and what about your
animals?"

"I've been thinking about that. Until I get a license
and a car, I'll just hitch Henny up. She can take me
to town. The animals have always been my
responsibility, so they are fine. I'm glad I have
them."

"Henny?"

"My horse."

The Sheriff looked like he wanted to say
something, but he didn't speak. I was too tired to
ask him, so I leaned back in my seat making a
mental list of what I'd need at the market and feed
store. A half-hour later we pulled up in front of Mr.
Bee's office. I got out of the car, and the Sheriff got
out as well.

"I'm just going to walk you to his office," he said.
It wasn't a question, and I experienced chivalry for
the very first time.

We entered the office, and Miss Donna called Mr.
Bee when she saw us. Mr., Bee came out to the
waiting room, and he and the Sheriff shook hands.
Mr. Bee thanked him for accompanying me and for
bringing me to his office.

"Should I stay?" The Sheriff asked Mr. Bee. "She's going to need a ride home."

"I can walk," I interjected. Although I knew if I walked I would be able to get food for me or the animals.

"I'll bring her home, Sheriff." Mr. Bee told him. The Sheriff nodded and then turned to me. He reached into his shirt pocket and pulled out a small rectangular card that had his name on it and two telephone numbers.

"Belle, if you need anything you give me a call."

"Thank you, Sheriff you are very kind."

"I may stop by and check on you once in a while, will that be all right with you?"

"Of course, I will appreciate the company."

That made the Sheriff chuckle yet again, and although I didn't know why, I knew I had made my very first friend.

"Belle, where should I have your Mom's body delivered?" The Sheriff asked as he put on his hat.

"My farm please." I saw him give Mr. Bee an odd look.

"The M.E. said she would be there the day after tomorrow. Is that okay?" He asked.

"Yes, that's fine. It will give me time."

"Time?"

"Yes, time to ready her grave."

The Sheriff blew out a long breath. I don't think that was the answer he was expecting.

"What do you mean, ready the grave Belle?" He asked almost cautiously.

"Why to dig it, of course."

The Sheriff muffled an exasperated gasp, and Mr. Bee simply grinned. He knew we had always dug the graves for our family.

Mr. Bee shot the Sheriff a look that told him to not to press the issue. I gathered from the Sheriff's reaction that digging a grave was not usual, but it was a tradition I did not plan on breaking.

Mr. Bee and the Sheriff bade each other good day, and I watched the Sheriff leave before turning back to Mr. Bee.

"I'm so sorry for your loss, Belle." He said ushering me to his office.

"Thank you," I replied growing anxious again.

He gestured for me to sit in a leather chair with brass rivets running along the side seams. It was opposite Mr. Bee's large wooden desk. The leather was cold against my legs, but I welcomed it.

"Belle, tell me what you know of your family's finances?" Mr. Bee asked, situating himself behind his desk and getting right to the heart of the matter.

"I know nothing."

"Nothing at all?"

"No, my Gigi said we were well off. My Gram found it crass to discuss finances, and my Momma..." I paused and sighed. "Well, my Momma just never got around to talking to me about it."

"You turn 23 next week, is that correct?"

"Yes."

Mr. Bee smiled gently. "I know you're an intelligent young lady, and I'm going to explain everything. If

there something you don't understand just ask; is
that acceptable?"

"Yes, I would appreciate your candor."

Mr. Bee sat back in his chair and opened a folder
that was on his desk. He pushed the folder towards
me, and I turned it, so it faced me.

Then he proceeded to explain that I was the
beneficiary of our half of the mountain, Green
Mountain. I also inherited a diversified portfolio
containing stocks, bonds, and other varying
accruing assets. He explained that the monies from
those accounts were what sustained our farm. My
grandparents had accumulated enough money to
live comfortably living the way we did.

"What do you mean Mr. Bee?"

Mr. Bee sat back in his chair and clasped his hands
over his waist.

"Well, until recently your family has always lived a
simple life. You did not have extra expenses, as you
do now for cable television and the phone. I don't
believe you will have money issues. However, the
bulk of your money is tied up in stocks and real
estate. If you ever needed a large amount of
money, I would sell some of your assets."

"Did you sell assets for Momma?"

Mr. Bee chuckled. "Yes, for the truck, and a few
recent shopping sprees."

"If I need money I just come to you?"

"Exactly. Your account at the Hardware store is
current I pay that bill monthly. I spoke with the
insurance company this morning, and you will have
money to buy yourself a car. There was a trust set

up for you if you ever decided to go to college. It can't be touched for any other reason, except if you do not use it, it is then bequeathed to your children."

"Oh, I never knew about that." I was a surprised about the college fund. My grandparents and momma had not wanted me to attend a regular school while growing up. However, they must have thought I should go to college. This revelation was interesting. A lump formed in my throat thinking about all the things I wish I could ask my Momma. I was feeling angry that she had not confided in me. I had known nothing about our finances, and it made me feel foolish. A sense of lonliness and vulnerability pressed down on me. I took a deep breath and forced myself to push away the enervating feelings.

I sat with Mr. Bee for three hours, and it wasn't until his secretary came in and said that she was leaving for the evening that I realized how long we had been talking.

When Mr. Bee got to the last two things in the folder, he stood from his chair. He took out a large map and opened it, so it lay on his desk. He then took the last paper from the folder and handed it to me.

"This is the deed to your property on Green Mountain. "This here," he said gesturing to the map on his desk, "is a survey map indicating your property lines." I noticed how the property line ran across the top of the mountain and stretched out along both sides of the mountain. It extended outwards from the base of the mountain to include our house, barn, and a goodly amount on either side of our long drive.

We owned more than 1,500 acres. I knew from listening to my Gigi that at one time our family had owned the entire mountain, but her parents had deeded the other side of the mountain to the State to be used as a National Park. She said it ensured that no one could build on it. My Gigi was so smart.

I saw that the date printed on the surveyor's report was from a month ago. I pointed at it and asked why the survey had been done. Mr. Bee looked slightly uncomfortable, and I knew I would not like his answer.

"Belle, your Mom was offered money for your property, quite a bit of money. She gave the interested party permission to do the survey."

I was astonished, and a myriad of emotions washed over me. I was hurt, angry, saddened, and mystified. How could my Momma even consider selling our home? How many other things had my momma kept from me?

"I can't believe it. Was she going to sell our mountain, Mr. Bee?"

"I know she was seriously considering it."

Mr. Bee folded the map and placed the survey back into the folder, along with the photocopied deed, and he closed it.

"This folder is for you to take home. The original deed to your property is in my safe."

Mr. Bee sat back down in his chair and remained quiet allowing me time to absorb what he had told me. I leaned back in my chair and blew out a breath mentally digesting all I had just learned. Mr. Bee organized his desk while I stared at my folded hands laying in my lap.

Mr. Bee finished with his desk and looked across to me. "Belle, do you have any questions?"

I looked up, suddenly feeling exhausted.

"A few, yes."

He spread his hands open with his palms up. "Ask me anything. I want you to understand. I need you to understand."

I nodded and smiled. Mr. Bee was a nice man.

"Well, am I correct that when my Gigi, Gram, and Momma came into town, the reason we stopped here first was to get cash?"

"Yes, for the supermarket."

"Is that a usual arrangement for people?"

"No, far from it actually."

"Can you tell me why we do this?"

"It began many years ago. I was fresh out of law school. Your Gigi got into an argument with a bank manager here in town. He refused to discuss business with her. He was emphatic that he should be dealing with the man of the house. Your great-grandmother explained to that bank manager that her husband was in the hospital. He insisted she come back with her dad, brother, or uncle; in other words, a male."

I smirked, "I bet that went over well."

"Your Gigi was so mad she walked right over here and hired me on the spot. I was a young lawyer, but I knew the bank manager had no legal grounds to keep the money from your great-grandma. It took me less than an hour to straighten it out. Your great-grandmother withdrew every dime she had out of that bank; at the time the sum she had in there was quite substantial. She even emptied her safety deposit box." Mr. Bee shook his head and chuckled. "She managed the family finances after that."

"How did we come to use you?"

"It was your Gram that talked your great grandma into using me as a financial go-between. Your grandma had come into town about six months after the bank incident to purchase a truck that was for sale by a local farmer. I happened to be walking past when she was negotiating the price with the farmer. I recognized her from when she and your Gigi would come into town. The farmer, like the bank manager, refused to deal with her because she was a woman. I couldn't believe how ignorant the farmer was being, so I walked up to him and lambasted him for his archaic thinking. I then proceeded to tell him if he had half as much smarts as your Gram did that he wouldn't be in the debt that I knew he was in.

The farmer was shocked, and your Gram laughed outright. He refused to sell her the truck after that. I offered to drive your Gram into Springfield to buy a truck, and she took me up on my offer. On the way there we bonded."

He chuckled again, "well, maybe bonded is too strong of a word. We had a mutual respect for each other. Anyway, the next day your grandmother brought your great grandma into the office, they sat right there, your great-grandma sat in that very chair you're sitting in."

I touched the arm of the chair picture Gigi sitting there.

"Well, we discussed a great many things that day. The world was changing. One difficulty your family was experiencing was that without a bank they could not cash or write checks. Their assets paid them with checks. I asked what they wanted, and I listened to them. Belle, they were intelligent women. They knew exactly what they wanted. I agreed with most of their ideas. I was able to convince them to diversify into a few areas, which thank goodness did pay off. Your grandma's appreciated that I treated them respectfully and listened to them without sexism. I think they were tired of how men treated women as if they didn't have a brain. I often thought that was why they preferred to live how they did."

He finished his story, and I knew that Mr. Bee had to be a pretty smart man himself to have garnered the respect and trust of my Grandma's.

I was a bit overwhelmed knowing that not only had I inherited the farm and the surrounding property including half of Green Mountain, but also I had stocks that paid monthly dividends. I also had a savings account that was to be used only in emergencies. Mr. Bee assured me I didn't have to

worry about money, but I did have to think about
the future.

I was relieved that I didn't have to think about
finances for a while. I would be lying if I said I
hadn't been worried about it. I could now stay on
the farm and continue living with my animals and
not worry about bills. I once again thought about
my Momma and the fact that she had been
contemplating selling the farm and our half of the
Green Mountain.

"So what happens now, Mr. Bee?"

"Well, the paperwork is minimal. Would you like to
continue using my services?"

I paused, alarmed that he may not want to.

"I have to ask, Belle. It's a legal thing."

I was instantaneously relieved.

"Yes, please."

Mr. Bee smiled and handed me a paper that I read
over. It was a simple contract. I signed it. Mr. Bee
charged our family monthly. The amount seemed
small, but what did I know? I did know that Mr.
Bee would never cheat me, and I was comforted
that he would continue to represent me.

"So last thing Belle. Your family has a unique Will.
In a nutshell, it states that the heir to your property
must be a blood relative." He produced a paper,
and I saw that Gigi's grandfather's name was on
top of the paper and below his name was Gigi
fathers name; they were both crossed out with
dates next to them. Then came Gigi's name
followed by Gram's and those had been crossed

out as well, lastly was my Momma's name and now that was crossed out too. My name was under hers. "If you would initial here and then sign down at the bottom all the property and investments will be transferred to your name."

I looked at the paper and tears slid down my face. My hand shook as I held the pen he had given me. "I'm sorry Belle, I know this is difficult." Mr. Bee said softly. I couldn't speak so I nodded then signed the paper.

"Mr. Bee, what happens when I?"

I couldn't even finish my thought.

"Belle, one day perhaps you will marry, and if blessed with children their names will go underneath yours. The Will stipulates only a blood relation to the heir can inherit. It's an unbreakable clause. It's in the Will so a husband, that's not a blood relative, can't take the property from his wife."

"And if I pass without leaving an heir?"

"The property goes to the State of Vermont and everything else goes to specified charities. Here's a list of those charities your family has as beneficiaries. Would you like to add one?"

I thought about it for a second.

"Can the library be added to the list?"

Mr. Bee smiled and said, "of course." He wrote a note to himself.

"So, do you understand what we've talked about today? I know it's a lot to take in."

"I think I understand everything. I just hope I remember it."

Mr. Bee chuckled. "You will. You're smart like your grandma's."

"Thank you, Mr. Bee." I noted he didn't say my momma, but I didn't take any offense. I understood that Momma was smart with other things.

Mr. Bee smiled at me compassionately and then stood up from behind his desk. "If you have more questions please call me. I've been a friend of your family for years, and I want you to know that you can count on me for anything. Now, how about if I take you home?"

"Yes, thank you. Umm, Mr. Bee could I run into the food store quickly and then would you mind if I picked up some feed from the Feed and Grain?"

"Of course, how about if I meet you out front in a half an hour, and then I'll take you over to the Feed and Grain, is that doable?"

"Yes, perfect."

Mr. Bee reached into his top drawer and handed me a one hundred dollar bill. "Will this be enough?" he asked.

"Yes, thank you." I watched as he made a notation in a book that was in the drawer before shutting it. I headed to the market, and I knew the news of my Momma's death had reached the townspeople. A few persons smiled sadly at me and the woman at the market who always rang up our groceries told me she was sorry for my loss. I nodded and thanked her.

She packed up my items in a box, and I carried them outside where I met Mr. Bee. He was standing by a shiny white Saab, a car that I knew from hearing radio advertisements, was good for the harsh Vermont winters. He took the box from me and put it in the back seat and then held the passenger side door open for me. We stopped at the Hardware store, which doubled as the Grain and Feed store. I signed for a large bag of feed for Bessie and Henny, another bag of feed for the sheep, and another for the pigs. Mr. Greeter carried the bags outside for me and put them in the back of Mr. Bee's car. He told me he was sorry about my Momma and I thanked him.

6

A half hour later I was home. We emptied Mr. Bee's car of my purchases, and he asked if he could help me take the feed to the barn, but I declined his offer. Mr. Bee told me he would call to check on me tomorrow, and again I thanked him.

I was exhausted; I'd been away from the farm for longer than ever before. I wanted to do my chores, check on Mimi, and go to bed. Tomorrow I would have to dig Momma's grave, and that would not be an easy task.

Josh rose from his perch on the front lawn where he had been waiting for me and moved gingerly up the steps to follow me inside. I put away the groceries and quickly changed into jeans, and a tee shirt. Since I'd been away all day, I first hurried to the sheep's corral to first see how Mimi was faring. She was moving even slower than this morning, so I knew I'd be sleeping in the barn that night to be near her. I opened the hatchway and herded the sheep into the small corral inside the barn. Mimi made her way inside too, and after I shut the hatch, I guided her to an unoccupied stall where she could be alone.

I put the chickens in their coop and fed the pigs and checked they had enough water. Then I put Bessie in her stall and fed and watered her. Lastly, I fed Henny and made sure there was plenty of water in her outside trough. I had put Mimi in the stall next to Henny's, and if Mimi gave birth she'd be bellowing, and Henny would get agitated, so I left her outside.

Satisfied that the animals were taken care of, I went back inside the house. I fed Josh and then made myself a peanut butter and jelly sandwich.

When my grandmothers had been alive, we had sat down for every meal; breakfast, lunch, and dinner, but lately my Momma had been forgoing that tradition. Sometimes she would even eat in the living room so she could watch her shows. My Momma had been our primary cook, and I bit back tears remembering how we had sat at the table as a family enjoying many delicious meals that she had prepared.

The sun was almost down, and I didn't feel like listening to music or watching television, so I sat out on the back porch with Josh at my feet and listened to the sounds of the day closing. I was so tired that my eyes drifted shut. I needed to be near Mimi tonight, so I shook off the fatigue, went back inside, and took a couple of blankets from the wooden chest in Grams room.

I retrieved the emergency light from the utility drawer in the kitchen and headed to the barn. The hay was in the loft, but I had thrown down a couple of bales the day before to use on the stalls. I spread some of the fresh fodder, creating a hay nest for me to sleep. I lay one blanket in the indention and used the other two as my covers. Josh circled at my feet before lying down against my legs. I turned off the light and hunkered down to what I knew would be another long night.

I loved the barn. I spent a good deal of my life in it, and I took comfort in the familiar smells around me. Yes, there were the pungent animal odors, but to me, they were soothing. The hay and the grain bins had their sweet smells, and the barn itself had a woodsy scent.

The sounds of the animals settling down for the night consoled me as I thought about my Momma. A fresh wave of tears overwhelmed my tired eyes, and I attempted to rub them away, but they continued to flow. A whimper slipped from my throat, and the sadness I'd been trying so hard to hold in check, burst free in the form of a deluge of tears and body racking sobs. Josh stood and walked up the small bed of hay to lick my cheeks, and I hugged him to me until he lay down next to me. The ache in my chest was crushing, and my head begged to be free from the heavy pressure of a headache I'd bore for almost twenty- four hours. I couldn't stop crying. My nose ran, and my throat was sore. I knew my eyelids were swollen; they felt uncomfortably heavy. I used my shirt to wipe my face as best I could.

I was a wreck. I was alone. I couldn't remember ever feeling so lost. I buried my face in Old Josh's tan coat and cried for my absent family, and even for myself. My life was going to change, it already had, and I was so frightened that my usually calm and logical demeanor was obliterated.

I awoke upon hearing Mimi's harsh bleating. I turned on the large emergency light and sat up from my hay bed. Josh got to his feet and shook off a few stray pieces of straw that clung to his fur. I flipped off the blankets that had covered me and stood quickly, shining the light towards where I knew Mimi would be.

Sure enough, she was on her side, and her large tummy rippled as a contraction tore through her. I went to the bucket of water that I had filled earlier and reached for one of the two clean towels that I had hung on a wooden peg near the stalls. I used the bar of Ivory that I had laid on the flat piece of wood near the bucket and thoroughly washed my hands all the way up to my elbows. Then I dried them and rubbed on antibiotic ointment all the way to my elbows. This was something my Gigi had taught me.

I carried the other towel into Mimi's small pen. I knelt near her, away from her hoofs, but close to her rear and although I wanted to calm her, by petting her I didn't want to dirty my disinfected hands in case I needed to help with the birth. Mimi's bleating grew harsher, so I spoke to her gently, hoping to encourage her. Mother Nature took over, and Mimi pushed her tiny lamb from her womb.

I helped clear the little lambs nasal passages and rubbed him vigorously with the towel before placing him at Mimi's side. Mimi began licking him clean. I made sure the placenta was fully discharged, and then I placed it in a clean bucket to discard of later.

Mimi stood up shakily, but I knew that it was a good sign when the Momma stood up after birthing. I was now able to clean the area around her with a brush and soap and water. I gave them fresh hay and feed and placed a clean bucket of water for her.

When I finished, I sat back in the wooden stall watching over Mimi as she lay back down on the clean hay to nurse her babe. I became aware that the other animals in the barn had started to move around, so I knew it was close to dawn.

I was tired, and my body was sore from sleeping on my makeshift hay bed, but I was relieved that Mimi had successfully birthed her lamb. I hated when we lost animals, and if this birth had gone badly, I would have really been knocked for a loop. A smile escaped me as I gazed at the tiny male lamb that was now part of my small flock. A wave of sorrow followed when I realized I had to name the lamb. That had always been my Momma's favorite thing to do.

I thought of male names, and the one that kept popping in my head was William, the Sheriff's name. He had been so kind to me so I figured I'd honor his kindness by naming the new lamb after him. I gave Mimi and tiny William a gentle rub purposely letting William smell my hands so he would become familiar with my scent. I praised Mimi, and I swear she smiled at me.

I needed to use the bathroom, but I held off. Since I was already in the barn, I decided to do my barn chores. I rushed through them methodically, and when I finished, I carried the eggs inside.

I entered the side door and toed off my barn boots in the mudroom before continuing into the kitchen. I saw on the oven clock that it was 6:30. I needed to shower, even though I knew digging Momma's grave would render me filthy, I hoped that the shower would rouse me. I also smelled like the barn, and although that was not entirely unpleasant, I wanted to enjoy baking my bread and drinking my coffee without that clingy animal smell on me, so I quickly showered.

I was ridiculously proud of myself that I held myself together in the shower even when I smelled my Momma's rose scented products. I gave myself a mental kudos for staying strong.

Clean from the shower I brushed my hair and braided it before putting on an old pair of jeans and a soft blue tee shirt. I made a pot of coffee and then I realized that I had made enough for two people. I had already ladled in two scoops of beans into the grinder before I realized what I had done. I could have easily taken them out, but I figured after yesterday and the early morning that I'd just had maybe I'd need an extra cup or two. I cranked the handle on the antique grinder and then poured the ground coffee beans into the silver filter. I added a pinch of cinnamon and plugged in the percolator.

Next, I mixed the ingredients for the bread. I liked wheat bread so I prepared enough to make two loaves' and placed the readied dough in a bowl and covered it so it would rise. After it rose, I would shape it and put it in a loaf pan to bake. Usually, I would prepare the dough the night before, and then after my barn chores I would bake the bread, but today I'd have to wait until later to bake it. I had a grave to dig.

I fed Josh and let him outside before making myself an egg and cheese sandwich. I took a mug from the cabinet and poured myself a cup adding in cream and two sugar cubes. Then I took my mug and sandwich outside to the front porch. From the front porch, I had a view of our front property. On the far left was a small pond, which I knew had been dug years ago in case we ever had a fire. The frogs were croaking happily as the early morning sun warmed their water and sent rays of silver into the murky surface. An old shed was also to the left, that's where we put the truck when the weather was bad. We also stored a plow in there along with the small tractor that we used to cut the lawn and some tools. There were thick woods behind the shed. Those woods went on forever and bracketed our driveway that led to the county road. There were no lights along the long dirt and gravel driveway, and at night the long drive sometimes appeared sinister with the moon casting shadows through the tree limbs. Our driveway was nothing more than a mile long dirt lane. It started as a circular loop in front of our house and ended at the country road that led to town. The County Road ended at the end of our drive. Years ago we had a gate at the end of our driveway entrance, but the gate was left open now. Gigi said it had been to discourage solicitors. No one ever came to the house, so we stopped shutting the gate.

To my right, beyond the grassy front lawn was a meadow, and on a hill in that meadow sat the family cemetery. I could see the tops of black wrought iron fencing from where I sat. In the distance, the front of our entire property had a backdrop view of three beautiful mountains tops. To my far right, I could see a part of the barn.

I sat in my chair on the front porch, the one I had been sitting in forever, and took in the three vacant chairs that were near mine. Tears dampened my eyes, and I wiped them quickly. I had never cried so much in my entire life. I felt sad when my grandmothers had passed, but I'd never felt this kind of sorrow before. I wished I could be stronger. My Grandma's would want me to be stronger.

I had always felt like I was a mixture of my family's different personalities. I had my Gram's tough, quiet, even temperament. I had Gigi's pragmatic disposition. I thought that I had some of my Momma's fun and gentle nature too. My heart ached knowing that I'd never get to talk to her again. I was still shocked that she may have wanted to sell our farm. "Momma why didn't you talk to me?" I whispered aloud.

I took a bite of my sandwich, but it sat like a rock in my stomach, and I just couldn't force down another bite. I sipped my hot coffee and as I looked out over the farm; my family's legacy, I anguished that it was now solely my responsibility. I hoped I was up to the considerable undertaking of keeping it up.

I finished my coffee and walked back inside. I needed to get started on the grave. The last time I'd dug a grave I had been with Momma and that had taken the two of us hours. It had been hard work. Momma had tried to keep our spirits up by telling me about all the new things she had read in her magazines. Digging the six by three-foot hole alone was going to be trying and time-consuming, and I knew I could not procrastinate any longer. I went into the mudroom and dug around in a large drawer in the dresser we had there. I finally found the string I had been looking for. The string would mark where I needed to dig and how far down I needed to dig. Momma had shown it to me when we had dug Gram's grave. I guess my great- great grandparents had fashioned it, way back when, and we were still using it. Lastly, I got down the thermos from the pantry and filled it with water. I was capping the thermos when I heard two cars pull down my drive. I dried my hands off and walked outside as Sheriff McDaniel's car pulled to a stop in front of the house followed by a truck. The Sheriff got out of his car, and I turned my attention to the person's getting out of the black truck that stopped behind him. A teenage boy hopped out of the passenger side of the truck. He was smiling and had a mop of dark glossy hair. He was taller than me, and gangly, like his muscles were still catching up to him. He smiled shyly at me, and I saw he had two dimples that gave off an adorable boyish charm. He walked over to stand by the Sheriff. I couldn't see the driver of the truck; the windows were tinted, so I turned to the Sheriff who had walked around his car to greet me.

"Morning Belle," he said extending his hand, which I took in mine and shook.

"This is my boy, Tommy." He said nodding at the young man standing next to him. I shook the boy's hand. "And that's my oldest, Brady." He said gesturing towards the truck.

I looked to where he had pointed and watched a man walking around the front end of the truck. He stopped and leaned against his grill. He crossed his arms, and the first thing I noticed was how defined they were. His whole body looked rock hard. He had dark hair and like his brother and it hung across his forehead in a gentle raven wave. He was looking down at the ground so that I couldn't see his face. I deduced that he was taller than me by a good 8 inches.

"Belle?" It was then that I realized I'd been staring and Sheriff Mac Daniels's had been speaking to me. When he realized that he had my attention again, he started talking.

"As I told you yesterday, your Mom will be arriving here tomorrow. I'm heading up to Springfield this morning; do you have an outfit you want to have her dressed in? I'll bring it to the Medical Examiner's Office; they can dress her for you."

The breath left me for a second in a small gasp. Just hearing that her body would be coming had sent a frightening shiver down my spine. I was so alone.

I nodded to indicate that I had heard him. The Sheriff was watching me closely waiting for an answer. I knew he was concerned for me. I didn't trust my voice not to waiver with tearful sentimentality, but I had to speak.

"Yes, I'll go get something." I turned and walked back into the house, my emotions surfacing once again.

I walked upstairs to my Momma's room and opened the door. This was going to be tough. Her scent was everywhere, her favorite things adorning her bedroom, but I couldn't break down now. The Sheriff was outside waiting for me, and I had no idea why he had brought his sons with him. I opened my Momma's closet and took out a dress that I knew was her favorite. I took the shoes that matched from the floor and even grabbed a pair of clean underwear and bra from her dresser drawer. I had no idea what they needed, but better to be thorough. I put everything in a small paper bag and headed back outside.

I handed the bag to the Sheriff, and he seemed somewhat relieved. I guess he knew that picking out clothes for my Momma to be buried in hadn't been easy, and he was probably thankful I wasn't a blubbering mess.

The Sheriff put the bag on his passenger seat and turned back to me.

"I called Mr. Bee, and he talked to Pastor John. He wants your Momma to be brought to the church first. I hope that's all right? He said he would bring your Momma and his church helpers at 2:00 PM tomorrow for the service." I knew they were the custodians at the church and they would be the ones to put the casket in the grave and cover it with the dirt from the hole that I was going to be digging today.

"Thank you," I said softly. I was grateful everything was planned, and that did ease my mind.

"I heard you tell Mr. Bee you were going to dig your Momma's grave today." The Sheriff said still watching me closely.

Again I nodded. Then I decided to add, "Yes, its tradition. We dig the graves."

"Well, my boys are here to help you."

I looked at the two boys, well one boy, and one man. Tommy was staring at me nervously, and Brady was still looking at the ground. Neither appeared happy to be there.

"Sheriff." I fought to keep my voice even. I wasn't mad, but digging the grave was my responsibility. "There is no need for your boys to help me. It is very nice for you to offer their services, but no thank you."

I watched Brady tip his head up, and that's when I saw his face. He was extremely good-looking, like the men I saw on television. He had dark stubble covering his jaw, and it made him appear rugged. His eyes met mine, and I felt my breath leave my lungs. Good grief the man was handsome. His

moss green eyes were like his fathers. He had been
frowning but his lips tightened. His expression
changed from sullen to surprises hearing what I
had just said to his dad. He was staring at me now,
so I averted my eyes quickly. I hope he hadn't seen
me looking at him. From the corner of my eye I
saw that he had unfolded his thick arms and placed
his hands in his front pockets.

"Belle, we are not negotiating this. My boys are
going to help you. They brought their own
shovels."

"Sheriff, really," I stuttered as words escaped me. I
was ridiculously nervous. I had never even spoken
to a boy before. The Sheriff wanted me to be alone
with two of them! I gulped anxiously, wringing my
hands in my tee shirt.

"When you're done, they will leave you be, but
until that grave is dug, they're staying." The
Sheriff's tone indicated that he was not going to
take no for an answer and deep down I knew I'd
probably need their help.

"Well then, thank you. It took Momma and me
almost a whole day to dig Gram's grave."

I heard Brady grunt. What was his problem?

"That a girl." The Sheriff said pleased as punch that
I'd accepted his boys help.

Tommy sauntered off to the back of the truck, and
he returned with two shovels. The Sheriff reached
into his passenger side of his car and came out
holding a picnic basket.

"My wife sent this for you three to eat while you
work." He put the basket down at my feet and

reached back into his car only to turn back to me and hand me two covered dishes.

"And these are for you. This here is a pot pie, my wife, makes the best pot pie around, and this is a plate of brownies."

"My Mom's brownies are famous," Tommy supplied with a cheeky grin.

I took the plates from the Sheriff. I was surprised by the food offerings. I should not have been. My Momma, my Grandmothers, and I had been sending food to neighbors for funerals, babies, weddings, and other occasions ever since I could remember. It was nice to know other's made the same kindly gesture.

"Thank you, Sheriff, and please thank your wife for me."

Brady walked over to the basket and hefted it up. I noticed he walked with a slight limp.

"Let me just put these plates inside, and we can get going," I said looking at Tommy and then to Brady.

"Boys I'll see you at home." The Sheriff said as he turned to get in his car. Tommy was carrying the shovels, and Brady was carrying the basket as they both followed behind me.

I couldn't open the front door with my hands full, so Brady opened it, and as I passed by him, I could smell a pleasing scent of leather and spice that came off of him. Tommy left the shovels outside and followed after me.

"Something smells good," Tommy said as he looked around my home. I was instantly on edge that they were going to judge me. My family was considered to be odd. I wondered if my home looked like other peoples.

Tommy was gazing towards the kitchen, and I realized he smelled the coffee.

"It's coffee. Would you like a cup?"

Tommy giggled boyishly, "I don't drink coffee. My Mom won't let me yet."

"Would you like a cup Brady?" I said my voice was shaky looking at the handsome man who was standing near my rustic wooden dining table.

"It does smell good. Yeah, a cup before we work will be good; thank you." He sat down putting the basket at his feet and Tommy followed suit.

I poured a cup for Brady and another one for myself. Then I poured Tommy a glass of milk. I placed the last of the bread that I'd made the other day on a cutting board along with the bread knife on the table then added jars of strawberry and peach preserves. I laid out three small plates and finally set out the cream and sugar before sitting down across from them.

"Please, help yourself," I said in what I hoped was considered good hostess manners.

Tommy took a large gulp of milk before slicing himself a hunk of bread.

"I never cut my own bread before," he said as he applied a heaping tablespoon of strawberry jam to his thickly cut bread slice. He took a large bite, and as he chewed, I could tell he wanted to talk, but his mouth was full.

"Mmmmm," he moaned with his full mouth shut, successfully conveying that he liked what he was eating.

I grinned, pleased that he liked it. I made good bread and put up a great jar of jam. I had added my own special ingredients through the years, and my Momma had said no one made better bread than me. That was a pretty big compliment coming from her because she had been the best cook ever.

"Good?" I asked with a tiny smile.

Tommy swallowed, "This is the best bread and jam I have ever had." He wiped his mouth with the back of his hand reminding me that I had not put out napkins. I stood quickly and reached into a drawer of the large china hutch and brought out three cloth napkins. I placed one near each plate.

"Where did you buy it?" Tommy asked his mouth finally totally clear of food.

"The bread and jam?"

"Yes, I have to tell my mom. She'll love this, so will dad. They're into that old-fashioned stuff."

I blushed slightly embarrassed, but it didn't bother me too much. I knew I'd been raised different and that we were considered to be old-fashioned.

"Tommy!" Brady admonished him quickly.

"What?" He looked up at his brother utterly unaware of what he had said.

"Sorry," Brady apologized.

"It's all right."

"What?" Tommy asked again.

"Tommy, Belle made the bread and probably the jam too."

I nodded confirming this.

"Wow, this is good stuff, Belle. Why did you holler at me?" He asked looking at his brother.

"Because you said..." Brady looked a bit flustered so I rescued him.

"We know it's a bit old-fashioned to bake our own bread and to put up the jam, but it tastes so much better than store bought, so we have just continued to do it."

"It tastes way better than store-bought." Tommy agreed as he took another huge bite making me smile.

Brady had sliced himself a piece of bread, and he spread strawberry jam on his. He smiled after he took his first bite.

After he swallowed, he grinned at me awkwardly. "This is wonderful, and the coffee is really good too."

I was so pleased with the compliments. "Thank you. We grind our beans and add a little cinnamon."

I realized I'd been saying 'we' and I sat back in my chair and fiddled with my napkin to organize the emotional chaos surging through me.

Tommy and Brady finished off their bread, and I stood to clear everything away. The boys stood, and Brady carried his cup and plate to the sink. He thanked me for the coffee and bread.

Once again I noticed his leathery spicy smell. Tommy brought me his glass and plate, and he thanked me as well.

"You know I didn't mean anything about the old fashion comment, right?" He said looking sweetly contrite.

I set down the dishrag and smiled gently at him. "Yes, I know," I assured him.

We left the house, and I shut the door behind me. Tommy was holding two shovels, and Brady was holding the basket. Josh had risen from his normal sunny spot on the porch and curiously eyed the two visitors.

"I have to check on the lamb that came last night and grab my shovel," I told them.

"Can I see the lamb?" Tommy asked jogging to me. "Sure."

We walked into the barn, and I was aware that Brady had followed us too.

"See," I said as I pointed at Mimi nursing William. "The Momma's name is Mimi, and the little guy is about four hours old, and I named him William."

"William?" Brady asked.

"Yes, after your father actually." I felt funny after I told him that but I wasn't sure why.

"You named that lamb after my Dad?" Tommy asked.

"Yes. He was very kind to me yesterday, and when I had to think of a male name, I decided to use your dad's."

"That's so cool! Wait till I tell him!" Tommy was beaming. "Can I pet him?"

"Not now. He's only a couple hours old, and the Momma will become agitated."

I saw that Brady was watching me closely and it made me nervous. I turned from the small pen and took the shovel off the wall that was near the door and walked outside where Josh met me. I gave his ears a sound scratching before starting to walk up the open field. I could hear Tommy and Brady following behind me. Tommy was whispering to Brady, but I couldn't hear what he was saying. The walk to the family plot took 5 minutes. There were six headstones, my great -great grandparents on my Momma's side, Gigi and her husband, and Gram and her husband. It was getting a little crowded.

Brady stepped even with me.

"Where do you want to bury her?"

I studied the small area and decided to dig in the upper corner of the plot. It was nearest the woods, and my Momma loved taking walks in the woods.

"Over there," I said pointing to the corner area.

We walked over to the patch of grass, and I dug out the piece of string I stuffed into my back pocket that morning.

I laid the string on the ground and Brady watched as I made an indentation at each end of the string with my shovel. I did the same on the other side, and then I folded the string in half and marked the top and bottom.

I rolled the string back up and stuffed it in my pocket.

"That's pretty handy," Brady said referring to the string.

"Yes, my great great-grandparents fashioned it. I didn't expect to be using it so soon after..." I let my sentence drop off because I had choked up.
Brady nodded solemnly. I think he knew I was teetering emotionally.
Tommy had finished reading the headstones and joined us.
I described what we needed to do. "We need to dig 6 feet down. We put the dirt over there so the casket can be lowered from either side and the preacher will stand there." I don't know why I said all of that. I suppose I wanted them to visualize it so it would be done correctly.
Brady dug in first, and we began the arduous task of digging my Momma's grave.

I had been worried about what to talk to the two of them about. I didn't have any practice speaking to persons near my own age, and I did not want to appear even more old-fashioned, as Tommy had alluded to. Luckily, Tommy did most of the talking. My Gram would have called him a regular chatterbox. He told me all about school. Summer break was beginning shortly, and that created a whole topic of conversation as he proceeded to tell Brady and me what he planned on doing during the three-month hiatus from school.
I enjoyed listening to him, and it made me grin when I saw Brady shaking his head as he spoke. I think he thought his brother was a chatterbox too.
I didn't wear a watch, but when we were finished, Tommy told Brady and me that it had taken us

four hours. We had stopped for lunch, so I figured
it had only taken 3 and a half hours. Mrs.
McDaniel's had made sandwiches and sent small
bags of carrots, apples, and nuts. She also had
included cookies and a thermos of lemonade.
About an hour into digging I realized I had left my
thermos of water at home, so it was a good thing
we had the lemonade. Digging a grave was thirsty
work.

The last hour had been tough because beside the
water jug I had also forgotten the bucket needed to
heft the dirt out of the hole. I glumly thought that
if my forgetfulness, regarding this task, was any
indication of how I was going to get on by myself,
I might be in trouble.

We all couldn't fit in the grave, so Tommy and
Brady stayed in the hole and tossed the dirt up to
me. I moved the dirt to a pile at one end of the
grave.

Brady's limping had become more pronounced the
longer we worked, and I felt horrible because I
could tell he was in pain. Sometimes his lips would
press into a thin line, and once in a while, he would
clench his jaw tightly together.

The grave was finally dug, and Tommy got down
on his hands and knees, and Brady stepped on his
back and pulled himself out. I'm not sure what
possessed me, but as he pulled himself from the
hole, I attempted to aid him by grabbing him
underneath his arms. His large body cleared the
hole, and he awkwardly tumbled on top of me, our
faces froze mere inches apart from each other. I

was mortified. It was the first time that I had even touched a boy, and humiliatingly it was with full body contact. My face flushed red, but he quickly rolled off of me. Brady remained on his knees and reached down into the grave to extend his hands to his brother. Tommy held them and walked up the wall as Brady pulled him upwards.

By the time Tommy was out, I had composed myself. We gathered up the shovels and Brady grabbed the empty lunch basket. I whistled for Josh who had run off to lie near the woods edge. That old dog hated being in the hot sun. Josh ran to me, and I rubbed his head affectionately.

We were walking back through the field each lost in our thoughts, and I was tuckered out.

"Belle?" Tommy was on one side of me and turned to look as we continued walking.

"Yes?"

"Won't you be scared out here on your own?" Brady tensed beside me. I wasn't sure why. Maybe he didn't like the question. I couldn't be sure.

"Well, I've only been alone two nights so far," I said contemplating if I could answer him any better.

"Were you afraid?"

I thought about it. "No, not last night."

"Why not?"

"I slept in the barn last night because I knew Mimi was going to have her lamb. I needed to be close in case she needed me."

I glanced at Brady who was starting to fall behind us, I presumed because of whatever was making him limp. I slowed my steps so we wouldn't get too far ahead of him.

"Keep walking," Brady bit out tersely.

I was taken back by his sharp tone and gasped.

"Brady!" Tommy chastised him loudly.

He quickly hobbled to move ahead of us. I looked at Tommy who just shrugged his shoulders. When we neared my house, I saw that Sheriff McDaniel car was in the driveway.

"Dad's here I can't wait to show him the lamb." Tommy yelled at his dad and started running towards him, which prompted Josh to run, leaving Brady and me alone for the first time.

"Thank you for helping me today," I said quietly hoping to lighten the tension that had grown between us.

"Your welcome." He stopped walking, and I almost ran into his back. "How the hell did you think you were going to do that on your own?" I was startled by his tone, and he made me feel foolish. I teared up.

"Oh shit. Don't cry."

I rubbed the tears away and held my gaze away from him.

"I would have gotten it done," I said quietly.

Brady sighed, and I felt his hand touch my arm, and I froze.

His hand fell away, but its effect was what he had wanted, and I was now looking at him.

"I know you would have gotten it done, Belle. It's just not right that you would have done it alone."

I didn't quite know what to say to that, so I nodded and just replied, "Well I didn't have to now, did I?" I said trying to sound stronger than I was feeling. Brady turned from me, and this time I caught his arm with my hand. I saw him look to where I was touching him and quickly pulled my hand back. Brady looked up at my face, and I swallowed hoping to garner some spit in my dry mouth. I couldn't believe how hard it was to talk to boys. "Why are you limping?" I asked with a tiny voice. Brady didn't answer right away, and I thought he might even turn from me, but he did not. Instead, he reached down to the hem of his jeans and pulled them up just enough so I could see a metal bar that ran inside his boot. He was an amputee.

He dropped his pant leg and stood up. I knew he was watching my face to gauge my reaction.

"How did it happen?" I asked calmly.

"I was a Marine. My buddy stepped on a mine, and I was walking next to him."

"I'm sorry. My great granddad was a Marine."

"I saw that on his headstone."

"When we buried him do you know that a Marine stayed outside with his casket the entire night?"

Brady smiled. It wasn't a big ole toothy smile, but it was enough to let me know he and I were okay.

"Yeah, it's a Marine thing."

"Did your friend survive?" I asked.

"No." His tone was somber. We started walking again.

"You know my Gigi was a nurse; some say she was gifted. She was called upon all the time to help our neighbors."

"That right?" Brady replied, lost in thought and just answering to be polite.

"Yes, and she taught me everything she knew. One of those things was how to rub the limb of an amputee."

Brady stopped walking, and the look he gave me could only be described as one of horror. I guess I wasn't good at talking to boys at all.

"What are you saying, Belle?" He was mad, I could tell.

"Well, since you helped me all day perhaps I could return the favor and rub your leg for you. I know it would help you feel better. I have the best ointment ever and."

"Geez, Belle stop." Brady was shaking his head. "That's not going to happen, all right?"

"I just..."

I let my sentence fall because we had reached the barn and I could hear Tommy telling his dad that I had named the lamb after him. Putting distance between Brady and myself, I walked inside the barn, as the three men followed behind me. I hung my shovel up and walked to where they were leaning over the small stall looking in.

"He's a tiny little guy." The Sheriff said.

"He was born last night."

"Did you help birth him?"

"No, Mimi did all the hard work, I just helped at the end."

The Sheriff chuckled.

"Thank you for naming him after me. I'm honored."

I grinned. "You were so kind to me yesterday. It is my honor to do so."

"Is the grave dug?" The Sheriff turned and looked at Brady who remained quiet.

"Yes, all finished."

The Sheriff looked at his son and then me, and I thought I saw his lips turn upwards ever so slightly, but I hadn't been around many men, so it was probably nothing.

"Brady I'm taking Tommy to choir practice. I'll see you at home."

Brady nodded, and we all left the barn. The Sheriff and Tommy said good-bye and then just as I thought that I was about to be alone again Brady asked for a glass of water. We'd run out of the lemonade a half hour before we finished so I was thirsty too and didn't think anything odd about his request.

"Sure, have a seat on the porch."

"Can I wash up first?"

"Oh, of course." I showed Brady where the mudroom bathroom was and I went to wash my own hands in Gigi's bathroom. I took the soothing balm, which she and I had made years ago, from the medicine closet and put it in my back pocket. Then I went to the kitchen, poured two glasses of water, and walked outside. Brady was sitting in one of the chairs looking deep in thought. I handed him his glass and then reached into my pocket, and placed the small glass jar on the table that was between us.

Brady took a big sip of his water and then pointed at the blue jar. "What's that?"

"That's the balm I told you about."

I observed his facial expression, hoping I hadn't gone too far. I wasn't sure what boys and girls were supposed to say to each other, but I knew if I had a friend who was in pain that this is what I'd do for them.

His eyes darkened and a frown settled on his lips. I thought he was going to stand up and leave, but he didn't.

"Belle, my leg. It's not pretty. It's badly scarred. It's nice of you to offer, but honestly, I don't think you realize what you'll be seeing, much less touching."

Oh, so that was it; he was worried about me seeing his leg. I smiled gently at him and moved to sit on the ottoman that was in front of him.

"Brady, I understand how you're feeling, but you're in pain, and it's because you dug my Momma's grave. I can ease your discomfort." I sighed and stood up.

"Where are you going?"

"I'm going to get you a beer to help you relax, and then I'm going to rub down that leg." I turned and walked inside and I was pretty sure I heard him chuckle. It was a nice sound.

When I came back outside, I sat back down on the ottoman.

"Here you go," I said handing him the Budweiser. There had always been beer in the fridge. My Gram liked to have one after being outside all day. My Momma didn't care for the taste; she liked champagne. I liked beer, and I liked champagne. I just didn't drink very often.

Brady took a long pull on his beer, and I reached to pull the leg of his jeans up.

He put the beer down and gently batted my hands away. "I can do that."

He lifted the thick denim material, and I could see that he had been amputated below the knee. The prosthetic was a metal bar attached to a hard plastic sleeve, and even though I couldn't see it yet, I knew that above his knee there was a strap holding it in place.

"That's great that they could save your knee," I told him. Brady looked at me and then shook his head. "Are you always this matter-of-fact?"

"Actually, yes," I said, which got another chuckle out of him.

He was having difficulty undoing the strap because his jeans wouldn't lift up past his knee and I could see that he was getting frustrated.

I carefully put my hands up inside of his pant leg to help him, and his entire body froze. I quickly went to work unbuckling him, and after I undid the straps, I gently pulled off the prosthetic and put it on the ground next to us. I scooted the ottoman closer to him and placed his scarred stub on my lap. Brady hadn't moved since I had touched his leg and it made me a little nervous.

"Are you okay?" I asked as I twisted the lid off the jar and laid it back on the table.

"Yeah, this is just a little weird. I haven't even allowed my parents to see my leg and here you are, a stranger and I'm going to let you rub some cream on me."

"It's not cream, it's a balm, and it will make it feel better."

I rolled his jeans up as far as they would go then dipped two fingers into the jar scooping out a tablespoon of the special salve. I remembered to warm it first, by rubbing my hands together. When I felt it warming in my palms, I lay my hands on his stump and began to massage him. I closed my eyes letting my fingers feel the scars, and I concentrated on remembering everything Gigi had taught me. Brady moaned so softly that I almost hadn't heard him. I looked up worried that I was massaging him too hard. His head was resting comfortably on the high backing of the chair, his eyes were closed, and he a faint smile on his lips. He looked completely at ease. I was inwardly thrilled that I was helping him and that he had allowed me to do something nice for him.

I reapplied more ointment and manipulated every little knot from his muscles above and below his knee. I gently massaged the angry red scars and the irritated welts until; the redness turned to a light pink. When I finished, I looked up to find that he was watching me.

I blushed under his scrutiny.

"Does it feel better?" I whispered.

"It feels so much better Belle. I can't believe it. I thought I'd be hurting for days."

"Doesn't your doctor do this for you?" I asked as I reattached his prosthesis.

"Yes and no. I go to the VA Hospital in Springfield for appointments, but no one since it first happened has tended to it like you just did."

"Brady you need to rub it down all the time. It's good for the circulation, and it will help with chaffing and keep blisters at bay."

He smiled and tapped my nose with his fingertip, which surprised me. "Yes, I know all that Miss Logical, but there isn't a Physical Therapist near here, and I've been a tad busy trying to get my act together."

"I'll be your Therapist."

Brady laughed outright. "And you'd be a good one, but I can't ask you to do that."

"I offered, but you do what you want. You know where I live."

Brady smiled and stood up, so I did too.

"Thank you, Belle, for, you know, doing that. I know it's not something anyone would want to see."

He seemed embarrassed. His hands went back into his pockets.

"I didn't do it to look at it, Brady. I did it to help you." This man was a strange one. I think he was trying to say something else but darned if I knew what it was.

"Can I ask how old you are? I know it's not a very polite question to ask a woman, but I'd like to know if you don't mind?"

He wanted to know my age. I wonder why. "I'm 22. How old are you?"

"25."

I picked up the jar and replaced the cap.

"Thank you for helping me today. I'd probably still be out there."

"Yeah, you probably would be," he said with a teasing tone, which made me smile.

I walked him to his truck, and after he got in, he started the engine up and then turned to me.

"Belle, do you have my dad's phone number?"

"Yes, he gave me his card the other day."

"Good, don't be afraid to use it."

"Okay." I didn't know why I would need to use it, but my answer put a grin on Brady's face.

As he started to drive away, he waved and said, "See you tomorrow."

What? Why was he going to see me tomorrow? Tomorrow was Momma's funeral. I watched as the dust settled in his wake. I was alone again.

I was bone tired, but the animals needed bringing in and feeding, so I did that first. When I finished, I fed Josh and then I put the potpie into the oven and watched television until it was ready. I wanted to shower, but that would have meant walking past Momma's room, and I was sure I'd left the door open after I had gotten her clothes to be buried in. Physically and emotionally drained and still filthy from the digging I sat at the large kitchen table staring at the empty chairs around me and ate half of the delicious potpie.

I cleaned up my lone plate and knew I couldn't put off my shower any longer. I didn't think I could bear to pass by her open door knowing she would never be in there again. Soon enough I would need to pack away her belongings as Gram had done for Gigi, and my Momma had done for Gram. I guess that was another Green/Janson family tradition.

I finally got up the courage to go upstairs; I needed a shower. I jumped past her open doorway and then chastised myself for being silly.

My heart was pounding when I entered the bathroom. I didn't know why I was so jumpy. Momma's bath products still permeated the air and this time I didn't deny the tears that fell down my cheeks. I didn't cry as hard or as long this time, and like last time releasing my tears was cathartic.

I changed into my pajamas, but I couldn't bear to sleep upstairs. It felt so wrong that Momma wasn't in the next room. I quickly moved past her room and walked downstairs. I lay on the couch, pulling the soft Afghan over me. Josh circled nearby until he dropped placing his chin on his paws. I closed my eyes and wished my Momma would come in the front door and tell me I'd been having a nightmare. Fresh tears rolled down my face, and instead of holding them back I sobbed uncontrollably into the couch cushion. Josh picked his head up to check on me, and I swear that old hound was crying too.

7

I was dancing and laughing, but something was niggling at me that I shouldn't be happy. I pushed the thought away and kept dancing. I was being spun around, and when I stopped twirling, I was breathless and looking up into Brady's green eyes. He had a sly grin on his face until his lips contorted into a pained expression and I watched him collapse. He lay on the ground helplessly, and that's when I noticed that he had only one leg. I asked him where his prosthetic was and he started screaming at me to stop looking at him. I backed away from him shocked. Kaleidoscopes of floating unfamiliar faces were laughing at me. I woke up with a start.

I let my eyes adjust to the light while I calmed my breathing. What had started as a happy dream ended up being a nightmare. I hoped that wasn't an omen of things to come. My Momma believed in all that superstitious, paranormal stuff; I didn't, but still, the dream was odd.

I must have kicked off the afghan because it lay on the floor next to the couch. Josh was sitting near to me waiting patiently for me to let him out for his morning ritual.

I sighed deeply, sat up, and stretched my sore muscles. Digging that grave had been a hard workout and two nights of sleeping on the old couch and one in the barn hadn't helped either. It was 5:00 AM, and I had a full day ahead of me. Momma was coming home today, and Pastor John was coming to eulogize her. I got up, made coffee, and put the bread I'd made yesterday into the oven. The rooster crowed waking the animals up, and after changing I made my way outside to the barn. My first stop was to see how Mimi and William were doing. He was nursing, and Mimi greeted me by putting her nose in my hand. It was going to be a warm day, so I decided to leave them in the shade of barn for one more day. I shoveled the small stall, replenished the hay, and refilled the water trough and grain bucket.

Bessie greeted me with a swish of her tail and a little moo. I led her outside, and Henny trotted over to greet me pushing my hand. She knew I had a sugar cube for her. I always did. I laughed and fed it to her. I went back to the barn and mucked Bessie's stall and put out fresh hay for when I brought her inside later. I moved to the pig corral next and threw their feed into their trough. Then I tended to the sheep, feeding them as well. I uncoiled the hose and put fresh water in all the outside troughs. Lastly, I let the chickens out, and then I put fresh hay in their coop and scattered feed and collected the eggs.

When I went back inside, I put the eggs away and took the bread from the oven and poured myself a cup of coffee. I took the coffee outside and sat in my chair on the front porch. Today I would bury my Momma, and I knew that was going to be very sad. Her body would be arriving shortly, and I needed to prepare food for the repast. I knew Pastor John would come back to the house and I thought Mr. Bee would too since he had also attended Grams. I remembered that Brady had said that he would see me tomorrow and I wondered if he was coming so I decided that I better prepare extra food just in case.

It was 10:00 AM by the time I finished showering and thankfully I didn't break down this time. I dressed in jeans and a tee shirt, nothing fancy since I was only going to bake and clean the house. I put a chicken in the oven and made potato salad. I wasn't sure how much to make, so I doubled my potato salad recipe. Momma had always made the potato salad, and she would mix in hard-boiled eggs making it more of an egg-potato salad. It was delicious, and when I was younger I always asked her to make it, so when I turned 10, Momma had taught me how to make it. Next, I made a large container of sweet tea and set it on the back porch in the sunlight. In an hour I would take out the tea bags, add sugar, and then put it in the refrigerator. My Momma had also taught me to make sweet tea; that was her favorite drink. Little memories like that kept popping into my head as I prepared the food and tidied the house for the funerals repast. I opened the windows and turned on the ceiling fans to cool the house down. I had one more thing to do. I made myself a peanut butter sandwich, and as I walked to the side garden, I ate it. In the garden, I cut a large bouquet of wildflowers and tied them with string. These would go in a vase in the living room. Next, I cut a bouquet of red roses. These would go into the grave. My Momma had loved red roses. She had told me once that my father had given her a bouquet of red roses when they'd been dating. She didn't elaborate when or where that had happened, but the dreamy look she got in her eyes when she looked at the beautiful fragrant blooms told me all I needed to know. I also realized it was why she liked the scent of roses so much.

I went back inside and put the one bouquet of wildflowers in a vase and placed the vase on the table. I put the roses in another vase of water to keep them fresh. I looked at the clock and saw it was 1:15 PM. A lump formed in my throat. I had to rinse off, and I knew I couldn't use my usual shower. I couldn't risk breaking down so close to the funeral. I took a clean towel from a closet in Gigi's room used the bathroom that was between her and Gram's downstairs bedrooms. The bathroom had a combination shower-tub. I ran the tub and tossed in honeysuckle blooms. I only filled the tub a few inches. I just needed enough water to rinse off and feel clean again. My soak took a few minutes, and I loved the honeysuckle scent left on my skin. Feeling refreshed, I jogged back upstairs with the towel wrapped around me. In my mind I was running through everything I had done to prepare for the funeral, hoping I hadn't forgotten anything. I changed into a black skirt and a black blouse. I tied my blond hair back with a black scarf and put on a pair of black flats. I then added Gigi's pearl necklace and Grams pearl bracelet. I took a fortifying breath and bravely went into my

Momma's room. I hurriedly rifled through her jewelry box to find her pearl earrings. Thankfully they were right on top. Before I left her room, I opened her top drawer and pulled out one of her rose scented sachets putting it in my skirt pocket. Back in my room I put the earrings on and studied myself in the full-length mirror.

I seemed to be in order. I opened my top drawer and took out an embroidered handkerchief, which I folded and placed in the waistband of my skirt. I went back downstairs just as the timer went off signaling the chicken was done, so I took it out of the oven and placed it on the counter. I heard Josh bark, and that's when I heard the cars.

The church's hearse pulled up first followed by Pastor John's car, which was followed by the church truck with the two custodians. The next car was Mr. Bee's, and I was touched to see Mrs. Bee was sitting in the passenger seat. Then to my surprise came the Sheriff's car and he had a woman with him, I assumed that was Mrs. McDaniel's, and last in the line of cars came Brady's truck, with Tommy sitting in the passenger seat.

My eyes returned to the first car. I knew my Momma was in there and my stomach twisted, as a lump formed in my throat. I became anxious seeing all the people and instantly hoped I had prepared enough food. I took deep breaths trying to thwart the tears threatening to fall. As each person got out of their car, I noted that every one of them carried a covered dish or plate, and Brady carried a large jug of what Tommy excitedly told me was his

Mom's lemonade. I thanked everyone but was too afraid to talk too much since I was emotional. The women came inside with me and helped me put away the food, while the men remained outside in the shade on the porch. I couldn't remember a time when so many people had been to the farm. I sadly thought how my Momma would have loved to entertain them, and I rubbed away a tear that broke free and ran down my cheek.

We arranged the food on the table so it would be ready when we came back. There were cold cuts and a tomato salad, a pasta salad and a fruit salad. Mrs. Bee had brought a vanilla frosted cake and chocolate chip cookies too. I put out my bread, plates, glasses, silverware, and napkins. When we finished setting up, I took the red roses from the vase, and we walked back outside. Now came the hard part.

Outside I noticed that the hearse, the church truck, and Pastor John were gone. I knew that the pine box casket with my Momma inside had been transferred to the church truck and that the men had taken it up to the plot so it would be in the grave before we arrived. My guests became quiet as I started walking towards the field beyond the barn. Josh walked next to me, and everyone else followed behind us. I was battling mixed emotions; I appreciated the space they were giving me, yet I was feeling isolated. I was thinking about the last time Momma, and I had walked to the cemetery, and I wished more than anything that I could go back to that time. A time when I wasn't so alone.

I heard someone step next to me, and when I looked up, Brady was walking next to me. He looked over and gave me a sad grin. "You okay?" I shrugged my shoulders. "There have never been so many people going to the cemetery before," I answered nervously.

"They want to support you, Belle."

"It's very kind of them."

The closer we got to the iron enclosure the harder I found it to breathe. Brady must have noticed. I forced one foot in front of the other, keeping my eyes plastered on the ground. I was trying to hold myself together, but I could feel a panicky feeling swelling up inside of me.

"Breathe, Belle just breathe." Brady whispered to me. "In. Out. In. Out. Breathe; you'll get through this. I promise."

His words calmed me, and before I knew it, we were standing around the open grave. Momma couldn't have asked for a nicer day. Blue skies, a slight breeze, and she would have been so honored by all the people who had come. Pastor John stood at the head with his bible open, and I stood where I had always stood, but this time I was alone. Everyone else stood on the other side of the grave. Josh had run off to find shade. I wish I could too. I couldn't believe I was burying my Momma. It was surreal.

Pastor John spoke highly of my Momma, and I couldn't keep the tears away, even though I really tried. My lips trembled and my vision blurred behind the watery tears. We ended the service by saying The Lord's Prayer, and then I stepped forward and looked down into the open grave to see a beautiful shiny pearl white casket. I looked up at Pastor John; surprise registered on my tear-stained face. We had always used simple pine caskets.

"You're Momma would have liked this Belle," he said quietly. "It's why I wanted your Momma brought to the church first."

I looked across the plot at Mr. Bee, and he winked. They were right my Momma would have been so happy. The casket was perfect, and somehow that made me feel better.

I watched as each person filed past the grave, each one saying a whispered goodbye, last to go was Pastor John. Then I was alone with my Momma. I tossed in my bouquet of red roses and said a silent prayer to her, thanking her for my life, for all she had taught me, and then I prayed to God to keep her safe until we were reunited. I then took out the rose sachet from my pocket, kissed it, and tossed that in as well. I stood looking down at the casket for an undetermined amount of time. A small breeze blew across the field, and the rose scent drifted up to me. Somehow I knew that I had just made my Momma very happy.

I blew a kiss down to the casket and then another up to heaven, and then I headed back down the small hill.

Brady was waiting for me a little ways from the iron gates. When I reached him he didn't say a word, he just turned and walked next to me. I found that to be comforting.

When we reached the house, I saw that no one had gone inside and I loved how respectful everyone was being. I immediately donned my hostess cap and ushered everyone inside. I took the sweet tea and lemonade from the refrigerator and poured everyone a glass.

I asked the Pastor to please start the buffet line, which he did and within minutes everyone was either sitting around the table, or they were outside on the back patio sitting at the picnic table.

I walked around refilling glasses until Mrs. Bee took the pitchers from me and Mr. Bee steered me to the table.

"You need to eat Belle."

"I know. I will. I just want to make sure everyone is comfortable."

Mr. Bee chuckled. "You are such a mix of your grandmothers and your Momma. They were all so proud of you, and I know they are smiling down at how strong you are being."

I let his words sink in, and I felt a bubble of emotion start to rise inside of me.

"Thank you Mr. Bee, and thank you for all your help. The casket was lovely. My Momma would have loved it. "

"You're very welcome my dear. Next week would you like to get together to discuss any questions you might have?"

"Yes, that would be perfect. I was so out of sorts the other day that I barely remember what you told me."

"Yes, I figured. Your Momma had to come to see me three different times after your Gram passed." He smiled gently, and I returned his smile letting him know I appreciated his words.

Mr. Bee loaded a plate for me and then he escorted me outside to the picnic table. Tommy moved over, and I found myself between him and his mother.

"We haven't been properly introduced." His mother said, and I was immediately horrified that I had not introduced myself when she had helped me set up earlier. "I'm Sheila McDaniel's." She stuck out her hand, and I shook it.

"It is very nice to meet you," I said. "Thank you for the pot pie and the brownie's and lunch yesterday." "It was no trouble at all." She smiled gently at me, and I liked her immediately.

Tommy was prattling away about something, and then I realized he was talking about William the new lamb. I blushed when he announced that I had named it William after his Dad.

"Looks like I have two namesakes." Sheriff Mac Daniel's exclaimed loudly with a laugh. I realized Brady's formal name must be William.

I looked around and saw Brady leaning against the fence that separated the small back grassy lawn from the back hay field. He looked deep in thought, and I wished I knew what he was thinking. I could not help but to notice how attractive he was with his dark, hair, beautiful eyes, strong chin, and equally strong stature. He was honorable too. He had served our country, and as a Marine, which totally fascinated me. He was sweet too. I appreciated how he had waited for me so that I wouldn't have to walk home alone after the service. That had been unexpected and thoughtful. I small tremor of nervousness fluttered in my belly, and I placed my hand on my stomach to hopefully squelch the odd sensation.

"Are you feeling ill, dear?" Mrs. Bee asked noticing that I was clasping my stomach.

"I, uh, no, I, I'm fine, thank you." I stuttered. I picked my fork back up and glanced back at Brady. His eyes were on me, and I could not decipher from his expression what he was thinking. I wondered if a strong, capable man like himself was struggling with losing his lower leg. He seemed so sure of himself though, unstoppable, focused, yet I saw a vulnerable side to him yesterday, and that made me feel sad for him.

I realized I had been staring at him, so I lowered my gaze and fed myself a few forkfuls of the egg-potato salad. Perhaps that was the wrong move. The sweet mayonnaise concoction reminded me of Momma. Gigi was gone, Gram was gone, and now Momma was gone. I stood quickly with my plate, but my eyes were clouded with tears forcing me to stumble.

Two strong hands latched on to my upper arms helping me to regain my balance. I looked up to find that Brady was standing in front of me and had managed to stop my clumsy misstep with his steadying grip.

He leaned closer and in a whisper voice, "Easy Belle. You're doing great." Once again he was able to calm me.

I nodded at him, and in a hushed tone, I thanked him, which he answered with a small grin.

Carrying my plate and glass, I made my way into the kitchen to find Mrs. Bee washing the dishes, and Mr. Bee drying them and putting them away. They had even stored all the leftovers. The dishes that the food had arrived on were washed, dried, and ready for their owners to take home.

"Belle, we put the leftovers away in plastic bags and Tupperware's." Mrs. Bee chirped.

"You'll be eating well for a couple of days." Mr. Bee chimed in as he finished drying the last dish.

"Thank you. I could have done this."

"Of course you could have dear, but now you don't have too." Mrs. Bee replied happily.

"Thank you."

My guest chatted quietly with each other and complimented each other on the food and dessert. I was feeling robotic moving from guest to guest asking if they needed anything.

The desserts were cleared and stored away for me, even though I tried to get my guests to take home the leftovers. There was no way I could eat the rest of the cake. I'd probably try though. I had a sweet tooth. I could have frozen the cookies, but they were my favorite, and I could eat those all day long. There were a few brownies left. Tommy was pointing at his pocket and smiling, so I knew he had managed to wrap a couple up for himself. I gave him a thumbs up gesture, and he returned it. I thanked each person as they left my home. They wished me well, and each one told me to visit them.

The last person to leave was Brady. I walked him to his truck, and I could hear the sheep baying and Bessie was mooing belligerently. They were hungry; it was almost 6:00 PM.

"What are you going to do the rest of the night?" Brady asked.

"Well right now I need to change and take care of my animals. I can hear Bessie mooing for her dinner."

"Bessie?"

"Our, I mean, my cow."

"Do you want some help?"

"With my animals?" I wasn't offended by his question; I was more shocked that he offered. I could not remember a time that I hadn't taken care of the animals by myself. They had always been my responsibility. I cared for them every morning and every evening without fail, and I had always done it, alone. I only remember one time, when I had the flu that Momma had insisted I stay in bed. I hadn't been sick too often as a child. I guess that was because I wasn't around other children, getting their germs. At least that's what Gram had said. So when I was sick, it was a big deal.

"I, um, I can do it, but thank you."

Brady put his hand on my arm and then took it off. "Belle, I know you have to be tired. Let me help. What if you ever need me to do it for you? How will I know what to do?"

"Why on earth would I ever need you to do my animals for me?" I asked a bit tersely. I knew he was simply being kind, but to me, it was a strange offer.

"Well, what happens if you decide to somewhere and your car breaks down, and you can't get home right away?" He was smiling, and I realized that he was teasing me. "If that ever were to happen, you could call me, and I could come over and be your farm hand."

I laughed out loud at the audacious scenario he had created.

"Brady, I don't have a car or a license so that's not going to happen."

Brady grinned at me, his green eyes shining with mirth and it sent a shiver up my spine. It wasn't a foreboding shiver, it was different, and it felt kind of pleasant.

His voice lowered. "Belle, show me how to take care of your animals."

I cocked my head and put my hands on my hips just staring at him wondering what his true motive for helping me was. Then I just threw my hands up in the air and chuckled.

"Well okay, if you want, but you're going to get those nice clothes dirty."

"Nope, I have a change in my truck." He was smiling from ear to ear, and his exuberance made me laugh.

"Okay, then you can change in the downstairs bathroom," I told him as I turned back to the house. "Meet you in the barn," I called over my shoulder.

My heart was beating a mile a minute, and I knew then that it was because of Brady. I was attracted to him. I had all the classic signs. My Momma had told me all about this. He made my hands sweat when he was near me, and my heart sped up. I couldn't talk straight, and I even got clumsy. He was an attractive man, and I liked that he was thoughtful. As I made my way to my bedroom I realized I had no idea what I was supposed to do about these feelings; or if I was supposed to do anything.

My Gigi and Gram were adamant that men should do the courting. Perhaps Brady only liked me as a friend? I was in trouble here because I'd never even had a friend, much less a guy friend, so I was, what Gram liked to say, 'up a creek without a paddle.' Brady was leaning against the barn door when I came back outside. He had changed into a pair of jeans and a tee shirt. I noticed he had changed into work boots too. I was dressed similarly except I had my rubber barn boots on.

I walked him through my chores with the animals. I showed him how I fed the pigs and brought Bessie inside and fed her. I made sure the sheep were okay and refilled all the water troughs. I gave

Henny a cube of sugar and rubbed her down. I shooed all the chickens back into their coop and made sure they had fresh water too. Lastly, I checked on Mimi and William. They were doing so well that I told Brady that I would let them outside with the others tomorrow.

It took almost an hour, and I had to admit it had been nice to have someone helping me. Brady was strong, and he had lifted the grain sacks easily, and he didn't even spill any. He had wrapped up the heavy water hose too and helped rub down Henny.

"So every day, huh?" He asked as we walked back to the house.

"Yup, every morning and every night."

"You're so good with them Belle, you should be a veterinarian."

I chuckled. "My Gigi wanted me to become a vet. She taught me all the medical training she had learned, so I just alter it for the animals if they need treating."

"You're good with people too."

I blushed I couldn't have stopped it if I tried. I was so unaccustomed to compliments.

"What? You're blushing! You are good with people."

" Brady," I paused a little exasperated, "I have no experience with people, just my family. Your dad's the first person I ever spoke with without a family person being around. You and Tommy." I chuckled, "You and Tommy are the first boys I've ever spoken with; ever."

We had walked back to the back porch, and we both sat down. Josh lay at my feet, and I scratched his back.

"Really? You've never spoken to a boy before?"

"Nope."

"Do you have friends?"

"No, just the animals."

"That's… I don't know; don't you get lonely?"

I shrugged my shoulders. I was lonely last night. I'd never felt lonely before. I did always feel that I was missing out on something, but I never knew what that was.

"Do you know that there were more people here at the farm today than any other time that I can remember?"

"Was it too much?"

"Honestly at first, I was taken back. Then I was concerned that my chicken wasn't big enough to feed everyone." Brady chuckled, and I smiled. "No, I think it helped to have everyone here."

"They're worried about you Belle."

"I'll be fine," I answered quickly.

"I'm sure you will be too, but it doesn't hurt to have people you can call on to help you; if you need help, that is." he quickly added the last part so I wouldn't be offended.

"I guess I'm just not use to that. Everyone that was here today I know from town, but not socially." Brady nodded, "But they cared enough to come."

"Yes, that was kind of them."

"And my family, we're going to be there for you too."

I looked at him and decided I might as well ask some of the questions that had been plaguing me. "Brady, I've known your dad for two days and you for one. I don't understand why you would care?" He chuckled and sat back; his arms rested comfortably on the armrests of the chair. "Two days ago my dad came home after driving you to Springfield, and he could not stop talking about the resilient, smart, young woman he had just met. You made a wonderful first impression on a man that is very, very hard to impress. He's pretty old school, and you completely charmed him."

"I charmed him? I wasn't trying to be anything like that." I blushed and looked away.

"Not charmed in a romantic sense, more like 'you're a special person' sense."

"Oh, but, what about you?"

"Me?"

"Yes, I cannot believe that you and Tommy were thrilled that you were recruited to dig a grave and then forced to come to a funeral for someone you didn't even know."

Brady chuckled, "You got that right."

My jaw dropped hearing his answer, and I looked away, mortified, but Brady chuckled and tapped my arm with his fingers so I'd look at him.

"I gave my old man hell for insisting we come dig that grave, but he put his foot down and when he puts his foot down it stays down."

"I'm sorry about that."

"It all worked out." His eyes held mine.

"How so?"

"Well for one it made me get my ass in gear, and my body got a good hard work out. I needed that. Ever since I lost my foot, I've been laying around. Yesterday, I went to bed feeling good that I pushed myself. My dad was right, you are extraordinary, and I'm glad I have gotten to know you. After spending one day with you, me attending your Mom's funeral was a no-brainer. I was happy I was going to see you again." He finished softly.

My cheeks colored so darkly at his compliment that I felt hot and I had to stop myself from fanning my face.

"Too much? Did I embarrass you?"

"A little."

"See you're different Belle. You don't act coy or flirty. You speak your mind, and I like that."

"Brady, I'm the way I am because of how I was brought up. I wouldn't know coy or even how to flirt. We just got a television last month. I am just now realizing how different I am. It's actually scary."

"Well, I for one don't want you to change too much."

Brady stood up and stretched his arms over his head fighting back a yawn.

"I guess I better head home. You going to be all right?"

"Yes, I'm pretty tired. I may even try to sleep in my own bed tonight." Before Brady could question what I just said I shook my head and said, "Don't bother asking, but don't worry I'll be fine."

He got an adorable smile on his face and stepped off the porch.

"See ya, Belle."

"Bye Brady."

I stood on the front porch as he drove away and then called in Josh. I headed upstairs for the night and felt the emptiness of my house. I opened my bedroom window before I got into bed hoping the sounds of the nights would fill in the void of being alone.

When my Momma had been home, I would hear her moving around her room that was next to mine as she prepared for bed.

I said my prayers and at the end where I usually said Amen I added a thank you for sending me the people who came today. I was exhausted and sad, but a small tingle of excitement permeated my solemnness. I had no money concerns, a home I loved, and now I had even made, what I dared hope, was a friend. Brady.

I slept in my own bed that night, and the next and the next night. Every night I slept better than the night before. I realized it could also be from sheer exhaustion. I cried every night right after saying my prayers. I wondered if I'd ever stop crying. The next morning, I slept until the rooster's crow woke me. The sun was rising, and I could see from my bed that the sky was cloudless and a beautiful blue. It was my birthday. I was twenty-three. I stretched and got out of bed feeling better physically than I had in days. I knew it was because I was getting some sleep. I used the bathroom and threw on my usual barn attire before heading downstairs. Melancholy blanketed me because I knew I'd be spending this birthday alone, well except for my animals of course.

My morning routine was usually cathartic, but today I felt the solitude that surrounded me. On my other birthdays, one present had always been waiting for me when I'd gone down to the kitchen in the morning. My Momma would also prepare anything I wanted for dinner, and then after dinner, I'd get another present. There was always cake too. I loved cake. My favorite was vanilla, on vanilla with buttercream icing. I choked down a small whimper of distress and took a deep breath.

"Happy Birthday to me, now quit your bellyaching," I said out loud to myself.

I made coffee and the bread. Then I headed out to do the animals. Tending to the animals never failed to make me happy, even they seemed to be in better spirits. Mimi and her babe had joined the other sheep. I noticed how she carefully watched over William as he navigated his tiny body around the older, larger sheep, making sure they accepted him.

Back inside I poured myself another cup of coffee and headed to the front porch. Funny how we did things, well I did things, out of habit. In the mornings we had liked to sit on the front porch, and in the evenings we had sat on the back patio. A pang of loneliness sliced through me but I tamped it down as I made a mental list of what I needed to do that day. I even smiled, remembering how Gram use to say, "even birthday girls have to do chores."

The two pressing chores I had were to mow the lawn and tend the garden. They would easily take up most of my day. I did not need to make anything for dinner or even go to the store because I still had plenty of leftovers from the repast. I decided that if I got my chores done early enough that I would go for a celebratory birthday swim. It certainly was going to be hot enough. It would be a present to myself. Just the thought of going to the old swimming hole made me happy.

Mowing the lawn was easy since we had purchased the small John Deer tractor. I sat on the seat with a straw cowboy hat on my head and daydreamed while the mower did the work. When I finished, it was almost noon. I hosed off the tractor making sure I got the blades cleaned and then left it in the sun to dry.

Inside I drank a glass of sweet tea and ate two chocolate chip cookies. Then I headed out to the garden. Weeding was my least favorite thing to do. I loved the fresh vegetables, and pretty flowers, but I hated the tedious chore. The sun bore down on my back, and I knew if I hadn't been wearing the hat my neck would have been burning. As I pulled the weeds and placed them in a bucket, I decided that the current garden was too big for one person. The thought saddened me, but I needed to be practical. I had to downsize. I thought about other changes I needed to make.

I knew I had to get a license and then get a car, or did I need to get a car first and then the license? I would have to ask Mr. Bee about that. I also knew I needed to reduce how many pigs I kept. We sold our pigs every fall and then would get new ones in the spring. I knew we received a goodly amount of meat products as part of the barter. After my Gram passed, Momma and I discovered that our table scraps weren't enough to feed the growing pigs, so we were spending money on feed to supplement. When Gigi and Gram were alive, we had no less than four pigs ever. Momma and I had downsized to two.

I was never happy when the pigs were carted away at the end of fall. I knew where they were headed and even though I loved pork roll, ham, and bacon, I wasn't sure if the ends justified the means. The only problem was that we sold the pigs to the butcher. Those pigs supplied us with enough meat for the year, and I was a meat eater. I especially loved cheeseburgers on the grill. Momma had put the cheese inside the burger, making the burgers even juicier. I liked cheese, so for me, it was a win-win. I'd have to think about the pig situation a little more.

I finished the weeding and tied the tomatoes vines that were starting to lean to stakes before taking my bucket and leaving the wire enclosed area. I was wet with sweat; my day's chores were clinging to my skin and clothes in the form of grass and dirt. I dumped the weeds in our compost bin and went inside to get my book, the Ivory soap, a small bottle of biodegradable shampoo, and a towel. I took off my clothes and put on an oversized billowy muumuu that my Momma had made for me many years ago. When Momma had first made it, the muumuu had been so long that it dragged on the ground, now it was hung at my knees.

I loved to skinny dip, and I did it as often as possible. It was June 10th, and it was still a little early to be swimming. I whistled for Josh, and we headed for the swimming hole behind our house. The stream's water flowed down from the mountain, our mountain, and that water was darn cold.

I walked on the small trampled down path in the back hay field and made my way to the two birch trees that marked the opening to the worn trail that led to the stream. As I walked down the heavily wooded trail towards the swimming hole, it struck me that I'd never been for a swim alone. I also realized I'd left my rifle hanging above the door. We never headed into the woods without that rifle. I had learned to shoot when I was ten. Gigi had made me practice until I could hit a can 50 yards away. I liked shooting; I knew how to take the rifle apart and clean it, and I was the best shot in the family. When I was sixteen, we bought a new rifle, a Henry. It was so much lighter and easier to handle. I don't know what happened to the old rifle, but the new one took over the place of honor hanging above the mudroom door.

The trail turned left when it reached the stream but continued running adjacent to the gurgling water. I walked fifty more yards until I reached a sun-filled space where the pine trees gave way to an area that had formed a flat grassy bank next to the swimming hole. The hole had been created when beavers had constructed a dam. Their hard work had barricaded much of the water and forced the stream to widened and become deeper naturally. It was perfect for playing in. The cold water moved much slower over the large partially submerged boulders, and with the sun bouncing off them it was mesmerizing. Little rainbows appeared in the air just above the water when the water collided with the rocks. I sighed remembering how much Momma had loved how pretty our private swimming hole was.

Josh headed right into the water. He drank first then walked around in it splashing up enough water to cool himself down before laying down right where the water met the bank. I spread my towel on the small grassy ledge, put my book down, and pulled off my oversized covering. I jumped down the small ledge to touch the running water and the cold bit my toes. The first weeks of June were early to be venturing into the stream, but I was determined to have a birthday swim. I waded in up to my knees going to the flat rock; we actually named it the flat rock and placed the soap and shampoo on it. The small fish swimming around my feet nibbled at my numbing toes. I wadded further out, away from the rock until my knees were submerged. Years of swimming in the cold Vermont waters had taught me that one could not slowly wade into the water hoping it might eventually get warmer. Nope, in Vermont, you needed to jump in, comparable to ripping off a Band-Aid, do it quick and it won't hurt as much; so that's what I did.

I did my customary doggie paddle for about three feet as my body adjusted to the waters freezing temperature, allowing for me to take a breath since the cold water always knocked the air from my lungs. Finally, I was able to immerse myself completely.

I swam around the small swimming hole keeping a watchful eye on the brush across the way. I was uneasy not having my rifle with me. Wolves, bear, and moose had been known to make their way to the hole for a drink, and they weren't the kind of animals that liked to share their watering hole. I was able to partially relax because I knew if Josh heard or smelled anything he would alert me.

I paddled back to flat rock and using the soap and shampoo cleaned the grime from my goose-bumped skin. The water was cold, very cold but I loved how invigorating it was. After washing, I floated on my back soaking in the warm sun. When I was little, my Momma had gotten me a black tire tube, and I played on that tube for hours. She even played with me. We would try standing on it, diving through it, and sitting across from each other before we eventually upended into the water. A tear slid down my face, and a sob broke loose from my throat. I turned over and dove into the cold water furiously rubbing my face free of the tears. When I surfaced, I solemnly walked out of the water after gathering my soap and shampoo from flat rock and lay on my towel.

I finger combed my hair, which was no easy chore because of its length and then fanned it out around my head to dry. I attempted to read, but after rereading the same page three times, I gave up. I must have been tired because I soon fell asleep.

8

Brady

I was driving to Belle's farm. I'd been thinking about her for the last couple of days, and I wanted to see her, I just couldn't come up with a good enough excuse. Luckily, my mom asked me to bring Belle cookies that she had just made; I could have kissed her.

The night before I had tossed and turned thinking about how alone Belle must be feeling. I never slept well anymore anyway, but that night it was because I was thinking of Belle.

Night terrors often plagued my dreams as I relived that fateful day when I lost my friend and my foot. The first night home from the hospital I had experienced a terror-filled dream, and I had woken up the whole house with my agonizing screams. My parents and brother had run to my room to find me drenched in sweat and yelling so loudly it hurt my throat. My Dad broke through the awfulness, and when I woke up, I saw my mother was weeping, and my brother was pale, even my dad looked shaken. I didn't have the dream every night, but when I did my family knew what I was dreaming about, and my dad always came in to wake me from hell.

I turned down Belle's driveway, and when I reached her house, I was surprised that Josh hadn't met me. Belle had told me he was too friendly to be considered a professional guard dog.

I knocked on the door, and when no one answered, I walked to the barn and not finding her there, I walked towards her back patio. It concerned me that she wasn't there. I didn't think she had gone into town or had an appointment, at least she hadn't mentioned that she did. It was then that I noticed the freshly trampled small trail through the thigh-high hay field. Belle had said there was a stream behind her place maybe she'd gone for a swim. It was hot for June day. I headed down the path pleased that my training was coming in handy. I had trained to be a trail guide when I was in high school and had led groups of campers and hikers through State trails during the summer months. As a Marine I had become a lead scout for my platoon, learning from a three-tour veteran, who did not re-up for a fourth tour, leaving me to lead the way.

My scouting for the Marines was a hell of a lot different than leading eager tourists through the woods. I had to become a crack shot and had used every bit of knowledge Captain Jack had taught me. When I had worked as a trail guide during the summers, I had looked for animal tracks and different plant life to point out to my groups. In Afghanistan, I looked for indications of snipers, IED's, and dangerous terrain, while keeping my platoon headed in the correct direction whether we were in a mobile convoy or on foot.

I walked the small trail of freshly stepped on hay until I came to a stream. I followed it to the left noticing little shoe and large paw prints on the trails soft dirt. I had gone about thirty yards when I heard Josh's loud howl. I hoped he was howling because he had smelled me, but I was still concerned, so I started running, well as best I could. Josh met me after I'd lumbered about twenty more yards and that's when I was treated to a momentarily glorious sight.

Belle was buck-naked standing near the stream's ledge fighting to pull on a colorful cover up.

I froze, well most of me froze, one part of me moved, and that piece of manhood had not moved in a long time, so I became thoroughly flustered. The accident had left me with erectile dysfunction, and although the doctors assured me that it was not a permanent condition, my dick hadn't so much as twitched since the accident. Bombarded with the knowledge that it, meaning my cock, wasn't broke, and seeing Belle's gorgeous naked body; I had the biggest, cheesiest smile on my lame ass face.

It wasn't until I heard Belle yelling that I snapped out of my befuddlement.

"Bradeeeee! What the heck!" Belle screeched. The hideous billowy dress was now hiding her bodacious curves, and when I finally realized Belle was genuinely upset, I held up my hands in an 'I surrender' gesture.

"I'm sorry. I'm sorry. I heard Josh howling, and I was worried."

Belle didn't look pleased, and I knew the color on her face was not from being sunburned.

She crossed her arms looking indignant.

"Belle, honestly, I didn't see anything."

That seemed to calm her so I knew I'd keep to that story.

"Really?"

I limped towards her, the running had chaffed the skin under my prosthetics band, and I grimaced. Belle noticed how I was hobbling and walked towards me.

"Brady what did you do?" She said referring to my limp.

I shrugged my shoulders relieved I was out of hot water.

"I ran."

"Because you heard Josh howl?"

I looked away from the beautiful girl because I couldn't stop thinking about her perfect body and although I wanted to stroke myself just to make sure my dick was indeed working, I knew if she saw anything close to a bulge in my pants she would lose it.

"Brady?"

I took a deep breath and looked back at her. "Well yeah. I was hoping Josh had smelled me, but out here in the early summer there are a ton of animals all with their young."

He didn't need to explain further. Belle was smiling at me. I knew any Vermonter worth their salt knew the dangers of animals protecting their offspring.

"I know. I forgot my rifle. I don't know what I was thinking?"

I smiled back at her. "You have a lot on your mind." I defended her forgetfulness.

"I guess. Still, it wasn't smart."

Belle turned to walk back to her towel, and I followed like a puppy. My limp was more pronounced after sprinting down the uneven trail, and I hated looking like a crippled in front of her. She stepped off the grassy ledge and patted the ledge indicating that she wanted me to sit, so I did. Belle kept her eyes on mine and slowly knelt down in front of me. So many thoughts went through my head right then, and I put my hands in my lap in case my Johnson decided to move again.

She untied the laces on my boots and slid off the boot and sock before rolling my pant leg up. She then rolled my other pant leg up and reached up my loose fitting jeans to undo the leather band holding my prosthetic in place.

Her soft hands just above my knee could have unmanned me, but I was so conscientious that she was going to see my stump again that my cock remained still.

"What are you doing?" I asked shakily.

"I'm going to help you to soak that leg. This water is cold, and it will feel good. I promise."

"Belle, I don't..."

"Brady, we've been through this. You trust me right?"

I nodded.

With my prosthetic off Belle stood up and held out her hand to me.

"Lean on me I'm going to help you to flat rock."

"Flat rock?"

"That rock right there. You're going to sit on it."

I looked where she had pointed to and was relieved it wasn't too far from the edge.

We made it to the rock, and I sat. My pants were getting wet, and so was the bottom of my tee shirt, but the water felt great. Belle once again knelt down in the water in front of me, and the damn dress billowed around her in the water allowing me a fleeting glimpse of her backside.

"It's pretty cold," I told her attempting to distract myself from what was under that dress.

"How long have you been out here?" Belle started to rub my leg where the band had chaffed me, and it felt great.

"I don't know. What time is it?"

"It's probably around 4:00."

"Well, I came out here for a swim around 3:00." I needed to strengthen my lie about seeing her naked. "So why don't you keep swimming while I sit here."

Belle looked up and me, her face was crimson. "I, uh, don't have a swimsuit."

"Oh," I said smiling at her. "I won't look." I winked.

That made her laugh.

I reached behind me and pulled my tee shirt over my head. I jammed it into a ball and threw it to the grass. The sun felt great, and the cold water had taken the sting from my leg. Belle had stopped massaging me, and when I looked at her, she was staring at me with her mouth slightly opened. Her blue eyes were big as saucers as she perused my chest and I was immediately glad that I had kept lifting weights.

"Belle, I want to try to swim."

My voice jolted Belle back to me, and she stood up almost tripping from the weight of the wet dress.

"Is that okay?" I asked.

"Yes, yes, of course. Can you swim in those pants?"

I knew they'd be heavy when they got wet. I had to buy ones that had wide legs to fit the prosthetic.

"Would it be appropriate if I swam in my boxers? I'd be completely covered." I added quickly.

"Uh, I guess so." I could hear how quiet her voice had gotten, and I didn't want it to be weird between us, but I really wanted to see if I could swim.

Belle turned away from me, and I shimmied out of my pants tossing them to the shore. Then I pushed off the rock and floated out to the middle of the small swimming hole.

"This feels great!" I said excited that I was swimming, well; treading water, and it was effortless.

Belle swam out near me, and I could tell she was struggling in the weighty dress.

"Belle if you want you can put on my tee shirt and swim. It will be less cumbersome than the dress, and you'll still be covered."

She appeared to be debating my suggestion, and then she headed for the bank.

"Turn around, okay?"

I rotated, so I was facing the bushes on the other side. I didn't want to think about her being naked only a few feet from me, so I took in the swimming holes surroundings. The first thing I noticed was the small trail between two bushes across the way that animal had forged. It was definitely a watering spot for animals; Belle should always have her rifle with her when she was here. I made a mental note to ask her about her rifle and if she was experienced handling it.

"Okay." I heard her call from the bank.

I turned back around, to find Belle standing shyly on the bank in my tee shirt. The water had to be less than 60 degrees but my body heated up, and my cock jumped and swelled in my boxers. Belle looked better in my shirt than I did. Her wet body had the thin cotton sticking to her feminine curves. Her nipples jutted out provocatively, and I could make out the swell of her breast. If I were normal, if she were normal, if I'd had two legs, I would have walked out of the water and kissed her silly. If she let me, that is.

I stopped my blatant perusal of her body by turning away from her and playfully yelling for her to get in the water before I dove under the surface. When I resurfaced, Belle was treading water near me. I could see she was concerned that the hem of my shirt was drifting up past her stomach, so she swam with one hand holding the shirt down.

"We're a fine pair," I said with a grin. "I'm swimming with one leg, and you're swimming with one hand!"

Belle laughed gaily before disappearing into the water. I felt her yank on my leg trying to pull me under. I dove and tried doing the same to her. The only problem was that I was treated to an exquisite view of her naked behind. I sucked in water and came up for air coughing.

Belle giggled thinking I just wasn't as good as she was playing the water game. No way was I admitting that I was choking to death because I saw her sweet posterior. When I was able to talk again I laughed along with her and then we started splashing each other. Using two hands, I was clearly the victor. We stayed in the water until our teeth were chattering and our fingertips were wrinkled. I was physically tired from the exertion and the cold water, but it was a good tired.

We were horsing around, each trying to dunk the other and every time she'd try to dunk me I'd escape. She'd sneak around the back and grab me, and I'd use a move I learned in the Marines, and she'd end up ass over teakettle in the water.

"How do you do that?" She asked after one rather good dunking.

"I'm using simple self-defense moves on you."

"They're pretty neat. Teach me one."

We spent the next hour in the water with me teaching Belle some easy self-defense moves. I explained the vulnerable parts of a man and where she should specifically try to land hits. There was one move she got down pat. It was a fake kick to the groin and then a hard kick to the back of the leg. Most men protected their groin by lifting their dominant leg and turning the knee inward. I showed Belle that when a man did that they usually became unbalance, so a well-placed leg kick could take a man down. It would at least give her time to run. The impromptu self-defense lesson ended with Belle executing the move successfully against me, sans the hard kick.

Belle helped me out of the water and honest to goodness I tried not to look at her luscious wet body in my tee shirt, but that was like telling a starving man not to eat something that was right in front of him. I didn't make it obvious though. It also helped that I was very occupied trying to maintain my balance. I still got a pretty good look at the gorgeous woman with my tee shirt clinging to her wet skin. One that I was going to visualize the first chance I got to test out my hopefully, still functioning dick.

Belle had laid out my pants and her dress in the sun, so they were dry by the time we put them on. Belle asked me to turn around again as she slipped out of my shirt and back into her oversized dress. I took off my boxers and pulled on my pants, going commando. Then I pulled on my sock, boots, and my prosthetic. Belle leaned down to help me reattach it, and it was then that I recognized I wasn't self-conscious around her anymore.

We walked back to her house with Josh leading the way. That's when she realized that I had found her, so she asked how I had.

I told her about the summer job that I had in high school and college and how that had led me to become a scout for my platoon. I explained that a seasoned veteran had trained me and after he retired, I had become the platoons only scout. By the time I had finished my story, we were back at her house. I noticed that she had grown quiet.

"What?"

Belle turned to me in that gosh awful excuse for a cover-up and put her hand on my forearm. I could feel my heart speed up with her touch.

"That's why it's been so hard for you."

"What do you mean?"

"You feel like it's your fault."

I went ridged under her soft scrutiny.

"I...I... it was. I should have noticed the change in the road." I answered quietly.

"Brady, I can't even begin to understand what you're feeling, but there is no way I believe that you did nothing less than your best when you were there."

She took my breath away. How does she already know me so well?

I needed to change the subject. "This was fun today."

"It was. I'm so glad you found me!"

"Me too. Oh, my Mom made you cookies. I put them on your porch."

"That was sweet of her, please thank her for me." I nodded replying, "of course."

I shifted uneasily, "Belle, what are you doing tomorrow?"

"My chores and then I was going to call Mr. Bee so I could go get my license and maybe get a truck too."

"I can take you to get your license. Do you know what you need to get it?"

"Yes, I have all my ID's ready and I've studied for the test."

"What about the driving test?"

"I think I'll be fine I've been driving around the farm since I was twelve."

"Can you K turn?"

"Yup."

"Parallel park?"

Belle kicked at a loose stone under her foot. "Not well, I've never had the need too, but I've studied how to do it."

I grinned, she was priceless, "I'll come get you tomorrow, and we can practice parking before we drive into Springfield for the test." I let loose a smile that I'd been holding back. Why was it so darn important that I see her again?

"That be great! Thank you. I won't be keeping you from something will I?"

"No my schedules clear."

"Can we go first thing in the morning?"

"Sure, what time?"

"If you come here at 8:00 I'll be ready. We will need to stop at Mr. Bee's though so I can get money."

"Okay, I'll see you tomorrow."

Belle had walked me to my truck and waved to me as I drove away. The smile I had on my face remained there the entire way home.

9

Belle

I had so many thoughts churning through my brain that I barely remembered bedding down the animals that night. I had a lot to do; like study for the driving test again. Go through all the papers Mr. Bee had given me. Plant flowers on the graves. Then the questions came. Could I keep the farm up? Did Brady see me naked? Yeah, that was one I kept coming back too. I was sure he had, but he had been so polite and insistent that he had not seen anything. I had enjoyed swimming with him. It had been difficult to keep that darn tee shirt in place, but I'm glad I changed out of the cover-up. I recalled the image of him sitting on flat rock, in his boxers with his muscled chest and arms flexing naturally as he moved. Seeing him like that had made my insides flop around. I knew that I had gawked at the man, but in my defense, I'd never seen a man's bare chest before. Well, I'd seen them on television a couple of times, but Brady's chest put those men to shame.

I ate leftovers, and called Mr. Bee to tell him Brady was taking me to get my license, and I explained that I would need some money for the test. He and I discussed the financial and practical logistics of me getting a car. He agreed with me that I needed something that was safe and reliable, but also practical for the farm. I told him I didn't need a new vehicle and he thought it best that I lease one. That way I could build up my credit. I thought that was smart. He asked if Brady would be taking me to get the truck after I passed the test and I said I wasn't sure, but I hoped so. I didn't know if I'd get one right away, even though I needed one. Maybe Brady would take me to look at them.

That night I slept free of any nightmares. I was physically tired from mowing the lawn, weeding, and then playing in the water. However, I knew my calm frame of mind was all because of my new friend Brady. After my head had emerged through the darn muumuu, I saw him standing at the edge of the clearing and what I noticed first was the strange expression he had on his face.

Then when he limped over to me, I saw pain mixed with some other emotion etched on his face. He always seemed to be hiding the fact that his leg hurt. I figured he was dealing with a whole bushel of issues. I hated that he was embarrassed about his loss of limb and even worse that he shouldered the blame for the hit his platoon took.

I had the feeling that he didn't think too much of himself and that bothered the heck out of me. He was kind and strong and just talking with him I could tell he was smart. I wondered what he planned to do with the rest of his life. I also thought he was handsome as all get-out. It surprised me that he did not have a girlfriend. Maybe he did. Ouch, that thought actually made my stomach pitch.

I completed the morning chores and dressed for Springfield. I wore a sundress my Mom had made. It was a very simple light blue, A-line, with an empire waist. The neckline was low in comparison to the few other dresses I had. You could almost, almost see my cleavage. My Mom thought I looked great in the dress and I'd worn it to town a few times. There wasn't much call for me to dress up. I put on my white Ked's sneakers because they would be most comfortable to take the driving test in.

Downstairs I went out to the shed and climbed on the lawnmower. I know Brady had said he'd help me, but I didn't want to bother him, so I spent ten minutes practicing how to parallel park. Satisfied with my efforts, I went back inside, poured a coffee, and went back outside to wait for Brady. It was going to be another warm June day. I could hear the barn animals and saw that Henny was hanging her head over the fence looking at me. I needed to brush her; maybe I'd do that when I got home later.

Josh howled, and then I heard Brady's truck in the distance. In the mountains, you can hear cars on roads that were quite far away. The distinct sound of a truck coming down the drive had Josh wagging his tail and barking happily. That darn dog loved company. I went inside, put my mug in the sink, grabbed up my Identification papers and one of my momma's purses. When I got back outside Brady had just pulled to a stop. I walked to the truck and smiled when Brady jumped down from the cab to open my door for me. Momma would have loved that. Heck, who am I kidding, I loved that!

"Thank you and good morning."

He was grinning and replied, "Your welcome and good morning." Then we were off.

"Remember we need to stop at Mr. Bee's office first, okay?"

"Sure thing. Do you have everything you need?" I knew he meant the I.D.'s."

"Yes, birth certificate, proof of residency, my library card."

"Your library card?"

"It has my picture on it," I told him.

I heard him chuckle. "Do you have any other cards with your picture on it?"

"No, just that."

"Well let's hope that's enough."

We pulled up in front of Mr. Bee's office and once again Brady jumped out and opened my door for me. We went inside, and Miss Donna, who had been sitting behind her desk popped up quickly and walked to meet us. I was wondering why she did that until I saw how she was looking at Brady.

"Well hello there," she said, her voice a notch higher than usual. She smoothed down her form-fitting dress as she approached us.

"Belle, how are you dear?" She addressed me like I was a child and I knew for a fact she was only slightly older than me. My Momma had told me.

"I'm fine, thank you, Miss Donna." I don't think she even heard me she was too busy ogling Brady.

She was smiling at him, and I noticed that he was returning her smile.

"And who have we here?" She reached her hand out to Brady and didn't even give me a chance to introduce him to her.

"I'm Donna Romella."

Brady took her outstretched hand.

"Nice to meet you I'm Brady McDaniel." Their hands lingered together for a second longer than I thought necessary.

"McDaniel, hmm? Are you related to the Sheriff by any chance?"

Brady smiled, "Yes, he's my father."

"What a nice man he is. He was so kind to our poor Belle here. I guess you've been appointed her driver now so your dad can concentrate on more important matters?"

My mouth hung open at the unmistakably snarky comment. I'd never met someone who had been outwardly unkind to me, so I was in foreign territory here.

I looked at Brady and saw anger flash through his green eyes. He stepped closer to me, and best of all he put his hand on the small of my back.

"We're here to see Mr. Bee. Please tell him we are here." Brady's tone left no uncertainty as to how angry he was.

Miss Donna didn't hear the disdain in his voice though because when she walked to her desk, there was an extra sway in her derriere that brokered no doubt that she was trying to attract Brady.

Miss Donna rang for Mr. Bee and then told us to go back to his office. Mr. Bee greeted us and told us to have a seat.

"Brady it's nice to see you again. Thank you for driving Belle. I'm going to compensate you for your gas and trouble."

"No." Brady interrupted. "Sir, all due respect, I'm doing this because Belle is my friend."

I grinned like a loon, and Mr. Bee seemed quite pleased as well.

"Well then, in that case, Belle here's everything you might need. He handed me a large manila envelope and when I looked inside there were stacks of crisp 100-dollar bills.

"I've given you $4,250.00 in cash. Fifty is for the driver's test. The two hundred is for you to spend as you please, and the $4000 is a down payment on a car if you happen to see one that you like."

"You're getting a car today?" Brady asked.

"I was hoping we could look. If it's too much trouble, I can go another time?"

Brady appeared somewhat unnerved, and I got a twisty feeling in my gut. I felt as if I was imposing on him.

"It's no trouble." He answered. I knew he was thinking about something I just didn't know what it was.

"Brady, I can take her tomorrow." Mr. Bee interjected. I felt like such a burden, and I hated how that felt. I was buying a car today for sure. I needed to be independent. I couldn't keep relying on other people.

"It's okay Brady. I appreciate that you're taking me for my license."

"No, we can car shop. It's no problem."

I looked back to Mr. Bee who was penning something on to the back of one of his cards. He handed the card to me.

"Go to Quigley Chevrolet on the Highway, give him my card."

I took the card from him and stood up. "Thank you, Mr. Bee."

"Belle, I also put a debit card in the envelope. Do you know what that is?"

I shook my head.

Mr. Bee explained to me about how the card worked, and I listened carefully.

"I think Momma had one of these," I said.

"She did. Have you looked through her wallet?"

I hung my head slightly and shook my head no.

"I already deactivated all the cards she had. Your grandma's never liked credit cards, but your Momma did." Mr. Bee chuckled. "When you go through her wallet just cut up the cards and throw them away."

"Okay, thank you I will."

Mr. Bee and Brady shook hands, and we walked down the short hallway back to the waiting area. Miss Donna was watering the plants near the big bay window, and I noticed she had freshened her pink lipstick and the floral fragrance of just applied perfume hung in the air.

"You two have a nice day now." She said walking towards us. I reached for the door, but Brady got

there first and opened it for me. Yup, Momma
would have liked this guy. Miss Donna stepped
close to Brady as he was following me out, and
covertly handed him a small piece of paper. I didn't
want to stare, so I kept my head forward, but out
of the corner of my eye, I saw him jam the paper in
his front pocket.

"Bye now." Miss Donna called from the doorway.
"Brady, I hope to see you again." I turned back to
wave and caught her winking at Brady.

My stomach knotted. What was the heck wrong
with me? Brady's handsome; of course, women
want to meet him. I had no claim on him. He said
it himself; we were friends. Then why did I feel like
clawing pretty Miss Donna's eyes out?

Brady opened the passenger door for me and
walked around the front of the truck. Miss Donna
was standing in the open doorway with her hand
perched daintily on her slim hip. Her one leg jutted
forward making her appear even slimmer than she
was. She had a smile on her pretty face that even I
had to admit looked captivating. I studied her
openly. I wondered if this was what men liked. I
mean like, as in fell for romantically. Did Brady like
her? I hated that he might.

I saw Miss Donna wave; I waved back only to
realize she was looking at Brady and that he too
was waving back at her. I folded my arms across
my stomach and counted to ten. My Gigi had
taught me to do that many years ago. She told me
that whenever I felt angry, sad, mad, or any other
unbefitting emotion, especially when in the

presence of company I should count to ten. The
first thought I had when she gave me that advice
was that we never had company, however I was
smart enough not to say that out loud. When I
asked her why I needed to count to ten, she
explained that counting to ten gave the body and
the mind a chance to calm down. She further
explained that many times people spoke or
physically lashed out when they first experience
unpleasantness and the outcome was never good.
That advice had saved me a few times when
Momma and I had butted heads. I reached ten and
unfolded my arms and snuck a peek at Brady.
He was driving, but he was looking over at me too.
"You okay?"
I nodded, "Yes." I stared back out the front
window wishing I had gotten my license when I
had turned seventeen as normal kids did. Then I
wouldn't feel indebted to Brady, or anyone else, for
carting me around. I could have driven to
Springfield myself to identify poor Momma. I
would have never become friendly with the Sheriff
or his son.
"Belle, talk to me I know something has upset
you."
I looked out the side window, but I could see
Brady's reflection in it, and he kept glancing at me
waiting for an answer.
I decided to be partially honest with him. I sure as
heck was not going to tell him that I felt ugly next
to Miss Donna and hated how she had looked at
him.

"I just don't like being beholden to anyone."
"Belle, I don't mind taking you to Springfield. I think looking at cars with you will be fun too."
I had to count to ten again because I wanted to blurt out 'why would he want to be with me when beautiful Miss Donna obviously would have jumped at the chance to spend time with him.' I didn't say that though.

Instead, I opted for, "I just feel bad about taking your time."

Brady had his lips set tightly together. I knew that look; he wasn't happy. The next thing I knew Brady had pulled to the side of the road and turned towards me.

"Let's get something straight right now." He said with a bit of vinegar in his tone. "I don't do anything I don't want to do."

I was anxiously twisting my hands in my lap. I was not a fan of being yelled at. Well, he wasn't yelling, but the tone he was using felt like he was yelling. He must have realized how terse he sounded because he speared his hand through his hair and I heard him take a deep breath. I wondered if he was counting to ten.

"Belle, I enjoy spending time with you, okay? This isn't a chore. I'm looking forward to taking you into Springfield. I know you have only been there once, my dad told me. It's going to be an adventure for you, and I'm going to be your guide."

His words were kind and gentle and made me feel better.

I nodded because for some dang reason I was feeling emotional and I didn't want to spill tears. Men hated when women cried; Gigi had told me that.

"Belle, say something."

"Are you sure?"

Brady chuckled, "Yes, very sure." He looked pensive, and I knew he wanted to ask me a question.

"Spit it out, Brady."

"Sheesh, how do you do that?" He asked with a lopsided grin that made me smile.

"I can read your face. That's all." He laughed after I said that.

"I guess I should never play poker with you." He chuckled. His fingers drummed the seat between us.

I grinned cheekily; I didn't even know how to play poker. Brady still wanted to ask me something, so I remained quiet and waited.

"Belle, are you comfortable being with me?" He finally asked. He ran his hand through his hair again, a clear indicator that he was stressing about something. "I mean we get along pretty well, right?"

"Yes, we do."

"You don't mind me driving you do you?"

"No, I appreciate it, really I do."

"Would you rather Mr. Bee had brought you?"

I thought about his question for a second, and I could see he was anxious as to how I might answer it.

"Oh Brady, no. It's just that I've never had a friend before. It's all so surreal. Everything is new to me. So much has changed and so quickly. I like being with you. My Gram wouldn't be happy that I'm talking with a man." I added with a chuckle. "Yesterday was fun, and I'm excited about today. I just don't want you to feel like you have to..." I almost couldn't finish my sentence, but Brady waited patiently for me to go on. "I don't want your pity or for you to feel like you have to do anything for me or with me."

"Whoa, girl. Where did that come from?" Brady blew out a breath that sounded more like an exasperated sigh. "Belle, I do feel bad for you because you lost your ma and you're alone, but I promise you I am right where I want to be." He seemed pleased with his answer, and he gave me an adorable wide grin. When I returned his smile, he decided to tell me more.

 "I wanted to see you yesterday, even before Mom asked me to deliver the cookies. I want to take you into Springfield. I want to help you shop for a car. I want to show you around Springfield." His voice was getting softer, drawing me in. "I want to watch you use that debit card for the first time, and take you to a store you've never been in before."

I interrupted him. "There are quite a few of them," I whispered, making him chuckle.

"I want to spend time with you Belle because I enjoy it. You make me smile; cripes you make me laugh. I haven't laughed a whole lot lately."

He broke eye contact with me, and I felt the loss immediately.

"So you get me, Belle?"

"Yes, thank you."

"No Belle, thank you."

My heart soared, and I gave him a grand smile. I may not have had the smile Miss Donna had, but I sure tried to give him a good one.

Brady smiled back at me, and then we headed towards Springfield once again.

"So what kind of music do you like?" Brady asked a few minutes later.

"I like all kinds," I answered honestly.

"But do you have a favorite genre?"

"I am partial to country music. I was brought up listening to my Gigi's music, which was classical and jazz. Then when she passed my Gram listened to the Blue's, it sort of fit her personality. Then when she passed my Momma took over the radio, and we listened to anything she could dance to." I paused thinking about Momma dancing around the kitchen and was surprised the memory didn't hurt quite so much as others before had. "She liked Motown, and the Beach Boys, oh and Michael Jackson."

Brady was chuckling. "She liked to dance, huh?"

"All the time. She'd be dancing around the kitchen before breakfast and then after dinner while we cleaned up. She also would sing the songs as she danced."

"Did you dance with her?"

I laughed. "Sometimes. Do you dance?"

Brady's features hardened and he then looked sad. It was only for a nano-second, but because I had memorized his facial features I'd caught it.

"I use to."

"You don't dance anymore?"

"Belle you know why I don't dance," he said softly. I remained silent, not sure if I should state the obvious. Then I decided I should.

"You can still dance. You're pretty mobile."

I saw him sneak a glance in my direction. "Pretty mobile, huh?"

"Actually, very mobile judging by how you flew down the path yesterday."

He laughed; he laughed really hard and loudly, and I saw that beautiful smile light up his face, and darned if I didn't feel all tingly knowing that I had put it there.

We passed the rest of the ride talking about the driver's test and what I should expect. He even quizzed me with possible test questions, which I was able to answer, thank goodness.

When we arrived at The Division of Motor Vehicles, I started to get nervous. I'd never seen so many people in one place before; there were lines of people. My palms were sweating I was so anxious. Brady sensed my apprehension, so he guided me to the correct line and stood with me. I told him he could sit down, but he insisted on staying with me, and honestly, just with him standing near me made me feel better.

Finally, it was my turn at the window. The man took my Identification's, including my Library card and I paid, and then he pointed for me to go into another room where I would take the written test. Brady couldn't go with me, but before he let me go inside, he looked to see who else was in the room. I guess it looked okay to him cause he gave my upper arm a gentle squeeze and wished me luck.

I finished the test quickly. It wasn't hard, and the computer checked my answers right there. A woman stamped something on a card and told me I needed to take the driving part of the test. I left the room and found Brady, who was chatting with a young man. When he saw me, he stood up. I told him I passed and he said he knew I would, and then he walked me to a door where a man who would oversee my driving abilities met me.

"We forgot to practice parallel parking," Brady whispered sounding concerned.

"I practiced on the lawn mower this morning." Brady chuckled, and I heard him say "Smart girl," under his breath. I used Brady's truck for the test, and even though it was bigger than what I'd been used to driving, I passed, even parallel parking.

I was smiling ear to ear when I exited the truck. I went back inside, and Brady ushered me to another line, and that's when I got my picture taken. A couple of minutes later the lady handed me my license. I couldn't stop staring at it. I had my license!

Brady guided me back to his truck. He kept his hand on my back the whole time. I think he was

worried that I was going to trip since I couldn't
stop staring at my license.

"Hold it up," Brady said standing behind me.

"What?"

"Hold up your license I want to take our picture
with it. You know to commemorate this day."

I couldn't help but laugh as Brady took out his cell
phone and snapped our picture.

He helped me up into the truck and got in and
then held out his hand.

"Okay let me see it."

I gleefully handed over my laminated license. I was
watching Brady's face and saw him frown. His
brows furrowed and I thought maybe something
was wrong with my license.

"Belle, your birthday was yesterday?"

I was still smiling. "Yes."

Brady didn't look pleased. "Why didn't you tell
me?"

"I don't know. The subject never came up."

"Sheesh Belle, you were alone on your birthday."

"Uh no." I laughed. "We swam remember?"

He still looked upset. "That's not what I meant."

"Brady, swimming with you was as good a present
as I've ever had. It was fun."

He cocked his head a little. I knew he was thinking
hard about something. I waited for him to speak,
but he didn't. Instead, he buckled himself in, and
we headed out of the lot.

"Okay, let's go look at some cars." He said
enthusiastically.

"Trucks." I corrected him.

He chuckled, "let's go look at some trucks."

We spent an hour at the car dealership that Mr. Bee had suggested we go too. At first, a young man was helping us, but when I gave him Mr. Bee's card he left us looking at trucks and another, more distinguished gentleman came to help us.
When he asked what we were looking for, he looked at Brady, and I felt my temper rise a bit. Brady however deflected nicely and told the man that he was not the one buying the car and that I would be making the decision so he should sell me not him.
I mouthed 'thank you' to Brady who winked at me, and that silly wink made me not hear what the man had said, so I had to ask him to repeat it.
I was torn between two trucks. They were both V-6 engines; both certified used, one had 28,000 miles on it and was light blue. The other was gold and had 30,000 miles on it. They both had hitches and power everything. It really came down to color.
"Brady I don't know which one to pick," I whispered.
"How about if we go get lunch and look around Springfield and then we will come back. Maybe by then, you'll know which one you'll want."
"Good idea."
I told Mr. Dennison the sales manager who was serving us that I was probably getting one or the other today, but I was going to decide later on. I could tell he didn't want me leaving the lot without buying car, so he countered his original offer,

lowering the price of the blue truck by $500 and the gold truck by $400. He said the offer was only good for five minutes.

Brady looked mad, but I was pleased that he had lowered the price, so I said, "Okay I'll take the blue one."

Mr. Dennison rubbed his hands together looking happy. Brady scowled and whispered, "Belle, you don't have to decide right now."

I whispered back, "I wanted the blue one." I winked at him, and Brady cocked his head and chuckled.

Mr. Dennison walked us to an office to complete the paperwork. One hour later I owned a blue Chevy Silverado. I loved it! Brady asked Mr. Dennison to keep the truck there telling him we would pick it up when we were heading home. Mr. Dennison said he would get it cleaned and gassed up for me. I was on cloud nine!

Brady drove into the heart of Springfield and parked in a metered spot. We then walked down the sidewalk heading towards a restaurant that Brady said had the best food.

I'm not sure what I expected, but it wasn't what I had stepped into. Suzie's was a loud and busy eatery. It consisted of a small room with eight tables and more seating at the bar. Above the bar were four large televisions all tuned to various sports games or sports talk shows. The clientele varied in age and gender, but more men were

sitting at the bar. A waitress in a checkered apron
came out of the kitchen area carrying a large tray.
"Well Lordy, look what the wind blew in." She said
as she passed us.

"Hi Suzie, how's it going?"

"It's all good. Let me deliver this food, and I'll be
right over. Why don't you take that table in the
corner."

Brady guided me to the table, and we sat down. My
face must have given away how I felt because he
laughed when he saw my expression.

"So I take it you didn't eat out much?"

"We didn't eat out ever," I answered in a hushed
voice.

"That lady with the tray owns the place. Her name
is Suzie. My dad arrested her about twenty years
ago for disorderly conduct. It turned out she had a
no good husband, and when she got up the
courage to leave him, she got a job here on a
recommendation from my dad."

"So she bought this place and changed the name?"
I asked delighted with the happy ending story.

"Nope, the original owner's name was Suzie also.
She took this Suzie under her wing, and they
became best pals. You see old Suzie had left a no
good husband of her own, so the two women
forged a pretty strong friendship despite the age
difference. When original Suzie retired, she gave
the business to this Suzie."

"That's a nice story, except for the no good
husband part," I added quickly, which prompted
Brady to laugh out loud.

Lunch was awesome. We each had a burger with fries and Brady had a beer, and I had soda. Brady introduced me to Suzie, and when we left, she hugged me. I thought that was very friendly of her. Brady guided me around the busy town, and he willingly stopped in any store I showed interest in. Momma had told me once that men didn't like to shop, but I was excited to see inside the various shops, and Brady acted like he was enjoying himself, so I hoped Momma was wrong.

Two hours later Brady dragged me into a little bakery. Oh my, it smelled heavenly. The market in our town had a bakery section, but it was nothing like this.

I stared at the array of goods, my sweet tooth begging me to buy something.

"What's your favorite kind of cake?" Brady asked.

I didn't even have to think about it. "Vanilla on vanilla with buttercream icing. Are we going to have a piece?"

"No, I'm buying you the whole cake. We can eat it when we get back to your place. Is that okay?"

"Really? The whole cake?"

"The whole cake," he said and chuckled seeing my obvious delight.

"Thank you; I love cake, of course, we can eat it when we get home. It will be the perfect ending to this day."

Brady took the square box from the lady and then he bought me a cream filled, delicious looking pastry called a cannoli. "Here this should curb your sweet tooth until we get you home." He said as he handed me the treat.

I didn't remember telling him I liked sweets, but it didn't matter when I took a bite of the cannoli and unabashedly moaned at how good it tasted. Brady was watching me, and when I moaned, he got the cutest little smirk on his face.

"What? Is it on my face?"

I wiped my mouth with my fingertips.

"No, your face is fine."

He still looked like he had something to say.

"Brady!"

"I just like seeing you happy, is all."

I grinned, "That's a pretty nice thing to say." I told him.

"Well, you're a pretty nice person."

The warm and fuzzy's were back, and I knew I was blushing. I quickly took another bite of the pastry and with my mouth still full I offered the half-eaten cannoli to Brady. He took a bite, and when he moaned at how good it tasted, I had to laugh.

The day flew by. We had gone into so many stores. I couldn't believe all the different clothes that were available. I mean, I knew there were clothes other than what my Momma had sewn or the few that ones we regularly purchased, but I never imagined the variety. My wardrobe consisted of jeans, jean shorts, tee shirts, flannel shirts, and a few dresses. I never really needed anything else.

I bought a fancy pair of jeans, and Brady informed me that they were to be worn someplace other than in the barn. That made me laugh. They were so feminine and soft. Who would have thought jeans could be so girly looking! They fit a bit snug, and they had embellished back pockets. Brady assured me I looked really good in them, his words. I also bought three shirts and a belt for the new jeans. I found a skirt that wasn't too short; the sales lady assured me it was fashionable. I bought a handbag, a pair of sandals, and a pair of stall muckers. I had needed new ones.

Momma would have approved of my shopping spree, but I shuddered when I thought what my Gram would have said.

Brady showed me how to use the debit card, and my gut feelings were that not paying for goods with actual money might be too easy and that people might spend more than they should. I knew my Momma must have loved having a debit card. It reminded me that I still had to clean out her room. That was going to be a hard task.

Brady purchased a few things as well. I was able to buy him a small thank you gift for driving me without his knowledge. It was a little silver compass that worked. It could hang from a car's rear view mirror or even on a shirt pocket button. I thought it was fitting. It reminded me of how he had tracked me down at the swimming hole yesterday.

We were both done with shopping. We got in Brady's truck and headed back to the Chevy dealership to get my car. I must confess that I was nervous about driving back home by myself. When we got there, my truck sat out front gleaming from being recently washed. I once again thanked Mr. Dennison and asked him to fax the paperwork that I had signed to Mr. Bee for safekeeping.

Brady helped me to adjust my seat once I got in and I fixed the mirrors.

"You ready?" He asked.

"I am," I answered nervously.

"Don't worry; you'll be fine. I'll meet you at your place. Do you know how to get there?"

"I think so, but how about if I follow you?"

"Sounds good. Drive carefully. Flash your lights if you want me to stop for any reason, okay?"

"Okay."

I think he knew I was anxious. "You'll be fine Belle."

I nodded feeling oddly out of sorts. Was it that I was about to drive by myself or was it that I wasn't going to be with Brady? Brady shut my door, and I quickly turned the radio on so I wouldn't feel so alone.

10

Brady

I kept checking my rear view as we drove. I knew
Belle was nervous. I saw that she kept two hands
on the wheel and she was completely focused on
driving. Her truck was perfect for her, and I liked
the blue one better than the gold one, so I was
secretly pleased when she'd chosen it; I just hadn't
liked the guy being so pushy.

We had had a fun and productive day. I hoped she
thought so too. She got her license and bought a
truck. Our lunch at Suzie's, the bakery, the stores,
everything was so new to her, and I love that I got
to be with her when she experienced them. Some
of the shops she had not liked. One of the clothing
stores was expensive, and she scoffed at the prices.
She had held up a scarf, and then I watched her
mouth drop when she saw the price tag. It made
me laugh.

I got to know her; really know her. The little
snippets of information that she unknowingly
revealed told me so much.

She loved to be outdoors. She loved animals; I
already knew that. She was extremely intelligent.
She showed that at the car dealership. She liked
sweets. She was not up to date on current fashion,
but she didn't seem to care. She was her own
person, and I liked that. Her taste in clothes was
simple, but not dowdy. She had helped me to pick
out a shirt, and when she said it matched my eyes, I

was pleased because that meant she had noticed them. She was different than any girl I had known. I was familiar with the Miss Donna's of the world. Well, until I lost my foot.

Did I like Belle because I was comfortable around her? Would I have even looked at her a year ago when I was a whole man? I probably would have just because of how beautiful she was. I hated doubting how I was feeling about her.

It bothered me that she spent her birthday without any sort of celebration. She and I were going to celebrate with the cake I bought, but I had another surprise for her too. While she was busy at the dealership, I had called my Mom, and instead of going to her house we were going to mine. We were going to have dinner there, with my family. I hope she didn't mind. I also had bought her two birthday gifts. I hoped she liked it.

When we reached the town limits, I pulled off to the side of the road and Belle followed. I got out of my truck and walked back to her and asked if she would mind following me to my house before going back to her place. She said she didn't mind, but she reminded me that she did need to get home to the animals. I assured her she would be home before it got dark.

We pulled up to my parent's home, and I was pleased that Dad had managed to get home. When we walked inside my wonderful family yelled, "surprise!"

Belle jumped. I mean honest to goodness jumped, when they yelled surprise, and I felt bad because she placed her hand against her chest. I knew she was frightened. I put my hand on her back and whispered into her ear.

"I wanted you to have a birthday dinner. Is this okay?"

She looked at me with those huge blue eyes and when she smiled at me I friggin melted; melted. "This is so kind of you," Belle said to my family. Then she looked at me. "How did you do this?"

"I called my Mom when we were at the Dealership."

"I don't know what to say? Oh, wow, we can share the cake!" I laughed when I saw her dash back outside to retrieve the cake from her truck. It gave me a moment to thank my parents.

Belle came back inside and handed my Mom the white box. "For dessert!" She said happily.

We sat down for dinner. Mom had made chicken parmesan, one of her best meals. I knew she had been planning on hamburgers, so I mentally made a note to thank her.

After dinner, we sang Happy Birthday to Belle, and she giggled as she blew out the candles. She looked happy and was smiling, but I knew she had to be a little sad. Her Mom had only been gone for a week. Belle had been through a lot.

After enjoying the cake, which Belle exclaimed was the best cake she'd ever tasted she got another surprise. My Mom placed three wrapped boxes on the table in front of her. I looked at my Mom, and she smiled and shrugged. I mouthed a thank you. My Mom was awesome.

"What is this?" Belle asked in a hushed tone. I knew she had not expected presents and I could tell she was getting emotional.

"Duh, Belle, they're birthday presents." My brother said teasing her without hesitation. I could have hugged him because that made Belle laughed out loud.

"It's all so much," she said looking at all of us. Tommy handed her a box, "open this one. It's from me." Belle giggled seeing his exuberance. She tore open the box. Inside was a coffee mug that had a picture of two sheep on it. It had 'Coffee is wooly good' printed under the sheep.

Belle laughed and thanked Tommy.

My Mom handed her another box, which Belle accepted. I could see a tear gathering in her eye, and I rubbed her shoulder. My Dad watched me comfort her and gave me a wink. Dad was probably Belle's biggest fan.

Inside this box was a pair of work gloves. They were very girly looking, tan with pink trim and leather palms.

"Oh my goodness, these are so, so pretty. Thank you."

The next box Belle opened was an emergency kit for her new truck. It was from my dad, and it had everything in it including a small medical kit. Belle clapped her hands together gleefully and gushed out a thank you. I don't know how my Mom had managed all this in the short notice I'd given, but she had. I would give her a big time thank you later.

Then I put another box down on the table. I was nervous buying it for her, but it seemed perfect. Belle gave me a shy smile. "When did you buy this?"

"Today, pretty stealthy of me right?"

"Very stealthy." She agreed with a giggle.

She opened my box and started laughing. Inside was a bathing suit cover-up. It was blue and yellow and even had pockets and a little hood. Belle started laughing, and that got me laughing.

"I guess I know what you think of my muumuu!" We then had to explain how we had gone swimming yesterday. I left out the part about seeing her naked, of course, but leave it to my little brother to figure out she didn't have a swimsuit.

"You mean you skinny dip all the time!"

"Tommy!" Mom admonished.

Belle just giggled and shrugged her shoulders. "I've been doing it since I was little. I don't even own a suit. But when Brady and I swam yesterday we were covered up." She added quickly blushing brightly.

Tommy stared at her and then he turned bright red. I had to slap the back of his head because I knew just what his teenage mind was picturing.

I then handed Belle a small bag with one more gift I had bought for her. Belle took it, but I could tell she was flustered.

"Another? Brady, really it's too much." She was embarrassed, and that only endeared her to me more.

Belle reached into the fancy green bag with the pink decorative tissue and pulled out a small Lily Pulitzer wallet. It had a place for a couple of credit cards and a zippered area for coins and cash, but the main reason I had bought it was because it had a clear pocket, designed specifically to hold a license.

"Oh, my." Belle was looking at like it was gold instead of a simple wallet. "It's beautiful." Her voice was hushed, and I could tell she loved it. I felt like a King at that moment.

"It's for your new license," I said proudly pointing at the plastic area.

Belle jumped up, and we all watched in alarm as she ran out of the dining room. I thought that maybe I had overdone it, but I relaxed as I watched Belle run to her purse pulled out her license and run back to us.

She picked up her new wallet and put her license in the slot.

"This is wonderful Brady, just wonderful. I love it!" She then turned to my dad. "Do you want to see my license?" She asked with so much excitement in her voice that it was contagious.

"I sure do." My Dad answered, and Tommy and my Mom also asked to see it.

While they were commenting on what a nice picture it was I studied Belle, really studied her. I don't think she had any idea how remarkable she was. She was stunning, beyond beautiful. She had a big heart, and her face was so expressive. I knew she'd never played organized sports, but I'd bet my last dime she would have been a terrific athlete. I wondered if she skied. Then I remembered I couldn't anymore. The thought took my breath away.

I caught Belle glancing at me with a worried look on her face. I needed to keep my emotions in check, that girl could read me like a book.

Belle thanked my family, and we gathered up her new presents and headed out, but not before my mom put the rest of the cake in foil for her.

"Oh thank you, but why don't you keep this for your family?"

"Belle, this is your birthday cake, enjoy it." My Mom said patting her hand.

"Thank you, I will and thank you so much for the dinner and my gifts." Belle was looking very happy, and I was thrilled seeing her that way.

"Okay, you want to follow me back to your place?" I said placing her gifts in the passenger seat.

"Oh, Brady you have done so much already. Why don't you put my address into this little OnStar thing and I'll follow that."

"Really? I don't mind." I was disappointed; I wanted to follow her home.

"No, I insist. I've had a great day thanks to you. It will be an adventure driving my new truck home and using this On Star thingy."

I had to laugh. "Okay, but would you mind calling me when you get home. You have our house number on the card dad gave you."

"Okay, I will."

It was awkward standing next to her. I wanted to kiss her, even hug her, but I didn't want to wreck the great day by doing something she may not like. We got along great. I just didn't know what we were, or where we could be headed. She had so much on her plate right now. I didn't want to add anything to it. I decided slow and steady was the course to take with this special woman.

I showed Belle the button to press, and the woman's voice asked how could she help, and I said directions and when prompted Belle relayed her address.

Belle whispered "That was easy." and I grinned because she was whispering.

Seated in her truck, Belle rolled her window down. "Bye Brady thank you so much for today, for everything."

"You're very welcome. Bye Belle, call me when you get home."

Then she drove away and darned if I didn't like it, not one bit.

11

Belle

I didn't dare turn the radio on for fear of missing
the directions from the On-Star lady. When I
arrived home, I called Brady and thanked him
again. I had the feeling he would have like to have
talked for a bit, but I wanted to do the animals
before it got too dark. It was already twilight.
I fed Josh first, and he accompanied me on my
rounds. I didn't muck the stalls that morning, so I
did that before letting in Bessie. It was going to be
a pleasant night, so I left Henny out. I left the
sheep outside too. They seemed pretty content.
The pigs hastily ate the grain while I freshened the
water in their trough. Lastly, I shooed all the
chickens into their coop.
Back inside I showered and looked at all the
fabulous gifts I had received. I also tried on my
new clothes; again. That's when I realized that I
had forgotten to give Brady his present.
It was too early to go to bed, so I put on my
pajamas and sat out back watching the fireflies and
listening to the sounds of the night. I loved doing
this. Sitting outside, with no noise other than what
came from the barn and forest, was incredibly
relaxing and one of my favorite things about
summer.
When Momma was alive, she would have been
quilting or baking, until we had gotten the
television that is. After we got the television, she

watched it every night. It wasn't until Momma went to bed that I could enjoy the quiet of the night. A lump grew in my throat, and I chastised myself because I'd give my eyeteeth if she were inside watching television.

I had such a happy day, but my thoughts about Momma had saddened me, and I wept softly into my hand. After a few minutes, I dried my tears. My life was already changing. I had someone I considered to be a friend. Was it okay to want to kiss a friend? I had wanted to hug Brady so many times today, but no idea if that was appropriate and I had not wanted to spoil the fun we were having. Heck for all I knew he was calling Miss Donna at that very moment. That was a sobering thought, and I groaned out loud. Josh lifted his head to look at me, and after realizing that I was all right, he went right back to snoozing.

I had to clean out Momma's room tomorrow. That wasn't going to be fun. I remember cleaning out Gram's room. Momma and I had both cried as we packed away her items. Things we wanted we kept, but most everything else we gave to Goodwill. I thought it would be hard to give Gram's things away, but turned out it made me feel better knowing someone in need would be using her clothes.

I did not sleep very well that night. I think just knowing I was going to have to clean Momma's room had me anxious, or it could have been the extra piece of cake I ate right before going to bed; I loved cake. As I lay awake, I heard many unbeknownst sounds that I'd never given much thought too before. When I was little, and I'd hear a strange noise, my Gigi would always say that it was the house settling.

I pushed out of bed before the rooster crowed and Josh and I headed downstairs to start our day. The rooster finally sounded his morning wake up while I was grinding the coffee beans. I chuckled to myself thinking of the adage 'up before the rooster crowed,' my Gigi loved to be up before the rooster and would then add that she'd cook that rooster if he didn't do a better job. She was just kidding; I think. I was weary from lack of sleep and a bit melancholy, as I took my cup of coffee to the front porch. I didn't need to start the barn chores just yet.

The morning air was crisp but refreshing, so I pulled on my barn coat to thwart the chill. I loved how the grass glistened as the rising sun hit it. The birds were unquestionably happy; I could hear them chirping away, and the frogs from the pond were already croaking loudly. A small rustling of the nearby pine trees sent down their fragrant scent, making me look to the hill where I could see the top of the cemetery's iron fence. I got nostalgic thinking that everyone I'd ever loved lay in the small plot on the hill. I'd have to bring some flowers up there soon. I wanted to tell Gigi about getting my license, Gram about buying the truck, and Momma about Brady.

I finished my coffee and headed to the barn with Josh right behind me. Thirty minutes later we left the barn with four eggs in my hand. I put them in the basket in the kitchen and set about making myself breakfast. I decided on a piece of cake, why not? Halfway through eating it my phone rang.

"Hello?"

"Hello Belle, it's Mr. Bee. I hope this isn't too early?"

I looked at the clock and saw that it was 8:00 AM. It wasn't too early for me.

"No Mr. Bee I've been awake for some time now."

"Good, good. Did you have a good time yesterday?"

"I did, thank you for asking. I bought a truck."

"I know my friend called me and he faxed over a copy of the agreement. I heard that you drove a tough bargain."

"I think I got a good deal. Brady said I did." Just saying Brady's name had me smiling.

"Belle the reason I'm calling is that the person that approached your Mom about buying your property would like to make sure you understand that the offer still stands."

I was silent.

"Belle?"

"Mr. Bee, right now, I don't want to sell. I like it here. It's all I know."

Mr. Bee was quiet.

"Mr. Bee?"

"Belle, how about if I come over there this afternoon and we can discuss it?"

"That would be fine. I'd like to show you my new truck."

"Yes, I'd like to see it

"Thank you, Mr. Bee, for everything."

"There's no need to thank me. This is what I've done for your family for years."

That made me smile. Thank goodness at least one thing was remaining the same.

I hung the phone up and took my cake and another cup of coffee outside. It was odd realizing that I had to make decisions like whether to sell or not by myself. I finished my cake and sat in my chair unmotivated to start the task I had planned. The sun climbed higher into the sky, but I still couldn't get myself to move from my perch. I was feeling sluggish because I had started my day eating the sugary cake. I had to take better care of myself; the animals had only me now. I pushed out of my chair and headed inside. This job had to get done.

I went downstairs into the cold cellar to bring up a large plastic storage bin. When I was younger, going onto the cellar had scared the be-jinkers out of me. It had a dirt floor with stonewalls that served as the foundation for our home. We used the cellar for storage, and it was the perfect temperature to keep the fruit and vegetables we canned and the jams we jarred. It was very organized, thanks to my Momma. There were clear plastic bins containing everything from Holiday decorations to my Gigi and Gram's personal things that we just couldn't bear to let go. There were handmade wreaths of dried flowers hanging from the ceiling beams. These wreaths hung on our front door, and Momma changed them out monthly. She had made every one of them. That reminded me that in a week I'd need to put up the one we use for The Fourth of July.

An old, oversized empty wooden hutch sat against one wall. On the floor next to it were crates holding the preserves we put up. There was another crate on the floor that had china dishes that were wrapped protectively in newspaper. They had little roses on them. They were my Momma's; she loved roses. I wish I'd asked her why we never used them.

I grabbed an empty plastic bin and an empty cardboard box and hurried upstairs giggling. Who was I kidding? The cellar still scared me. I headed upstairs and opened Momma's door. I hadn't been in her room since the day I buried her.

Dust danced through the beams of sunlight, and I glumly thought that I was going to have to start cleaning the house now. That had always been Momma's chore. There were so many things I had to do to keep the house and farm up; take care of the animals, the barn, all the farm equipment, the garden, the lawn, and the inside of the house. My shoulders sagged at how daunting it seemed.

I looked around Momma's room, and the tears pricked my eyes. A hint of rose scent still lingered in the room. Everything was in its proper place. My Momma was fastidious when it came to housekeeping, so her room was perfectly tidy and organized. I started the arduous chore of packing away Momma's things. I began with her closet. She had a quite a few new dresses, tops, and even a fancy gown that I'd never seen before. I had to wonder why she'd bought that. I took the clothes off their hangers and folded them and put them in the cardboard box. My system was simple. Items I wanted to keep, I would lay on the bed. Things I wanted to keep, but not use, would go into the bin to go into the cellar. Everything else would go in the box to go to Goodwill. I ended up only keeping one item from all the clothes hanging up, a dress. It was store bought and still had a tag on it. It was red and simple with a V-neck; the material was soft and clingy. My Momma would have looked great in it. I really liked it too. It was different than her other new clothes, which were too glitzy for my taste. A whimper escaped me when I thought how sad it was that she'd never get to wear the pretty dress. On the floor of her closet were her shoes. We had the same size feet, so I kept most of them, a pair of black heels, a pretty pair of blue flats, a pair of sneakers, and a pair of Teva sandals. Next, I cleaned off her closet shelf. I discovered a brand new pair of hiking boots that were still in the box. They were superior quality boots and something I would have picked out for myself. There was another box on the closet shelf, and when I pulled it down, I saw there was a blue ribbon wrapped around it, with a small card affixed to the top. 'Happy 23rd Birthday to my beautiful daughter.' I stared at it for about three seconds before I burst into tears. My chest squeezed so tightly that it hurt to breathe. My Momma had bought me a birthday present. It took a few minutes, but I finally got my emotions under control and opened the box. Inside I found a gorgeous cable knit sweater. It was white and soft, and I loved it. I placed the box on the bed. I was so happy with the present my Momma had bought me. I felt a little guilty that I had been thinking how selfish she had been the last few weeks; going out at night and not doing her share of the work around the house. Now I knew that Momma had been thinking about me and I also knew I would cherish the lovely sweater forever. I cleared the rest of her closet and then started to empty her dresser drawers. Every once in a while I'd have to wipe away tears. I didn't even realize I was crying. The family Bible that sat on top her dresser was a definite keeper. Names and dates of births and deaths had been meticulously recorded inside the front cover. I'd have to add Momma's death date next to her name. A lump formed in my throat. I pushed the self-pitying tears away. I had to keep working. I wanted to complete this task. There were a few items that I had placed on the bed that I was keeping, my sweater, of course, the new boots, along with the other shoes, the pretty red dress, a red, white, and blue scarf, and a thin leather belt. Everything else I packed for Goodwill. The belt that I had placed on the bed slipped off, and when I leaned down to pick it up, I saw a metal box under her bed. When I unlatched it, I found a leather-bound journal. As I gingerly leafed through it, I saw that the pages were filled with my

Momma's impeccable handwriting. Just seeing her perfect script had me tearing up again. I read a paragraph and realized that what I was reading was a journal, an obviously private journal since I knew nothing about it. I shut the book and held the precious keepsake on my lap. My hands were shaking, so I counted to ten. I knew I would read it at some point but now was not the time. I hoped that reading it might answer some of the burning questions that plagued me.

I placed the journal on the bed and found there were legal looking papers and a few photographs in the box as well. I placed the papers back in the box. I was not going to look through them now, or I'd never finish cleaning Momma's room. I sifted through the photographs; many I had seen before. One of them was of my Momma and me sitting on the split rail fence near the barn. I looked so much like her. Another was a faded picture of my Momma and a man with blond hair. They were hugging and smiling at each other. On the back of the picture, my Momma had written the name, Elias. I stared at the picture for a long time. I'd never heard of anyone named Elias. I wondered if this could be a picture of my father. It bothered me that my Momma never shared anything about him with me, and now seeing this picture, I was a bit miffed that if this was a picture of him, that she had never shown it to me. There were other family photographs, some that I had not seen before. I choked up seeing the photographs, each one evoking a special memory and reminding me just how unique my family was. There was one of my Momma standing next to an elaborately decorated cake that she had made. Another of me when I first rode on Henny, I had the biggest smile on my face. There was one of my Gigi holding a tiny lamb, and one of Gram on the tractor, with a grand smile on her face. There was only one photo of the four of us together, and I immediately remembered when it was taken. We had just come home from swimming, and we were wearing the colorful muumuus that my Momma had made for each of us. A lady, whom I did not know, was sitting at our back picnic table, waiting for us, with a crate of strawberries. They were a thank you gift for Gigi because Gigi had helped to deliver her baby the month before. My Momma just happened to have her camera with her with her, and the lady offered to take our picture. This was a big deal because we could never take a true family picture since someone always had to be taking the picture and therefore couldn't be in it. So with our wet hair and colorful outfits we posed for what was our only family portrait. Once again tears leaked from my eyes. Life had been so simple back then. I put the picture of my Momma and the man back in the metal box along with the journal. The priceless family pictures I put on the bed.

I continued to work. The dresser was now cleared out, and the last thing I needed to tackle was her nightstand. In a bottom drawer, there was a tubular shaped item that I realized looked like a man's penis; I cringed and tossed that into the garbage bag. There were a small notebook and pen in the top drawer. When I opened it I saw a notation, 'Belle's birthday.' Underneath my name, she had written sweater, and there was a check next to it. Hiking boots with another check, Red dress with another check. I realized those items were my birthday presents! This time I smiled. They were great presents. I said a little prayer thanking Momma.

In the middle drawer, I discovered travel brochures. Some of them Momma had drawn stars next to the large imprinted titles. They appeared to be recent. One was for a cruise to the Bahamas', another was to Italy, another to Las Vegas, and the last one was to France. I knew my Momma had always wanted to travel, but it seemed strange that she had not shared the brochures with me. Typically, she would have laid them out on the table and showed me every detail. There were two more brochures, and when I pulled them out, I saw they were for two colleges. One was for University of Vermont, and the other was for the University of New Hampshire. I felt a little queasy as things began to click into place. Momma was going to sell the farm, send me off to college, and use the money to travel. There was no way we could have kept the farm if she was traveling and I was away at college. I was now positive my Momma had been seriously considering selling our home.

I sat down in the wing chair next to her bed. Why didn't she talk to me about any of this? Momma had been acting differently lately, but she had told me everything, or so I'd thought. She had been my only friend, and until recently, I had been hers. Hurt bloomed in my chest, and I stared out her window lost in thought.

Josh's howl brought me out of my contemplative state, and I went downstairs to find Mr. Bee pulling up.

It was good timing I needed a distraction. I made him coffee and put out bread with peach preserves, which I knew was his favorite because we always gifted him a few jars at Christmas. I sat across from him with my third cup of coffee of the day in front of me.

"So how are you, Belle? Really."

"I'm doing well, thank you."

"Your truck is very nice looking. The color suits you."

I smiled. "I do like it. I like that I can drive myself now."

"Yes, you are like your grandmother's and mother in that respect. You have their independent streak."

I took that as a compliment. "Thank you."

"So let me get right to it okay?"

"Yes, please."

Mr. Bee pulled out a sheet of paper and slid it towards me. I righted it so I could read what it said. It was a contract for my property. The price offered was one million dollars, and I gasped when I read that.

"A million dollars?"

"Yes, it's a very generous offer."

I knew that monetary amount would have dazzled my Momma. I just wished she had spoken to me about it.

"Mr. Bee I don't doubt that my Momma would have wanted to take this offer. I know she wanted to travel."

"Oh, she shared that with you did she?"

I lied, "Yes."

"She wanted you to go to college too." He said thoughtfully.

"Yes, I know that too."

We sat quietly for a few moments as I tried to formulate my thoughts so I could relay to Mr. Bee how I was feeling.

"Mr. Bee, I can go to college even without selling the farm, correct?"

Mr. Bee chuckled. "Yes, there is the trust I told you about."

"Do I have enough money to fix up the farm? Buy new things for the house?"

"Belle, you do have a good amount money available. What are you thinking?"

"I don't think I want to sell the farm, and I've been thinking about downsizing, just a little, to make it more manageable. I also want to fix it up and make this home my own."

"You are a smart one." He grinned at me.

I smiled. I trusted Mr. Bee and was so grateful I had him.

"Please tell the buyers thank you, but no thank you. Please convey to them that if I change my mind that I will let you know and you can call them."

"I think waiting a bit is a smart plan, Belle."

"Why do they want my property, do you know?"

"I asked, but the man didn't say."

I looked around the downstairs of my home and came to a decision.

"Mr. Bee I'd like to purchase some new furniture and hire someone to help me around the farm. I need someone who can repair things and help me with the animals, the garden, and the property. Is that possible?"

"Yes, of course. It's a wonderful idea. There is a furniture store in Springfield. I will call and set up an account for you. Any other items you want just use your debit card; you have a limit of $5,000. Would you like for me to look into hiring you a hand?"

"Yes please."

"Mr. Bee I'm also thinking of taking some college classes. It's one of the reasons I'd like someone to help me on the farm."

"I think that's a splendid idea. May I make a suggestion?"

"Of course."

"Why don't you start with a few courses at the Community College in September. If you like it, you can take more classes, and if you decide you want to go somewhere full time, well then we will cross that bridge when we come to it."

"That's a good, good idea, Mr. Bee," I answered excitedly and Mr. Bee chuckled at my enthusiasm. I was pleased with my decisions and felt as if a great weight had been lifted from me. I had a plan.

I was going to fix up the house and make a few upgrades to the barn and corrals, and I was going to take college classes. My first thought was that I couldn't wait to tell Brady.

I pushed the piece of paper with the offer back to Mr. Bee. "No Belle you can keep that, it's a copy."

"So you'll tell them?"

"Yes, they knew I was talking to you today."

Mr. Bee stood up, so I did too. "So what are you thinking of doing in here?" he asked.

"I'm not sure yet. I just thought about it while we were sitting here. It just came to me that I want to make this place my home."

"It's a wonderful idea, Belle. Let me or the Mrs. know if you need any help."

"Okay, thank you."

"I'll call you when I find a helper for you."

"Thank you." It seems like I was always thanking Mr. Bee. He was a good man.

After Mr. Bee left I headed back upstairs to Momma's room; I was almost finished. I took the magazines she had stacked in a corner and put them in a garbage bag along with the travel brochures. Her books from the library I put in another bag; they needed to be returned. I put some of her knick-knacks in a small plastic bin. I didn't want them, but I couldn't bring myself to throw them out. The delicate figurine she had on her dresser of a mother and daughter hugging I relocated to my dresser. I also kept the few pieces of jewelry that had been passed down from Gigi to Gram, then to her, and now they were mine. Lastly, I stripped her bed and folded the beautiful quilt she had made back and placed it at the bottom of her bed

I placed the paper with the offer for my ranch inside the metal box, along with the journal, the other papers, and the one picture of Momma and the man. I put the box on the shelf in her closet. The other pictures and the college brochures I put in Momma's nightstand drawer. I wanted to get the pictures framed. I hoped they could be made bigger too. I'd have to ask Brady how to go about doing that. The college brochures I would look at another day.

I carried all the bags and boxes downstairs. Her clothes and a few other items I was taking to Goodwill, so I placed that box by the front door. The bags I was throwing out, so I put by the door as well. I would take them to the dump.

I carried the plastic bin containing the few mementoes that I couldn't part with to the kitchen and opened the cellar door. After pulling the string to illuminate the bare bulb at the top of the steps, I hurried down the wooden steps. I placed Momma's bin next to Gigi's and Grams. A shiver ran up my spine; I felt as though I was being watched, which was, of course, ridiculous. I quickly ran back up the steps, flicked off the light, and slammed the door closed. I leaned back against the door holding my palm over my pounding heart. I felt foolishly dramatic and chastised myself for overreacting. No sooner had I moved away from the door I heard a heavy thud sound coming from the cellar. I cautiously moved away from the door listening for more sounds, but none came. I was breathing hard as I stared at the door fearing the cellar monster would open it and pop out. After a few nerve-wracking moments, I started nervously giggling. The cellar monster! I hadn't thought of that in ages. When I was younger, I told my family that I refused to go in the cellar until the cellar monster had left. My Gigi and Gram had covered their grins after seeing how serious I was. My mother, however, told me I had an overactive imagination and she threatened to take the Science Fiction book I had been reading away if I kept talking nonsense.

Once I calmed down, I realized that I had probably just heard the house settling.

"You should be done settling." I tersely said out loud to the empty house.

Feeling satisfied with my day's efforts I treated myself by eating another piece of cake. I was feeling drained but oddly exhilarated. I had accomplished a lot today, and my chat with Mr. Bee had been productive as well.

While eating my cake, I looked around the kitchen, dining, and living room. I had always liked how all three rooms were blended into one. There were three doors in the kitchen. One opened to the mudroom. Inside the mudroom, there was a half bath, the laundry machines, shelves, and a door that led to the outside. Another door in the kitchen was for the spooky cellar and right next to that door was a walk-in pantry. The appliances in the kitchen were still usable, and I had always loved the big gas oven, so I was keeping that. I did not need a big refrigerator, so the one I had was fine. The kitchen did not need any upgrades.

I turned my attention to the living area. The furniture was old and worn; it's funny how I never really noticed it before. When I had walked into Brady's home, I had been awestruck with how homey and put together it was. I wanted that feeling when I walked into my home. I envisioned furniture and accent pieces that were blue, green, and yellow. Those colors made me happy. I wanted happy!

I walked into my Gigi's downstairs room. It was the largest bedroom in the house with built-in bookshelves and an attached bathroom that she had shared with Gram. I walked into the shared bathroom and into Gram's room. It was smaller than Gigi's, but it had a small bay window with a bench seat that overlooked the front yard that I loved.

I decided I was going to move onto Gigi's room. I was so excited over my plan that I happily clapped my hands together, and Josh circled my feet feeling my excitement. I got the measuring tape from the kitchen drawer and took down the dimensions of the room and the two windows. One window looked out on the side yard, and the other looked out onto the backyard.

The walls were painted white, and I decided to paint them blue. I was also going to buy new furniture for the room. The floors in the room were hardwood, and I loved the wide dark brown planks.

It was after 2:00 PM when I got in my truck. First I dropped the bags at the Goodwill box, which was behind the market in town. Next, I took two bags of garbage including the one bag filled with my Momma's magazines to the dump. Then I headed for Springfield for the second time in two days.

The On-Star guided me to the Home Accents Store. I was secretly happy that it wasn't all the way in downtown Springfield but was located on the outskirts of the large town. I didn't know if I was ready to drive in heavy traffic just yet. A woman met me as I walked through at the stores front door and asked if she could help me. I thanked her and explained that I was going to look around first. I walked through the three rooms of furniture. I liked how it had been organized so that the pieces were arranged to resemble rooms. I found a living room set that had a couch and love seat upholstered with a brown, soft, leather-like material. To my delight, I discover that the ends of the couch reclined. Pretty pillows of yellow, green, and blue embellished the couch, and a comfy looking oversized chair upholstered with material matching the three pillows pulled together the living room ensemble. I wrote down the style numbers on each piece and went to another part of the store.

I picked out a beautiful bedroom set. It included a sleigh bed, a dresser, armoire, and nightstands. It was on sale and advertised as classic country. I measured the pieces and decided that the queen bed would be the perfect size for the room. I was pleased that the store sold mattresses as well, Gram's bed had been a full, and so I needed one. I wrote down the style number of the bedroom and practically skipped to my next area, lamps. There were so many to choose from. I was going to need a little help with this, so I found the lady who had asked if I needed help.

I showed her the two complete room sets I was going to be purchasing and then asked her to recommend lamps.

She helped me pick out two lamps for the bedroom. They were tall with bases of thick cut glass. The woman explained that bedside lamps should be tall so that when I was sitting in bed, I could easily reach under the shades to turn them off or on.

For the living room, I decided on two beautiful lamps that were made from pottery. They had the same colors of the couch pillows running through the base, and I knew they were perfect. Next, I chose throw rugs, one for my bedroom and one for between the kitchen and dining area. I also bought a large 12 X 15 rug to go under my living room furniture; it was yellow and white and tied my whole room together.

Lastly, the woman showed me curtains. I had not planned on purchasing curtains. My Momma had made all the ones in our house, but I realized that they would not match the new furniture. So I bought curtains for the living room, one for over the kitchen sink, two that would bracket the sliding doors in the living room and lastly ones for my bedroom. My home was going to look great!

I paid the salesperson who then wrote down my address. She said my furniture would be delivered the day after tomorrow. That gave me a day to paint, so it was perfect. She explained that the company delivering the furniture would take the old furniture away if I wanted and I told her that would be perfect.

On the way home I stopped at the market and bought an already roasted chicken and some other staples. When I got home, I found Brady waiting for me. Josh was sitting by him clearly pleased that he had a companion.

He walked to meet me as I stepped out of the truck. "Hi. Where have you been?" He sounded weird, almost sad, that I hadn't been home.

"Hi. I've had such a good day. Well, not better than yesterday, but still good. Want to eat dinner with me? I bought a chicken. It's already cooked. How cool is that!"

Brady laughed. "Yes, I'd love to eat dinner with you. Let me just tell my mom." he took out his cell and put it back in his pocket. "You don't get cell service here?"

"No."

"Can I use your phone?"

"Of course," I said cheerily. I heard Brady tell his Mom where he was and then he hung up and sat down at the table.

I put the chicken on a plate and made a green salad. Brady helped by setting the table; it was nice having company. I set the dishes on the table and poured us both ice tea.

"Okay, tell me what has you smiling like that?" Brady chuckled as he helped himself to the food.

"So many things Brady. Okay, first Mr. Bee came over and showed me an offer that someone made on my property." Brady froze, his fork midway to his mouth. He put his fork back down on his plate.

"Wait. What?"

"Someone wants to buy Green Mountain, well my side of it."

"And?"

"I told Mr. Bee to tell them thank you, but no." I visually watched Brady's shoulders sag with relief.

"Okay, go on." I think he was nervous as to what else I may tell him.

"So while Mr. Bee was here I decided to redecorate my house, you know paint rooms and buy new furniture, and I decided to move into my Gigi's bedroom. I'm also going to hire someone to help me around here."

Brady interrupted me. "You are?"

"Yes, even Mr. Bee thinks it's a good idea. I can't keep this place up by myself."

Brady still hadn't started eating again. "If you are staying here I think that's a good idea too."

"I also decided to take some courses at the County College."

"That's a great idea," Brady said finally taking a bite of his chicken.

I was beaming.

"So where were you today?" he asked.

"I went to Springfield, to the furniture store, and bought a living room set and a bedroom set. Oh, and I also cleaned out my Momma's room, dropped things at the Goodwill box and went to the dump. "

Brady started laughing, "Wow you did have quite a day."

"I did," I said spearing a piece of chicken and eating it. "Hey this is pretty good," I said pointing my fork at the chicken. "I always saw these in the market, but Momma would not buy one. She loved to cook and refused to believe the market could make one better than what she could." I laughed thinking about it.

We talked about the changes I wanted to make and how I needed to buy paint. I told Brady that I hoped Mr. Bee could hire someone for me tomorrow because I needed help painting. Brady offered to take me to get the paint, and I said that would be great. We decide to do that tomorrow morning, so I could start painting right away.

"Brady I'll feed you dessert, but I need to bed down the animals first."

"Okay, I'll help you, and we'll get to that cake quicker."

We worked in compatible silence. Brady was a quick study and at ease among the animals. Henny nudged him with her nose, and I told him that meant she liked him. We finished quickly and headed back inside.

I brought out the last of the cake, and Brady laughed when he saw how little was left.

"What? I like cake." I said trying to appear offended, but I too happy and started laughing.

We sat out back eating the cake and watching the sun dip behind Green Mountain. When I asked Brady what he had done that day he replied that he had run errands. He gave no details, and I didn't press him for any. I secretly wondered if he had met with Miss Donna.

It was dark when Brady decided to leave, and I was tired. I walked him to his truck, and we stood facing each other. He was tall enough that I had to tilt my head back to look at him. Once again I was struck by how good-looking he was. He was looking at me, and I knew he wanted to say something. This time I waited and hoped he would speak without me prompting him. He did.

Brady tucked a piece of my hair away from my face and realizing that he had just done something intimate put his hands in his pockets. "Belle, I know you've had a rough time of it. I also understand that we've only just met, but I want you to know that I like being with you."

"I like being with you too Brady," I told him softly. "When I'm not with you I think about you." He admitted shyly.

I felt my face heat with a blush.

"Do you think about me Belle?" he asked nervously.

"Yes," I answered so softly that he had to lean in to hear me. "Today when I came to all those decisions about the farm, the house, and college, I wanted to tell you. It was my first thought."

Brady smiled. "I like that."

I smiled up at him, and somehow we moved closer together.

His hands came out of his pockets, and he gently placed them on my waist. I think he waited to see if I moved away from his touch; I didn't. His voice deepened, "I want to kiss you. Can I?"

"I've never been kissed before." If it hadn't been so, dark Brady would have seen that my face was flushed crimson.

"Is that a yes?"

"Yes," I said breathlessly

"I'm glad. I want to be your first." My heart thudded so hard in my chest I had to put my hand over it.

Brady leaned in and put his lips on mine. His strong arms held me gently and my chest pressed against his strong upper body. His lips brushed softly against mine, and then he opened them slightly, and I felt his tongue touch mine.

I pulled back feeling awkward.

"Are you okay?" He asked not releasing me completely.

"Am I doing it right?" I had seen people kiss on the television but the tongue thing I hadn't been prepared for.

Brady chuckled. "Yes, it's perfect; you're perfect." He leaned into me, and this time his kiss was more urgent, electric. When his tongue once again touched mine, I realized we were supposed to stroke them against each other. It was so sensual and exciting. I moaned with how incredible it felt. We must have kissed for ages because Josh barked letting me know he was done waiting to be let inside. It was past his bedtime. We slowly pulled apart. Brady did not take his eyes off me, and the way he was looking at me gave me goose bumps, the good kind of goose bumps.

He had a small grin on his face that I knew mirrored my own. I touched my lips with my fingertips, and he smirked happily.

"That was a good kiss," he said keeping his eyes on mine. "I hope we do that again; soon," His hands rubbed my back. I felt like purring I was so content.

"Me too," I agreed, which made him happy because his smile got even wider and his green eyes sparkled. Yup, Brady was definitely happy. I hugged him because I wanted to, plain and simple, I liked how he felt. My cheek rested on his chest. He whispered in my ear. "So I'll see you tomorrow?"

"Yes," I answered remaining against him. I thought of his well-defined chest that I had seen when we swam, and I wished he didn't have his shirt. Whoa, where did that thought come from?

"How about if I come by early to help with the animals? Then we can go buy the paint."

"Brady you don't have to help me with the animals."

"I actually like doing it. Don't do the animals without me; I'll be here at 7:00." He gave me a sweet but short kiss and then climbed into his truck and drove off.

Upstairs, getting ready for bed I looked at myself in the bathroom mirror. The woman looking back at me had mussed hair, rosy cheeks, and swollen lips. Seeing my reflection reminded me of Momma. I looked like she had looked when she had come home a few of the times that I had waited up for her. It made me happy that Momma had been kissing someone. I wish I knew who that had been, but it didn't really matter; Momma had been happy. I giggled and hopped into bed. I'd had two very good days in a row!

12

Brady

I kissed her, and it had been fan-friggin-tastic! She
was soft and so responsive, and darn it was mind
blowing knowing she had never kissed anyone else.
When our tongues had met, I could tell she was
trying to mimic me, and it was a sensual
experience. I'd gotten so hard that I had to keep
my hips away from her. When we were pressed
together, I could feel the swell of her breasts, and
her nipples had beaded tightly. If she'd been any
other woman, I would have gone further. It's not
that I needed the release. Since I'd re-acquired the
use of my cock, I'd been beating off every chance I
got. All I had to do was picture Belle's perfect little-
naked body, and it was as if my dick was reacting to
a direct dose of Viagra.

When I'd heard that she'd had an offer on her place
I darn near bit my tongue. I was worried she was
going to take it, move away, and leave me to fall
back into my miserable existence before I'd met
her.

Since I'd met Belle, I'd been working out with a
purpose, and I'd even gone back to Physical
Therapy. I was happier, noticeable happier, even
my dad commented on it. I was no longer sitting
home feeling sorry for myself. Granted I still was
not the man I'd been before, but being with Belle
made me feel better. She didn't look at me like
other people did. People who knew me when I

wasn't damaged smiled and talked to me, but I knew they pitied me, and I hated that.

When I got home, I talked to my dad, and then I called Mr. Bee. I wanted to be Belle's handyman. I sure as hell wasn't letting anyone else get close to her. She was my found treasure.

Mr. Bee said he thought that would be fine, but then he said something I wasn't expecting.

"Brady." He said. "I've known that girl since she was born. She's led a very sheltered life. She's intelligent and kind, and very, very trusting. I've also known you since you were a baby. If you're toying with her boy, I don't care who your daddy is; I will whip your ass."

I had to hold in a chuckle because even with me in my prosthetic Mr. Bee had no chance of whipping my ass. However, I appreciated that he was looking out for her.

"Sir, I won't hurt her. I like her. I do."

"I know you've had your share of ladies, son." I knew what he was getting at so I cut him off before he pissed me off.

"I understand completely, Mr. Bee."

"Okay then, as long as you have her best interest at heart, you're hired."

"Thank you."

"Now let's talk pay."

Here's where it could get dicey. I took a calming breath.

"Mr. Bee I don't want any money. Could you donate my salary to one of Belle's favorite charities? Just don't tell her okay? Is that agreeable?"

"I don't know Brady, don't you need the money?"

"I could use the money, but if I take it, I'll lose my disability status and right now I need that for medical reasons."

"Oh, I see. You're a smart man Brady. I believe you'll be a good friend to our Belle."

"Yes, Sir," I said pleased with his compliment. When I got off the phone I told my mom and dad what I was going to be doing and my mom got all teary-eyed, and I had to look to dad for an explanation as to why my usually very stable mom was crying.

"Son, we've been worried about you. I think your Ma is just happy you've taken an interest in something."

I shook my head, "I'm sorry if I've been difficult." Mom started crying harder, and my dad chuckled and put his arm around her.

"It's been a bit stressful," he admitted candidly. "First losing Chelsea, and then your foot. We were hoping it wouldn't be too much for you."

Hearing Chelsea's name, I swallowed and smiled uneasily. "Hey, her loss," I said with false bravado.

"Damn right her loss." My mom snuffled loudly making both my dad and I laugh.

I headed upstairs to my room. I hadn't changed a thing about it since I'd moved back home. It still had my high school posters on the walls and old trophies on the shelves. The things I had planned on taking to what I thought was to be Chelsea's and my apartment were still sitting in boxes in the basement.

The next morning I was up and out the door even before my dad. I got to Belle's and saw that she and Josh were sitting on the front porch. She remained sitting in her chair, and when I reached her, she handed me a cup of coffee.

"Thanks," I said taking a seat next to her. She was looking at me as if she was summing me up.

"Are you sure you want to be my work hand?"

"I guess you've talked to Mr. Bee?"

"Yes, last night."

"Do you have a problem giving me the job?"

She hesitated, and it made me uneasy. "No. I just wonder if this is really something you want to do?"

"Yes, I want to be your hired hand," I told her sincerely.

"Come on." She said in a frustrated tone. "You cannot seriously want to be a handyman on my little farm? You have a college education. You are a Marine!"

"I'm handicapped, and I need a job!" I countered quickly.

Belle gasped. "You are not handicapped!" I could tell she was mad.

An uncomfortable silence stretched between us.

"You aren't," Belle whispered.

"Belle, I am. I'm classified. I even have a tag for my car that states that I'm handicapped."

Belle looked at my truck. "I don't see it."

"I don't display it."

"See, you don't think of yourself as being
handicapped."
"I don't want to discuss this." I abruptly stood up
and put my mug on the table between our chairs
and started walking.

13

Belle

He was going to leave. I wanted to call him back, but my pride wouldn't let me. Well, I thought sarcastically, I guess he didn't want the job after all. What a disappointment. It then hit me like a hammer, the proverbial light bulb flashing on. I now understood why Gram and Gigi and kept our family female only. Men sucked! One serious discussion and Brady bolts. Men always leave. I took another sip of my now tepid coffee and watched Brady head to his truck. He opened his door, reached inside, shut the door, and started walking towards the barn. I saw that he was now holding a pair of work gloves in his hand. He stopped walking and turned back to where I was sitting.

"Well come on, let's get these animals done."
He turned away from me again and started walking towards the barn. I knew my mouth was hanging open and I shut it quickly before getting up to follow him.

As we worked, I saw Brady inspecting the coop, the fences, and other little deficiencies in the barn and corral areas.

Momma and I had done our best to keep up with repairs, but once Momma had started going out at night, she had slacked off. I was embarrassed at the sad state of my little farm. I should have talked to Momma about getting a helper a long time ago. I just didn't know that we could afford it and I was sure she would have balked at having someone invading our private lifestyle.

Brady and I didn't speak while we worked and when the chores were done, I told him I was going to make us breakfast. He nodded and remained behind in the barn.

I had mixed emotions surging through me. I was worried that my new friendship with Brady was fractured. I had no experience with people. I'd had minor disagreements with my family but they were simple, really trivial, like what should we name the new rooster or what we should plant in the garden. I was also annoyed with him. What the heck was his problem? How could he think he was disabled? He could walk and talk and think just like everyone else. Doggonit, if you didn't know him, you'd never know he was missing his lower leg. I'd obviously hit a nerve. I didn't understand what topics could or couldn't be discussed with him. The worst feeling that was bombarding me was a sense of loss. If Brady pulled away from me, I knew I was going to have a tough time going back to my solitary lifestyle. Brady had shown me how much I needed and enjoyed being around people. I also wasn't happy that there would be no more kissing. I liked kissing. I liked kissing him.

I made us a breakfast of eggs, potatoes, and bacon. As I was putting his plate on the table, I heard him come in.

He stood by his chair uncertainly.

"Please sit and eat," I said to him taking my own seat.

We ate in silence and to say it was uncomfortable was an understatement.

I finished eating and took my plate to the sink. My emotions were frayed, and I was holding back tears that threatened to fall. I kept my back to him.

I heard him get up and then the most wonderful thing ever happened. He put his arms around my waist and pulled me back into his chest.

"I'm sorry Belle. I don't want to argue with you."

I leaned back into him and placed my hands on his forearms holding him to me.

"I don't want to argue either. I feel like I need an instruction manual."

"An instruction manual?"

"Yes, something that could guide me through all these new things that are popping up between us."

He turned me around, so I was facing him and tilted my chin up.

"You don't need any manual telling you what you should say or how you should act around me. It's one of the things I like about you."

"But when I spoke my mind earlier you got mad."

"So we disagreed about something, and yes I was mad. I'm sorry, it's a sore subject."

"I still don't agree with you. You're not disabled; far from it."

He smiled gently. "Yes, I know you feel that way, and I thank you for that."

Brady kissed me so sweetly that my tummy somersaulted. He pulled back from the kiss.

"Is it all right that we are kissing?"

I cocked my head, not understanding. In my mind, I was screaming, kiss me more!

He looked down at me with his green eyes burning into mine.

"Belle, if you want to just be friends with me, please tell me now."

I was slightly confused; maybe I just wasn't up on terminology. "So we aren't friends?"

"We are, but we can be more than friends too."

"I enjoy being with you Brady. You're the first friend I've ever had."

He knew I had more to say. "And?"

"And I also like kissing you? I'm wicked aren't I?" I said blushing deeply.

Brady chuckled. "No, you are far from wicked Belle."

"So you and I can still be like we have been and still kiss?"

"Yes, I'd like that."

"I'd like that too," I admitted putting my arms around his neck, and Brady wasted no time diving back in for a lengthy kiss.

His body was plastered against mine, and I felt something hard pressing against my stomach. When I realized what it was, I kept kissing him, but I was blushing furiously. Gram and Gigi would have been mortified at my promiscuous behavior, but I really liked kissing Brady, so I quickly pushed that thought away.

My body was responding to Brady's kiss in its own way. My insides were churning, my breasts were achy, and I felt wet in my private parts. I wanted to rub against Brady in the most decadent way, but I was sure if I did that he would run for the hills thinking I was a hussy.

Brady pulled back from the passionate kiss and rested his forehead against mine.

"I really like kissing you," he whispered.

"I like kissing you too."

"As soon as I get myself under control why don't we go buy some paint?"

I nodded, and as he stepped back from me. I figured out that 'under control' was guy speak for waiting for his erection to go down. Brady had a large bulge front and center of his jeans. He saw me look there and grinned.

"You have that effect on me."

Once again I cocked my head not understanding him.

"Belle, you do realize how desirable you are right?"

"Desirable?"

"Yes, sexy, beautiful, want to do more than just kiss you, desirable."

"Oh." He could tell I had something on my mind. "What?"

"Nothing," I quipped quickly. It was too embarrassing. I'd have to go to the library and research this 'more than just kiss' thing. I knew about male and female anatomy, where babies came from and how they were made, but I had a feeling there was a lot more to men and women being together that just that. Brady proved that when he kissed me.

"Come on, tell me?"

"No, it's embarrassing."

Brady looked apprehensive, and then he looked uncomfortable.

"Uh, do you need to talk to my mom? Is it a female thing?"

I knew I was red as beet now.

"Oh, no, no, it's not, I mean, no it's not that," I stammered.

"Come on Belle, tell me."

I sighed nervously. "What do you mean 'more than just kiss'? Are you talking about procreating?"

"Procreating? You mean having sex?"

"Well, yes."

"Oh boy." He said running his hands through his hair. "Why don't we sit down for a minute, okay?"

We moved to the sofa. It was ironic that we were sitting there because that's where I had been sitting when my Gigi, Gram, and Momma had explained to me about the birds and the bees.

"Belle, there are many things men and women do with each other when they care about each other."

I nodded.

"Kissing is one of them," he continued cautiously.

"I like kissing," I whispered making him smile.

"I like kissing you too, and that's important. I like kissing you. I wouldn't enjoy kissing just anyone. Do you understand that?"

"Yes. I would not want to kiss Mr. Bee as I kissed you."

Brady chuckled. "Exactly. Aside from the fact that Mr. Bee is married, it's important that you feel something special towards a person before you do the 'more than kiss' things."

"Well, what are those things?"

Brady hesitated. "Belle how about we shelve this conversation for a bit?"

"But I want to know."

"Yes, and I want to show you."

"Show me?"

"Belle there are things I want to do with you, to you that require time."

"Brady, I'm getting really confused here."

"Crud, okay, for example when we were kissing you know how your nipples got hard?"

I gasped. "Yes," I stammered out meekly.

"Well, I would have liked to touch them. I'd like to kiss them and use my tongue on them."

My insides quivered, and I felt tingly, flushed, and the juncture where my legs came together was on fire.

"Oh," I said breathlessly.

Brady smiled. "You would feel good when I do that, and it would be very stimulating for me too." My nipples were achingly hard, and I wanted to rub them. Brady looked at my face and then to my chest. When he lifted his hand, I froze. I don't think I was even breathing. He slowly moved his hands towards my breasts, and he gently cupped them before he swiped his thumbs over my needy points.

"Ohhhhh," I moaned softly. Brady leaned in and kissed me, keeping his hands on my breasts. He kneaded them through my tee shirt so tenderly, but what was so incredible was how he used his fingers on my nipples. My lower private parts were wet now, and a foreign ache down there had me squirming. After a few minutes, Brady pulled back and took his hands from my breasts.

We were both breathing hard. "Did you like that Belle?"

I nodded; there was no way I could talk yet. I saw his jeans were once again inflated in the front. He saw where I was looking.

"You make me so hard, Belle." His voice was shaky.

I have no idea what possessed me, but I ran my hand over his bulge, and he groaned. I snatched my hand away thinking I'd hurt him.

He took my hand and placed it back on his hardness and right before he leaned back in for a kiss he whispered. "I like that you're touching me. Keep touching me."

His voice was husky, and I liked it. He moved my hand with his so I was rubbing him up, and down and I could feel the shape his penis through his jeans. I added some pressure and Brady moaned. This time I knew he liked what I was doing to him. He put his hands back on my breasts and this time I moaned.

We stayed like this for many minutes, and when Brady lay down on the couch and pulled me on top of him, I let him. His hardness was aligned with my private parts. He placed his hands on my hips and encouraged me to rub on his hard manliness.

His penis was stroking my covered clitoris, and the feeling was unbelievable. We kept kissing, and I kept moving, and a heated tornado began to turn inside of me. I had to stop kissing him because I couldn't breathe.

"Brady." I hushed out as I rubbed against him.

"Keep moving Belle. Let it happen."

I groaned as an intense feeling pushed through me. My clitoris was zinging from the stimulation.

Brady put his hands on my rear and pressed into me and then it happened. A volcanic wash of ecstasy burst forth, and my body erupted in a most overwhelming way. My eyelids fluttered, and my body convulsed as I moaned Brady's name over and over again.

Brady was kissing me again, and he was whispering to me, but darned if I knew what he was saying.

"You came Belle. You came."

I regained some control. "Is that what that was?"

"Yes, You climaxed, you came."

"I liked it," I said breathlessly. "Did you come too?"

I had read a medical journal that described orgasms, and I knew men ejaculated when they had an orgasm, but Brady was fully clothed so I couldn't tell if he had.

Brady was smiling at me our faces were so close together.

"No Babe."

"Don't you want to?"

Brady groaned and kissed me. "Yes, but I think we need to stop for now."

It didn't look like he wanted to stop. "Are you sure?"

"Belle, we have all the time in the world." He said sweetly.

I still knew I was going to be doing a little research on this 'more than just kissing' stuff, but for the moment I was just going to enjoy what I'd just experienced.

My body felt lazy and warm. Brady gave me another short kiss and rolled me to the inside of the couch. He sat up keeping one hand on my hip. "We have paint to pick out." He said. He then leaned down to kiss me once more before he stood up.

"I'm going to use the bathroom before we go." He said standing up. He adjusted his bulge. I think he had to so he could walk. I watched him walk away feeling euphoric.

I finally got off the couch and went into my Gigi's, soon to be my bathroom. I froze when I looked into the mirror. My Momma was once again staring back at me; mussed hair, swollen lips, and a very content look on my face was what I saw. My Momma must have been with a man for sure when she had been going out. Again I wondered who it had been.

I used the bathroom noticing how wet my underwear was. I came out of the bathroom and found Brady sitting on one of the chairs. Because my hair was a mess I wanted to use my hairbrush and I also wanted to change my underwear.

"I'll be right down," I told him as I climbed the stairs. I could feel Brady's eyes watching me as I jogged up the wooden staircase.

14

Brady

I couldn't stop thinking about her. Even though we had been fully clothed, I had held her breasts in my hands, brushed her nipples with my thumbs and given her what I believed was her first orgasm. I'd almost spewed in my pants when she convulsed on top of me. I had to stop thinking about it. It had taken me a while for my erection to go down and if I thought about that sweet moment, I'd get hard again.

I watched her climb the stairs and her little heart shaped bottom swayed sexily as she retreated up the steps. My mind was blown away by how responsive she had been. I was going to love teaching her about sex. I had not been with anyone since Chelsea. That was twelve months ago.

We had dated all through college. She had been my best friend, along with my friend Kip. She was my lover, my everything. We knew we were going to marry someday. We never really spoke about it, it was a given. She lived in the next town over, and we met during freshman orientation. We were inseparable. My family loved her, and her family loved me.

After college, I enlisted. I wanted to serve my country, plus having military experience was a good stepping-stone if you wanted to pursue a career in law enforcement or Wildlife management, which I did. My parents didn't want me to enlist. My Dad said he'd help me get a job, but I wanted to do it on my own.

I spent two years in Afghanistan, and the training I received was invaluable. I knew I'd made the correct decision by enlisting. I was trained specifically to scout ahead of my platoon. I could shoot better than any of my brothers, and I learned to hone all my senses to keep my platoon safe.

When my tour was over, I figured Chelsea and I would move in together and then get married. I'd find a job in one of the State Agencies. I was leaning towards being a Sheriff, like my dad, or maybe a Game Warden.

When I got back to the states, I discovered that Chelsea had changed. When I'd been away we had kept in touch as best we could with the time difference. Unfortunately, I had been naive thinking we were in a solid relationship.

While I was overseas, she had not been faithful to me. My first night back from Afghanistan Chelsea never came to my house. I called her, but she never answered her phone. I waited for her thinking she would arrive any minute. Cripes, I was surprised she hadn't met me at the airport.

Two days later and I still had not seen her. I finally drove to her apartment, and that's when I found out she had been seeing someone else. The guy was there, and I wanted to put him through the wall, but I was equally mad at Chelsea. To say I was hurt

and pissed was an understatement. The next day I
re-upped, and I shipped out a month later.

My accident happened halfway through my second
tour. When I was in the hospital stateside, my mom
said Chelsea had stopped by to see me. I knew I'd
see her; she was a nurse in the hospital; she worked
in pediatrics. She was so good with kids. She would
have been a great mom. I told my mom not to let
her in, and my mom assured me she would keep
her out. I knew that request had to be hard on my
mom since she and Chelsea had been close. When
I was in the hospital, I think Chelsea had snuck in
when I was sleeping. I was so high on pain
medication that I couldn't tell if I had dreamt it. I
felt her hand on my brow, and I think she was
crying. I also think she kissed me before leaving.

I still thought about Chelsea and couldn't believe
she had so easily thrown away what we had. A few
months ago, I heard from my mom that Chelsea
and the guy had broken up. I tried not to care but
secretly I was glad. We had been so good together.
She was pretty, loved being outdoors, and had a
great sense of humor. Everyone who had met her
loved her. We had learned how to have sex
together. We had even bought a book that
explained different positions to try.

I'd been back from Afghanistan for six months
now. The first two weeks I had spent in the trauma
hospital in Afghanistan. Then I was flown stateside
where I spent another two weeks in the local
hospital. When I was discharged, I had kept to
myself. Since meeting Belle, I was starting to do

things again. Going to Springfield with Belle had been a first, in a way, for me too. I still hadn't been out to a bar. I had been avoiding my friends. I wasn't the same, I was damaged, and I'd kept my pitiful self-locked away. Belle was drawing me back out. I wondered what my friends would think of her. Part of me wanted to take her out and show her off. Belle was gorgeous and so sweet. I was always smiling around her. I knew if I went out publicly with her that it would get back to Chelsea that I was with another woman. Part of me couldn't wait for her to hear that. I hoped it stung. Belle came back downstairs, and I saw that she had brushed her hair. She was smiling, but it was a shy smile. I stood up and took her hand. We needed to buy some paint.

Belle

We took Brady's truck to the hardware store. I picked out a pale blue for the bedroom, a yellow for the bathroom, and a white for the living room and kitchen. I was going to paint the other rooms too, but these were the areas I wanted to fix up first. We bought tape and rollers, and brushes and I used my debit card. Before we left town, I told Brady I needed to stop at the library, and he said he had to go into the pharmacy anyways, which was right next to the library, so it was perfect.
When I entered the library, Mrs. Bee came from around the desk and gave me a warm hug. We chatted for a few minutes, and I did not want to be

rude, so I told her I was Brady and that he was at the pharmacy, so I needed to hurry. I found a book called exploring human sexuality, and I also took out a Steven King novel, and a Harlan Coban mystery. When I went to check the books out Mrs. Bee gave me a little smile seeing the Human Sexuality book, and she patted my hand and told me that if I ever needed someone to talk to her door was always open. I thanked her. She looked behind her desk, and I saw she was eyeing a paper bag. It was the magazine bag that she had always saved the old magazines for my Momma. She looked back at me, and I shook my head.

"My Momma sure liked reading those."

"I wasn't sure if you read them also. I didn't want to throw them out if you, did."

"Thank you, Mrs. Bee. I'm good with my books." I tucked the books under my arm and headed out. Brady was waiting at the truck. He was leaning against the passenger side door, and he looked troubled.

"Hi," I said, as I got closer. "You look deep in thought."

He didn't offer up what he had been thinking about. He opened my door and helped me in. Then he saw the title of my one book.

"You got a book on Human Sexuality?"

"I did."

He got a cute little smile on his face. "I don't mind teaching you." I knew he was being cheeky.

"And you are a very good teacher." I playfully answered.

He was quiet on the way back to the farm, and I thought he seemed contemplative, but I just dismissed the little apprehensive niggle that surfaced.

We spent the rest of the day prepping and painting. I couldn't believe how much a coat of paint could transform a room. It looked great. I couldn't wait for my furniture to come tomorrow. We cleaned up, and I saw that it was after 5:00 pm.

"I have to do the animals." I told Brady," then, if you want, I'll fix us dinner?"

"I have to pass on dinner, but I'll do the animals with you." I was a little hurt that he didn't want to have dinner with me, but I knew it was dumb to think that way.

We walked out to the barn, and I saw that one of the stall doors that had been broken now hung on the stall.

"You fixed the stall door?"

"Yes, when you were fixing breakfast."

"Thanks," I said as I swung the newly fixed door closed.

"No need to thank me, that's what a hired hand does."

"There is so much that needs to be done," I told him sounding exasperated.

"It will get done. I made a mental list. I'm going to need to get some things from the hardware store though."

"That's no problem. I used my debit card today, but I'm sure I still have an account there."

We finished bringing in the animals. This time I brought in Henny and Bessie because the clouds had started to darken and the leaves on the trees had flipped to their shiny side. My Gigi had taught me that was a sure sign of incoming weather.

I walked Brady to his truck, and he gave me a quick kiss goodbye on my cheek. I was actually hoping for a bit more, but maybe that's not how things worked. I only knew how I felt and I felt like I wanted to kiss him more.

I was so excited about getting the new furniture the next day I barely slept. When I deemed it time to get out of bed, I did so with so much giddiness that even Josh was wagging his tail. I made coffee, then bread and then waited on the front porch for Brady. When he arrived, I gave him a cup of coffee, and we discussed what had to be done that day.

Organizing the inside of the house was paramount before the furniture truck got there. Brady thought it would be best if I organized the inside of the house while he did the animals He also wanted to start fixing a few more things in the barn area. I agreed, so we got to work.

Two hours later Josh howled, and I heard a large rumbling indicating something large was coming down my drive. Sure enough, the furniture truck came into view, and I walked outside to meet the men. Brady came out from the barn, and I couldn't help but notice that he was sweating through his tee shirt and it was sticking to his muscled chest.

His skin gleamed, and his hair was matted to his forehead. Whatever he was doing was making him sweat.

An hour later my new living room and bedroom furniture were in place. I had hung the curtains and just as I finished Brady, who had retreated back to the barn, came in. I nervously waited to hear what he would say.

"It looks great." He said plopping himself down at the dining room table.

"I sat across from him. "It does, doesn't it?"

"I like the colors you used."

"Me too. It's me." I said happily.

"It is you." He agreed.

It was after 5:00 PM and Brady stood up slapping his work gloves in his hand. "Okay, well I already put the animals in, so I'm going to head home."

The disappointment I felt when he said that was like a wet blanket thrown on my happy party.

"Oh, okay. I guess I'll see you tomorrow."

"Yup, tomorrow." Brady left, and this time I didn't even get a kiss. He had been acting a little off all day and even though I was a total novice regarding boy-girl stuff I found it very hard to believe that one could be intimate one day and then turn it off the next day. It was time to start researching human sexuality.

That night I made myself an omelet for dinner, and after dinner, I took my book out to the back porch. The book was very detailed. School-aged children referred to the 'more than just kissing' in terms baseball terminology. 1st base was kissing, 2nd base was touching the breasts, 3rd base was when a male touched the female's lower private parts, and the 4th base was having sex.

I read until the mosquitos got to be too much. It was fascinating, and I was so glad that I had borrowed the book. I had no idea how many different sexual things could be done with a partner. The other eye-opening fact was that there was a whole chapter on self- stimulation. I knew what I'd be trying before I went to bed that night. It also explained that rubber thing I'd found in Momma's drawer; gross.

I had not bought sheets for my queen-sized bed, so I remained in my bedroom upstairs for one more night. I lay on my bed and shut my eyes and pretended that Brady was touching me. I rubbed my clitoris and the same wonderful feeling pulsed through me and exploded leaving me breathless. It felt fantastic, but it wasn't quite as good as when Brady had led me there.

I woke to Josh howling, and as I sat up in my bed still half asleep, I heard Josh running down the steps. I looked at my clock and saw that it was 3:00 AM. I groggily got out of bed and followed Josh downstairs wondering what the heck he had heard. Josh stood at the front door with his tail wagging, and when I opened the door, he dashed out. I sat down on one of the front porch chairs and watched Josh run down the driveway and then turn back around. I figured he had heard a deer or something, but it was really out of character for him to react to just an animal. The only thing that made sense was that whatever animal it was had probably gotten very close to the house. I called Josh back inside and went back to bed.

The next morning Brady arrived before I had even made the coffee. He didn't come to the house looking for me he just went to the barn. I tried to justify his behavior, but I honestly couldn't. The last couple of days he had not been as attentive as he had been and he seemed almost to be avoiding me. He wasn't smiling as much, and he barely made eye contact with me. It was very odd, and I hated how awkward it felt.

The only thing that made sense was that after our intimate liaison he had decided that I was not to his liking and he was trying to distance himself romantically from me. It hurt to think that he didn't like me in that regard anymore, but I was not going to let on how I was feeling.

I put a cup of coffee out on the front porch and walked to the barn. Brady was fixing the grain bin area.

"I put a cup of coffee on the porch for you," I told him. "I'll be back later." I quickly left the barn and walked to my truck. I was, of course, hoping he would ask where I was going or even better chase me down and kiss me silly, but neither of those things happened.

I drove into Springfield, and the OnStar navigated me to Macy's. Momma had loved Macy's. I bought an ensemble for my bed. It came with sheets and pillowcases, a comforter, bed skirt, and pillow shams. Next, I purchased new towels and washcloths for the bathroom.

I put everything in my truck and went back inside to look at the clothes. An hour later I had bought a skirt, shoes, another pair of jeans and a really cute dress. I returned to my truck and headed home. I saw that it was close to 3:00 PM and even though I had been away from the farm for a while I just didn't want to go home and see Brady. I was feeling very discombobulated.

On the way home I passed a country western store, and I pulled in on a whim. I left that store with a pair of cowboy boots and fun, very feminine shirt, a jean skirt and beaded belt; the whole outfit looked great together. I had no idea where I'd wear it, but I couldn't help myself.

I returned home after 5:00 PM and saw that I had indeed missed Brady. The animals had been brought in, and he had left a note on the front porch.

Stopping at hardware store tomorrow so may be late. Want to fix the fences. Brady

I took the note inside and fed Josh and made myself a grilled cheese. I washed the sheets, and while they were washing, I read more in the Human Sexuality book.

I had gotten to a chapter, which described a variety of sexual positions that couple could try for maximum stimulation, and I was absolutely flabbergasted. I became aroused and looked at the pictures probably longer than I should have. I leafed through the next few chapters until I got to one that discussed relationships. There were many different kinds of relationships. Some were based entirely on sex, some rooted in love and some were a combination of both. Brady had given me that little speech about doing more than just kiss with someone you cared about, but I was beginning to think that he was what the book described as someone who says things just so the other person would have sex with them. My Gram used to say that men would say anything to get in girls pants. I had been too young to understand what that meant, and back then I could not even understand why a man would want to get in my pants, but my Gram was looking smarter and smarter every day. I closed the book, and after making up my bed, I climbed into my new bed in my new room.

I was so pleased with the room and how everything seemed to be coming together, but my sense of loss because of Brady's distant attitude had me feeling melancholy.

I was awoken out of a sound sleep by Josh's howling again. He ran out of my room, and I heard him whimpering at the front door. I threw back the sheets and padded in my bare feet on the cool wood floor to see what had Josh in a tither. I opened the door, and Josh flew past me barking loudly as he ran into the darkness.

I walked out onto the porch and scoured the area hoping to see what Josh was chasing. He disappeared down the drive and then I heard a car engine startup. It was close enough that I knew that the car was near my house, but far enough down my driveway that I couldn't see it. My heart pounded anxiously, then I heard Josh yelp in pain, and I cringed.

I ran back inside and grabbed my Henry from the kitchen doorframe, slipped on my boots, and quickly made my way back to the front porch. I heard the car driving away, but since I had no idea if anyone was still on my property, I kept my Henry ready while I called for Josh. I heard him whimper in pain and knew he was hurt; I prayed he wasn't hurt badly.

I couldn't hear the car anymore, so I cautiously ran down the driveway looking for Josh. When I came to the curve in my driveway, I saw a dark lump in the middle of the dirt. Josh was whimpering, and I flew to his side. My eyes had become accustomed to the dark, but it was so much darker down the drive under the trees that I could barely see anything. I ran my hand over his side and felt where there was wetness. It was warm, and when I looked at my hand, I saw that it was covered in blood. I ran back to the barn and got the large wheelbarrow.

A half hour later I had managed to get Josh to the front porch. I turned on the light and was horrified to see a broken crossbow's arrow sticking out from his side.

Someone had shot Josh then broken the arrow off. Tears blurred my vision seeing how much pain my poor friend was in. I left Josh on the porch, boiled water, took out the medical bag, gathered towels, and lastly washed my hands.

I knew what I had to do. I'd seen my Gigi do this on a neighbor's sheep that had been accidentally shot with an arrow. I talked calmly to Josh and felt around the small shaft. I didn't think it had hit a bone and if that was the case, Josh just might survive.

I poured alcohol over a stretching device and a large pair of tweezers and deftly dug out the arrow. Josh knew I was helping him, but he continued to whimper, and he even tried to nudge my hand away with his foot, but he had lost so much blood that my poor dog was weak. I got the arrow out and made quick work of suturing his wound with x type stitches. I placed large gauze pads over the wound, and lastly, I wrapped his torso with gauze wrap.

I wiped the blood off the porch floor as best I could. Then I carefully slide him onto a blanket. I quickly cleaned up the medical equipment and myself and changed into a pair of flannel pants and a sweatshirt. I took two blankets outside. I laid one next to Josh, and then I lay down next to him and covered us both with the other. I kept my hand on his chest praying it would continue to rise and fall.

15

Brady

Her timing sucked. Two days ago Chelsea had gone
to my parent's house and had refused to leave until
she had spoken to me. When I had been waiting
for Belle to come out of the library, Tommy had
called me. My Mom wasn't home, and he was at
our house entertaining my ex-girlfriend, and he
wasn't too happy about it. I had him put her on the
phone, and then I told her I didn't want to see her
or talk to her.

Chelsea would not take no for an answer, and I felt
terrible for Tommy and I sure as heck didn't want
my Mom to have to deal with her so I finally told
her I would call her later. She made me promise,
and I felt like a damn kid promising her, but she
knew me, and she knew I would never break a
promise.

The whole ride back to the farm I wanted to tell
Belle about her, but I just couldn't. Chelsea was still
an open wound. Her betrayal and then losing my
foot had been two crushing blows. It wasn't just
that she had cheated on me; it was the entire idea
that my planned out perfect life was gone. I
couldn't wrap my head around the fact that Chelsea
didn't want us to spend the rest of our lives
together; we'd been so perfect together. Then after
losing my foot, I figured no one would ever want a
life with me, and I had wallowed into months of
self-pity. Chelsea had devastated me; how could I

explain that to Belle without sounding like a coward. It would also mean I'd have to tell her about Chelsea and I had some pretty unresolved feelings regarding her.

That night I called Chelsea as I promised and the conversation had gone better than I anticipated. She had not begged for anything or demanded that I see her, she just wanted to talk, and so we did. The next night she called me again, and once again we talked. The old connection that we had was still there. The things we had in common, our friend, likes, and dislikes. She asked about what I'd been doing, and I told her I was working on the Janson farm. I didn't say anything about Belle. She told me about her job and how she had been taking classes that would certify her to work in the Emergency Room.

Before I hung up with her, I had agreed to meet her for dinner the next night. I didn't sleep well that night. I had befriended Belle, kissed her, more than kissed her, led her to believe I liked her more than a friend, and now I was meeting the girl I had thought I would marry. I was a lout, and I felt like it.

I could tell that Belle knew something was up. I was such a chicken shit. I don't know why I couldn't just tell her, but I couldn't. Mr. Bee was going to kick my ass. I think my dad might even help him. Chelsea was like a drug though, one that I couldn't just give up. That hurt she had put on me was slowly evaporating. She had not indicated that she wanted anything more from me than just friendship, but we quickly slipped into our comfortable camaraderie.

I had been keeping myself distanced from Belle. I was telling myself it was for her own good, but it was because I didn't know how to explain to her that I was getting close with another girl, and not just any girl. The girl I thought I'd marry. I should have explained everything to Belle as soon as Chelsea had called. I was kicking myself. Sweet Belle knew something was different between us. I hated myself.

On my way to Belle's that morning I was determined to tell her about Chelsea. I mean I technically wasn't exclusive with Belle, and I had not done anything other than talking to Chelsea. Yeah, then why did I feel like such a heel? Could I date them both?

I pulled down the drive and saw Belle sitting on the porch wrapped in a blanket drinking coffee. I noticed that Josh had not run to greet me and that's when I saw that he was laying on the porch wrapped in a blanket.

Belle

I heard Brady's truck, and Josh lifted his head, but I patted him and told him to relax. I watched as Brady made his way to the porch and I knew the second he realized something was wrong.

"What happened?" he said kneeling awkwardly by Josh.

"Someone shot him with an arrow."

"What?"

"He was shot with an arrow." I pointed at the broken piece I had dug out of Josh and placed in a plastic bag.

"Are you taking him to the vet? Did you call my Dad?"

"The vet will be here shortly. No, I did not call your dad." Her voice was clipped, and she looked exhausted.

"Why not?"

"Brady I just didn't. It was probably some kid playing with his dad's crossbow."

"Belle, I'm calling him."

Brady went inside to use the phone; I was too tired and barely hanging on to my emotions to fight him. I sat down next to Josh. I'd lain awake most of the night praying for Josh and thinking about Brady. I was mad at Brady. How dare he pretend to care for me more than just a friend. I was livid that he said what we had done on the couch should only be done with someone you care about. For him to distances himself like he had was infuriating and baffling. The absolutely only reason I came up with was that Brady realized I wasn't someone he wanted to be romantic with, but for goodness sakes, just tell me! Could we have just remained friends? Maybe. Honestly, I thought we had connected in a special way. Obviously not. I had zippo experience with men, heck, with anyone. I may have to watch some of those Reality shows my momma liked. I was a fish out of water when it came to understanding friendships and 'more than

friends' relationships. Still, what a jerk Brady
turned out to be. I slammed my hand on the arm
of the chair; I didn't need a friend that badly.
Brady returned. "My Dad's on his way."
I nodded stiffly. "Can you sit with Josh while I
shower?" I refused to be nice.
"Sure, go ahead." He watched me get up, and I
swear he looked sad.
I went inside and showered. I could hear people
talking on the porch, so I quickly dressed, brushed
out my hair and hurriedly went outside. Sheriff
McDaniel was there, and so was our vet, Dr.
Lachlan. Their conversation ceased when I
appeared.
"Did you look at him?" I said to the Doc.
"I did. You did a good job patching him up Belle, a
real good job. I'd like to take him back to the clinic
with me and start him on antibiotics and monitor
him for a few days.
"He can't stay here?" I felt tears gather in my eyes
and I bit my lip to stop them from quivering. Brady
stepped next to me, and when he tried to put his
hand on my shoulder to comfort me, I stepped
away from him. There was no way could I deal
with him pretending to care for me, while worrying
about Josh.
The doc asked Brady to help him lift Josh to her
truck. They used the blanket as a stretcher and
walked him to the truck. I followed along behind
and kissed Josh good-bye on his head. The vet
buckled him in so he wouldn't slide around, and
then she shut the lift. I watched them drive off, and

although I'd felt alone after Momma passed, this was worse. I'd lost Brady, and now my trusted companion Josh was leaving me too. I walked back to my porch keeping as far away from Brady as I could. I was crumbling inside, and I wish I were alone so I could cry.

"Belle can you tell me what happened." Sheriff McDaniel asked gently.

"Would you like some coffee?" I deflected.

"Belle, Honey sit down and tell me what happened."

I sat down and folded my hands in my lap.

"Josh heard a noise. I let him out. I heard a car. I heard Josh yelp. The car left."

"That's it?"

"That's it."

"Did you see the car?"

"No."

"Did you hear anyone talking?"

"No Sheriff." I wasn't trying to be short with him; I was seriously exhausted.

"Did you use your gun?"

"No, but I had it with me."

The Sheriff was quiet, and I stood up indicating as politely as I could that the conversation was over.

"I need to do the animals," I said.

"I'll do them," Brady said.

"No thank you, I'll take care of them." I looked at Brady as anger swelled inside of me. "Actually, I don't think I'll be needing your services."

"Belle." His voice was soft. I noticed his dad was staring daggers at him.

"Sheriff the arrows shaft is in that bag there. You can take it if you want, but I'm sure it was just a terrible accident."

I headed towards the barn, and I could faintly hear Brady and his dad talking. A few minutes later Brady came into the barn.

"Belle we need to talk."

"About what?" I played dumb.

"Us."

"Us? There is no us Brady. We're friends that's it."

"But we were headed down a different path."

"Yeah, that's what I was led to believe," I said tersely

That shut him up. I may have been naive and socially awkward, but I wasn't dumb.

"Belle I'm sorry. Can I explain?"

"No, no you cannot explain anything to me. You let me believe we were more than friends. I think those were your words, weren't they? I may be an odd ball, the weird girl in town, but I am not stupid Brady. You cannot toy with me like that. I won't let you! Now get out. You are no longer my handyman." By the time I finished my little tirade I was yelling. Brady's face looked as if I had slapped him. He turned away and left. I heard his truck leave, and I crumbled into the nearby hay and cried.

I must have been really tired because I fell asleep. The animals were still in their stalls and coop, and I felt like the worst person ever that I had not taken care of them before falling asleep. I let them out and fed them extra grain and changed out their water before going back inside my house.

I loved how my house looked now. The furniture the colors, it was so me. I wished my family could see what I'd done. I called Dr. Lachlan to check on Josh, and she assured me that he was doing well, but she was keeping him sedated so he would not pull the stitches. I was relieved that Josh was in a safe place and being taken care of, so I went to the garden and weeded. Afterwards, I grabbed a towel and headed for the stream. I didn't take my new cover-up. I was just going for a quick dip, and then I'd just change back into the clothes I'd worn there. I waded in until I had to dive. I couldn't stop thinking about Brady. I wish I had another female to talk to. I couldn't believe that all men were like that. The thing that kept sticking in my craw was that I had been the one to orgasm, not him. So if he was just using me for sex, that theory didn't make sense, because I was the only one to get something out of it. No, it had to be that I wasn't what he wanted. Somehow between kissing and the orgasm he gave me, he had decided I wasn't what he wanted; that hurt.

I redressed and headed back to the house. It was close to 5:00 PM but because I'd left the animals inside for so long I decided to give them more outside time. I opened my refrigerator debating what to have for dinner. I was famished because I realized I'd had nothing but a cup of coffee all day. Seeing nothing that I cared to eat, I decided to do something I'd never done, ever. I was going to town, and I was going to eat at the diner.

I changed into my new jeans and a light blue tee shirt, brushed my hair, and headed into town. The new tee shirt was powder blue, and it made my eyes pop. I did not wear makeup, but I couldn't help but wonder what mascara would look like on me. Maybe I'd go back to Macy's and let one of those cosmetic girls show me how to put it on. Momma was very good at it. She didn't wear a lot. She told me that the trick was to look like you were not wearing any.

I parked in front of Mr. Bee's office I wanted to tell him I needed a new farmhand but I saw that he was gone for the day. I walked down the street to the diner and hesitated before going inside. I felt decadent going to a place and letting them cook for me, but I figured today I needed a little pick me up. I was reminded when Brady and I had eaten out in Springfield. This time I was alone. The hostess showed me to a booth in the corner, and I sat so I could people watch.

I ordered a hamburger and fries and flipped through a mini jukebox on the wall next to the table. I read the instructions on the glass and learned that if I fed the machine a quarter, it would play a song. I didn't want to disturb the other patrons, so I just busied myself by looking at what songs were on the little machine.

The door to the diner opened, and a pretty woman stepped through followed by Brady. I sunk down into my seat. He didn't see me and I watched as he and the woman were led to a booth on the other side of the diner. Luckily the woman sat facing me and Brady had his back to me.

My heart was pounding, and for some reason I was embarrassed, maybe it was because I had let myself believe that someone as handsome as Brady could have been interested in me. The woman was grinning happily at whatever Brady was saying. Two men came in after them and sat with Brady and the woman. One was a big man, not fat, just huge. I didn't get a good look at his face. The other man was not as tall as Brady or the other man, but I could see from his tight tee shirt that he was muscled and when I snuck another peek at him I saw that he was attractive. I could hear the group of them laughing even from where I sat. I felt so foolish.

One of the men, the shorter of the two, caught me looking their way and he smiled at me. I ducked my head, and luckily the waitress brought my burger right then, so I concentrated on my meal. Unfortunately, I now had no appetite.

The waitress came back to the table to refill my water and when she saw I wasn't eating she asked if something was wrong. I told her I forgot that I needed to be someplace and she nicely offered to wrap my meal up for so I could take it with me. When she came back, she gave me a slip of paper and said to pay at the cash register at the door. I left her a tip; I'd seen Brady do that, and then made my way to the cash register. I prayed Brady wouldn't see me.

The man that was sitting with Brady was watching me, and he got up from the booth and walked towards me. I tried to avoid eye contact with him, but he stepped into my path.

"Hi," he said. I looked up to find that he was smiling at me. He was a few inches taller than I was with sandy blond hair, brown eyes, and a wide white-toothed smile. I was nervous, but I smiled back and returned his hello.

"I haven't seen you around here before." He said grinning at me.

"I have never been to the diner before," I told him, my voice shook a little. I wasn't afraid of him; I just wasn't accustomed to speaking with strangers.

"No, I mean." He never finished his sentence.

"Belle, what are you doing here?" Brady asked stepping next to his friend.

I looked at him, and I wanted to say something witty, but I just choked out. "Eating."

"You know her?" His friend said.

"Yes." He didn't explain how and his friend stuck out his hand.

"I'm Dirk Keith."

I took his hand to shake it.

"Belle Janson," I said shaking his hand.

Dirk continued to hold my hand even though I tried to pull it from his grasp.

"Knock it off Dirk," Brady said tensely.

I snatched my hand back and stepped to the cash register putting my back to Brady and his friend.

I knew both men were still there, but I refused to turn around. I finished paying and pushed open the door to leave.

"Hey there Belle what's your hurry?" Dirk said following me. Brady must have followed me too because I heard him say.

"Dirk come on, leave her alone."

Then I heard Dirk say, "What's the deal Brady, you got Chelsea back. What do you need another girl for?"

I couldn't resist turning around, "Yeah Brady, whatever would you want another girl for?" I said starchily.

I hurried across the street, hopped in my truck, and headed home.

The tears started falling as soon as I hit the outskirts of town. I was so done with men. Brady was a jerk, he had a girlfriend, and his friend was creepy. Crud, the first two men I meet and one turns out to be a jerk and the other a total ass.

I was going to call Mr. Bee in the morning and tell him that not only had Brady not work out, but that I did not want another farm hand. Yup, that was exactly what I was going to do.

16

Brady

Dirk was watching Belle's truck pull away. I knew
that smile he was wearing. He was attracted to
Belle. Well, shoot, who wouldn't be.
"Wanna tell me how you know her?" Dirk asked.
"I, uh, I have been doing some work on her farm."
That wasn't a lie.
"Can you give me her number?"
"No."
Dirk gave my shoulder a little punch.
"Come on man. You know I'll get it eventually."
"No," I said as I headed back to the dinner. I knew
he was like a dog with a bone when it came to
women. I also knew women thought he was good
looking and I'd seen him charm the pants off
women, literally and physically. I settled back into
the booth and Chelsea, of course, wanted to know
who Belle was.
"I met her a couple of weeks ago. She lives off of
Totes Road. Her mom passed recently, and I was
helping her around her farm.
"Wait a minute," my friend Kip said, "Are you
talking about the family that owns Green
Mountain?"
"The recluse?" Dirk asked.
"Yeah, her family owns Green Mountain. Well, the
east side of it. The west side they sold to the
National Forest years ago, and yes, I guess she's
probably considered a recluse."

"My Mom said she was homeschooled and only grew up with her mom and grandma's," Dirk added.

"Yeah, well her mom died, and she's alone now."

"That's sad," Chelsea said.

"She's hot," Dirk voiced with a smirk.

Chelsea put her hand on my thigh. I should have been flipping happy that she was touching me intimately, but all I could think about was Belle. I was screwed, royally screwed.

After Belle had told me to leave that morning I had gone home and sulked on the couch watching television. My Dad came home and asked me to join him in the kitchen. I knew what was coming.

"What happened Brady?"

"What do you mean?"

His fingers drummed the kitchen table impatiently.

"Between you and Belle?"

He looked mad, and I honestly couldn't blame him. My Mom who had been at the grocery store walked in. I took a bag from her and started unloading it, hoping to thwart my Dad's scrutiny.

"Thanks." My mom said as she put the other bag down. "So why are my men home at this hour?"

"I wanted to talk to Brady."

My mom looked at my Dad then to me. She silently began unloading one of the bags.

"Something happened out at Belle's place last night. Her dog was shot with a cross bow's arrow."

"Oh dear, that's awful. Please tell me that old hound is alive. I don't think that poor girl could take any more heartache."

I didn't think I could feel worse, but I did now. I swallowed uneasily. Tommy came into the kitchen and rifled through the one bag pulling out a bag of chips.

My dad looked at my Mom. "When I was there, Brady tried to comfort her, and she clearly did not want our son anywhere near her."

Mom stopped unpacking the bag and looked at me. My father continued. "In fact, she told him he needed to leave her place."

"It's cause of Chelsea isn't it?" Tommy said with a mouth full of chips. I shot him a laser beam look that conveyed that I was pissed and he shrugged and left the kitchen.

"Chelsea?" My Mom asked. I watched as my parents looked at each other and then back to me. Mom put the cold food away, and sat down at the chair gesturing for me to take a seat.

"What's going on Brady?"

I sighed and figured maybe if I explained to them what had happened they could give me some advice. I told my parents that I liked Belle that I had fun with her and didn't feel handicapped with her.

"You are not handicapped!" My Mom said vehemently reminding me of my conversation with Belle.

"Anyway a few days ago Chelsea came here, and she wouldn't leave until I promised to call her. I didn't want her in the house. I know how hurt you were Mom when we broke up, and I didn't want you to have to talk to her, so I promised to call her."

My mom patted my hand, encouraging me to go on, but when I looked at my dad, his lips were pressed tightly together.

"So I called her, and we've been talking."

"I don't understand?" My Mom said.

"I do." my dad said. "Our son had Belle thinking they were more than friends and then he changed gears as soon as Chelsea came back in the picture."

"Brady?" My Mom asked. "Did you?"

"Yeah, I kissed Belle, and I did hint that we were more than friends. Then when I started talking to Chelsea again, it just felt wrong to act like that with Belle, so I kind of distanced myself."

"You should have told her." My Mom said.

"Which one Chelsea or Belle?" I asked frustrated.

"Oh dear." My Mom said, and at the same time my dad said, "Both of them."

"Are you still in love with Chelsea?" My Mom asked.

"I don't know. I was angry and then dealing with my leg and all; I don't know if I ever got over her. Now, talking to her again, it's comfortable."

"What do you feel for Belle?" My Mom asked.

"I really like her."

"But?" Mom prompted.

"But do I just like her because she's the first person that I've let get close to me after I lost my leg? Do I just like that she never knew me before, so she accepts me for the man I am now?"

"You're the same man, Honey." My Mom said softly.

We sat quietly for a few seconds. "Any advice?" I asked.

My Mom looked at my Dad. "I think you need to figure out what's happening between you and Chelsea."

"I'm not happy that you have hurt Belle." My dad said.

"Just go and explain things to her." My Mom suggested.

"She hates me," I said glumly.

"Well, what did you expect to happen?" My dad said running his hand through his hair. "You take her to Springfield, bring her here for a birthday dinner, give her gifts. You led her on son."

"I know. I know."

"Figure out how you feel about Chelsea. If you discover you don't have feelings for her maybe you can mend things with Belle."

I nodded appreciating my Mom's advice.

"I think you should steer clear of Belle." My dad interjected surprising both my Mom and myself.

"Will?" My Mom said looking at her husband.

"That girl does not need anyone unsteady in her life. She needs people around her that she can trust, who will help her through what she's dealing with."

"Dad," I said feeling worse than before.

"Son I love you. I know you've been through a lot too, but right now I feel bad for Belle. I'll say this too since I'm already in the doghouse with your ma." My dad said, giving my Mom a cautious glance. "I don't trust Chelsea. I know you were head over heels for her, but what she did to you was low. Tigers don't change their stripes." Then my dad stood up, bent over and kissed my Mom on the cheek and left.

My Mom once again patted my hand. "Figure out how you feel about Chelsea. Brady. If it's meant to be, you'll know. Whatever happens, you know we love you."

"Thanks, Ma." I stood and kissed her before heading out to my truck.

I had left the house and driven around the old back roads just thinking. My Mom was correct I needed closure first and then, or if it was meant to be, a new beginning with Chelsea. What my dad had said about her though stuck fast in the back of my mind. I wondered if I'd ever trust Chelsea again.

"Brady. Brady!" I heard Chelsea then felt her hand squeeze my thigh bringing me back to the conversation in the diner.

"Oh, sorry. What?"

"Kip said some of your friends are at Rustic and he wants to know if you want to go over there?"

"Sure." I had not been around anyone since I'd been back. I figured I might as well see everyone and get it over with. It was funny, I thought, no one had even brought up my injury. Belle had no problem asking me about it. Part of me was happy that no one was asking about it, but another part of me was thinking that they probably all had questions, but were too apprehensive to ask them. Kip was my oldest friend. We'd been best friends since he had moved to Vermont from South Carolina when he was in the 8th grade. He was a big guy, but my Mom called him a gentle giant. I use to laugh when she said that and told her she didn't play football with him. He was a beast. We even attended the University of Vermont together. When I met Chelsea I started spending more time with her, but Kip was dating the head cheerleader, so we doubled all the time.

Kip played football for the University until his junior year when had he torn his ACL during spring ball. He rehabbed himself and could have recaptured his starting job on the offensive line, but he decided to train for his Fire Fighters physical. Ever since I'd known Kip, he had wanted to be a firefighter. His little cheerleader dumped him when she found out that he was done playing football and Chelsea and I had consoled him for weeks. The three of us had been inseparable our senior year.

When we graduated, I enlisted as I had planned. Kip was going to enlist with me, but a firefighting job opened up in our hometown and Kip applied for the position, and he got it. I was nervous that I was going into the Marines alone, but I knew that Kip had to take the job. Our town only had four full-time firemen, and there was no telling when the next job would be available.

Dirk was a good friend too, but he could be a jerk, and Kip and I didn't like the drama that seemed to follow him around. More often than not we had saved his bacon when he talked tough or tried to mess with another guys girl. Dirk was a notorious womanizer. I hated that he had met Belle. He wanted her, and I knew when he wanted a woman he was relentless.

We paid for our dinners and Chelsea, and I walked to her car. She had insisted on driving so she could show me her new little sports car. It was a small red convertible. Personally, I thought it was impractical considering where we lived, but it wasn't my car, so I just kept nodding and smiling when she pointed out the cars finer features. Kip and Dirk followed behind us as we headed down the road to Rustic, the only bar in town.

"So tell me more about Belle?" Chelsea asked. I could see that she was watching me with her peripheral vision.

"Not much to tell. She's really nice, and she's led a very sheltered life."

"Brady."

"What?"

"It's me. I saw how you looked at her."

We pulled into Rustic's dirt lot, and I exited the car. "So you're not going to talk about her?" Chelsea said as we walked in.

"No," I answered firmly. I was annoyed that she was questioning me about another woman. She had long since given up that right.

It was early evening, but the bar was packed. I realized it was Friday and we had arrived during Happy Hour.

People who knew me greeted me warmly, and Randy the bartender shook my hand, thanked me for my service, and told me anything I drank that night was on him. We took over a booth and some guys that I had been friendly with in high school pulled chairs up.

A few women that I had not seen in years also joined our little group, and my quiet night out with Chelsea became an impromptu reunion. Chelsea remained glued to my side, warding off any potential attempts by other women to flirt with me. She was staking a claim, re-staking it actually, and I wasn't sure I liked it. I began to realize that even though all of the people I was with knew I'd lost my lower leg no one cared. I mean I'm sure they cared, but they weren't treating me differently than they did before. That had been my greatest fear and why I had avoided my hometown friends for the last few months. It was good reconnecting with them, but I was different now, jaded from war, Chelsea, and losing my leg. These people were my childhood friends, but I was feeling a disconnect.

We had been drinking for a couple of hours, and I was feeling the alcohol. I had not drunk much in the last three years. The Happy Hour crowd mixed with the night out crowd, and soon the little wooden floor in the middle of the bar was filled with men and women dancing to songs that the old jukebox was kicking out.

"Come on," Chelsea said grabbing my hand. She wanted to dance.

"Chelsea, I haven't danced in forever." I didn't want to dance, but Chelsea was insisting.

"I'm sure you haven't forgotten how." She said pulling me up and laughing coyly.

I apprehensively let Chelsea drag me into the middle of the fray and slowly started moving to the music. The longer I danced, the more confident I felt. Chelsea was moving her body provocatively against mine, and I knew she was attempting to get me aroused. I saw Kip watching me, watching us, and he gave me the thumbs up, as he danced nearby with a friend of ours named Jeannie.

We danced through four songs, and my legs started to ache. It was my straps that chaffed my skin. It brought to mind how Belle had soothed my leg that very first day that I had met her. A slow song began playing, and Chelsea put her arms around me, and I had no choice but to do the same, without creating a bit of a scene.

She placed her head on my shoulder, and it evoked memories of her and I dancing this way back in college. We would talk and kiss and work ourselves up as we slowly rubbed our bodies against each other. That would ultimately lead us to leave wherever we were.

Chelsea was doing her darndest to recreate the sexual heat we used to share, but it just wasn't happening for me. I thought about what it would be like to dance with Belle, and that brought a smile to my lips. Chelsea saw my smile and smiled back.

"I'm glad you're having fun, Brady." She said flirtatiously.

She thought I'd been thinking about her. "I am," I told her, but I couldn't help but wish that it were Belle in my arms. The thought rocked me enough that I stopped swaying to the music.

I knew then, in that very instant, that I had made a grave mistake with Belle. Luckily the song ended, so I sat down in the booth and didn't let Chelsea coax me up for any more dances. My leg hurt anyways.

A popular song began playing and our table headed to the dance floor, all except Kip and myself. Chelsea had given up trying to get me to dance again.

"So you and Chelsea?" He asked spinning his bottle of Bud.

I looked at my best friend and shrugged. "I don't think so."

"Really? Could have fooled me."

I looked at Chelsea moving sexily on the dance floor, and when she saw me looking at her, she blew me a kiss. Kip saw that too.

"Does she know that?"

I didn't want to talk about Chelsea. My stomach was in knots. I wondered what Belle was doing at that moment. I wondered what she had done all day. I hoped Josh was all right. I felt sick; I had messed up a good thing with Belle.

Chelsea was putting on a show, and it was all for my benefit. I had to fix this mess.

"So how is everything at the Firehouse?" I said changing the conversation. My dad had told me Kip was on track to become the youngest battalion chief in the state.

"It's good. I've been studying Arson. I'll have my certificate within the month, and that will bump my pay."

"That's great," I told him honestly.

"What about you?"

"Me?"

"Yeah, what are you going to do?"

"I don't know."

"You should think about law enforcement. Your time in the Marines is valuable. It's the reason you enlisted."

I listened to my friend and wanted to physically shake him. Instead, I snapped at him, "Kip, stop."

"What?"

"I'm an amputee, man."

"So?"

"No Civil Agency would look at me seriously."

"Bull shit. That's your excuse?"

I was annoyed that our conversation had taken this route.

Thankfully, Chelsea and Jeannie came back to the table. Unfortunately, Chelsea plopped herself down on my lap. Kip tipped his beer to me and nodded to Chelsea who now had her arms wrapped around my neck. I knew she was about to kiss me and I didn't want her too.

I unpeeled her hands from my neck, and I could tell she was taken back. "I need to use the restroom," I announced lifting her from me and stood up.

I used the restroom and washed my hands; I felt emotionally drained. It had been great seeing my friends, and even though Kip had pissed me off he was still my best friend, and I had missed him. I left the restroom and headed back to the table. Kip was standing with Dirk while Chelsea and Jeannie sat next to each other chatting.

"Kip, can you give me a lift home?" I asked him quietly.

"Sure. I'm ready."

"I'm heading out," I said to Chelsea and Jeannie. Chelsea jumped up from her chair I could see she was perplexed.

"Brady, you came with me."

"I know, but I'm ready to go, and you're having fun. Kip's is leaving now."

"I'm ready to go too." She insisted.

I looked back at Kip, and he shrugged. "Okay, then let's go," I said to Chelsea.

I made sure she was okay to drive, and she told me she had stopped drinking earlier. Satisfied that she was sober, I got into her car.

"Did you have fun, Brady?" She asked.

"Yes, it was nice seeing everyone."

"Dirk said you've been keeping to yourself."

"I haven't felt much like going out," I replied honestly.

"I'm glad you came out with me."

I didn't answer her. We pulled into my parent's driveway, and I knew I had to tell her how I was feeling, something that she should have had the decency to do with me before she cheated on me. Chelsea turned towards me expecting me to kiss her but I remained as far away from her as I could get in the little car's front seat.

"Chelsea I had fun tonight, and it's been nice catching up, but I'm not interested in anything more than friendship with you."

I think it took a second for her to understand what I was saying. Then her face registered shock, and I watched as tears fill her eyes and fell down her cheeks.

"Brady I'm so sorry I cheated on you. It was the worst mistake of my life. Please don't give up on us."

I hated when she cried, and I felt terrible, but then I remembered how I had felt when I found out she had been unfaithful and it gave me the confidence I needed to stay strong.

"If you'd like to remain friends, we can try that, but just friends, nothing more."

Chelsea was sobbing, and she kept wiping the tears away. "It's that girl; Belle isn't it?"

"No, she hates my guts," I replied glumly. "It's a lot of things. Tell me, Chelsea, why did you cheat on me?"

She stopped crying, and I saw that she was embarrassed. "I was lonely. You were gone. It was a terrible lapse in judgment."

"You devastated me, Chelsea. I loved you."

"I loved you too. I still love you."

"No, no you didn't. When you love someone, there is no way, lonely or not, that you would even want to be with another person."

I sighed remembering that I had alluded to that very thing when Belle and I talked on the couch.

Chelsea's voice quivered. "How can you say that? You have no idea what I was going through while you were away. I was lonely." I listened and what I heard was her, being concerned for her. At no time did she say that she missed me or was worried about me. It was all about her. She had been lonely.

"Brady, we were perfect together, and you know it."

"We were kids. It was great, but it's over. As I said, I'd like to remain friends with you. I know we will see each other around and I don't want it to be awkward."

She wiped her eyes and glared at me. "Fuck you, Brady." She spat out. Then I watched sweet, flirtatious, Chelsea transform before my eyes. "I'm the best thing that ever happened to you. You think you can do better than me. Now!" She said nastily pointing at my leg.

I opened the door and got out. What she said hit a nerve. It's what I had been telling myself.

I slammed the car door shut, and as I walked toward my front door, I heard her tires peel out in the driveway.

17

Belle

I brought the animals inside and got into my
pajamas. The food from the diner sat in the
refrigerator still untouched. I just wasn't hungry.
Outside on the back porch, I tried to read my
Stephen King novel, but the words kept colliding
together, so I gave up and just sat back in my chair
looking out at the mountain that was now a dark
silhouette in the beautiful star-filled sky.
The mosquitoes started to bite, so I decided to turn
in. I got ready for bed still marveling at the
transformation of my new bedroom. I said my
prayers and lay in my new room thinking about
Josh, then Brady. The last I spoke with the Doc,
Josh was doing well, and I had thanked God extra
especially for that miracle.
Telling Brady off in the barn at the diner had been
cathartic. His dad had looked super mad at him
too, and that made me feel slightly vindicated.
I was proud of myself. I had accomplished so
much in the last week. I knew my family would
have been pleased with how I was carrying on
without them. As I thought about the good things
that had happened that week, the falling out with
Brady kept creeping into my thoughts making me
sad and angry. I fell into a restless sleep.
I awoke abruptly, something wasn't right. I smelled
smoke, and I bolted from my bed running into the
kitchen to look out the window at the barn. I didn't

see any flames or smoke. I realized the smoky smell was coming from upstairs. I took the stairs two at a time, and when I reached Momma's room, I saw that her one window was open and that a small fire burned near the wall, and was spreading to the nearby curtain. I grabbed the throw rug near Momma's bed and tamped out the fire. The wall was scorched, and I quickly pulled down the curtain, rod, and all, and ran into the hall tossing it in the bathroom shower and dousing it with water. I ran back into the bedroom frantically looking for any signs of flames. Smoke hung thickly in the room, and I cautiously lifted the throw rug I had used to find the wooden floor beneath the rug was deeply singed.

My heart was racing. I shut Momma's door and opened the other windows in the room to help air out the smoke-filled room. I looked out the window that was open and peered outside. I saw nothing, no person, no car, nothing. Making sure that the fire was out I ran downstairs and got my Henry. I took a flashlight from the kitchen, turned on my front porch light, and cautiously walked out the front door, ready to confront the person who set the fire. No one was there. It was eerily silent, and I gulped down fear so heavy I felt nauseous. I quickly made my way to the barn. I needed to make sure my animals were safe.

I listened to any out of place sounds as I walked, but heard nothing out of the ordinary. I moved stealthily around the outside of the barn and shined my light around the corrals, the sheep's pen, the

pig's area, and the chicken coop. Satisfied that
nothing was amiss, I went inside the barn. I turned
on the overhead light and Bessie mooed thinking
she was about to get fed; I shushed her. I moved
from Bessie's stall to Henny's and then looked
around at the rest of the barn. I even climbed into
the hayloft. I was so frightened I was shaking. I
clutched my Henry; it's weight reassuring me.
The animals weren't acting skittish, and I knew
they would be if a stranger were in their barn. I
turned off the barn light and headed back inside
and back up to Momma's room. Most of the
smoke had cleared from the room, but the heavy
cloying smell of smoke remained. I studied the
charred area and realized that the fire had been
started using one of Momma's bed pillows.
I knew I should call the Sheriff, but something held
me back from making the call. I didn't want to
appear helpless. I didn't clean up the mess though.
I decide to leave it just in case I changed my mind,
and the Sheriff wanted to see it. I took the throw
rug that I had put the fire out with, and the pillow
into the bathroom ran them under the shower
water, and then I carried the thoroughly soaked
curtains, the remnants of the pillow, and the throw
rug outside to my back stone patio. I didn't want to
take any chances of leaving them inside in case any
embers remained. They were sopping wet, but I
didn't want to chance it.
I went back upstairs and felt the floor and wall to
make sure the fire was truly out then I closed
Momma's door and went back downstairs.

I was too amped up to go back to bed, so I lay down on the couch with my Henry next to me and turned on the television.

I did fall asleep, but it wasn't until the early morning light had begun to creep through the front windows. I must have slept through the rosters crow because I woke up to my phone ringing. I groggily made my way to it.

"Hello?"

"Belle, it's Mr. Bee."

"Hi, Mr. Bee."

"Belle I heard about Josh. Are you okay?"

"Yes, I'm fine, thank you."

"I'm going to be there in a half hour. I need to talk to you. I just didn't want to stop by unannounced."

"Okay, I'll see you soon."

After I hung up, I changed and made some coffee. I went outside and took care of the animals in record time. I picked out the eggs, and when I was walking back to the house, Mr. Bee pulled up, so I walked to meet him. He opened the front door for me, and as soon as he entered the house, I knew he could smell the smoke.

"Belle is that smoke I smell? Was there a fire?"

I put the eggs in the basket and motioned for Mr. Bee to follow me upstairs. I showed him Momma's room.

"Belle, why didn't you call me? Did you call the Sheriff? How big was the fire? How did you put it out?" He was upset, and I felt bad that he was so concerned.

"Why don't we have some coffee first?" I suggested calmly.

Sitting at the table with our coffee I explained to Mr. Bee what had happened. He then asked about Josh, and I relayed to him that story as well.

"I'm calling the Sheriff, Belle." He went to my phone, and I heard him talking with someone. He came back to the table and gave me a good looking over. I must have looked as tired as I felt.

"Honey, you look exhausted. Why don't you come spend the night with Mrs. Bee and I. Brady can watch the animals."

I grimaced hearing his name. "About that Mr. Bee. Brady is no longer working here. I think it is best that I handle my own affairs."

Mr. Bee looked like he wanted to ask me a question but the Sheriff's car pulled in. I walked to the door and let him inside before he could knock.

"There was a fire?" he asked looking around the room.

"It was upstairs."

Just then another car with a Fire Marshalls insignia on the side of the door pulled into my little drive and out stepped a hulking big guy in a uniform and a baseball cap, with an official seal of some kind on it. I recognized him as one of the men that had been with Brady at the diner.

"That's Kip; he's a fireman in town," the Sheriff said. "I called him."

Kip walked to the door that I held open for him. He looked at me and smiled widely. The guy was impressively big. His nameplate read Lt. R. Kippers.

He shook hands with Mr. Bee and the Sheriff. Both men addressed him as Kip. He then stuck out his hand to me.

"Hi I'm Randy Kipper, my friends call me Kip. I'm here to investigate the fire."

I shook his hand, and it dwarfed mine. Unlike his friend Dirk, Kip released my hand immediately. The big man had a charming smile, and his blue eyes were magnetic. His sandy blond hair was short, but it wasn't like the Sheriff's. In fact, he had an adorable curl that he kept pushing back off his forehead. Kip had a kind face with a square jaw and a cute dimple on his chin. He was very good looking. For some reason that made me think about Brady, but I quickly pushed away that discombobulating thought.

"Hello, I'm Belle Janson." I told him holding his gaze. Gigi had said to always look people in the eye when talking to them. She said the eyes are the windows to the soul.

I took the men upstairs. Mr. Bee followed along for a second time. When I got to Momma's door I opened it and stood back letting the men go inside. I remained in the hallway and watched them.

Kip had his cell phone out and was taking pictures of the room and the charred area. He also made notes in a little notepad. He visibly grimaced seeing how badly burnt the wall was. Kip turned to me.

"Did both curtains catch fire?" He asked pointing at where the curtains should have been.

"No only the one. I put the fire out with a throw rug. I soaked the curtains, the rug, and what was left of the pillow in the shower and then put them on my back patio.

Kip grinned, "Good thinking."

"Were these windows open?" Kip asked.

"None of them were open when I went to bed. After I put the fire out, I noticed that one," I pointed at the window he was standing near, "was open. After I got the fire put out I opened the other windows to let the smoke out."

The Sheriff turned to me. "Belle, did you hear anything? See anything?"

"No nothing. My bedroom is downstairs and with Josh at the vet." I didn't need to finish the sentence. "Anyway, I was asleep until the smoky smell woke me up."

Kip was kneeling near the ashy area. I watched him look around the room. "So there were two pillows on your Moms bed?"

"Yes, whoever set the fire must have used one of them to start the fire; it was engulfed in flames when I got upstairs."

"I agree; whoever started the fire used the pillow to set it."

Kip stood up and told the three of us that he was going to look around outside. He asked the Sheriff to join him. We walked back downstairs, and Mr. Bee and I sat back down at the dining room table again. I figured the men would come back inside, so I poured them each a cup of coffee, sliced my freshly baked rye bread and put out the peach preserves that Mr. Bee liked and also a jar of strawberry jam that Momma and I had jarred a few months ago. I set the table, so everyone had a knife, spoon, plate, and napkin. Lastly, I added more cream to the small pitcher and double-checked that there was enough sugar.

"You're a wonderful hostess Belle, just like your Momma."

I smiled at Mr. Bee, "Thank you that's a nice compliment."

The men came back inside as I sat down.

The sheriff smiled seeing what I had done, and I saw Kip look at the table and what I had prepared and then he too smiled.

"Please help yourself," I said as I passed the bread." The three men prepared their bread and Kip got the biggest smile on his face after tasting his slice that he had spread strawberry jam on.

"This is delicious," he said before taking another bite.

"Belle makes the bread, and the jam is homemade as well. You should try the peach preserves." Mr. Bee handed Kip the jar, and I was pleased when I saw Kip take another slice of the bread and spread the peach jam onto it. He took a bite of that, and he groaned. "This is so good Belle."

"She's a pretty special girl our Belle." Mr. Bee said making me blush.

Mr. Bee looked at the Sheriff, and I knew he wanted to say something to him, and I was afraid it would be about Brady, so I decided to avert that awkwardness.

"So, what do you think?" I asked Sheriff McDaniel and Kip.

They looked at each other and the Sheriff spoke. "Belle someone deliberately set that fire upstairs. I think you know that. They broke into your house and if you hadn't acted quickly your house would have burnt down."

"That's what I thought, well figured," I answered with a sigh.

"So what did you do after you put the fire out? Why didn't you call me?" The Sheriff asked.

I shifted uncomfortably in my seat. "Well, the first thing I did was grab my Henry." I pointed at the rifle hanging over the mudroom door. "Then I went out to check on the animals and the barn." The Sheriff looked angry, and I really liked the Sheriff, so I didn't want him to be upset with me.

"Please don't be mad at me," I said softly.

"Oh Belle, I'm not mad at you. I'm concerned for you, and I wish you had called me. I hate the thought that you went outside last night, alone, and that whoever set that fire could have been waiting for you."

"I had my gun," I said weakly realizing that I could have been a sitting duck.

"Belle." Kip interrupted my self-lamenting thoughts. "You're not that tall. How do you get that gun down?"

I stood from the table and picked up the walking stick that stood next to the door. I pushed it up under the guns forearm, near the trigger guard,

successfully dislodging it from its iron holder. I
caught it as it fell and held it out for them to see.
"Shit." I heard the Sheriff say. Mr. Bee was smiling
"Is that loaded?" Kip asked.
"Yes, but the safety's on."
"Belle that is just not safe." The Sheriff said
shaking his head.
"I've been doing this since I was ten Sheriff. I was
the best shot in the family." I told him proudly
causing Mr. Bee to chuckle.
"How do you get it back up there?" Kip asked with
a grin.
I turned back to the door, and with practiced ease,
I tossed the gun up so that it landed back on the
two iron arms.
"Oh boy," Kip said. I think he was trying not to
laugh.
"Do you have a license for that?" The sheriff asked.
"I don't know. Do I Mr. Bee?"
"You know, I don't know." He answered. He too
looked like he wanted to laugh.
I sat back down. "Would anyone like more coffee?"
I asked.
The men declined more coffee, so I started
cleaning the table.
"So can I clean the ashes up now?" I asked Kip.
"Yes, I have what I need."
"Belle, I don't like you being out here alone." The
Sheriff said. I could tell he was still upset.
"Sheriff, I'll be fine. I won't deny that I'm a little
scared, but Josh will be home soon."
"Josh?" Kip interrupted.

"My hound dog, Josh."

Kip nodded, and the Sheriff spoke again.

"I still don't like you being out here alone. First Josh got hurt and now this. Is anyone mad at you for any reason?"

"No, I don't know anyone for them to be mad at me."

I was secretly thinking that his son was probably not too happy with me, but then I wasn't too happy with him either."

"Mr. Bee, can you think of anyone that might have a beef with Belle?"

"No, I have no idea who could be behind this." The men stood from the table, and I walked them outside. Mr. Bee left first. The Sheriff turned to me before getting in his car. "Belle I'm going to have my men start patrolling here on a regular basis. I will want them to drive down your driveway. Please don't shoot any them." That made Kip laugh out loud, and I even smiled at his jest.

"I won't Sheriff. I promise. Really, I'm a good shot."

"I believe you," he said before leaving.

Kip remained outside of his car. "I saw you in the diner last night," he said.

"Yes, I was there." I had been thinking that Kip was a nice guy so I was hoping he wasn't about to say something that would put him in the same category as Brady and Dirk.

"I'd like to show you something if I may," he said.

"Sure." I had no idea what he was getting at. He led me to under Momma's open window.

"Whoever set that fire probably climbed up that trellis." He said pointing at Momma's beloved rose trellis.

"I recommend that you take that trellis down. It is a pretty easy climb to that window."

"My Momma loved that rose trellis," I said quietly.

"She liked roses?"

"Loved them. She liked all flowers, but she loved roses best. I think it had something to do with my dad."

"Is your dad around?"

I paused then shrugged. "I have no idea."

"Belle I noticed that your windows have no locks on them."

"We've never needed them," I told him honestly.

"I have no idea what your financial situation is, but I highly recommend that you get new windows."

"That sounds expensive."

"It's not cheap, but with you staying out here alone, I think it would be a prudent purchase."

"Okay, I'll talk to Mr. Bee about it."

"Is he a relative?" Kip asked, and I had to giggle.

"No, he's an old family friend. He is our family lawyer, and he also handles my families, well my finances."

"Do you want me to talk to him about the windows?"

"No, that's nice of you to offer, but I have to call him later." I realized that Mr. Bee had never told me why he had come to see me because he had gotten sidetracked with the fire.

Kip headed towards his car, and when I thanked him for coming, he turned back to me, tipped his baseball cap in a mannerly way acknowledging my thank you, and gave me a really nice smile. The man was big, in every way; big body, big hands, and a big smile too. His size was intimidating, but for some reason, I could tell he was a gentle person.

18

Kip

I drove down Belle's driveway and the further away
I got the worse my stomach knotted thinking how
vulnerable she was. I had seen her in the diner, but
I'd only gotten a quick glimpse of her. I knew she
was pretty, but holy smokes she was my kind of
gorgeous.

She was about 5'5" I could estimate that because I
was about a foot taller when I'd stood next to her.
She had wavy long blond hair. It wasn't colored it
was the real deal. When we had walked outside into
the sunlight, I could see different shades of blond
and a few strands of strawberry blond woven
through her long mane.

She had a curvy athletic figure. She wasn't so thin
that she looked fragile, but she wasn't big either.
Her skin was smooth, and she had a few sun
freckles across the bridge of her nose. The other
thing that I had noticed was her dimple. She had
the cutest little dimple that was only on one side of
her face. It was closer to her eye than a regular
dimple, and it only appeared when she smiled or
laughed.

However, what had me almost made me stumble
was when I'd looked at her eyes. They were the
prettiest eyes I'd ever seen. They were blue, but
they were a pale illuminating blue, and boy were
they ever captivating.

Her personality was something else too. I had to
hold back a laugh when she had tossed that rifle
back up in its rack. I thought the Sheriff was going
to have a heart attack. When she said, she was a
good shot it was stated with no boastful intention.
I knew from town gossip that her family owned
one side of Green Mountain. When we were
younger, Brady and I had discovered a small
waterfall up on her mountain. We knew we were
trespassing, but we were so far from the house we
knew no one would know we were there. The
waterfall plunged into a body of water that was
surrounded by large boulders. It was a pretty
spectacular place, and I wondered if Belle knew
that it was on her property.

It bothered me that she had not reached out to
anyone when she'd discovered the fire last night.
Heck, it was darn lucky she had even woken up.
She didn't have any smoke detectors.

I knew she had been homeschooled, and that her
family had been reclusive, but it bothered me that
she didn't feel she could call anyone. She seemed to
be close with Mr. Bee but not close enough to call
him when it happened. I thought about Brady and
wondered how friendly he had gotten with her. He
said he had been working for her. Brady was my
best friend, and he was a good guy. I felt bad that
he'd been injured in Afghanistan, but he was tough,
and I knew he would get through all the crap he
was dealing with. If he worked for her, I wondered
why she hadn't called him.

I thought about how tired Belle had appeared. As tired as she was she had generously offered us coffee, and that coffee was one of the best cups I'd ever had. The girl could bake too. I'd eaten two pieces of bread, and that jam had been unbelievable. Her home was different, but I liked it. It was comfortable and utilitarian. She did not have any knick-knacks cluttering the empty spaces, and I couldn't remember seeing any photographs either. I could tell that her home had been expanded upon through the years. It had probably been a one or two room place when it was first built and had been added to as her family had grown. I understood she had been raised unconventionally and that she was used to being self-sufficient, but I couldn't help feeling a little sad for her. I thought she was lonely.

The barn was old, and I had seen that she had a horse and a cow in one of the small-attached fenced in areas. I had heard sheep bleating but hadn't seen them. The place was an awful lot for one little slip of a girl to manage on her own, but with her feisty disposition, I did not doubt that she could. Again, I wondered what Brady did for her. I pulled into the fire station and saw that Joe, my Chief, and Austin were checking the rigs equipment. There were only four full-time fire fighters in Lansing. Joe was the Chief, and he was already talking about retiring. Austin and Larry were older than me, but they were happy being firefighters. I was the youngest of the four at

twenty-six, but all the extra classes I was taking
ensured that I would be the next Chief.

Joe walked out the open garage door and met me.
"How did it go?"

"It was arson," I told him. "Someone climbed a
trellis and set the fire using a pillow from the bed.

"Damage?"

"Minimal. Could have been bad though."

"Thanks for coming in on your day off."

"No problem. I'll see you Monday morning."

I handed him the keys to the department's one car
and headed towards my jeep. Then I turned back
and went inside the station, grabbed three smoke
detectors and returned to my car. I drove to my
home, which was just on the outskirts of town and
changed into jeans and a tee shirt. Then I grabbed
my toolkit and got back in my car. I don't know
when I decided to do what I was going to do, but I
headed back to Belle's to put up the smoke
detectors and take down that trellis. I hoped she
would let me. She was an independent little thing.
On my way, I stopped at the market, and at the
meat department, I had them make up two
sandwiches. I also bought soda, chips, and a plastic
container of brownies.

When I drove back down Belle's driveway, I was a
little anxious as to how I would be received. I knew
her family had liked their privacy. She probably did
too. I stopped near where I had parked before and
got out of my car.

"Kip, up here." I looked up, and Belle was hanging precariously out of the window above the trellis with a screwdriver and a hammer in her hands.

"Geez Belle, be careful," I called up to her. I couldn't keep the smile off my face; she was something else.

She laughed and told me to come inside. When I reached the room she was in she had pulled herself back inside.

"Did you forget to ask me some questions?"

"No, if it's okay with you I'd like to put up a few smoke detectors and help you take down that trellis. I had a feeling you'd try to do it alone."

"You didn't have to do that. I just started working on it."

"You know I was thinking," I told her cautiously. "If we are careful we might be able to salvage some of the roses. We can move the trellis to the barn and transplant them."

Belle gave me the grandest smile, and I felt like I'd just won the lottery. "That's a great idea," she replied enthusiastically.

"We need to get a spot ready for them, then dig up the roots. I know we won't be able to save the ones that are growing way up here, but we should be able to salvage the ones that are lower on the trellis."

Belle was grinning. "Thank you. I have been dreading the thought of killing Momma's roses. My Gram made this trellis for her. It was a birthday present."

I thought a flicker of sadness passed over her eyes, but it passed quickly.

We walked downstairs, and I went to my car and got out my tool kit and the bag with our lunch in it.

"What's that?" She asked pointing at the bag.

"Lunch."

"Oh, please go eat. I'm sorry I should have offered you something."

I chuckled. "No Belle its lunch for you and me. Are you hungry?"

She got an adorable grin on her face. "I'm always hungry." She replied with a laugh.

"Me too!" I admitted. I was thinking holy cow, can this girl be any more perfect? She actually admitted that she likes food.

Belle led me inside, and I took out the food from the bag.

"This is a feast!" She exclaimed.

Belle put out plates and napkins and glasses to pour our drinks in, and then we sat down to enjoy the sandwiches.

" So tell me about yourself," Belle asked between bites.

"Not much to tell. My family moved here from South Carolina when I was in 8th Grade. I went to high school here, pretty normal stuff. I attended the University of Vermont, played football for three years, but then I got hurt. I was going to enlist right after college like Brady did."

I watched her face when I said Brady's name, but she didn't reveal anything to me.

"We knew it would look good on our resumes when we applied for our dream jobs, mine being a firefighter. Then a position opened right here in town, and I applied and got it, so I didn't enlist. I've been a firefighter since graduating college."

"That's nice that you're doing something that you wanted to do, and that you obviously like."

"I love my job," I told her honestly. "What about you? Tell me about yourself."

Belle snort-laughed and I chuckled when I heard that. "There isn't much to tell you. I was born and raised right here. I was homeschooled. My family used to own Green Mountain but now we, well I, only own half of it. I just got my license, and I bought a new truck. I guess you know my Momma just passed. It's just me and the animals." She finished almost reflectively.

"So are you going to get a job? What are your plans?"

She smiled. "I want to take college classes at County. I like living on my farm, and I love animals. I learned about medicine from my Gigi; she was my great-grandmother; I've done a little doctoring on the animals. I think I might like to be a veterinary assistant or something like that."

"Sounds like a plan," I said watching her smile. "Can I ask about Brady?" I cautiously added.

"What about him?"

"He said he was working out here."

"He was," she hesitated for the briefest moment. "It didn't work out."

"Was it because he's handicapped?"

"He is not handicapped." She said rather forcefully. "He can do anything he puts his mind to!"

I chuckled, "I just told him the same thing." I told her. "He's had a rough go of it."

Belle didn't respond to that, so I didn't press her. She hesitatingly put a Frito chip into her mouth, and I watched her lick the salty goodness off her lips before she ate another and another.

"These are delicious," she said finishing off the ones left on her plate.

"Yeah, they're my favorite too."

She stood up and brought her empty plate to the sink, and I followed her with mine.

"Thank you so much for lunch Kip. That was so good."

"You are very welcome. You ready to get to work?" She nodded, and I followed her back outside.

It took two hours, but we succeeded in taking down the trellis. We separated the roses as best we could from the lattice to transplant them. Belle added compost to the holes before we put the roots in and we carefully arranged the rose vines on the trellis that I had leaning against the barn. Lastly, I affixed the trellis using the power screwdriver I had brought with me, and luckily I had the perfect screws for the job. When we were done, we stood back and looked at our finished work.

"It looks perfect there," Belle said happily.

"It does. I hope the roots take. You may lose some roses, but I bet they grow back."

"I hope so." She said wistfully.

I packed up my tools and stood up. "I have another job I'd like to do, aside from putting up the smoke detectors if that's okay?"

"What is it?"

"I want to make you a rack for your rifle that you can reach. Will you allow me to do that for you please?"

I was so relieved when she laughed. "I guess I scared you all this morning."

"Yeah, just a little," I chuckled.

We headed inside, and after I drank a glass of Belle's sweet tea, which was homemade, of course, I walked around the kitchen and living room looking for a safe spot for her gun.

"How about here?" I said pointing to a space above her stone fireplace.

"But it's stone."

"I'll put two pieces of wood here." I showed her where "and then screw it into your mantle using special screws I have. I'll use the same racks that you use now and attach them to the wood."

"Oh, that would be great if you used my old iron racks. My Gram made me those. She fashioned them from an old lamp post we had out front."

"Okay then, let me get started. Do you have any wood stain?"

"Yes, in the shed. I'll show you."

I followed Belle outside, and before we went to the shed, I asked her to show me the barn. I could tell she was happy introducing me to the animals. The barn was in need of repair. I could see a few things

that looked as if they had recently fixed; I
wondered if that was Brady's handwork.

"It a lot of work keeping this up, isn't it?"

"Yes, I'm trying. I know I have to downsize. I don't
think I'm going to raise pigs next year, and I know
I'm going to cut the garden in half. Taking care of
the garden is my least favorite thing to do. That
had been my Momma's job."

We headed towards the shed and inside she handed
me a can of stain that looked pretty old, but I
thought it would work.

"I'll just get to work," I told her bringing my tools
inside. "If you have to do something go ahead."

She hesitated and then grinned. "It's nice of you to
do this, and I do appreciate it. If you don't mind
me leaving you alone, I do have chores to do."

"Nope, I'm good here."

Belle headed outside, and I got to work.

Belle

Kip was a nice man. He came back on his day off
to help me with the trellis. I would have never
thought to try to transplant the bushes and relocate
the trellis to the side of the barn. I was just going to
take it down. It looked great where we put it; I just
hoped the roses didn't die.

He brought lunch for us too, which I thought was
incredibly thoughtful. I didn't want to appear
unworldly, but I had never had a Frito chip before,
and I found that I really liked them.

Then for him to offer to move my gun rack, well that was just plain sweet. I decided that later on, I would make him some bread as a thank you.

I carried the fence posts and rails that Brady had left near the barn the morning I booted him off the property, around to the corral that needed fixing. Henny was glad to have company. As I took out the old crumbling posts and replaced them with the new ones, she kept nudging my arm so I'd stop working and pet her.

The sun was beating down on me, and I was sweating through my tee shirt. I kept wiping my brown with the bottom of my tee shirt hem, and that soon became grimy and wet. I heard Kip walking towards me, and when he saw what I was doing, he jogged towards me.

Without hesitating, Kip helped me, and before too long, the new post and rail were up.

"Thank you, Kip."

"No problem. Your smoke detectors are up, and the new rack is too. Want to see?"

"Of course, " I answered immediately.

When I walked in, I couldn't believe how perfect it looked there. I looked at the mantle, and a small wooden box sat under the Henry.

"What's this?"

"I found it in the shed when I put the stain back. It looked old, and someone had carved Green into the front of the box. I cleaned it up and stained it." He opened the box. "I thought you could put your shells in here."

"On my goodness Kip that's wonderful! That was my great grandfather's box. I have no idea what he used it for. My Gigi said she thought he kept nails and stuff in it. Thank you! Thank you so much! You're amazing!"

Kip was grinning, and darned if he didn't look especially handsome at that moment. His eyes were twinkling, and his smile showed off his straight white teeth.

Next, he showed me that he had installed smoke detectors in the kitchen, just outside my bedroom and in the hall of the upstairs. Once again I thanked him.

"So what will you do for the rest of the day?" He asked.

I looked at the kitchen clock and saw that it was after 4:00 PM.

"I think I'll go to the old swimming hole for a swim. I'm hot and sticky."

"Me too. Can I join you?"

I blushed profusely and looked at the floor.

"Or I could just head home." He said sensing that he may have overstayed his welcome.

"Kip, it's just that, well, I don't have a suit."

"Oh," then it sunk in what I had just said. "Oh," he repeated louder.

I smiled shyly, "I've just never needed one."

"I understand," he said. "Hey if you have an old tee shirt I'll make you a swim top, and if you have a pair of old shorts, you could wear those."

"You're going to make me a swim top?"

He laughed. "Believe it or not I had to make a swim outfit for my sister one time. We went camping, and she left her bathing suit at home. She wanted to swim, so I made one for her out of an old tee shirt."

"Well, I do have an old tee shirt. I probably could just wear that with shorts."

"Yeah, but it will float up around you. If you don't mind me cutting the tee shirt, I'll be happy to make one for you that I guarantee will make it easy for you to swim in. It will only take a few minutes."

"Okay, I have one that I've thought of making into a barn rag, and I know I have a pair of old shorts."

"Great! Go get me the tee shirt, girl!" he said cheerfully.

I ran upstairs to my old room where I still kept some clothes and came down with a thin, light blue tee shirt that I'd had for years. It was stained with paint and was a little tight on me.

"Put it on," Kip said, so I put it on over the tee shirt I had on. I saw that he was holding the shears from my kitchen. Kip cut a few areas of the shirt and then told me to take it off so he could fashion it properly.

While he worked, I asked what he was going to wear.

"I keep a pair of swim shirts and a towel in my jeep. I always carry extra clothes and stuff."

Kip held up the tee shirt, and he told me to put it on again. He had cut the sleeves off and cut holes from the neck to the shoulders. He had notched a v in the front of the shirt from the neck, but it wasn't so deep to be indecent. The shirt was also cut almost in half except two longer strips hung down the front.

"What are these for?" I asked lifting the two pieces. Kip took them in hand and tied them together. "It will keep the shirt against your skin. See?"

"That's ingenious," I told him looking down at my makeshift bathing top.

"Yeah, well don't tell anyone that I'm a closet fashion designer. I'd be teased until no end."

I laughed and took the shears from the table where Kip had laid them down and ran into my room to change. I took off my tee shirt and bra and put on the shirt Kip had made me. It fit pretty well. It was tight enough so I knew it would not ride up and it wasn't too revealing. Then I took out my old denim shorts. I cut them underneath the rear pockets and made little slits at the side of each leg so they wouldn't be too tight. I put them on and realized I couldn't button them, so I just zipped them up and left the button undone. The shorts were now really, really short on me, but I giggled thinking that I was more covered than most store-bought bathing suits afforded, so I figured I was decent.

Next, I put on the cover-up that Brady had bought me. I pulled off the tag, and I was momentarily saddened that I was wearing it for the first time and he wasn't going to see me in it. I sighed; he had a new girl, and I wasn't going to waste any more time thinking about him.

I walked back into the living room to find that Kip had changed into swim trunks that hung to his knees and he had his tee shirt on and a towel hung over one of his broad shoulders.

"Ready?"

"Ready," he echoed.

We walked single file through the hay field and into the woods. When we emerged at my little swimming hole, I could see Kip was checking out the surroundings. I realized I'd forgotten my rifle again. What was up with me?

"This place is great." He said tossing his towel then his tee shirt to the ground.

"It's one of my favorite places. I forgot my rifle though." I said taking off my cover-up and tossing it to the ground.

Kip looked at the bushes across the way.

"Yeah, we'll make enough noise to keep the animals away though."

That made smile. "Yeah!" I said then I yelled like a banshee and ran towards the cold water.

I could hear Kip running right behind me, and I jumped in grabbing my legs to my chest. As I came up for air, a tidal wave of water hit me in the face, and I realized the big man had also cannonballed into the cold water.

Kip

Holy smokes that shirt and those tiny shorts had me stirring. She was pulling off her cover-up, and I saw those undone jean shorts and how low they sat on her slim hips and my mouth went dry. When

she turned to run into the stream, I had to follow
her. Her little ass was peeking out from under the
hem of her frayed shorts, and I got so hard it hurt.
I did not want her to see me like that, so I ran for
the water right behind her. It was damn cold, but
just what I needed to settle my dick down.
We swam and had competitions for who could
hold their breath the longest or how many laps we
could swim underwater from the rock to the log
that was on the other side of the small swim hole.
I dunked her a few times, and she laughed and tried
dunking me, but I was way too tall and big for her.
She climbed up on my shoulders, and that became
a game. I would launch her up in the air, and she'd
do tricks before splash landing into the deep end of
the little swim area. Man, she loved that! Then she
tried to balance on me and jump off; first from my
shoulders and then she tried to balance while I held
her by her feet and lifted her over my head. I
couldn't remember the last time I'd had so much
fun in the water. We were laughing so hard that we
didn't even hear Brady arrive.
I looked over, and he was standing on the ledge
and he looked pissed. It probably didn't help that
Belles jeans had wiggled higher exposing more of
her perfect ass, and her tight tee shirt was plastered
to her chest leaving little to the imagination.
I had her rear in my two hands, and I was lifting
her to launch her again. We were going for
maximum height this time but when I saw Brady I
stumbled, and she fell on top of me grabbing
around my shoulders to steady herself. She was

laughing hard, and I had been too. All that stopped when we saw Brady.

"Hey, I didn't hear you," I said.

"Obviously," he answered sarcastically.

Belle had gotten real quiet, and I didn't like that Brady had wrecked the fun vibe we had going.

"What are you doing here Brady?" She asked, and it wasn't with her sweet voice either.

"My dad told me about the fire. I came to make sure you were all right. I guess you are." He said glaring at me.

What the hell? I thought.

"I'm fine," Belle answered.

"I called you." He said looking at me.

"If you called when I was here I don't get service."

"You need to be more aware; you're one of only four firemen. Thought you had to be plugged in 24-7?"

Well, that was a dick thing to say I thought.

"I'm off today. The Chief knows where I am. What the hell Brady?"

Belle chose that moment to walk out of the water, and Brady's mouth dropped open when he saw her outfit. She wrapped the towel around herself and sat down.

I walked out and wrapped my towel, around my hips and sat down next to her. The silence was awkward, and I was annoyed. I was having fun with Belle. Brady had no claim over her that I knew of. Then why did I feel like I was missing something?

"I saw you finished the post and rail?" He said looking at Belle.

"Yup, today, with help from Kip."

"And the trellis?" he asked.

"Kip." She answered smiling at me.

Belle wasn't finished letting Brady know that she was getting along just fine without him. "He made me a new rack for my gun too." She said shooting me a sexy grin, "and he fixed up an old box, that was my great grandfather's, for my bullets."

She was not happy with my friend Brady, and she was letting him know it.

"You've been busy," he said looking at me.

"We got a lot done today." I acknowledged.

"And don't forget about the smoke detectors and lunch." Belle prompted.

Brady looked defeated. "Lunch?"

"Kip brought us lunch, and I had the best things ever, Fritos!"

I chuckled, and even Brady grinned ever so slightly hearing how excited the girl got about eating Fritos. "You liked those did you?" He said gently.

"I really did. I'm going to buy some the next time I'm in town."

"Well, I'm sorry I interrupted your fun," Brady said walking towards the trail.

"Are you ready to head back Belle?" I asked her quickly. I liked Belle, I really did, but Brady was my oldest and best friend. Bro's before Hoes, but in this case no way could I classify Belle as a Hoe.

"Yeah, suns lowering anyways."

We silently followed along behind Brady. I was comfortably sore from all the work I'd done that day plus playing in the water. I must have tossed Belle into the water 50 times. She had loved it.

We got to the back of Belles house, and because I was still wet, I didn't want to go inside.

"Belle, I had fun swimming. I hope we can do that again." I told her sincerely.

"It was fun, thank you. And thank you for doing all the work around here today."

"Listen you be careful tonight," I added.

Brady just stood there listening to us.

"I will."

"I wanted to look around the house for other ways someone might be able to break in, but I got sidetracked."

"I can do that," Brady said quickly.

"That's not necessary," Belle told him firmly.

Wow, whatever my boy did to get on her bad side must have been a doozy. Brady looked like a chastised puppy. She had slapped him down good.

We walked around to the front of the house, and Belle stopped near her porch and looked at me.

"Thanks again Kip."

"Have a good night Belle," I said and headed towards my car. I knew Brady would follow me.

I opened my car door and put my towel down on my seat then I put my tee shirt on.

"What are you doing with Belle, Kip?"

He had just picked the wrong fight.

"I'm not doing anything that concerns you, Brady."

"Do you like her?"

"Who wouldn't? She's awesome."

I got in my car and left him standing there. He needed to cool off, and I needed to think things over.

19

Belle

After I said goodbye to Kip, I showered and
changed. When I came outside the guy's cars were
gone, as I expected them to be. I went to the barn
to do the animals. To my surprise, I discovered
they'd already been put away for the night. I figured
Brady must have done it. Kip didn't know how.
I didn't understand Brady at all. How could he be
with another woman, right after being with me, and
then think I would be right as rain with him? It just
didn't make sense. If we were just friends then yes,
but he had flat out said that we should only be
intimate with someone whom we felt was special. I
thought I was special. Maybe he had a lot of
'special' friends. I for one was taking, myself out of
that friendship group of his.
Now Kip, on the other hand, was not an enigma.
He was awesome. That man was someone who I
could be put in my 'special' category. He had been
a tremendous help all day today, so I knew he was
kind. He brought me lunch and made me a gun
rack, and the bullet box had been such a wonderful
surprise; proving he was thoughtful. Then
swimming had been one of the best times I'd had
in a long time. I had had a great day with Brady
when we'd gone to Springfield, but that fun
memory was marred with his deceitfulness. I was
tired from working and then romping in the water

with Kip. With the animals all in for the night, I had some much-needed downtime.

I went back inside and called Dr. Lachlan. I was happy to hear that I could pick up Josh tomorrow. She said he had to be kept inside for a couple of days, except for bathroom breaks, but at least he'd be home.

I made myself eggs for dinner and settled down to watch television.

I heard a car coming down my drive, and I cautiously got up and standing to the side of one of the front windows I peered out. The sheriff's car drove in and then immediately drove out. Two hours later, right before I was about to turn in, the same thing happened, except this time it was a Deputies car.

That night I thought I would have a great night's sleep because after a good swim I always slept better. Unfortunately leaving my bedroom window open, like I did every night I woke up every time the sheriff or one of his men drove down my drive to check on me. I was grateful that they were making sure I was safe. I was concerned and secretly quite frightened that someone had been inside my home the night before, but I was thoroughly exhausted. I hadn't slept well in a few days.

I finally got out of bed, once again before the rooster crowed, and started my daily chores. At 7:30 AM my chores were done, and I was sitting on the front porch with a coffee when the Sheriff's car pulled down my drive. I walked out and put my hand up to stop him.

"Morning Belle, everything all right?"

"Yes, Sheriff, but with the cars coming down my driveway all night I didn't get any sleep, and with Josh coming home today I know he will be howling whenever you and your men come to check on me. I don't mean to sound ungrateful, but I'm pretty tired right now. Can we stop the checks? I'm sorry."

The Sheriff nodded, and I could tell he felt bad that his attempts to watch my home had resulted in me not sleeping.

"Okay, Belle we won't come down your drive anymore. I'm sorry we disturbed you."

"Thanks, Sheriff. I know you're just watching out for me."

"I am worried about you. I can't believe you're not a little afraid?"

"I am afraid, but there isn't much I can do about it. There is no way I'm leaving my animals."

"I understand. Stay safe."

"I will," I told before he drove back down my drive.

I had many chores to do so I began my day. I mowed the lawn, threw hay down from the loft. Added a bag of grain to the grain bin. Fixed a broken board in the barn. Reattached some of the wire fence around the garden that had fallen, and lastly, I baked three loaves of bread. One I was keeping, and two I was giving to Kip.

After the bread came out of the oven, I covered the loaves with a dishtowel and left to pick up Josh. Dr. Lachlan had said I could get him between 3:00 and 4:00, even though it was a Sunday, because that's when her assistant would be at the clinic. The bell over the door rang as I entered the small clinic. I could hear dogs barking and then I heard Josh's distinctive howl. A woman in jeans and a tan lab coat came out and introduced herself as Mary. She retrieved Josh for me, and I paid with my debit card before we left.

Judging by the speed of Josh's wagging tail I knew he was excited to see me. I was just as happy to see him. I had to keep him calm so as soon as we got home, I made sure he did his business, and then I brought him inside. I needed to go to the food store, but I was going into town tomorrow to bring Kip his bread, so I put off going to the market until then.

I wrapped Kips freshly baked loaves up in foil and went down to the scary cellar to bring up a jar of strawberry jam that I was also going to give him. I made an omelet for dinner and knew I'd have to get my act together regarding feeding myself. I was getting tired of eggs.

After dinner, I took Josh out again. He didn't seem to have any energy, and his back legs were shaky. I hated that he was hurting. I let him inside, and I sat on my back patio reading the Steven King novel I had. It got too dark to read, so I went inside and turned on the television. I was asleep on the couch within minutes.

I slept hard and only woke up because Josh licked my hand that hung over the couch. I sat up and stretched my sedentary muscles. Josh moved awkwardly to the door to be let out, and I thought he looked worse than the day before. After letting Josh out, I ground my coffee beans and took a cup outside. It was much later than I usually wake. I even slept through the rosters wake up call.

I finished my coffee then fed and put out the animals. I could tell it was going to be another warm day. I had another cup of coffee and toasted a piece of bread, which I ate with butter. Then I changed and headed into town with Kip's bread and jam.

I knew he was working today and he had said his shift started at 8:00 AM. It was after 10:00 AM so I knew as long as he wasn't dealing with a fire that he would be at the firehouse.

I pulled into the paved firehouse's drive and parked next to Kip's jeep. The garage housing the large red rig was open, and when I walked into the oversized garage I started calling, "Hello, anyone here?"

Kip came through a door that was in the back and a broad smile lite his face when he saw me.

"Hey, this is a nice surprise," he said.

"I wanted to bring you a thank you present," I told him handing him the two wrapped loaves of bread and the jam.

"Oh, no way. Your bread?"

"Yup, one rye, one white."

"Thank you I love your bread," he said lifting the bread to his nose to smell, which made me giggle. I handed him the jar of jam.

"And your jam?"

I blushed. "Thank you for everything you did yesterday and for swimming with me."

"It was a good day. Everything okay at your place?"

"Yes, all's well. Josh is home now."

"That's good."

"Well, I just wanted to drop this off. Thanks again." Before I could turn away, Kip touched my arm.

"Would you like to go out with me?"

"Um, aren't you working?"

Kip grinned. "Yes, I meant Saturday night."

"Okay, Saturday night."

"I'll pick you up around 6:00 PM is that okay?"

"Yes, I'm looking forward to it." I left the firehouse with a giddy feeling in my stomach. I sure hope I wasn't in for another disappointment, but for some reason, I could not imagine Kip doing anything that would cause me pain.

After I left the firehouse, I stopped at Mr. Bee's office. Miss Donna was smiling away and perfectly coiffed as usual. My heart dampened with sadness thinking about the last time that I had been there; I had been with Brady. He had been so attentive and sweet. I remembered how jealous I had been of Miss Donna's overtures towards him and now, for all I knew, she may have connected with him too. Brady was obviously what my Human Sexuality book referred to as a 'player.' Well good luck to her, I thought sarcastically, I sure wasn't able to hold his interest. If he liked someone like her, there was no way he would have any interest in me.

Miss Donna told me to go back to the office, and Mr. Bee greeted me warmly. He first asked how I was and he reminded me that if I changed my mind, I could stay with him and Mrs. Bee. I thanked him but told him Josh was home and I was fine.

He then went on to tell me that he had told the persons that wanted to buy my property that I had said no and that they had upped the offer. When I saw the new proposal, I gulped.

"What can they possibly want with my land, Mr. Bee?"

"Honestly I have no idea."

"They know I only own half of the mountain right?"

"Yes, I made sure they understood that."

"It's so much money."

"It is Belle. You need to think about this. You have money of your own, but with this money, you could pretty much do anything you wanted."

"Can't I do that now?"

"Well, yes. You can't go crazy, but you can easily live off of the money you have."

"And keep my land?"

"And keep your land."

"I'll think about it Mr. Bee, but right now it's still no."

He chuckled. "I figured that, but I had to extend their offer."

After I left Mr. Bee's, I went to the market and filled up my cart. I didn't need meat. I had a freezer full in my basement, but I needed milk and butter, and I bought two bags of Fritos along with enough other groceries to fill four shopping bags. I hurried home to put everything away.

That night I woke up to a strange sensation. Josh wasn't howling, but he was awake. I heard the upstairs floorboards creaking as if someone was walking on them. I pushed back my covers and shut Josh in my room. I took my gun off its rack. It was loaded, it always was. I clicked the safety off and tiptoed up the stairs.

My heart was pounding so hard that I had to pause halfway up to steady myself. I listened and heard a floorboard creak. I drew in a deep breath and let it out slowly before I climbed the rest of the stairs. I had not turned on any lights, and I could only see what the natural light shining in from the moon illuminated. That made it even scarier.

I moved down the hallway peering cautiously into the two bedrooms and the bathroom and saw nothing out of place. I went back into the hallway and waited for a minute to see if I'd hear anything, but I did not.

I went back inside each room with my gun at the ready, and this time I turned the lights on. I even looked in all the closets. There was no one there. It was quiet as could be.

I had heard footsteps. I swear I did. I wondered though if there had been someone in the house why Josh hadn't barked? I walked back downstairs, flipped the safety back on my gun, and put it back on my rack. Kip had chosen a perfect place for the gun rack. It was right outside my new bedroom, and easy to reach.

I climbed back into bed and decided that maybe I had just dreamt that I heard footsteps. The next morning when I woke up I changed and went to the kitchen to make my coffee. As I headed out to the front porch with my mug in hand, I glanced at the fireplace and saw that my gun was not on the rack. In fact, I didn't see it anywhere.

I put my coffee down on the dining room table and walked towards the fireplace. I know I'd put it back. I called Josh back inside and made him walk with me through the house. I didn't find my gun or anything out of place. Now I was scared.

I knew I should call the Sheriff. My legs were shaking. I made the call, and while I was waiting for him to come, I quickly fed the animals and let Bessie out with Henny.

I finished just as a Deputy car arrived. A man in uniform stepped out and introduced himself as Deputy Graham. I told him what had happened last night and he followed me inside. I pointed towards the mantle and froze. My rifle was there, back on the rack. The Deputy gave me an odd look.

"I, I don't know. It wasn't there earlier." I stammered.

I was embarrassed. "Really, it wasn't there before."

"Why don't I take a look around? Would that be all right with you?"

"Yes, thank you."

I followed him as he went through my home looking into every closet and even going in the scary cellar. We ended back in my living room.

"Miss Janson I don't see anything out of the ordinary. Did you?"

"No, but the gun was gone," I said softly.

He made a few notes on a small pad. "I know you've had a rough go of it. Sometimes when we are stressed our mind plays tricks on us."

"No this was real," I said foolishly pleading my case.

The Deputy left, and I felt sick to my stomach. I busied myself by preparing a stew for the crock-pot that my Momma had bought a few months ago. She had loved that thing. She would make all these fancy stews and soups, and they would cook all day making our cabin smell delicious. I put in stew meat, potatoes, and vegetables, covered it, and turned it on low before heading for the garden. Today I had to stake the tomato vines so the tomatoes would not touch the ground and rot.

I finished in the garden an hour later, and when I went back inside, I heard my phone ringing.

"Hello?"

"Belle. It's Sheriff McDaniel. Are you okay?"

"Yes."

"You thought someone had taken your gun?"

"Yes, but then when I came back inside with the Deputy it was back on the rack."

"Did you hear anything out of the ordinary?"

I hesitated. "Um, well I thought I heard footsteps last night, but Josh didn't howl, and when I looked around, I didn't see anything."

"Deputy Graham looked around?"

"Yes, he did."

"Have you been sleeping, Belle?" I knew then that he didn't believe me either.

"Yes," I said quietly. "I mean, I guess as well as could be expected," I added.

"Honey, why don't you go stay with Mr. Bee?"

"No, I'm good I promise. I'll take a nap today." I told him knowing full well I wouldn't. I just knew it would be something he would want to hear.

I thanked him for calling and headed to the barn to clean the stalls.

That night I sat in my living room on the floor and rubbed Josh's ears thinking about the fire, the footsteps, and the gun. I was talking to Josh and noticed that he was not reacting to my voice. I left him on the floor and went to the kitchen, so I was not in his line of sight. Then I called him.

He didn't move. I rounded the kitchen corner moving closer to him and called him again.

Nothing. Closer still, nothing. It wasn't until I was right on top of him did he realize that I was near him.

I slept fitfully that night and even kept checking that the gun was still there. By the time the rooster crowed, I was in serious need of sleep. I had my coffee and did the animals, but I was barely holding it together. Besides the fact that I was exhausted I knew something was very, very wrong with Josh. I loaded Josh into my truck and headed back to Dr. Lachlan's. She was just pulling in when I arrived. She knew I was upset because I kept wiping tears away.

"Belle, what's the matter?"

"It's Josh. I think he's deaf."

She nodded solemnly and told me to bring him inside. We walked back to the examination room, and I noticed Josh's gate was off. Dr. Lachlan noticed too.

She and I picked Josh up and put him on the large table and Dr. Lachlan examined my friend.

She took the stethoscope out of her ears, and I knew she was about to deliver bad news to me.

"Belle, do you know old Josh is?"

"Um, I think we got him when I was 8."

"He's led a very good, long life." Dr. Lachlan said.

"Yes." I nodded afraid to look at her.

"Belle, he's suffering right now, and it's going to get worse."

"But he was okay. You had him here."

"He recovered well from his wound, but honestly I think that may have taken a lot out of him. His blood pressure is low, and his heart is beating erratically. His organs are shutting down. Did he eat anything last night?"

I thought back to his food bowl and remembered he had not eaten much if anything."

"No."

"You know the humane thing to do is, right?"

Tears streamed down my face. "Are you sure?" I choked out between sobs.

"Yes, I'm sure. I'm so sorry."

Two hours later I was back at my farm with Josh in my truck under a blanket. I took a shovel from the shed and got back in my truck and drove Josh's lifeless body up to the family cemetery. I had the option of cremating him, but I declined that. I dug Josh's grave by myself, and I could not stop crying. My Josh, my friend was gone. My heart ached as I dug down four feet. I didn't have to dig as deep or as long of a grave as we had for Momma. I hefted Josh from my truck, placed him on the edge of the open grave, then got into the hole and lifted him down into the dark earthy pit. I sat down next to him and cried even harder as I talked to him. I climbed out of the hole and began to cover him with dirt. Each shovel full of dirt I tossed into the grave sent painful daggers of grief through my body. When I finished, I said a prayer, and then I fell onto the freshly churned earth and sobbed.

I cried out my anguish and prayed that he was in a better place. I prayed to my family to watch over him. Then I got back in my truck and drove back to the house. I was filthy and sweaty, and my entire body ached, but I still had to take care of my other animals.

That night I slept in the barn I just needed to be near the animals, near something alive. I was sad and scared, and I didn't want to be alone. For the first time, I was seriously considering selling my farm.

The next morning I barely made it through my chores. I let the chickens out of the coop but didn't even bother collecting the eggs. I fed Henny and Bessie, the pigs and sheep, and headed inside. I sat down at the dining room table. I didn't have the energy to shower, and I didn't want to soil my new furniture, so I just sat at the dining room table in a daze. My phone rang, but I didn't even get up to answer it.

A half hour later I heard a car coming down my drive. I knew I had to look a mess; there was straw in my unruly, not brushed hair. I smelled like dirt and sweat. I didn't care.

"Belle." I heard someone call from outside the door. They were knocking frantically. "Belle!" The door opened, and I watched as Brady walked in. He took one look at me, and that's all it took for me to start sobbing again.

Brady gathered me in his arms and pulled me down onto his lap. I cried into his chest, and I must have fallen asleep because when I woke up, he had somehow managed to put me in my own bed.

I opened my eyes slowly. They were swollen and scratchy. Brady was sitting at the end of the bed. He got up and handed me a glass of water that had been sitting on the night table.

I took it from him, but my hand was shaking so he helped me to hold it and I sipped it greedily.

"I fell asleep?" I asked stupidly. I had obviously fallen asleep.

"Yeah, you were exhausted."

"What time is it?"

"It's near 8:00. You've been asleep for about twelve hours."

I slowly got out of bed, and Brady came around to help me. I let him.

"Come on you need to get cleaned up." He said as he walked me to the bathroom. Brady turned on the faucet for the tub to fill it and before I knew what was happening Brady was slowly stripping the clothes from my body. There was nothing sexual about it at all. He left my bra and underwear on and after he checked the temperature of the water temperature he held my hand helping me to step into the tub.

Brady washed my body and my hair. I was completely lethargic as he soaped and rinsed me off. This was not a sexual encounter, this was Brady taking care of me, and that thought had me weeping again. I missed him.

"Belle, Honey, you'll be okay. I know you miss Josh. I know you miss your family." He thought I was crying because of them. I didn't correct him. He unplugged the drain and helped me from the tub.

Brady gently toweled me dry, and I did start to feel better, but then the embarrassment of how pathetic I must have looked hit me. I wearily shooed Brady from my room and changed into a pair of flannel pants and a tee shirt. I didn't even put on a bra. Brady was waiting for me in the living room. I was feebly trying to brush my hair, but my arms were sore. Brady stood up, guided me to a dining room chair and then he took the brush from me and brushed my hair. It felt so good. I was inwardly cussing at myself for being weak and allowing Brady to help me.

When he finished, he walked me to the couch covered me with a quilt that he had gotten from my bedroom, and then he made me toast with jam. He sat next to me, and he made me eat every bite and drink the entire glass of milk that he had poured.

When I finished, he took the plate from me, and when he returned to the couch, he turned on the television.

"Try to sleep Belle," he said. He gently lowered my tired body to the couch and positioning my head, so it rested on his thigh. His hand lay on my hip, and within minutes I was asleep.

I woke up in my bed. I must have really been exhausted because I did not even feel Brady carry me in. The rooster crowed, and I padded to the bathroom and then out to the living room where I found Brady sprawled on my couch.

I didn't wake him. I ground the coffee beans and started up the percolator. Then I went back into my room and put on jeans and a tee shirt. If it had been anyone else other than Brady that had found me I would have been concerned about the care of my animals, but Brady knew what to do, and I knew he had taken care of them,

"Morning," Brady said as I reentered the living room. He moved to sit up, and he stretched his arms over his head.

I sat next to him. "Thank you, Brady."

He grinned. "You're feeling better?"

"Yes, thanks to you."

"I'm so sorry about Josh."

"How did you find out?"

"Dad saw Dr. Lachlan in town, and she told him, and my dad told me."

"So you decided to come out here?"

He shrugged. "I know you're not happy with me. Hell, you probably hate me, but I was worried about you. Dad was going to come out, but I offered."

"I appreciate all you did. I know you took care of the animals too."

"So I guess I'll get out of your way." He said standing up.

"Would you like a cup of coffee first?"

"No thanks I have an appointment." He hesitated, looking uncomfortable. "Belle, Kip called last night to remind you about your date tomorrow night. He said he hoped you feel better. He would have come, but he is in Montpelier taking a class, and he won't be back until tomorrow. He said he would call you later."

"Oh, wow, I had forgotten."

I walked him to his truck and watched him drive away. I was still smarting over the way he had treated me, but the initial sting was now gone. What he had done for me yesterday, and last night had been selfless. That was the Brady I had first met. The one I had been falling for. I wondered if his girlfriend knew he had been here. I hope she didn't get too mad at him.

I spent the rest of the day doing light chores around the house and barn. I gave Henny a good brushing and even rubbed Bessie down. She wasn't as keen as Henny was about being pampered. I made myself a sandwich and took that to the swimming hole with my Steven King book and this time I remembered my rifle. I swam and tanned and even napped in the strong afternoon sun. That night, after the animals were taken care of, I sat in my bed and continued to read. The phone rang, and I had to get out of bed and run into the kitchen to get it. When I answered, I was breathing heavily because I had run and also because the phone ringing had scared the bejinkers out of me. "Hello," I said breathlessly.

"Belle, it's Kip. Are you okay?"

I chuckled as I sat down in a dining room chair holding the phone. "Yes, I was in bed, and I was reading a scary book, and then the phone rang, and it startled me. I had to run to answer the phone."

I heard Kip chuckling. "I think you need to read a different book." He said.

"Yeah, probably not my brightest idea," I admitted.

"So did Brady tell you I called?"

"Yes, I was a bit out of it."

"That's what he said. I'm sorry about Josh."

"Thank you. It's a little lonely out here without him," I admitted softly.

"I wish I was there." I could tell that he sincerely meant it.

"I have to get used to being alone I guess."

Kip was quiet for a second. "Do you want me to call Brady and have him come back out?"

"No, I'll be okay." I was thinking that Brady's girlfriend would definitely not like him coming to my house again.

"So where are we going tomorrow night?" I said changing the subject.

"I thought I'd take us into Springfield to dinner and then maybe some dancing if you're up for it?"

"I've never been dancing. Springfield's pretty far though."

"We could stay in town and have dinner and go to Rustic, that's the local bar."

"I'm up for anything Kip. I know we'll have fun."

"Okay well, I'll be there at 6:00. Now Belle put that scary book away and get some sleep."

That made me laugh. Kip always made me feel better.

The book was suspenseful, and I was a bit spooked, so I just got back into bed and tried to fall asleep even though it was only 8:30. I got weepy thinking about Josh again, so I thought about Kip and our date instead. Funny thing, though, it was Brady whom I was thinking about as I fell asleep.

Once again I awoke to what sounded like someone walking on the second floor. I got out of bed, and this time I ran up the stairs with my gun in hand. It sounded like someone was running down the hallway, but when I got to the top step and turned the hall light on I didn't see anyone.

My heart was racing. I was seriously afraid. My hands shook as I clutched my Henry as I anxiously checked the two rooms and the bathroom. Once again I found one of the windows opened in my Momma's room. I knew they had all been closed. I was so terrified that my skin was tingly with goose bumps and my chest heaved from my nervous heavy panting. As afraid as I was there was no way I was calling the Sheriff again. I shut the window and cautiously made my way back downstairs. I didn't put my gun back on the rack. Back to my bedroom, I shut my door behind me, and for the first time in my life, I locked my bedroom door. Then I put my rifle on the floor next to my bed and lay awake for the rest of the night listening for footsteps.

I dozed off near dawn, and when the rooster crowed, I actually rolled over and fell back to sleep. I woke up, and I knew it was late in the morning because of where the sun was shining into my room. I looked at the round clock face on my nightstand and saw that it was after 10. Ugh! I am such a bad person I thought as I hurriedly threw on my jeans and boots, and leaving on the tee shirt that I had slept in, sans a bra. I had to feed my animals.

Henny and Bessie appeared irritated that I was so late and I apologized as I walked them outside adding extra grain to their bins. The chickens literally flew the coop when I opened it. Their little feathers flew as they scurried for the feed I'd tossed on the ground. The sheep were fine, and I added water to their outside trough and grain to their bin. Will was looking good but remained close to his Mom. Lastly, I checked on the pigs.

When I was younger, I always named them, but I stopped that after I understood what their fates were in the fall and I couldn't stand thinking about their awful demise. Maybe I wouldn't raise pigs after this year. I'm sure I could afford to buy meats. That thought made me feel better.

The pigs greeted me noisily. I liked to think that they recognized me, but I knew they only wanted what I had in the bucket I carried, their food. I collected three eggs from the coop before I headed back inside.

After depositing the eggs in the basket, I made my coffee and sat on the front porch. With the sun already beating down there was not much refuge under the porch roof, so I went back inside and sat at the dining room table.

As I sat there, I thought about the mysterious footsteps. Then I remembered my rifle was on my bedroom floor, so I quickly got up and retrieved it, putting it back on the rack where it belonged. Curiosity made me hesitate at the foot of the steps, and as I looked up the steps, I listened. I didn't hear anything unusual. I climbed the steps, hoping that maybe looking around in the daylight would reveal where the sounds had come from.

I checked out each room and even every closet. Nothing. I went back downstairs and fried an egg and placed it between two pieces of bread. As I ate my breakfast, I thought about my date with Kip. I had already decided what I would wear. I just wasn't sure if I should wear sandals, flats, or my new cowboy boots. I decided I'd ask Kip when he arrived.

The lawn needed mowing, so I hopped on the little tractor and went to work. I finished in time to go to the swimming hole where I swam, then bathed, and washed my hair. Then after an hour of drying off in the warm sun, I put my cover up back on and returned home to get ready.

Kip arrived a few minutes before 6. He was dressed in a polo shirt and a pair of jeans with a belt that had silver embellishments. When I opened the door to his knock, he smiled and handed me a beautiful bouquet of flowers. I thought his gesture very sweet. I thanked him, but inwardly I felt bad that he spent his money on something I could have picked from my own garden.

"Kip what should I wear on my feet?" I asked, and then pointed at the three pair of shoes I had sitting on the floor.

He grinned and told me any of the choices would be fine, but the flats or boots might be more appropriate for dancing. I decided to wear the flats since it was summer. I could wear the boots when the weather turned colder.

We started driving and the more we talked I could tell that Kip was tired.

"You look a little tired," I said hoping not to insult him.

"Yeah, I am. I just got back a few hours ago."

"Then why don't we stay local?"

He paused thinking for a second. "Honestly I'd like to but."

"But what?"

"Well, everyone will be at Rustic, it's the only place in town."

"Oh." My gut pinched. He didn't want to be with me around his friends.

"What are you thinking?" He said seeing my face.

I blew out an exasperated and very heavy breath. "I think you should just take me home Kip, please."

"What?" he pulled the car to the side of the road and turned to me.

"Are you sick? Is something wrong?"

"You're obviously tired, and if you're too embarrassed to be seen with me, I'd rather shut this whole thing down now," I said as I pointed to him and then me.

"Oh shit, no. Belle." He chuckled, and I almost went for the door handle.

"Wait, Belle, you have this all wrong. I don't want to go to the Rustic with you because I want to spend time with you alone."

"Oh," I whispered.

"My friends will want to meet you. I'm sure Dirk will be flirting with you. Brady may be there too. I just wanted it to be us."

I hung my head "I'm sorry I just thought. Well, you know what I thought."

"Listen, we have fun together. I like being with you. I don't know where we are headed, but I'd like to find out."

"How will we find out?" I asked.

Kip laughed out loud. "I love that you don't hold back and you just say what's on your mind."

"My Gram said it's the best way to communicate, but I think sometimes it's also smart to just listen and not blurt out what you might be thinking."

"Maybe, but I have to tell you that I find it refreshing to be with a girl that says what she means."

"So... how are we going to find out?" I repeated the question.

Kip grinned and pulled back onto the road. "Okay, you're direct, so I'll be direct too."

"Good."

"Tonight when I bring you home I plan on kissing you." He gave me an adorable wink.

"Ohhhh," I said softly.

"If there are fireworks when we kiss we are going to do a lot more dating."

"Fireworks?"

"Yeah, fireworks. When your brain explodes, and your body sizzles, and you lose your breath and can't think straight."

"Ohhhhh. And if there are no fireworks?"

"Well I'm hoping that there are, but honestly if there are not I think I could use a new friend and I'm hoping you could use one too."

I was quiet for a second as I let what he said sink in. "Kip that's about the smartest and nicest thing anyone's ever said to me," I told him with a grin. Kip decided we would eat dinner in Massey, a nearby town that had a reputable Italian restaurant and then we would head back to Lansing and dance at Rustics. He asked if I liked that idea and I told him I thought it was perfect. He wouldn't have to drive far. We could spend some time alone together, and we'd get to go dancing.

Dinner was an experience. There was so much on the menu. The tables were covered with red checkered cloths and candles stuck in colorful; empty wine bottles served as centerpieces. A man with a violin sat in a corner and played. I had lasagna and Kip ordered chicken masala. We shared a bottle of red wine that was sweet and delicious.

The menu alone had been revealing. There were so many other meals I could try to make, besides the basic meat, potatoes and vegetable meals I'd grown up eating. I was going to the library on Monday and take out a recipe book. I shared this with Kip, and we talked more about food. He told me about his week, and I told him about mine, but I didn't share that I'd heard footsteps. I didn't want him to think I was crazy.

He held my hand from across the table, and it felt pleasant to be touched like that. Kip was sweet and handsome. I saw how other women looked at him. I felt like a plain Jane, as my Gram would have said, next to him. I had on a new outfit, but it wasn't fancy, and I wore no makeup. I told Kip was I was thinking.

"You're beautiful just the way you are Belle."

"You're just saying that so I'll kiss you later." I teased, which made him chuckle.

"No, really you don't need any makeup. You're naturally beautiful, however, if you do want to try wearing make up my friend Jeannie manages the pharmacy in town. She's the pharmacist, but because it's such a small store she is also the store manager. She knows all about makeup. My sister and Mom go see her all the time."

"Will you introduce me to her? I'd feel silly just walking in and asking her to help me."

"Sure, she may be at Rustic tonight. I heard there was a new band playing and Dirk told me they are excellent. She likes to dance, so I bet she'll be there."

"I've never gone dancing you know."

"I kind of figured that. Don't worry; it's easy."

"Do you dance a lot?"

"I like to dance, so when the music's good, I get on the floor. I think we'll have fun tonight. I just don't want you to be overwhelmed."

"There will be lots of people there I assume."

"Lots and they all be drinking, and sometimes they get stupid."

"Are you going to drink?"

"I'll have a beer or two; I won't overdo it. How's your wine?"

"It's excellent, but I don't think I should have anymore."

"Yeah, better safe than sorry." Kip agreed.

We finished dinner and Kip, and I walked back to his car slowly. He was holding my hand and again I liked how it felt. He opened the door for me, and before I slide inside, he stopped me and gave me an unhurried soft kiss on my lips.

His large body dwarfed my smaller frame, and his one hand cupped the back of my head while his other warmed my back. I followed his lead, and since he never used his tongue, I didn't either.

When he pulled back, I said, "I thought we were going to do that later?"

"Yeah, but I just couldn't wait."

"Fireworks?" I asked.

"Too short of a kiss," he answered, and we both laughed.

It had been a gentle kiss, and I did like kissing him, but there were no fireworks for me either, so I had to assume that the kiss was like Kip said; too short to register.

We pulled into Rustic jam-packed parking lot.

"This band must be great; the place is packed," Kip said as he placed his hand on my back to walk me inside.

I could hear the music from out in the parking lot, and there were people in the lot too. I saw one couple kissing like crazy on the hood of a car, and a few other people were standing near the door smoking cigarettes.

"I'm a little nervous Kip," I whispered moving closer to him.

"I got you, Belle. At any time if you want to leave say the word."

"Okay." I gulped nervously.

Kip pushed open the door, and the loud music, dim lights, and the cloying smell of stale beer assaulted me. The sheer number of persons standing hip to hip or dancing in front of the band had my mouth gaping open.

Kip leaned down and had to shout in my ear to be heard. "You okay?"

I nodded. "This is wild," I shouted back.

Kip guided me through the throngs of bodies. His height afforded him to see over the large crowd, and he maneuvered us quickly through the packed bar. When we emerged from the main mass of patrons he steered us towards a table in the corner of the room. Brady was sitting at the table, along with Dirk, two other men, and four women.

I felt like a fish out of water. The women were eyeing me warily, and the men were staring as well, but I had no idea what they were thinking. I snuck a look at Brady, and he did not look happy. His jaw was clenched, and his eyes held no sparkle; more like sparks. I knew he and Kip were best friends and it bothered me that there was possibly discord between them. I just couldn't figure out why Brady would be upset. He had a girlfriend, why couldn't Kip and I date?

Kip pulled out an empty chair that was near the table and gestured for me to sit down. He sat next to me in another chair.

He leaned over the table and shouted, "This is Belle. Belle these are my friends."

He pointed at each woman and said her names, "Jeannie, Courtney, Ashley, Sara." I noticed how Kip's eyes lingered on Jeannie.

I smiled at each one of them anxiously. He then introduced me to the men at the table.

"This is Fred, Austin, and you know Dirk, and Brady. Austin is a firefighter too." He added.

The men were grinning, and I felt self-conscious as if there was a joke I had not been made privy too. Dirk was undressing me with his eye. He had on a baseball cap, and he was smiling at me. I'm sure he thought that he was charming; I didn't. Brady acknowledged me with a nod; he looked miserable. I wondered if one of the women at the table was his girlfriend.

It was too loud to try to talk, so I turned in my chair to watch the people dancing. I had never danced in public before, but I had danced in my room when songs came on the radio that I liked. How I danced was similar to how everyone else seemed to be moving. One difference was a few of the couples moved sinfully on each other; it was very provocative looking.

Kip shouted into my ear. "What do you think?" I shouted back, "It's very interesting. Um, what kind of dancing is that?" I said gesturing to a couple where her rear was rubbing against his front.

Kip chuckled, "Yeah, that's called grinding."

"Seems like it would be rather stimulating."

Kip laughed, and I watched Brady get up from the table and walk away.

"Where's his girlfriend?" I asked Kip.

"Not sure."

The band went on a break, and even though music began playing from the jukebox, I was relieved that it was not as loud as the band had been.

"I've never seen you around here before," Jeannie said sliding her chair closer to mine.

"I've never been here before."

"I love your belt." She said. "Where did you get it?"

I told her the store I had bought it in, and that started a whole discussion about clothes that the other girls joined in on. It was interesting. I learned that many of them bought their clothes at a boutique in the town that Kip and I had dined in. They also liked a store called Stein Mart, and they told me that the mall that was just outside of Springfield had fantastic stores. I made a mental note to visit them.

"So where are you from?" Fred asked.

"I live here, in Lansing," I told him.

"How is it that I've never seen you before?"

I was about to answer that I just didn't get out much when Dirk answered for me.

"She's the girl that lives at the base Green Mountain."

"Oh." Everyone else nodded and looked at each other. They knew I was 'that girl' the one that didn't go to school. The one whose family kept to themselves.

Jeannie leaned in, "I'm sorry about your mother."
She said patting my arm.
I took an instant liking to Jeannie.
"Jeannie, Belle may come visit you in the drug store."
Jeannie knew exactly what Kip was referring too.
"You come anytime you'd like." Then she leaned and whispered, "But Belle you don't need makeup, you're naturally beautiful."
I grinned widely at her and Kip smiled. "Told ya."
A waitress stopped at the table and put two empty glasses down in front of Kip and me and then placed a pitcher of beer on the table.
"Would you like a beer or something else?" Kip asked politely.
"Beers fine."
Kip poured the amber colored liquid into our mugs.
Much to my dismay, the band was getting ready to start playing again. I had enjoyed listening to everyone talk. Like my Gram had said, 'you can learn a lot from just listening.'
I learned that Ashley hated her job in the bakery at the supermarket in Massey, Sara loved her job as a Kindergarten teacher, and Courtney worked in the post office and was engaged to Austin, Kip's fireman friend.
Dirk was obnoxious as ever and flirted with everyone. I could tell he was well on his way to being drunk. Fred turned out to be the son of the man who owned the Feed, and Grain and I realized that he was the boy who had tried to talk to me all

those years ago. When I asked him if that had been him, he laughed and said it was. He told me that my Gram had scared the heck out of him and that his dad didn't want to lose my families business, so whenever we had gone to the store, he had to go into the back room.

I said I was sorry about that, but he laughed, saying it was in the past. He seemed like a nice guy. I asked why I didn't see him in the store anymore and he said he managed the Feed and Grain that was in another town.

Brady came back to the table, and I saw that Kip was looking at him like he wanted to say something to him, but he didn't.

He sat on the other side of me, and I hated that I felt his magnetic pull. "How are you?" He asked me quietly, trying to keep our conversation between just us.

"I'm fine. Thank you, and thank you again for, well you know."

Kip, of course, was listening. Brady looked at him. "So where did you two go to dinner?"

"Amalfi's."

"Nice place." My Mom loves it there.

"I had lasagna." I piped in.

Brady smiled. "I like their lasagna too."

"I'm going to learn how to make it," I told both men.

Brady smiled, and Kip was grinning. "If your cooking rivals your bread making you'll make it better than Amalfi's," Kip said.

I laughed at the compliment. "We'll see."

The innocuous conversation melted away the tension between Kip and Brady, and I was relieved. Dirk kept staring at me, making me feel extremely uncomfortable. I kept my eyes averted from where he was sitting; the man gave me the creeps. The band started playing, and the girls jumped up from their seats to dance.

"Come with us, Belle," Jeannie said grabbing my hand and pulling me up.

I looked to Kip for help, but it was Brady who spoke up.

"Go dance. You'll have fun."

Kip nodded and chuckled, so I followed the girls to the dance floor. I leaned into Jeannie and whispered. "Jeannie, I've never danced like this before. I mean I've danced before, just in my room, alone."

I know I shocked her, but after a momentary pause, she smiled. "Just move your body to the music."

I nodded, and as the song progressed, I became more comfortable with dancing in public. No one around me was even paying any attention to me, they were enjoying the music, and dancing, so I relaxed and danced like I was at home, alone. I glanced over at the table, and both Kip and Brady were watching me. Brady had a grin on his face, and Kip gave me a thumbs up. I waved at them, and Jeannie laughed seeing the two men watching me.

"They both like you, Belle."

"Oh, we're just friends. Brady has a girl and Kip and I, well we get along very well. We're going to kiss later and see if there are fireworks." Jeannie exploded with laughter. I wasn't sure what I had said, but she grinned and said I'd have to tell her how that goes.

Three songs later and the men joined us on the floor. I was already sweating. Dirk was trying to grind on Sara, who kept pushing him away. Austin and Ashley were dancing slowly with each other even though the music tempo was fast. I actually found that to be sweet. Brady was the only one not dancing.

The evening was turning out to be much better than I first anticipated. Kip's friends, except for Dirk, were very kind and had been welcoming. Brady and Kip were talking amicably, so I was pleased with that. I danced a lot and Kip, and I had even slow danced to a song.

We were sitting around the table, and Kip got up to use the restroom. The band began playing a popular song, and the women jumped up to dance. They tried to get me to join them, but I politely refused. Dirk, Austin, and Fred went to join the women on the dance floor leaving me alone with Brady.

At first, we sat quietly watching everyone dancing, and it was a little awkward.

"Why aren't you dancing?" I asked extending an olive branch of sorts.

"I just don't feel like it." He answered stiffly making me feel bad for asking.

"Sorry." I didn't know what I was apologizing for.

"How have you been? Really?" He asked moving closer to my chair so that we could hear each other.

"I'm okay. I miss Josh."

"Yeah, I bet. Are you getting any sleep?"

I looked away from him, debating whether to tell him what had been happening.

"Belle, talk to me."

"Okay," I exhaled, "I woke up again last night. I keep hearing someone walking upstairs. When I go up there, I don't see anyone."

Brady's mouth morphed into a tight line.

"I don't like this Belle."

"The Deputy said it was probably my mind playing tricks on me." I shared with him.

"What do you think?" He asked.

I looked at Brady and knew I could trust him with my personal thoughts. "Brady I'm scared. I swear I really hear those sounds. The other day my gun was missing, and then it just reappeared, I think maybe I'm losing it." I said pointing at my head.

"Belle you're one of the most stable people I've ever met. There has to be another explanation. Do you think an animal, like a raccoon, has gotten inside and that's what you're hearing?"

"I don't know, maybe, but I haven't seen any signs of one. And a raccoon wouldn't steal my gun and put it back." I replied sullenly.

"Would it be okay if I came out one day to look around?"

"Sure, I guess."

We were quiet again.

"I wish I had been the one to dance with you for the first time," he said softly. His green eyes locked on to mine and I felt my heart speed up. Then I remembered he had a girlfriend.

I blushed, "Brady you have a girlfriend. Let's just try to be friends."

"No, I don't."

"You don't want to be friends?"

"I don't have a girlfriend."

"But," I said, and before I could say more he interrupted me.

"I don't have a girlfriend. I did, not when I was with you though, but, it's a long story, so maybe when you have some time, I could explain everything to you." He paused. "I know I hurt you. I was an idiot." I was stunned by his admission. Kip came back to the table at that moment.

"What I miss?" he said looking between the two of us.

"We were just catching up," Brady answered, and I nodded. I was still letting the fact that he didn't have a girlfriend digest.

I excused myself to use the restroom. Kip pointed to where it was located. I entered the small hallway and turned into the two-stall lavatory. After I washed my hands and combed through my hair with my fingers, I walked out the door.

Dirk was standing outside in the hall waiting; I hoped not for me. I tried to walk past him, but he stepped into my path and remained close to me. I put my hands on his chest trying to push him back, but he was a solid mass of muscle. His hands gripped my arms as he backed me up into the wall behind me. His arousal was disgustingly evident as it pressed against my stomach. I was afraid, mad, and nauseated all at the same time.

"I can show you how a real man treats a lady." He slurred his words as his alcohol-infused breath washed over my face making it hard to breathe.

I shoved him back as hard as I could and because he was drunk I was able to move him slightly.

I tried to twist away, but he grabbed my arm, holding me in place. He shoved his other hand under my skirt to cup my rear intimately.

"Come on baby; I'll make it good for you." He said huskily.

I broke free but was so stunned by his crude behavior that I ended up slamming my back against the opposite wall as I tried to distance myself from him.

Just then Brady walked into the hallway followed by Kip. "What's going on?" Kip asked brusquely.

Brady took one look at my face, and I could tell he knew what was happening.

"I'll tell you what's going on!" I said pushing away from the wall. I was steaming mad.

"Your jerk of a friend here thought he would enlighten me as to what a real man was like."

You did what?" Kip was about to rain hell on the man, but this was my fight.

I stepped toward Dirk and began poking him in the chest as I spoke.

"If you think you're a real man you are sadly mistaken. You can't even carry the boots of a real man. You disgust me. If you ever try to touch me again, I will make you sorry you ever met me."

Dirk was laughing uncontrollably. Kip was ready to punch him, but when I looked at Brady, he had a little grin on his face. That's when I remembered that I could make Dirk sorry and Brady knew it.

Dirk giggled drunkenly looking at his friends. "This little girl thinks she can just waltz into our bar, act all coy, and then threaten me when I offer her what she obviously wants." He looked at me and laughed outright. "You have me soooo scared." He smirked sarcastically.

Kip moved to grab Dirk, but Brady put his hand on his arm holding him back.

"You should be," I answered with nervous bravado.

I stepped towards Dirk and quickly faked a knee hit to his groin. Just like Brady had said, Dirk swiveled and lifted his leg to protect his privates. I swiftly kicked him behind his supporting leg while he was unbalanced, and then slammed the heel of my hand into the front his neck. Dirk fell solidly onto the floor clutching his throat.

I knew I had knocked the breath from him. He lay on the hard wooden floor, his eyes wide with pain, gasping for air, utterly humiliated.

I looked up from my nemesis to find Kip staring at me with his mouth hanging open and Brady grinning proudly.

"It worked," I said to Brady giving him a wink.

Then I looked to Kip.

"He's lucky I didn't wear my cowboy boots, right Kip?"

Kip grinned. "Damn lucky." he agreed.

I bent down to Dirk and snatched his baseball cap off his head and threw it down on his heaving chest.

"Didn't your Momma teach you any manners? Never touch a girl unless she says it's okay, and a real man takes off his hat indoors." I then left the hallway, and yes, I had a big toothy grin on my face as I walked back to the table with both Kip and Brady following me.

20

Kip

I couldn't believe she had just laid Dirk out like
that. If I wasn't enamored before, I was completely
smitten now. I didn't know how Brady knew she
was going to do what she did, but he did. He had
stopped me from pummeling Dirk. We left our
friend on the floor in the hallway, and I didn't have
a shred of guilt. Dirk had been causing problems
for Brady and me since high school.
The way Brady looked at Belle was with unabashed
adoration, and when she had decked Dirk, I swear
he was proud of her. I had a feeling there was more
to him and Belle than him just being her farm
hand. I felt a little punch in my gut thinking that
maybe they had shared something that had gone
sideways.

Brady

She had put Dirk flat on his arrogant ass, and I
loved it. When she had winked at me, you could
have knocked me over with a feather. It was a sexy,
fun wink, and I knew right then that she had my
heart. She was here with Kip though. I hadn't seen
them doing anything overtly romantic, so it gave
me a little hope.
I was also genuinely concerned about what she had
confided to me. I was going to talk to my dad
about it first thing tomorrow.

Belle

I could see that the crowd had thinned out and I
was feeling euphoric; kicking someone's deserving
butt must have release mega endorphins. Kip and
Brady were talking. Brady and I were talking. I'd
meet four nice women, all around my age. The
men, all except Dirk, were easy to talk to as well.
Then the best part of the night was decking Dirk. I
liked that better than Kip's kiss; was that awful?
"Belle are you ready to leave?" Kip asked. We were
standing with Brady and Jeannie next to the table.
The band was on break so we could hear each
other without shouting.
"Yes."
Jeannie giggled. "Hope you have fireworks,"
Jeannie said with a silly grin on her face.
"Fireworks?" Brady asked.
I looked up at Kip and then back to Brady. "Kip
and I are going to kiss, and if there are fireworks,
we will go on more dates."

Brady

My heart sank. She and Kip were going to kiss. She
was going to be my best friends girl. I kept the
smile plastered on my face, but inside I was dying.

Kip

I was looking at Brady when Belle said that we were going to kiss and damn if my best friend didn't look crushed. He hid it, but I knew my man better than anyone. It was only for a second, but he had the same expression on his face when he had come to my house after discovering Chelsea had been cheating on him. He was devastated. The problem was that I liked Belle. I liked everything about her. She could be the one. We got along great. I loved her old world mannerisms. I just couldn't shake the feeling that there was more to Belle and Brady than either of them had shared with me.

Belle

I was nervous as we drove back to my place. We were going to kiss. I wanted to. I think I did. I definitely knew all about the fireworks that Kip had described. I'd felt them with Brady. Could I feel fireworks with more than one man at a time? Would that make me a 'player'? Dating more than one man at a time didn't seem right. I'd had a good time tonight, but talking with Brady had been a highlight, along with decking Dirk. I missed Brady. If I did feel fireworks with Kip, I hoped Brady and I could remain friends. The strange thing was that the more I thought about kissing Kip, the less I wanted to. I liked Kip, a lot, but my feelings for him were different than how I felt about Brady. I couldn't quite put my finger on why, but it was different.

Kip pulled to a stop in front of my house, and I realized I should have put a light on before I had left. It was spooky dark, and there were no stars or moon to illuminate anything.

"I should have left a light on," I told him feeling foolish.

Kip came around the front of the car and opened my door for me. He had wonderful manners. He took his cell phone out of his pocket and used its bright screen to guide us to my porch. I opened the front door, and Kip put his hand on my arm.

"Don't you lock your house?"

"I, uh, no we never have. I don't even know where the key is." I told him sheepishly.

I reached inside the door and flipped on the front porch light and then flipped up the other switch to turn on a lamp in the living room.

I turned back to Kip. My insides were fluttering nervously.

"Would you like something to drink?"

"No thank you. Can we talk for a second?" He asked.

"Sure." Kip sat down in one of the chairs on the porch. "Don't you want to kiss?" I asked anxiously standing near him.

He chuckled. "I do, but I want to ask you something first." He gestured to the nearby chair, so I sat down.

I could tell he was struggling with what he wanted to talk about.

"Belle, would you please tell me what went on with you and Brady?"

I blushed and pushed my hair behind my ears to give me a moment to compose my answer. I didn't want to hurt Kip, but I would never lie to him either.

"When Brady worked here we had gotten close. We even kissed, and well, I thought we were special, but."

"You thought he liked you more than just a friend?"

"Yes, we did boyfriend-girlfriend things." I was blushing furiously.

"Boyfriend-girlfriend things?" I saw the moment it dawned on him what I meant by that. "So you liked him?"

"I won't lie to you, Kip. I liked him a lot. I thought we had a connection, but what the heck do I know? I'd never even talked to a boy before I met him. Anyway, he started to distance himself from me, and that's when I learned he has a girlfriend."

Kip was quiet, and I wished I knew what he was thinking.

"I've known him a long time, and I'm pretty sure he likes you."

"I thought he did too, but then." I let my voice trail off.

"Chelsea," he added for me.

"Yes, I didn't know her name. He told me tonight they aren't together, but... I don't know. I'm a little confused."

"Yeah, he hinted that he wasn't with her to me too."

"I'm glad that you and he talked tonight."

"Me too; he's my best friend."

Kip stared out into the darkness, and I watched his brow furrow as he sorted out whatever was on his mind.

He left his chair and knelt down next to me. His strong hands pulled me gently towards him. I put my hands on his wide shoulders and let him lead me to his lips. The kiss was tender and warm, but it was nothing like when Brady and I kissed. I drew back and looked at his handsome face. He knew.

"No fireworks?"

"No," I whispered.

"I had a feeling." He said getting up from his knees. I stood up with him.

"Were there fireworks for you, right now, when we kissed?"

Kip shook his head. "There was a little sizzle, but I think I've known all along that you and I were just going to be friends."

I giggled. "A little sizzle," I huffed, pretending to be offended. I softly punched his thick arm playfully.

"I was worried about kissing you," I admitted.

"You were? You should have said something."

"I wanted to try it, you know to see if our kiss would be different."

"It was, right?"

"Yes, it was," I said with a sigh. "It's strange but the entire ride home I was thinking how much I liked you, but I wasn't sure if it was at your so-called fireworks level. I don't know what it's like to have a

brother, but maybe that's what this feeling is that I
have for you? Like a brother."

Kip chuckled. "I would be honored to be your
brother Belle."

"Are you sure? I just decked your best friend and
your other best friend, well who knows what will
happen with him."

"I'm sure. So I have tomorrow off. Want to go for
a swim?"

"I'd love it!"

And just like that, I had a new friend.

I stood on the porch and waved goodbye to Kip.
He was a special man, and I wished my Gigi,
Gram, and Momma were alive because they would
have liked him as well. I walked inside thinking that
I was going to have to find the key to the front
door, and the overwhelming scent of roses
enveloped me. I flipped the light switch and looked
towards the kitchen thinking I'd see Momma
standing there.

Goosebumps ran up my arms, and I was instantly
terrified. I swiftly crossed the room and took my
gun off the rack and cautiously moved around the
downstairs looking for what was releasing the
fragrant smell. I found nothing.

Guardedly, I walked up the stairs and noticed that
the pungent aroma was getting stronger. My
stomach was knotted as I released the safety on my
Henry. At the top of the steps, I pressed myself
against the wall and flipped on the hallway light.
Not seeing anything amiss I headed down the short

hallway. I peered into my Momma's room where the smell was sickeningly pungent. I turned on her dresser lamp with my left hand allowing me to keep my Henry butted against my shoulder ready to fire, I fearfully surveyed the room.

Except for the cloying smell of roses, it was exactly as I had left it. I crossed to the window where the trellis had hung. It was shut, as were all the other windows in the room. I was reminded that I needed to get new windows as Kip had suggested. I opened Momma's closet door, but there was no sign of anything that could have emitted the rose scent.

The sweet smell was so reminiscent of my Momma that an emotional lump formed in my throat. I once again looked around the room that was now void of all my Momma's personal effects.

A slight draft wafted across the back of my legs, and the curtain ruffled ever so slightly. I turned in a circle looking for the source of the breeze that had stirred the curtain and saw nothing. I clutched my gun so tightly that my fingers ached. I had never been so afraid.

The absolutely only thing that made sense was that my Momma had returned as a ghost. It went against all my sensible beliefs, but I knew that some people did believe in the spirit world. I'd just never been one of them.

"Momma?" I whispered. My body quivered with fear. "Momma are you here?"

I cautiously walked around the room; the offending smell of roses so permeating it was nauseating.

With my heart hammering in my chest I looked
under the bed and once again in the closet.
Nothing was out of place. Maybe I really was losing
my mind. I wished that Kip had come inside. If he
had, he would have smelled the rose smell, and
then I would know for sure that I wasn't going
crazy.

I opened all the windows in Momma's room as
wide as I could and shut her door. I wished I could
lock it, but Momma's and my door did not have
locks on them. Downstairs I opened the sliders
leading out to the stone patio and the front door as
well. A cool breeze blew through the room. I
boiled a small pot of water to which I added
cinnamon, nutmeg, and a cut up apple.

I left the kitchen to change into my pajamas and
when I returned I was relieved that the floral smell
was dissipating. The cross breeze through the living
room grew stronger, and I heard thunder rumbling
off Green Mountain. It was going to storm tonight.
I watched television until I was satisfied that the
rose smell had been replaced with the smell of my
cinnamon, apple, and nutmeg concoction. A crack
of lightning startled me, and the loud thunderclap
that followed made me jump off the couch. I
wasn't a big fan of storms and tonight I was already
on edge. I turned off the television, shut the front
door, and the backslider, and then turned off the
burner before heading to bed. Once again I
brought my rifle with me, and once again I locked
my bedroom door. I didn't even crack open my
window like I usually did each night. I pulled the

covers over my head like I had when I was young, and prayed that I wouldn't hear footsteps.

I was tired, but sleep evaded me. The storm outside was a doozy. I could hear tree limbs breaking, and the wind rattled the old windowpanes, slipping into cracks creating an eerie whistling noise.

I was frightened as I cowered under my covers, and not just because of the storm. Was I losing my mind? Was someone entering my house? If they were, how could they get in and out undetected? Had Momma come back as a ghost? My final thought, before I finally drifted off to sleep was who would take care of my animals if I were to be sent to the Looney Bin?

I woke to the rooster crowing and was relieved to see that the sun was shining through my window. Kip was coming to swim today, and I wanted to finish my chores early so that we could spend as much time swimming as possible.

I changed and made coffee taking it out onto the front porch. I stood looking at the front property surveying for any damage from last night's storm. Puddles had formed in the dirt driveway, and a few large tree branches had blown down that I'd have to drag to the woods. Worried that the small old shed may have taken a hit from one of the many trees that surrounded it, I looked towards it and was surprised to see that two of my sheep were lazily munching on the grass in front of it.

I quickly looked at the barn, but with only the partial view that I had of it, I couldn't see too

much. However, for my sheep to be out,
something had to be wrong. I put my coffee down
and jogged to the barn. Pushing open the sliding
barn door I immediately looked for Henny and
Bessie. They were both fine, but I could see that
Henny was wide-eyed and her nostrils were flared.
She was scared.

An unfamiliar large triangle of natural light ran over
my feet and widened towards the back of the barn.
My heart seized when I saw that a tree had crashed
through the corner of the barn smashing into the
area of the barn where the sheep slept. The damage
had torn a large enough gap in the barn wall that
the sheep had been able to escape their inside pen.

I stepped over the leafy branches and wooden
debris to inspect the damage better. When I peered
out the jagged opening, looking for the rest of the
sheep, I saw that the tree had also knocked down
part of the fencing that enclosed the outside corral.
So that's how the two sheep to escape I thought to
myself.

I climbed through the gap in the wall to see most
of the sheep were still inside the partially enclosed
paddock. A rush of pent of relief passed through
me when I saw that no sheep had been trapped or
hurt. The docile animals were scattered around the
downed tree as if it had always been there. I started
counting. Ten plus the two out front. Two were
missing! It took me a mere second to realize that
the two missing sheep were William and Mimi.
The two sheep in my front yard were safe where
they were, and the other sheep didn't have any

interest in leaving their familiar corral, but where the heck were Mimi and William? I walked towards the nearby wooded edge. Had an animal gotten to them? Were they lost in the woods? The woods near the barn were dense, and there was a small rocky ravine about 100 yards in, but sheep would never venture that far into the woods. I looked around the barn again then ran once around the house hoping to see them. I ended up back at the edge of the woods. I couldn't believe that Mimi would go into the woods. It was very un-sheep-like, yet I knew I had to look.

I stepped past the tree line beginning of the forest looking for any signs that my sheep had passed in that direction. My heart ratcheted when I saw a small tuff of sheep's wool stuck on a thicket branch. What struck me odd was that the tuff was approximately three feet off of the ground. I reasoned that last night's wind had blown it there. I pressed on.

Even though it was a sunny, cloudless morning, the forest was so thick with trees that the sun's rays only sliced through in a few spots. Moss grew on the tree trunks, and the leaf-strewn undergrowth was wet from last night's heavy rain. Orange salamanders crawled over the damp green moss, scurrying away from me. It was inconceivable that Mimi and William would have navigated so far into the heavily wooded area.

My feet were soaked, and I was about to turn back when I heard a faint bleating. I quickened my pace and followed the sheep's cry. When I got to the ravine, my heart clamored and dread sliced through me. Mimi stood at the edge of the ledge, with a huge tree limb around her. She didn't appear to be hurt standing among the thick limb, and she was looking into the ravine. William was nowhere in sight.

I stepped into the leafy fray of the large branch to kneel by Mimi's side, and I held my breath as I peered over the ledge. William was at the bottom of the ravine, and to my immense relief I could see that he was alive, but his front leg was broken. The lamb lay on the rocks and dirt below helplessly bleating for his mom.

"I'll get him," I told Mimi confidently.

I knew William was light enough and small enough that I could carry him. However, I'd have to climb back up the rocky face with one hand. I didn't know if that was doable. I didn't want to waste time running back to the barn to get a rope. I could see that Mimi was jittery, and she was snorting, which indicated that she was frightened.

The hair stood up on the back of my neck, and I realized there was a predator nearby that had Mimi wild-eyed with panic. I glanced around the wet, thick woods seeing if I could find the source of Mimi's fear, but I didn't spot anything. It could be a wolf or a bear, but my gut said it was most likely a mountain lion. If I left William in the ravine to get a rope, chances were high that he wouldn't be there when I returned.

I first extracted Mimi from the entanglement of the large tree limb. Then I dragged the heavy limb away from the edge. Mimi stepped over the branches as I moved the limb, going right back to her spot so she could resume her watch over her baby.

Carefully I began to make my way down the slippery rocky cavern, and as I cautiously negotiated my climb downward, I formulated a plan to carry William out. I would wrap William in my shirt and tie my shirt to me so I could use both hands for the climb back up.

The rocks jutted out, creating small feet and handholds, making the climb down easier than I expected. The only difficulty was that the rocks were slick from last night's rain. I knowingly avoided any area with moss.

I looked up to make sure Mimi was all right, but a large boulder that protruded out obscured my view. I looked down to William and hastened my ascent. A strange scraping sound from above me made me look up, just in time to see a tree limb crashing towards me. The thick branch hit my shoulder, and I lost my grip, my arms pin wheeling backward as I fell. Pain exploded through my body as I hit the ground, then my vision tunneled before my world turned black.

I have no idea how long I had been passed out for. I'd never felt such pain before, even breathing hurt. William was curled up next to me; I was relieved I hadn't fallen on him. When I looked up, I could see Mimi was still standing on the ledge looking down at her baby and now me.

I couldn't move my arm; my shoulder was dislocated. I was in such agony that I wondered if I'd also broken my arm. My shirt was ripped, and there was blood coating the sleeve of the arm that I couldn't move. My foot was seriously swollen inside my barn boot, and when I moved it the pain was so sharp, it took my breath away. I methodically assessed my body for other injuries. I had a cut on my cheek that must have bled profusely, but luckily when I had passed out, my head had lulled to that side, so my cheek had been resting on a rock, which had applied pressure to the wound and stopped the bleeding. Breathing was arduous, and although I didn't think my lungs were punctured, I may have broken a rib or two. My shoulder hurt so badly that I wonder if I had also cracked my collarbone. I knew I had bruises and scrapes in places I couldn't see, but I was alive. Now I had to stay that way.

I closed my eyes because the pounding in my head was making me nauseous and the pain from my shoulder spread to my chest making it difficult to take a deep breath. It hurt to move even the slightest bit, and although a sharp rocks edge was digging into my back, I didn't dare try adjusting my position.

I passed out again because I awoke hearing someone calling my name.

My mouth was desert dry, and I think I tried to answer, but I didn't know if I was making any sound at all.

"She's down here." I heard someone yell.

Tears slid down my face, and I prayed I wasn't hallucinating.

Someone was kneeling next to me. He had blond hair and piercing blue eyes. A ray of golden sunshine surrounded his head making him appear angelic. "Are you an angle? Am I dead?"

The stranger grinned and I realized that I wasn't dead and that I had said that out loud.

"Is she okay?" I heard someone yell from above. I was pretty sure that was Mr. Bee.

"She's hurt pretty badly."

I kept staring at the handsome man kneeling next to me.

"Belle we're going to get you out of here." My man angel said.

"And William," I said weakly.

"The lamb?"

"Yes."

My angel smiled at me, he was beautiful, and I wanted to touch his pretty face, but I couldn't lift my arm. I was borderline delirious.

"My shoulder." I attempted to speak coherently.

"Shhhh, you need to stay still until we get you out of here."

My angel took off his button up shirt and laid it over me. I hadn't realized I'd been cold.

"Thirsty," I mumbled feebly.

"Hang in there Belle. My Dad ran back to your farm. We have an idea how to get you out of here."

My mind was slowly becoming less foggy. "How?"

He smiled mischievously, and my heart thudded as I took in just how good-looking he was.

"I don't want to wreck the surprise." He tried joking with me.

I wanted to smile but I was in too much pain, and I groaned instead. I was really hurting, and my vision was tunneling again. I knew I was going to pass out. With my working hand, I grabbed my angel by his forearm arm.

My head was spinning, and I hoped that I was speaking out loud. "Promise. Get William out." As I blacked out, I thought I heard him say, "I promise."

I have no idea how long I was out for but when I awoke I was in excruciating agony, and I couldn't help the pain filled moan that slipped out.

"What's happening?" I heard Mr. Bee yell down. "She just came too. She's in a lot of pain." My angel yelled up to him.

I was in my angel's strong arms, and he was laying me in an inflatable rubber raft. As soon as I was situated, he placed a mewling William against my side. I saw that the raft had ropes affixed to both ends and one was also tied around the middle. "My surprise?" I faintly said, attempting humor. He grinned at me as he finished securing a rope. "Surprise," He said softly. He was sweating as he worked, and his blue eyes conveyed his concern. He stood back from the raft.

"On belay." He yelled. The raft began to move upwards, and when it bounced off the stony ravine wall, it wasn't as painful as I anticipated.

My angel climbed up the rocks alongside me as the raft was being raised. Every once in a while he had to adjust the raft when it caught on a rock. William was snuggled into my side as I held him tightly with my good arm. I hoped he wouldn't struggle because his little hooves would hurt my already sore ribs. My angel remained in my line of sight the entire time. I think he knew it reassured me.

When the raft breeched the ravine two faces peered down at me, one of them was Mr. Bee, the other man I didn't know, but I swear the second he saw me he blanched.

"Dad. Dad!" My angel was saying to the man I didn't know. The man that was staring at me shook his head as if to clear his mind and looked at my angel who must have been his son.

"Let's go." The man said quickly.

"Mimi?" I mumbled.

"She's right next to you." Mr. Bee said. Poor Mr. Bee looked so upset.

My angel carried the front of the raft, and his dad carried the back of it. Mr. Bee must have been in charge of Mimi because I kept hearing him trying to herd her behind us.

When we got to, the farm the two men placed the raft into the back of a large truck bed.

"Water?" I asked.

Mr. Bee ran inside my house and came out with a glass. I couldn't sit up to drink, so my angel helped me, but I still ended up choking. That hurt like heck and my vision spun again.

"Belle, we are taking you to the clinic. What should we do with William?"

With my tongue finally working from the tiny sip
of water I had choked down, I was able to speak.
"Can you ask Mr. Bee to take him to Dr. Lachlan?"
My angel carefully lifted William out of the raft and
handed him to Mr. Bee.

I watched as the handsome man handed little
William to Mr. Bee. He was so adept with William
that my addled brain formed a little crush on my
man angel.

"She said to take the lamb to Dr. Lachlan."

"My other animals," I panted laboriously. I was
distressed thinking of them not being fed.

"I'll come back and take care of them." He touched
my cheek softly before moving my blood-caked
hair off my face. His lips thinned with a noticeable
grimace. I assumed because he had just touched my
bloody face.

"You don't have to touch me." I gritted out as the
pain in my shoulder heightened.

He looked down at me and cocked his head with a
questioning look as to why I had said that. He must
have figured it out because the next thing he did
was to dampen a rag with the water from my glass,
and with a sweet smile, he began to gently wipe off
my face.

"You're so beautiful," he whispered almost shyly.
He then banged on the cabs back window, and I
felt the truck move.

I shut my eyes because the trucks motion was
jarring my shoulder. Tears slide down my face, and
my angel softly dabbed them away.

"You can cry, Belle. I know you're hurting." My angel was holding my good hand. I was so nauseous I couldn't respond.

The truck finally stopped, and the two men carried the raft, with me still in it, into the town's medical clinic. A nurse waved them into a room and then began asking so many questions that my head began to spin.

"Listen," The older man said harshly. "I will personally pay for this visit. Just get the damn doctor in here now!"

The nurse huffed and left the room.

The older man peered into the raft.

"Belle, I'm Samuel Fitzpatrick. This is my son, Adam."

"Hi," I managed to eek out.

"Can you tell us what happened?"

"I went down into the ravine to get William." I looked away trying to think. What the heck had happened after that?

"I'm not sure," I told him shakily.

The doctor came into the room.

"Miss Janson, I'm Dr. Travers. Can you tell me what happened?"

"I don't remember," I answered starting to panic.

"Don't worry, that sometimes happens. It will come back to you. I called the Sheriff."

I nodded, but then winced since even that movement hurt.

"Gentleman, I'm going to ask you to help me lift her out of the raft and onto the table, and then I'm going to ask you to leave the room for proprietary reasons."

I felt myself being lifted out of the raft and I couldn't help the small whimpers that tumbled from my lips. My angel Adam looked worried, and I wanted to ask who they were, but the doctor shooed them from the room.

Two hours later my shoulder was back in its socket, and my arm was in a sling that lay across my stomach. That same arm had stitches on the side of my forearm. My collarbone, which had broken, was held firmly in place with a big strap. My ankle was sprained, but not broken. The doctor had had to cut my new barn boot off. My foot was wrapped, and a constant changing of ice packs had begun. I had a mild concussion. If this was mild, I couldn't imagine what a non-mild one would feel like. The cut on my cheek had steri-strips holding it together. All in all, I deemed myself lucky. The nurse had washed me as best she could, and she had even untangled my hair. I was in a short blue hospital gown, on a bed in a white-walled room that smelled like lemons and bleach. I hadn't seen anyone except the doctor and the nurse since the doctor had sent the two Fitzpatrick men out of my room.

A knock sounded on my door, and Sheriff McDaniel walked in followed by the doctor. "Belle, how are you feeling?" The Sheriff asked walking to me. His hand grasped my good hand

and the fatherly squeeze he gave me let me know I wasn't as alone as I felt.

"My head hurts, and I'm pretty sore," I told him honestly.

"I gave her some pain meds." The doctor told him.

"And I still hurt? That can't be good." I said trying to joke.

The Sheriff and the doctor had the good grace to chuckle, but then the Sheriff sat down in the chair next to my bed, and his face looked serious.

"Belle, what happened?"

I sighed. "A tree crushed the side of the barn. The sheep got out. I went into the woods looking for William, and Mimi. I heard Mimi, and I followed her cries. William was at the bottom of the ravine. Mimi was standing in a big tree limbs branches. I moved the limb from the edge and went down to get William and." My voice trailed off, and tears rolled down my cheeks as I suddenly remembered what had happened. The tree limb, that's what I had forgotten. There is no way that tree limb could have fallen down the ravine. I had moved it too far from the edge.

The Sheriff must have sensed that I had just remembered something. "Belle, tell me."

"I think someone threw the tree limb that I had moved, down the ravine on top of me."

The Sheriff rubbed his face with his hand. The man looked uncharacteristically stressed.

"Belle, the tree that fell on your barn. I checked it out. I'm pretty sure someone cut it so it would fall."

I was staring at the Sheriff. I couldn't believe what he had just said.

"Belle, did you hear me?

"Someone wanted to hurt my animals?"

"Honey, I think someone is trying to hurt you."

"Why? Who?" I started to shake.

A knock on my door drew our attention, and the doctor opened it to the Fitzpatrick men standing there. The doctor left after allowing the two men to enter my room.

"What's the matter?" Adam said coming right to the bed to stand by me.

The Sheriff stood up. "I'm the Sheriff. Are you the men that brought Belle in?"

Samuel and Adam shook the Sheriff's hand.

"Yes, we found her. We were with Nathan."

I realized the men knew Mr. Bee by his first name.

"I'd like to talk to you two outside if I may?" The Sheriff said.

"First tell me why Belle's upset?" Adam said recognizing that I was distressed.

The Sheriff looked to me, and I could see that he was deciding what to say. I guess he decided to tell them the truth.

"I think Belle has been the victim of someone trying to hurt her. The tree that hit her barn had been cut, and I bet when I go to the ravine I'll find evidence that the limb that caused her to fall was thrown on her.

Adam looked at the sheriff then to me, and I saw his jaw tense. He did not look happy. He kept glancing at his father.

The Sheriff motioned to Samuel and Adam to follow him. Adam remained by my side.

"I'll be out in a second," He told the Sheriff. I could see that Sheriff McDaniel wasn't comfortable leaving me alone with Adam. The Sheriff looked at me, and I nodded letting him know it was okay.

"You look better," Adam said cautiously, giving me a little grin.

I smiled, but my cheek hurt, so I think it was a little lopsided. I put my hand on my cheek.

"I keep forgetting that's there," I told him referring to my cut. He took my hand from my face and held it gently. I don't know why I didn't mind him holding my hand. He felt safe.

"We took care of the animals." He said sitting on the bed's edge carefully, so he didn't jostle me.

"Thank you. Did you, I mean no disrespect, but did you know what to do?"

Adam was grinning. "Piece of cake."

"Really?"

"Yeah, we have a big spread, and I love working with the animals when I get a chance."

"Who are you? I asked quietly. "Why were you with Mr. Bee?" My eyes were growing heavy from the pain meds.

"We can talk about that later." He said rubbing his thumb on the top of my hand.

"So secretive" I replied sleepily

"I don't mean to be." He answered softly.

The doctor returned, and Adam left telling me not to worry about the animals. I was worried though. I knew they were probably okay, for now, but what

about in a day or two? The doctor checked my
heart rate and looked into my eyes and then gave
my hand a fatherly pat.

"You need to rest, Belle."

"I know. I'm just pretty sore." I said causing the
doctor to chuckle.

"Belle, you got hit by a tree and fell onto rocks.
You should be feeling sore, very sore. I'm going to
give you something to help you sleep, okay?"

"Okay, but I'm feeling sleeping now." No sooner
than I said the word 'now,' he pushed a syringe into
my arm.

The doctor marked some notes down on a tablet
that he had and as I watched him leave my eyes
closed and I was out.

I have no idea what time it was when I opened my
eyes again, but as my eyes adjusted to the light, I
looked out the nearby window and saw that it was
still light out. Adam was sitting in the chair next to
my bed leafing through a magazine. His one leg
was crossed over his knee, faded blue jeans encased
his long legs, and he wore brown cowboy boots
that were scuffed and well used. He had on a
different shirt than the last time I'd seen him. This
one was black with a pocket, and it stretched just
so perfectly over his sculpted chest and shoulders. I
could see that he had an athletic build. Not big and
muscled like Kip, and maybe not even as defined as
Brady, but he was clearly strong. His muscles were
formed from hard work, not a gym.

"Hi," I said drowsily.

He jumped up from the chair. "Hi."

How long was I asleep?"

"A few hours. It's after 5:00. My dad and Mr. Bee just went to get us something to eat."

I looked around the room self-consciously.

"Where's the doctor?"

"Are you hurting?" Adam asked quickly. "I can go get him."

"No, no it's just. I don't even know you, and you're sitting in my hospital room with me."

Just then Mr. Bee and Samuel came into the room. "Oh good, you're awake." Mr. Bee said hurrying to my side. He planted a fatherly kiss on my forehead. "How are you feeling?"

"Better, but I um, could you get the nurse for me?" The men looked flustered, and Samuel left the room quickly bringing back the nurse within seconds. The nurse came to my bedside, and I whispered to her that I needed to go to the bathroom.

"She's fine." She said to the men in the room who I saw appeared anxious. "She needs to use the bathroom."

All three men muttered various forms of "Oh," and I noticed that Adam looked especially relieved.

"We need a little privacy please." She said, and the men practically ran from the room.

The nurse, who told me her name was Margaret, pulled a plastic bowl shaped like a toilet seat from under the night side table. I recognized it as a bed toilet.

"Can't I use the real bathroom?"

"Not yet."

"Really?" I was whining.

"Really. Now come on and help me if you can."
The nurse pulled my sheet down, and I lifted my rear off the bed using my one leg as leverage as she pushed the bowl under my behind. She left the room, and I quickly did my business and wiped using the toilet paper she had handed me. Then I managed to pull the small bowl out from underneath me and put it on the nightstand. Margaret returned a minute later and praised me for not spilling on the sheets. After she emptied the plastic bowl out in the bathroom, she gave me a hand wipe to clean my hands off with, and then she let the men back into the room.

Adam used the remote to adjust my head, so I was sitting up. He was adamant that I was comfortable, and he kept asking if I needed a pillow behind me, or if the position he had the head of the bed in was okay. It was rather cute. Mr. Bee must have thought so too because he was smiling happily. When Adam was satisfied that I was comfortable, he slid a small table across my lap, and Mr. Bee unloaded food onto the table.

"Hope you like burgers, Belle?" Samuel said.

"I do." I nodded reaching for one. Adam was very attentive for someone who didn't know me. He took it from my hand and unwrapped it, and then he dumped a small bag of fries out alongside the burger organizing my meal for me.

"Thank you," I said making sure I made eye contact with him, so he knew how sincere I was.

His smile lite his whole face up, and I swear he blushed. I ate slowly because chewing hurt my face, and I still wasn't feeling well. I managed to eat half my burger and was picking at my fries, deep in thought, as the men talked. I wasn't even listening to them. I had no idea who Samuel and Adam were and I wanted to know why they were at my farm. Mr. Bee would never walk around my farm without asking permission first. It was unusual.

Mr. Bee broke through my deep thoughts. "Belle, Dr. Lachlan said to tell you that William is going to be fine. He has a busted leg, and she's going to keep him until it's weight bearing."

I put the fry down I'd been toying with. "Thank goodness. I was so worried about him." I looked at the three men in my room, and even though my head felt like a hammer was pounding on me, I decided enough was enough.

"So," I looked at Samuel and Adam, "can you please tell me why you were with Mr. Bee at my place?" The room got very quiet. My belly flip-flopped nervously.

"Maybe it's not the best time." Mr. Bee said with concern in his voice.

"It's a perfect time," I said picking up a fry. I watched the men uneasily. "I'm a captive audience." Once again I attempt humor to break up the tension in the room.

"Belle, did your Mom ever mention my name?" Samuel asked.

"No."

I saw him look at Mr. Bee.

"Belle, I was dating your Mom."

The air whooshed from my lungs as if I'd been punched in the stomach. I let that awkward snippet of information sink in. Now I knew why he had looked at me in the woods the way he had. I looked so much like my Momma. He probably thought he saw a ghost.

I still harbored doubts. "Why didn't you come to her funeral?" I asked skeptically.

"I was out of the country. I'm very sorry for your loss Belle. You're Mom, well she was a pretty special woman."

I nodded willing myself not to tear up. I also knew there was more to it. "What aren't you telling me?" I said looking from him to Adam then to Mr. Bee. My lower lip was quivering. I hated to appear emotional, but I was.

"Belle." Mr. Bee said coming to stand near me. "This is the man that wants to buy your property."

I let the fry in my finger drop back to my wrapper. Emotions and unease ripped through me.

"So, you're just here, being nice to me, because you want my property?" I choked out.

"No, no way Belle," Adam said vehemently. He looked genuinely upset. I wanted to believe him, but I had doubts.

"Why were you at my farm then?"

Samuel answered. "I found out about your Mom from Nathan when I got back to the States. I wanted to talk to Nathan, but I couldn't reach him. Adam and I were passing through town to go rafting this afternoon. We ran into Nathan this

morning at the diner, and I asked if he had given
you our latest offer. He said he had not. I
suggested that we all go to your house so I could
formally introduce myself to you. I also wanted to
pay my respects to you." His voice softened. "I
know your Mom is buried on your property. I had
hoped to say good-bye to her."

The room got awkwardly quiet.

Mr. Bee dispelled the unease. "It's true Belle. I had
tried to call you, and when you didn't answer, I
assumed you were in the barn. They followed me
to your house this morning. When we arrived the
sheep were in the front yard, and you weren't
around. When I saw the damage to the barn, well, I
knew something was wrong."

"We looked everywhere for you," Adam said softly.

"How did you find me?"

"We went into the woods, and Dad heard the
sheep."

I thought it strange that they would be looking in
the woods, but then I realized I had gone into the
woods myself looking for the sheep so maybe it
wasn't so far-fetched.

I was feeling drained, and my headache was making
me nauseous. The food that I had been enjoying a
minute ago sat like a lead ball in my stomach.

The men understood that I was processing
everything, and they had the good sense to remain
quiet. Adam appeared concerned, or was he simply
feeling guilty? I hated thinking that about him; after
all, he had saved me.

"Belle, would you like something else to eat?" Mr. Bee asked.

"No, no thank you. I'm actually a little tired." I wasn't really tired, but I needed to think. I just learned who the man was that had put that dreamy smile on my Momma's face night after night, and I also now knew who wanted to buy my property. I did not like that they were one in the same. If Momma had been going to Springfield to meet Samuel the night she died, then why did he say he was out of the country when she died? Was she meeting someone else? I had so many questions. Samuel and Mr. Bee left my room after cordially saying that they hope I felt better soon. Mr. Bee promised to return tomorrow. Adam remained behind. He was looking at me with anxious uncertainty. I think he thought I was going to yell at him.

"Belle, are you mad?"

"I don't know what I am," I answered honestly. Adam sat on the side of my bed and picked up my hand. "I'm sorry about your Mom. My Mom died too, but it was a long time ago."

"Did you know our parents were dating?"

"Not until today."

I sighed. I knew the pain medicine was wearing off because my body was beginning to ache, along with my head. I grimaced as I adjusted my back against the pillow.

"Are you in pain? Do you want me to get the doctor?"

The door to my room flew open, and Brady and Kip burst in. Adam jumped off the bed, putting himself between them and me. He was being protective and even though I knew I had to remain prudent around him because he and his dad wanted my land I couldn't help but feel grateful that even though he knew so little about me, he was protective of me. The three large, men stared daggers at each other.

Brady didn't take his eyes from me as he took in my injuries.

"Who are you?" Kip ask Adam a bit heatedly.

"Adam Fitzpatrick, and you are?"

"Friends of Belle's," Brady said pushing past Adam to stand near me and effectively making Adam retreat from my side. Brady took up the hand that Adam had just been holding and I saw Adam's expression harden as he observed Brady's obvious concern for me.

Brady's eyes remained locked on to mine, and I had to remind myself that he and I were simply friends.

"Belle, what happened?"

"Someone tried to hurt her," Adam told the men.

"What?" Kip was immediately concerned looking at me for details.

"I'm pretty tired, and I don't want to talk about it," I said wearily.

"You damn well better talk about it," Brady said heatedly.

"Don't you talk to her like that!" Adam said getting into Brady's face.

The two men stood facing each other and Kip wedged his body between them. The tension in the room was thick and thank goodness Kip had his head on straight.

"Guys, think of Belle." He whispered, but I heard him.

Brady looked at me then to Adam. He took a step back and then sat on the edge of my bed.

Adam turned to me. "Belle, I'm going to head out. Dad and I are staying in town for a week, maybe longer. I'll come see you tomorrow if that's okay?"

"Yes, thank you Adam, and thank you for taking care of the animals."

Brady's head shot up upon hearing that.

Adam came to the side of the bed that Brady wasn't sitting on and touched his fingertips to my arm. "I'll go back tomorrow morning."

"I'll be taking care of Belle's animals," Brady said glaring at Adam.

Adam looked at me then to Brady and shrugged his shoulders. I could tell he wasn't sure what Brady's and my relationship was, and I was annoyed that Brady had been rude to him. Adam had been wonderful today.

"It's okay Adam, Brady knows my animals."

My angel leaned down to place a kiss on my forehead.

"I'll be back tomorrow Belle. If you need me, call the B & B." That was an indirect message to Brady that he wasn't going away and Brady knew it too.

"Adam, thank you for everything you did today, saving me, taking care of my animals. Please come back tomorrow."

Adam smiled, and I knew I had successfully placated him.

After Adam left Brady seemed to calm down.

"Belle, please tell us what happened," Kip asked sitting down in the chair.

"And who was that guy?" Brady added tersely.

I shot Brady a look that told him I was not pleased with him and he hung his head and apologized. He knew he was out of line. I then told them about seeing the sheep on the front lawn and then how the tree had damaged the barn, which had allowed for the sheep to escape. I then told them that Brady's dad said the tree near the barn had been purposely cut. Brady stiffened, and Kip mutter something under his breath. I then explained how I'd gone looking for Mimi and William and what had happened at the rocky gulley.

"You mean someone threw a tree limb down on top of you while you were climbing into the ravine?" Kip couldn't believe it.

"Did anything weird happen last night Belle?" Brady asked.

"She was with me last night," Kip told him brusquely.

"I meant after," Brady said tiredly.

I looked at Kip almost apologetically. He knew nothing of the craziness I'd been dealing with.

"When I went inside, after our date," I said looking at Kip first, then back to Brady. "I smelled roses. It was overwhelming."

"Roses?" Brady asked.

"Her Momma liked the smell of roses," Kip told him.

"Oh." Brady didn't look too pleased that Kip knew that.

"I tried to find the source, but I couldn't. I think I'm going nuts. " I confided quietly. "I was thinking it was Momma's ghost visiting me."

Brady rubbed my hand with his. "Belle, you're not going nuts. I think whoever cut down the tree and tried to hurt you today has been getting into your house and messing with you."

"What else has been going on? Kip asked.

I sighed. I was worn-out, and the pain had become a steady pulse that was almost unbearable.

"I've heard footsteps. My rifle disappeared and magically re-appeared. A shut window somehow gets opened. You already know about the fire."

"Shit," Kip said.

"How damaged is the barn?" Brady asked.

"Pretty bad. I didn't get a good look at it. I was too worried about the sheep. Brady are you really going to do the animals, because Adam..."

"Don't even say it." He said holding up his hand interrupting me.

The doctor came into the room.

"How's my patient?" He said approaching the bed.

"I've been better." I tried to be upbeat.

"You haven't had any pain medicine in a while; I'm sure you are in pain, young lady."

"Can you give her something?" Brady asked the doctor.

"Yes, I'm going to give her something right now and then you two need to leave so she can rest. Rest is the best way for her to heal."

I smiled. "My Gigi use to say that."

The doctor gave me two shots this time and when I grimaced I swear Brady did too.

"Okay boys say good night."

Kip leaned down and kissed my cheek. "For the record, I called to tell you I couldn't swim today because there was a car fire."

"How did you find out about me being here?"

"Brady."

Kip left the room, but Brady remained at my side. He answered me before I even asked. "My Dad called me." Brady paused, and I could see by his expression that he was troubled. "Belle, I'm really worried about you."

"Me too," I answered him in a strangled whisper.

"I wish I had been there for you." He whispered back. His fingers stroked mine unconsciously.

"I'm just grateful someone found me."

"I'll take care of the barn and the animals. Don't worry about them. Please get better."

"Okay, thank you, Brady." I was feeling the pull of sleep, and I wasn't sure if I had even spoken my thank you out loud.

He tenderly brushed the back of his fingers across my cheek. My eyes closed and I succumbed to blissful unconsciousness.

Brady

I watched her drift off to sleep.
"I am so glad there were no fireworks," I whispered to her even though I knew she was already asleep.

21

Adam

The second I saw her lying injured in the ravine, I had wanted to protect her. She had that rare beauty that stole a man's breath away. It was all natural too. Her hair hadn't been colored. Her face was clear of makeup. When she had regained consciousness, she had tried so hard to be brave, but I knew how badly she was hurting. When she made me promise to bring up her injured lamb I knew I was a-goner.

After I left Belle's room the first time, I went to the clinic's lounge where the Sheriff was waiting for me. The Sheriff had just started to question my Dad when he got a call and had to leave. We agreed to meet in the same lounge in a few hours. That was fine with me because I wanted to change out of my dirty clothes and return so I could sit with Belle.

I had gone back to my room, showered changed and hurried back to Belle's room. I knew she had no family and I wanted to make sure that when she awoke, she would not be alone.

When she did wake up and saw me sitting in the chair, I could see the surprise on her face. I was a little nervous how she would react to me being there, so when she smiled at me my world literally tilted.

The second time I left Belle's room I was still chewing on the fact that I had left two men in her room, and one of them seemed pretty possessive of her, and I did not like it one bit. My phone pinged, and I saw that my dad had texted me to meet him and the Sheriff in the lounge.

When I got to the small room, the doctor was just leaving, and my dad was already inside the Sheriff. I guess the Sheriff was conducting all his interviews from here.

The Sheriff wanted to know why we had been at Belle's farm

My dad explained that he and I were with Mr. Bee to see Belle. He explained how we had found her and how we rigged the raft to bring her out of the ravine and then transported her to the clinic.

The Sheriff was pretty thorough, and he wanted to know specifically why we were there. My Dad explained that he had wanted to pay his respects to Belle regarding her mother.

The Sheriff asked my dad how he knew Eliza and my Dad asked if that was relative.

"I'm just trying to understand why you and your boy here were at Belle's farm." The Sheriff replied calmly.

"I met Eliza in Nathan's office two months ago." My dad answered.

"And you started dating?" The Sheriff had obviously done his homework.

"That's right."

"Seems odd that Belle didn't know about you two? The Sheriff tapped his pen on his knee.

I remained quiet because I was just as interested as the Sheriff in my Dad's answers.

"Eliza was going to sell me her property. She didn't want Belle to know."

"Where were you when Eliza was killed in the car accident?"

"I was in Europe. Spain, to be exact, you can check that out."

"I will."

"So you didn't know she had been killed?"

"No. I never called the house; she didn't want Belle to answer the phone. She always called me. When I didn't hear from her for a week, I called Nathan. That's when he told me the terrible news."

I noticed my dad was fidgeting. He wasn't the type to displaying emotions; I could sure attest to that. It was pretty obvious he did not like the Sheriff asking about his love life.

"So today, how did you happen to be at Belle's farm?"

My father answered. "We were having breakfast at the diner before we were going rafting. I saw Nathan, and I asked if he had told Belle of our latest offer. He said he had not. I suggested I meet with her in person and deliver the offer myself. I also wanted to pay my respects, and I had hoped Nathan would arrange that. Nathan said he would call Belle as soon as he got to his office and tell her we were stopping by. Adam and I decided to hold off on the rafting trip so we could meet with Belle. We left the diner and went back to the Inn to change."

"Change?"

"We were in board shorts and tee shirts Sheriff. We changed into more appropriate attire. I wanted to make a good impression."

"So you and your boy went back to the Inn and then what?"

"We." My father began, but the Sheriff held up his hand and pointed at me. "I'd like to hear from your son please."

My dad gestured to me, and I swear he grimaced. He liked to be in charge.

"Well like my dad said, we went back to the Inn. We changed, and then we met Nathan in front of his office."

"So you and your dad were together the entire time at the Inn?"

"Well, no. We have separate rooms." I said glancing at my dad.

The Sheriff paused for a second to write something down.

"Then what happened?"

"We met Nathan in front of his office. He said he hadn't been able to reach Belle, but he said she was probably in the barn. He didn't think it would be a problem to drop in on her." I added.

"So when you got to her farm?" The Sheriff prompted.

"Nathan commented that the two sheep that were on her front lawn should not have been there. He knocked on the door, and when no one answered, he started calling for her. He was surprised she hadn't met up when we drove in. We walked to the barn and that's when we knew something had happened. A tree had knocked the barn wall. It was the sheep's corral that was damaged. Nathan counted the sheep and told us that two were missing."

"Go on."

"Nathan was really upset, so we started looking for Belle, he said there was no way she would leave her sheep in her yard. Dad noticed some broken branches leading into the woods near that side of the barn. We fanned out, and Dad heard the mother sheep. I saw Belle lying in the ravine. I thought she was dead. Shit." I swore softly thinking about seeing Belle lying on those rocks.

"Take your time son." My dad said putting his hand on my shoulder.

"She was breathing, but I knew she was hurt. My dad ran back to the truck and got our raft and some rope. We hauled her up and brought her here."

I spread my hands out indicating that was all I had to say.

The Sheriff looked as if he wanted to ask more questions.

"So you never met Belle before? Never even been out to her place?" He asked me.

"No Sir."

"What about you?" he asked my dad. My dad hesitated before answering. Why did he sound so off?

"I've been there before. I was with the surveyors. Eliza had taken Belle into town. Eliza had told me

I would have an hour to do the surveying near the house. The rest was done up the mountain."

"And all the secrecy was because Eliza did not want Belle to know that she was going to sell you her families land?"

"That's right." My Dad answered firmly.

"So let's go back to last night." The Sheriff said looking at my dad.

"What time did you and your son check in?"

"Around 4:00."

"And you ate dinner, where?"

"The diner around 5:00."

"And then?"

"We turned in."

"Pretty early to turn in."

My dad shrugged. "I had work to do on my computer."

"And you?"

"I was doing work on my computer too."

"So neither of you left the Inn?"

We both told him no.

"Sheriff, do we need a lawyer?" My dad asked.

"You can always have a lawyer Mr. Fitzpatrick, but answering my questions without one goes a long way to my believing you."

"We have had a long day. We're staying at the B&B if you need us."

My dad stood up, and I followed suit.

"Why are you staying here for a week?" The Sheriff asked.

"I still want the property Sheriff. It's business."

The Sheriff shook his head, and I could tell he did not like my dad, and I recognized the feeling was mutual.

"One more question." The Sheriff said as we all stood. "Why were you in town?"

My father sighed and looked out the window. "Like I said before Adam and I were going rafting. The best river is Buck's bend."

I knew that was true and Buck's bend was only ten miles from town.

The Sheriff extended his hand to my dad. "Thank you for rescuing her."

My Dad shook his hand, and the Sheriff continued. "She's had a tough time lately, and my family has grown fond of her."

I shook the Sheriff's hand then my dad, and I left the room. I couldn't help but think that he was giving my dad and I a backhanded message. Belle was not to be trifled with.

As I went back to the B&B, I thought about the beautiful, brave girl lying in the clinic. I was going to be in Lansing for a week, and I was going to make an effort to get to know Belle Janson, not for business reasons but because she had made me want to be happy again. I hadn't been happy in a long while.

I had returned from Syria a few months ago. I had not re-upped, and I was feeling the Soldiers guilt knowing many of my friends were still in harm's way. War was a nasty business, and after graduating from West Point I served my country and although

I loved my country and was proud to serve I was also ready to move on.

I took some time to myself and stayed at our family home in Aspen, Colorado. I skied and hit the bars every night and then my dad said he wanted me to join him in his business. Dad's business was to acquire buildings, property, even other businesses, and resell them. When he bought a business, he would dismantle it or do a quick turn around the sale. He would knock down buildings and put up new one's; better ones, expensive ones. He would buy land because he knew someone else wanted it, and then he'd jack the price up. Sometimes he would be commissioned to buy property for someone who preferred to remain anonymous until after it was acquired. I wasn't sure I was cut out for his business. It was very profitable, and I knew the lifestyle I enjoyed was paid for from his hard work. I was still learning the business. I wasn't hardened emotionally like my dad, I didn't think I was, and in this business, you had to take out any emotional entanglement. Last week I had obtained my first property from a down on his luck rancher, and I sold it to a corporation that was going to redevelop the land into a housing development. When the farmer had signed his property over, the man broke down and cried. I felt horrible, but my dad was pleased as could be. He told me someone was going to buy the land and it might as well be us. I knew then that I needed to find a different job. The problem was that my dad was so happy that I was working with him and I didn't want to disappoint him.

Now I was in a real bind. My dad wanted Belle's property and when he wanted something he got it. I didn't want to disappoint my dad, but after meeting the woman that now own the land he wanted, I didn't think I could play the tough real estate investor if it meant hurting Belle.

Brady

When I heard what happened to Belle from my Mom, who heard it at the market from Mrs. Bee, I drove to Kip's house. If Kip was dating Belle, if she had felt those f-ing fireworks, and they were together, he needed to know. It killed me, but if they were going to be a couple, I was going to have to deal with it. The thought of them being together had me in knots, and I had even been contemplating moving from Lansing. I knew that was not a great way to deal with a problem, but I cared for Belle, a lot, and Kip was my best friend. I didn't know if I could handle seeing them all lovey-dovey day in and day out. I had to keep reminding myself that the last time I had run from a problem my damn foot had gotten blown off.

When I got to Kip's, I told him what I knew, which wasn't much, and he jumped into my truck as we headed to the clinic.

We were both thinking about Belle, so as I sped down the main road towards the clinic neither of us was talking. We had no idea how badly she was hurt, and that was scaring the crap out of me.

"There were no fireworks Brady," Kip said randomly, breaking the silence.

I almost veered off the road. I looked at him to see if he was joking.

The big ape had a shit-eating grin on his face.

"No fireworks?" I said hoping he wasn't yanking my chain.

"Nope."

"So you kissed?" I didn't like that they had even kissed.

"Just a small smooch, nothing crazy."

I glanced at him again. My knuckles were white as I gripped my steering wheel.

"Spit it out, Kip," I told him, not liking that he was drawing out what I needed to hear.

"We had a good talk. I like her Brady, she's different, special, beautiful, kind, and she is fun to be with."

"I know," I said softly. "I know."

"She told me that when you two kissed, there had been fireworks."

"She did?" I could not keep the stupid grin off my face.

"Yeah, and judging from how you're grinning, and how you've been acting I think you felt them too."

"Understatement," I admitted.

"I just don't get why you pushed her away? She liked you, and then you basically dumped on her. That's harsh."

"I'm an idiot. It was all because I was talking to Chelsea. She wanted to get back together. I didn't want to lead Belle on while I was figuring things out. I think I allowed Chelsea back in because I never had the closure I needed when our relationship ended. It was fast and unexpected, and when Chelsea started talking to me again, we slipped back into that comfortable, familiar zone. I don't know what I was expecting. Honest to God Kip the entire time I was with Chelsea, all I did was think of Belle. I realized I was totally over Chelsea and that I liked Belle far more than I thought I did. Chelsea lost it when I told her. She got pretty nasty. By then I had already lost Belle. Pretty messed up right?"

"I'm going to lay my cards on the table," Kip said looking at me while I drove.

"If Belle doesn't take you back I'm going to try to make the fireworks happen for her and me. Understand?"

"Yeah." I acknowledged him, "I understand. Whatever happens, I just want her to be happy."

Kip raised an eyebrow, "Okay then."

I had so much to do to win Belle back. I had no idea if I could, plus Kip was good looking, had a great job, and he was a genuinely good guy too. What the hell did I have to offer her?

We parked and jogged through the small clinic looking for her room. A nurse named Margaret pointed us to Belle's room. When I opened the door and saw that guy sitting on her bed holding her hand I saw red. Kip's hand on my shoulder was the only thing that kept me grounded. I could tell by how he gripped me that he hadn't been pleased seeing the man with her either.

After we left Belle's room, I saw Adam and an older man come out of a room down the hall, followed by my dad. Adam shot me a formidable scowl, and I gave it right back to him.
"How is she?" My dad asked when we reached him.
"She's asleep now. She really got hurt dad."
My dad chuckled. "She has a dislocated shoulder, a cracked collarbone, a sprained ankle, and bruises and cuts all over her little body. She's lucky she's alive."
Just hearing all of her injuries made me sick.
"Mom said it wasn't an accident?"
"Brady I really should not be discussing this." He said looking at Kip.
I interrupted him. "Do you know she's been hearing footsteps at night?"
My dad's eyes got wide, and he shook his head.
"And that last night she smelled roses throughout the house?"
"Maybe we should have a little sit-down." My dad said.
I tossed Kip my car keys, "I'll pick it up later okay?'
Kip nodded.
I followed my dad to his car.
Before I got in, I looked over the roof to him.
"Should we be leaving her here alone, unguarded?"
"The doctors here, well for a little while. A nurse will be nearby."

I rolled my eyes at my dad. If someone wanted to hurt Belle, a nurse was not going to be a roadblock. Dad got my point.

"Okay, I'll send over a deputy.

"Don't bother. I'll be staying with her."

"Brady they won't let you stay with her, you're not family."

"They will if you tell them too," I said as I got into the car.

I knew where we were going. We were heading to Belle's. On the drive there I told him everything I knew.

When we got to Belle's, we walked through her house and then out to the barn. Dad showed me where the tree had been cut. I could see that the sheep's corral had been patched up with material from the barn. It would work for now. I figured that guy Adam had done that. The animals were all in for the night, and everything seemed to be in order.

Dad and I made our way to the ravine, and I was shaking when I saw how big the limb was that had been tossed down on her.

"She's lucky Mr. Bee, and the Fitzpatrick's came by," Dad said.

"Who are they?"

"They want to buy Belle's property."

"No way!"

"Yeah, and I got to say this incident might be helping Belle to make up her mind."

"Sort of makes them suspects don't you think?" I said to my dad.

"Yes, it does," he answered.

We walked back to the house and looked around once more. There was a very faint smell of roses, but it was masked with a cinnamon apple smell. I smiled thinking that Belle had probably concocted something to get rid of the rose smell.

"Brady I know you want to protect Belle, but if she's still mad at you, I don't think that's such a good idea."

"We're talking dad," I said quickly.

"I'm worried about leaving her animals out here unprotected." dad said thoughtfully.

He was right, and I was annoyed with myself that I had not thought of that.

"Shit, you're right. I better stay here, but you have to put a deputy outside her room."

My dad smiled seeing how concerned I was.

"And can you come back for me around seven so I can go get my truck and see Belle?"

"7?"

"Dad, please? Oh, and can you bring me a change of clothes?"

My dad chuckled got in his car, and I watched him drive off.

After he left, I made sure the animals were secure and took note of what I needed to buy to permanently fix the fence and barn wall. I was rehiring myself as Belle's farm hand. I figured she would be able to leave the clinic tomorrow, and I didn't want her worrying about anything except getting better. I just had to convince her to give me my job back.

The sun was setting so I headed inside and made an egg sandwich for dinner. I settled on the couch for the night. I didn't feel comfortable sleeping in a bed, even though there were three spare rooms, especially since Belle did not even know I was in her house. I decided to call Mr. Bee and tell him that I was there.

"That's nice of you Brady." I heard him hesitate.

"Don't worry Mr. Bee; we're talking to each other."

"Oh, that's fine then, excellent actually. I'm sure she will appreciate you staying there." I could hear the relief in his voice.

"I'm planning on staying here when she comes home too," I told him. I didn't even know I was going to say that, it just popped out of my mouth, but as soon as I said it I knew it was exactly what I wanted to do. If she allowed me too, that is.

"Mrs. Bee and I were thinking that we should hire a nurse for her."

"Hold off on that. I'll talk to Belle tomorrow. I want to help her with the farm while she recuperates, and it's probably best that I stay here 24-7, so I can help her too."

"That's up to Belle."

"I hear you, Mr. Bee."

"Thank you for staying there tonight."

"No problem."

I took a pillow from Belle's room and used the throw as a cover. The pillow smelled like Belle. I inhaled her scent and thought about her. It had hit me hard seeing her in that hospital bed. Seeing that guy Adam holding her hand had been a double shock to my system.

I knew I had really messed up with Belle, but I planned on fixing that. I just hope she lets me. The first step was to get her to let me stay on the farm as her nurse and farm hand.

If I could get her to let me stay, then I had a chance to win her back. I also had to make some decisions, tough decisions. I needed a job. One that I liked, one that I could physically do, one that would put me back into the world of normal and productive people. Belle had been the main catalyst in bringing me back to life, so to speak. Now that I was living again, I needed to actually make a living. As I fell asleep, I thought of all the jobs that appealed to me. The one caveat was that all the ones I liked, every one of them, required rigorous physical capabilities. I knew I needed to test mine and then go from there.

The next morning I was up before the rooster crowed. I did not even attempt to make coffee. I had no idea how many beans to grind for a cup, so I just went to the barn and let the animals out. They had been inside all day yesterday, except for the sheep, and I knew they had to be antsy. I fed them and gave them fresh water. I fed Henny and Bessie grain and gave Henny an apple. I gave the pigs extra food too. Mimi was looking out of sorts without her baby, and I took a little time to pet her. I mucked the stalls and threw fresh straw down. The last thing I did was to gather the eggs and bring them inside, depositing them into the basket on the counter.

Inside I found a notepad, pen, and a tape measure that were in a kitchen drawer. I took them back to the barn and measured the size of the hole so I could get the correct sized boards to fix it. I also measured the rail and wire in the broken corral so I would buy the right sized materials for that job too. My dad drove up as I was leaving the barn. He handed me a cup of coffee and a bag with clothes in it.

"Yes, coffee!" I said excitedly making my dad laugh. It was tepid, but it still tasted great and was just what I needed. I ran inside, showered, changed, and got in the car.

On the way to get my truck, I spoke with my dad about possible job options. To his credit, he did not discount any of my aspirations. Instead, he explained what I would need to pursue each of them. They all required a physical test, but he also said there was nothing that would keep an amputee from getting a job as long as the physical test could be passed. The physical tests were tough, and many abled body people often did not pass them. It gave me a lot to think about, and if the size of the smile on my dad's face was an indicator, he too was pleased that I was thinking about my future.

After I got my truck from Kips, I stopped at the diner and got Belle a coffee and a blueberry muffin. Then I headed to the clinic.

By the time I got there, it was 9:30. Belle was sitting up in her bed, and I could see that she had already had breakfast, but I could also see that she had not eaten very much.

"Brady, you're here early." She said giving me a tiny sweet, but lopsided smile. My heart thudded in my chest.

"Morning, you look better. How are you feeling?"

"My head doesn't hurt as much, and I can now move a little without groaning, so that's a plus. I was worried about the animals, so I didn't sleep well."

I put the coffee and muffin on her little table next to her hospital breakfast and loved when she took a big sip of the coffee.

"I stayed at your place last night," I told her anxiously, hoping she didn't mind that I had done that.

"You did?"

"I didn't want your animals to be out there alone, especially after the day they had yesterday. I slept on your couch. I hope you don't mind. I told Mr. Bee."

"Oh Brady that was so, so nice of you. Thank you." In my mind, I was dancing a jig. Okay, next hurdle. "So that sort of touches on something I'd like to suggest. Please hear me out, okay?"

"Okay." I didn't like that she looked apprehensive. "First of all, I want to be your farm hand again. I know I hurt you, Belle. I'm so sorry for that, and maybe when you feel better, we can talk about that, but we are friends again, right?"

"Right." She answered hesitatingly. I knew she had no idea where I was going with this.

"So I want to be your farm hand again, and I want to stay at the farm full time, and help you convalesce."

"Stay with me at the farm?" She repeated stunned.
"Yes."

I waited. She was quiet, and the pause was tensely elongated as she contemplated what I had suggested. I had the awful feeling that the longer she thought about it that my chances were getting slimmer.

Finally, she spoke. "Brady I don't know about you staying there."

"Why not? I'll sleep in the barn if you don't want me in the house." That made her giggle.

"It just isn't proper." She argued.

"Listen, you need a farm hand. I am asking for that job back. You need someone to help you, at least until you can walk again. I want that job too."
She thought about it for a bit longer. "I know I'll need help with my animals. So thank you for taking that job back on. I'll ask Mr. Bee what he thinks about you staying with me full time."

"If I'm not the one helping you Belle you know you will have to hire a nurse."

She cocked her head. "I don't need a nurse."

"Can you walk yet?"

"Well no."

"How are you going to make yourself food or take a shower?" When I mentioned shower I know, she was thinking about when I had helped her clean up after Josh died because she blushed a deep red.

I put my hand on hers. "Remember when you massaged my leg that very first day?"

"Yes." She said.

"I want to return the favor. Let me help you, Belle." I said softly.

Belle peeled the wrapper from the muffin and pinched some of the moist cake between her finger and thumb bringing it to her lips and tasting it. I knew she was seriously thinking about my offer and that gave me hope.

"This is good." She said taking another small piece of the moist cake to eat.

"I'm sure you could make better ones," I told her honestly.

That made her smile. "Okay Brady, as long as Mr. Bee says it's okay. I don't want to get a bad reputation for living in sin. I don't have any friends, but I'd hate to lose any potential ones because they thought I was a loose woman."

That made me chuckle. "Belle first of all when friends live together they are just roommates, housemates, they aren't living in sin. Secondly, you have friends." It made me sad to think that she felt she had no one.

"Mr. Bee and Mrs. Bee, they are family friends I guess." She said thoughtfully.

"Kip and I are your friends."

"Yes, you and Kip." She repeated quietly.

"And I know Jeannie likes you."

That made her grin. "I like her too."

The Doctor chose that moment to come into the room followed by the nurse and then Mr. Bee.

"You have company early." The nurse said making me feel like it was a bad thing that I was there.

"Yes, he brought me coffee," Belle said.

"And a muffin," I said.

"And a muffin." She echoed.

"So Belle, how are you feeling?" Doctor Travers asked putting his stethoscope into his ears.

"Much better."

"Headache?"

"Almost gone."

"Your shoulder?"

"Very good actually, not as sore."

"Collarbone?"

"That throbs." She admitted.

"Ankle?"

"Just a dull ache now."

We all stood by quietly as the doctor checked her vitals.

"Well, I think you can go home as long as you have someone there to care for you."

That was my cue.

"That will be me."

Mr. Bee gave me a little eyebrow raise, and so did the nurse, but I didn't care.

"Um, would it be possible for me to speak with Mr. Bee alone?" Belle asked. I knew what she was going to be asking him.

I waited in the hallway, and a few minutes later Mr. Bee emerged shutting her door behind him. I wasn't sure if that was a good sign or a bad sign.

"Your offer is very kind Brady."

I knew he wasn't finished speaking so I waited.

"Are you sure you want to take care of her and the farm?"

"Yes."

"Well, I told her that she shouldn't care about what others think."

"But?"

"Perhaps for the first few nights you could get Tommy to come stay there as well. This way it would appear more respectable. I think Belle is worried for proprietary reasons. Remember she's a throwback, an old soul if you will."

"Yes Sir, that's a good idea; and for the record, I like that about her, the old soul and all."

Mr. Bee chuckled and slapped my back. "Okay son, take good care of her."

"I will Mr. Bee I promise."

I went back into Belle's room. "So ready to go home?" I asked.

"Oh boy, am I ever!"

"Okay, I need to run a few errands first. I'll have the nurse come back in and help you get ready. Then I'll come back for you. Is that good?"

"It's perfect. Margaret said he would help me shower, so if you can come back in an hour."

I kissed her forehead and left. I hadn't meant to kiss her, even though it was only on her forehead. It had been instinctive.

22

Belle

Yay! I was going home. Margaret helped me shower, and it was embarrassing how weak I was. She kept making comments about how long my hair was, and it made me feel a little self-conscious. Once I got over my initial shyness about being stark naked in front of her, I was overjoyed to finally clean off all the dirt and grime. It was the first time I got a good look at my battered body. I was sporting ugly purple bruises, and numerous cuts and scrapes. I tried not to think about the fall. Now that I knew that it wasn't an accident I was secretly terrified. All the strange things that had been happening in my house, and now this, had me pretty stressed out. I was honestly relieved that Brady would be staying with me. I knew I'd feel safer with him there.

When Brady returned, I was waiting for him in a wheelchair ready to go. Margaret wheeled me out while Brady walked next to me.

When we reached the front doors, I put my hand on the wheel to make Margaret stop pushing, so I could ask her a question that had been stewing in my mind.

"I've never been to a hospital before, do I pay now?"

Margaret chuckled and then told me that Mr. Fitzpatrick had already paid for my expenses.

"Oh," I said softly. I looked at Brady, and I could tell he hadn't liked hearing that.

"I'll have to reimburse him," I said out loud. Brady left us, and within a minute he pulled his truck right up to the front door. Margaret was going to assist me up into the cab of the truck, but Brady leaned down and gently plucked me up and placed me in the front seat.

He folded up the wheelchair, because I couldn't walk on my own yet, and put it in the bed of his truck. Brady made sure I was comfortable, and that my seatbelt was not too tight on my broken collarbone. He was so sweet and attentive like the old Brady had been. That thought made me sigh, and Brady gave me a look to make sure I was okay. I waved goodbye to Margaret as we pulled away. There were flowers sitting on the front seat between Brady and me, and he gestured to them. "I know you grow your own, but, well, I hope you like them?"

"They are very pretty, thank you."

"So," Brady said. "I called Tommy, and if it's okay with you, he's going to stay out with us for the first couple of nights. I'm sure you'll be getting some visitors, and this way, if anyone asks, you can say that the McDaniel boys are staying with you."

"Oh, Brady that's a smart idea."

"Yeah, well I wouldn't want your reputation to be sullied." He said with a silly grin.

I chuckled. "Thank you."

"It was actually Mr. Bee's idea, but I think it's smart too."

I saw the lumber and fencing material along with boxes of food in the back of the truck.

"What's all that?" I said gesturing to the truck bed.

"I bought lumber to fix the barn and material to fix the sheep's corral. I also stopped at the food store and picked up a few items."

"I was starting to run low on a few staples," I admitted. "Did you charge it?"

"No."

"Brady."

"We'll settle up later."

"Okay." I was starting to feel drained and didn't want to argue about money.

"My Mom is bringing over dinner tonight. Tommy and dad are coming too. If you're not up for company though, they will understand."

"I'm sure I'll be fine. I am tired though. How the heck can I be tired, I just woke up?"

"Belle, your body, took a beating and you've been stressed, and not sleeping well. You should be tired."

"I guess."

"After I wheel you around the barn area so you can see your animals you're going inside and taking a nap."

I stared at him and got a warm fuzzy feeling.

"What?" he asked after seeing my face.

"It's just that you knew I'd want to see the animals," I said softly.

Brady smiled widely and winked, and my traitorous heart pitty pattered. Yikes! I needed to reign that familiar emotion right in.

When we got to my house, Brady ran the groceries inside and then he came back out and brought the wheelchair around to my door. He picked me up and settled me into it. I had to admit that I loved being in his arms, even if it was for just a few seconds. Why was he back to being the old, nice Brady now? What had happened in the first place that made him pull away? I hoped we would have a chance to talk about it.

Brady wheeled me around to the fenced-in corrals,' and I got to pet Henny and Bessie. Mimi walked up to me, and through the fence, I was able to pet her too. I know she was missing William, I could see that she was depressed. Sheep had feelings too. Maybe when I got the use of my foot back, I could take Mimi to visit her baby. I'm sure little William was missing his Momma too.

At my request, Brady showed me the damaged wall in the barn, but he explained how he planned to fix it and I liked how enthusiastic he sounded about the project. I saw how the sheep's fence had been patched up and I wondered if that was Adam's work or Brady's.

Inside my house, Brady settled me on the couch. He elevated my ankle with a pillow and gave me the television remote. Then he brought me lemonade, my pain meds, and a bag of Fritos. I giggled seeing the bag.

"I love these things!"

"Yeah, I remember." I thought I saw a shadow pass over his face.

Brady started to leave. I knew he was going to get started on the barn. "Brady?"

"Um?"

"Will you talk to me tonight?"

He cocked his head, and I saw when it dawned on him what I was actually asking.

"Chelsea?"

"Yes," I said with a slight hitch in my voice.

He walked back to me, his eyes never leaving mine.

"I promise to tell you everything, absolutely everything."

"Okay," I said softly.

"I know you don't trust me right now, but please believe this Belle. I'm exactly where I want to be right now, and I hope to prove that to you."

He tapped my nose playfully.

"Now get some rest." He left going out the back sliding door leaving the door open but the screen closed.

I sank back into the pillow and placed my hand on my forehead. My insides felt like butterflies were playing tag and a ridiculous lopsided grin was plastered on my face. What the heck was I doing? I had to get a hold of my feelings. We were friends, just friends! I sat up again and took my pain pill and ate a handful of Fritos before settling back down into the comfy couch. I did not even turn the television on. I listened to the sounds of my farm. I could hear Brady hammering, the chickens clucking, Bessie mooing; even the frogs were enjoying the nice day. I loved my farm, but as I was quickly discovering there was life beyond my farm; one that I'd been kept from.

So much had happened in my secular little world in the last month, so much had changed. I still thought it was a good idea to take classes in September, but I had thought that I'd like to travel a little too. Not too far or for very long. I wasn't even sure where I'd want to go. New York City wasn't too far away, but it looked crazy. I'd never seen the ocean either. I drifted off to sleep so happy to be home and feeling safe knowing that Brady was there.

Brady

So far so good, I was seriously counting my blessings that Belle had allowed me back into her life. I wasn't going to push her. I had almost kissed her; it had been a natural response. Thankfully I stopped myself and had just tapped her nose.

I was determined to fix the barn siding in one day. The only times I stopped was when I went inside to see if Belle needed anything. I realized if she did need me I wouldn't be able to hear her. Luckily she was still sleeping.

I finished the barn and checked on Belle again. She was still asleep. I took a moment to study her. Her face was bruised, and she had a steri-strip on her cheek, yet she looked so peaceful. The thought of anyone wanting to purposely hurt her was unfathomable, and I knew I would do anything to keep her safe.

I walked back outside after drinking some water and went to work on the fencing. Currently, the sheep were roaming the enclosed area with Henny and Bessie. It was a little cramped, and I know the horse and cow could not have been keen on sharing their grass.

I was drenched in sweat when I finished but was pleased with everything I'd accomplished. I herded the sheep into their newly fixed area then changed out the water in their trough. While I had the hose out I filled the trough in Bessie and Henny's corral, and then the pig's pen.

When I entered the house, Belle was sitting up, and I could tell just by looking at her that something was wrong. I jogged to her side.

"What's the matter? Are you okay?"

"I have to use the restroom." She said shyly.

"Oh." I felt like a numbskull!

She looked uncomfortable, and I felt terrible that she had depended on me to care for her and I was already failing. I lifted her up and carried her into her room.

"Sorry, I'm pretty sweaty," I said to her.

"You've been working for a long time." She acknowledged.

I brought her into her bathroom and stopped in front of the toilet.

"Can you balance on one foot?" I asked her before setting her down.

"Yes, hurry, okay?"

I put her down gently.

She was still wearing the scrubs that Margaret had put her. The clothes that she had arrived at the clinic in had been cut off and unsalvageable.

"I'm going to hold you up until you can loosen your pants then I'll help you sit. I'll wait outside the door, okay?"

"Yes." If she was embarrassed, she didn't show it. She must have really had to go.

Two minutes later she called me. "Brady I'm ready."

I opened the door. She was balancing on one foot standing unsteadily using the wall to hold on to. "I want to wash my hands can you help me?"

"Of course." I helped her hop to the sink, and I held her steady by the waist as she used both her hands. My hands spanned her tiny waist; I loved holding her again and instantly felt like a cad. I suppose to be helping her, not copping a feel. I handed her a towel, and after she dried her hands, I lifted her into my arms and walked her back to the living room.

"Can you take me outside?" She asked.

"Sure thing. Front or back porch?"

"Front please."

I carefully placed her down in what I knew was her chair. Then I went back inside and got the pillow from the couch and a glass of water.

"Here you go," I handed her the water and propped her foot up using another chair.

"Thank you. You've been working hard Brady."

"Yeah, but it feels good to work. The barn is done, and so is the sheep's fence."

"That was quick."

"I had what I needed to do all mapped out in my head. I just had to measure, cut and hammer."

"Later will you take me to see it?"

"Absolutely. I'm going to take a shower upstairs. Do you need anything before I do? I won't be long."

"No, I'm good."

I showered quickly, and when I was walking down the steps, I heard Belle talking with someone. I hastened my steps.

"These look delicious." I heard Belle say.

I opened the front screen door and stepped outside. Adam Fitzpatrick was sitting next to Belle. He had brought her a box of what I knew was homemade chocolates from the market.

Adam stood when I stepped out the door and extended his hand to me. I shook it. I had to keep my jealousy in check.

"Hi, it's nice to see you again," I said lying through my teeth.

"You too. Belle says you fixed the barn already?"

"Yeah."

"He fixed the fencing too," Belle said smiling at me. Her smile was like a balm on a wound, soothing my jealousy.

"If you need me to help with anything I'll be here for the week. I'd be more than happy to pitch in." Adam said looking at me.

"Thanks, I think we're okay," I told him.

He looked back to Belle. "You're looking rested."

"I just woke up." She giggled. "I've slept the whole day away."

"You needed it," I said, and Adam nodded in agreement.

"Belle, the Sheriff said the tree falling on the barn and the tree limb was not an accident. What's going on?"

Belle looked uncomfortable with the question. She looked to me, but it wasn't my place to say anything.

"We think someone is trying to hurt me."

"Yes, but why?"

She shook her and laughed nervously. "I have absolutely no idea."

He looked to me. "She has no enemies," I told him.

"Adam, why does your company want to buy my property?"

Adam looked uneasy with the question. "I'm not allowed to say."

"Why not?" Belle demanded. I could tell she didn't like his answer.

"Sometimes we buy properties for other companies. I can't tell you who we are representing."

"Do you know why the other company wants it?" She asked.

"I do."

"But you're not going to tell me?"

"Belle I can't."

This guy was digging himself a hole, and I let him. "Please understand. It's nothing personal if I could tell you I would."

Belle sighed, she wasn't happy with what Adam said, but she accepted it.

"I understand." Crap, she was too good of a person.

"Have you been thinking about our offer?"

"I have."

My head swung to her quickly. Was she thinking about the offer?

Adam nodded and said, "good'" but had the smarts not to look too pleased with her answer.

"So you aren't dating anyone?" He said kneeling down next to her.

I noticed he didn't even look at me.

"No, I'm not."

Oh man, this was not good. I literally had to bite my tongue to stay quiet.

"May I take you out to dinner?"

I wanted to punch the guy's lights out, but instead, I sat uncomfortably waiting for Belle's answer. It pissed me off that he had had no problem asking her out in front of me.

"I don't think I can."

My hopes soared.

"I'm still hurting, and I'd be terrible company." Then plummeted.

"You could never be bad company." He said flirting shamelessly.

Belle giggled. Crud.

"I'll come back tomorrow, and we'll see how you feel then."

"I can't walk," she told him.

"It would be my pleasure to carry you." The guy was pouring it on.

"Adam, you can't carry me into a restaurant."

"Yes, I can!" He lifted her from the chair, and she laughed happily. I watched hopelessly as he carried her around the porch.

"See, you're light as a feather."

"Adam!" Her protest was way too weak for me.

"Since you're already carrying me can you take me to the barn? I want to see what Brady did today." My heart dropped.

"Your wish is my command." He said walking off the porch towards the barn.

I couldn't watch anymore. I went inside. I had some calls to make.

Belle

As Adam and I walked towards the barn, I looked over his shoulder and saw Brady watching us. All of a sudden I felt guilty. Then I got annoyed with myself. Why should I feel guilty that Adam was interested in dating me? I shouldn't! Brady had been the one to push me away. Adam had been nothing but a gentleman. He had been my rescue angel. Then why did it bother me to see Brady looking miserable?

Adam walked me through the barn doors, and we both admired the work that Brady had done. I mentioned that the animals were going to need to be brought inside soon and Adam placed me on a bale of hay, and I watched as he skillfully brought in the animals for the night.

"You do know what you're doing," I remarked.

"Yup, I love animals. I wish I could work a full time on a ranch."

"Why don't you?"

Adam looked embarrassed, and I immediately regretted asking it.

"It's kind of a long story."

"Well while you are here this week, we'll make time for it, okay?"

Adam knelt down next to and touched my cheek with his fingers.

"Belle, you are amazing, you know that?"

I blushed furiously.

"I'll tell you everything about me when we go on our date." He said.

"Adam I don't know about this date," I told him.

"Is it because of Brady? I sense there is something between you two."

"Yet you still asked me out in front of him? Are you that brave or that foolish?"

Adam chuckled. "Brave," he said giving me a little sexy wink. "I wanted to see if he would say anything, and since he didn't... Well unless you have other objections I think we are good to go."

"I really am sore, and I can only use one hand at the moment, and honestly, I do not want to be carried into any place."

"So we will wait a few days."

I hesitated. "Okay, maybe in a few days."

Adam picked me up again, and as we walked out of the barn, I saw the Sheriff's car coming down my drive. As we got onto the porch the Sheriff, his wife, and Tommy got out of his car. Adam placed me back in the chair and Brady came out the front door. He looked at me then Adam, I wasn't sure what he expected to see. He then went to help his mom with all the items she was pulling from the trunk of the car.

"What's going on?" Adam asked.

"The Sheriff is Brady's dad, and that's his mom and brother. They are coming for dinner."

"Oh." I could tell Adam felt uncomfortable and he stuffed his hands in his pockets. "Well, I guess I'll head out now. Can I come back tomorrow?"

Brady was just getting to the porch with his hands full, and Adam opened the door for him.

Brady turned his head to Adam. "There's plenty of food, would you like to stay for dinner?"

Wow, that was unbelievable nice of Brady. I knew he had shocked Adam too because Adam was speechless. Brady chuckled.

"I, um, well yeah thanks," Adam said.

I smiled at Brady and mouthed a 'thank you' to him. He nodded at me with a slight smile that didn't reach his eyes.

Mrs. McDaniel brought so much food that Brady, Tommy, and the Sheriff all had to carry bags inside. Mrs. McDaniel gave me a gentle hug and asked how I was. I introduced her to Adam. Brady came out and told his Mom that Adam was staying for dinner and I could see that threw her a little, but she recovered nicely saying there was more than enough food. She told Adam and me that as soon as she and Tommy set the table, we would eat. I felt odd that someone was in my kitchen working while I sat out front, but I would not have been able to help anyway. Brady took his dad to see what he had done in the barn. That left Adam and I sitting on the porch.

"They're very nice," Adam said to generate conversation.

"Yes, they are."

"Have you always been close with them?"

"No, I only met them after my Momma passed."

"They care for you. I figured you had known them for a long time."

"No, the Sheriff was the one who told me about my Momma. He took me to Springfield to identify her."

"That had to be difficult."

"It was. It's still a bit of a blur. I met Brady and Tommy when they came over and helped me dig her grave."

Adam blanched when I said that.

"Wait. What?"

"It's a family tradition. I didn't realize it was not an ordinary custom until, well, until I started to talk to other people."

"You have lived a very cloistered life, haven't you? My dad said you had."

"We did. I'm thinking now maybe too sequestered." I paused. "I wish my Mom had told me about your dad."

"Me too."

"You didn't seem shocked."

"I was, and I wasn't."

"He dated a lot?"

Adam hesitated, and I could tell he was grappling with an answer. Brady and his dad were coming back from the barn, and I watched them as they neared. Brady was looking at me and even though he and his dad were talking his attention was fixed on me.

I looked at Adam waiting for his answer. "Did he date a lot?" I repeated.

"I don't really know Belle. I haven't been around."

Brady and the Sheriff reached the porch.

"Where were you?" I asked Adam.

"I was in Syria, and then I took a couple of months off before coming home."

"You served?" Brady asked reaching the porch.

"Yes. Special Forces. I was in for four years."

"Brady was a Marine," I said proudly.

"Once a Marine always a Marine," Adam said.

The two men shared a knowing look.

Tommy came out and announced that dinner was ready.

Adam rose and turned towards me, but Brady deftly stepped around him.

"Would you like me to carry you in Belle or would you like to use the wheelchair?"

"The chair please."

I didn't want to feel any more awkward around Adam and Brady than I already did, so keeping my distance from both seemed wise.

Brady wheeled me inside and then helped me to sit in a chair. He got a small footstool and propped my foot up on it, and then he got a pillow and put it under my arm that was in the sling.

"Thank you," I told him. He was definitely wrestling with something. I could see it in his eyes. He sat down next to me, and I swear I think he was waiting for me to say that I wanted Adam to sit there.

Dinner was scrumptious. Mrs. McDaniel had made a meatloaf, mashed potatoes, gravy, and green beans. For dessert, we had peach cobbler. Adam and Brady exchanged stories about what they had done in the service, nothing gory thank goodness. Tommy was entertaining, as usual, telling us about what he had been doing all summer.

By the time dessert was finished I was barely holding my eyes open. Brady rose from the table and didn't even ask about the wheelchair he just scooped me up and told me to say goodnight to everyone, which I did with a tired giggle.

He brought me into my bedroom and as gentlemanly as possible helped me to change, and then he took me into the bathroom and waited until I called him back in. He held me up while I washed my hands and brushed my teeth and then he carried me to my bed.

Brady handed me a glass of water that he must have filled when I was using the toilet and my antibiotics and pain meds.

"You're a very efficient nurse," I said sleepily popping the pills into my mouth.

"And thankfully you are a very good patient." He answered playfully.

He helped me to lie down and then brushed a curl off my face.

"I'll be right out on the couch Belle. You call me if you need me."

"Why don't you sleep in one of the beds?"

"The couch is right next to your room. I'll hear you if you need me."

"Thank you, Brady," I said sincerely.

He turned to leave. "And Brady."

He turned back. "Thank you for asking Adam to stay for dinner."

Brady shrugged. "I just want you to be happy Belle."

"We never talked," I told him sleepily.

"We will. I promise. Get some sleep. I'm here, Tommy's here. Sleep tight." He shut my light out and closed my door. I lay on my back feeling safe for the first time in a while. There was no way my Momma's ghost would come with Brady and Tommy here, and whoever was messing with me would know I had someone here too because Brady's truck sat right out front. The pain medicine kicked in, and before long I fell asleep.

Brady

Everyone tried to help clean up after dinner, but my Mom shooed us out of the kitchen after a few minutes because there were, as she said, too many big bodies in her way. Tommy, Dad, Adam, and I sat on the front porch and chatted amicably. Mom came out, and my dad got out of his chair. We said goodbye to them, and I watched my dad drape an arm over my Mom's shoulders as they walked to his car. They had a good marriage. I was lucky.

Tommy stood up and said he was heading inside to watch television. I just told him to keep the sound low. That left Adam and me, alone.

"You want a beer?" I asked him.

"Yeah, thanks."

I got our beers from the fridge and settled back in my chair.

He gestured to my leg. "You're limping. Did you hurt yourself?"

"No." I didn't elaborate, and he didn't question me further.

"So really I would love something to do while I'm here. You can't put me to work?"

"I guess if you really want to work I can use you. I'm sort of the ranch hand around here."

"And her caretaker too, am I right?"

"Yes."

"So what can I do?"

"See that shed over there?" I tilted my bottle towards the aging shed. Adam nodded.

"I want to fix that up and stabilize it."

"Okay, I'm in."

"How about if you come back tomorrow afternoon? I have to cut the grass and weed the garden in the morning."

"Sounds good. Thanks."

Adam finished his beer and put it on the table. "Thanks, Brady."

"See you tomorrow," I said draining my bottle. I watched the dust in the drive settle as Adam drove out in his truck. I hoped I wasn't making a major mistake letting him get close to Belle. I mean it's not like I could have stopped him from seeing her, but now I just made it easier. The thing was that the more I got to know him, the more I discovered that he was a good guy. Kip was a good guy too. Sheesh, every dang guy that met Belle liked her and they were all great guys! I was in deep shit.

Tomorrow I would talk to her about Chelsea, maybe even let her know how I was feeling. I had to time it right though. I didn't want her to feel uncomfortable around me.

Dad had left me a small walkie-talkie that he had in his car. I wrote Belle a note and quietly put the walkie-talkie into her room on her bed stand.

She needed to be able to reach me no matter where I was on her farm. I was keeping the other walkie-talkie on me at all times. I walked upstairs to check on Tommy, who had gone upstairs to read. He was in Belle's old room.

"Hey."

"Hey, Adam gone?"

"Yup."

"He likes Belle."

"Who doesn't?" I replied a little sarcastically.

"If I were older I sure would," Tommy said with a mischievous grin.

"I hear ya."

"So tomorrow morning will you drive me to Carters?" That was Tommy's best friend.

"Sure. Thanks for staying here."

"It's a little creepy up here." He said looking around Belle's old room.

"I'll be right downstairs."

"Yeah, I know. I'm not afraid or anything. It's just..."

"Creepy." I finished for him.

Tommy shrugged.

I said goodnight and went back downstairs to lie on the couch. I was bone tired, and I had forgotten to grab a pillow, but I didn't want to walk back upstairs to get one. I pulled off my boots, jeans, prosthetic, and tee shirt, leaving me in just my boxers. Then I settled back on the couch and pulled the afghan over me.

I looked down towards the other end of the couch and a lump formed in my throat seeing one foot, my only foot, sticking out the end of the afghan. I was over the pity party I'd been throwing myself for months, but sometimes the harsh reality of it would hit me at the oddest times. The loss of my buddy and the memory of that awful day would surface and overwhelm me. This was one of those times. Seeing just one foot peeking out from the short blanket, without its companion next to it, was like a punch to the gut. I couldn't catch my breath and the horrible images of the moment when it had happened flicked through my mind like an old movie.

I quickly sat up and threw the covers off me trying to regulate my breathing. My hands were on my thighs, and I drew air through my mouth and exhaled out my nose until my heart stopped hammering. Then I drew in three deep breaths to calm me further. I had learned this technique when I was in the VA Hospital.

I sat back heavily on the couch and rubbed my hands over my face annoyed at myself for having the anxiety attack. When I'd first returned stateside, I'd had one almost every day, but the ones triggered by my nightmares were the worst. They had been so bad that I had needed medication, but that medicine made me loopy, which I hated even worse. Eventually, a therapist helped me so that I could now ward them off with the controlled breathing techniques Now that I thought about it I hadn't had an attack in a few weeks.

I still had the night terrors, but they weren't every night like they had been. I had worked hard to mend my body and my mind. Now I needed to mend my life.

Belle - Three days later

I was feeling better every day. Brady kept snapping at me because I was using my foot, but he wasn't being mean. I knew he was just concerned about my well-being. He and Adam had kind of ganged up on me, and the two of them were making sure I did as little as possible. Adam was spending his days at my farm. He and Brady had a bond of some sort. I think it had to be because they were both veterans. Meanwhile, I was bored out of my mind. Brady and I hadn't had a chance to talk yet, with Tommy around at night and Adam around all day. I wanted to hear what he had to say. I was imagining all kinds of excuses he'd have for how he had treated me and it was making me cranky.

Adam took every moment possible to talk to me, and we were really getting to know each other. The problem was that I couldn't shake that feeling that perhaps he was only acting interested in me because he wanted my property. I felt horrible for thinking that about him, but it did plague my thoughts. Brady would talk with me too when he could, but he was so busy around the farm that he didn't have the time that Adam did. Brady was restoring my little farm back to its original state of utilitarian glory.

Yesterday I had sat out on the front porch, bored out of my mind, watching the two handsome shirtless men transform my run-down rickety shed into a sturdy looking garage and workspace. Finally, Brady took pity on me and wheeled me out to the shed so I could hand him nails. Then later, when the shed was completed Adam had me point out the stuff that I wanted to be thrown away or put back in the shed.

That night, after Tommy, Brady, and I had finished eating another meal that his mother had dropped off, Jeannie and Kip came over to visit. I hadn't seen Kip since the hospital and Jeannie since the bar. I had to recount my entire story to Jeannie. She couldn't believe what I had been through and she said as soon as I was able we were getting manicure and pedicures to celebrate my being alive. She was adorably serious, and I started laughing so hard that my ribs hurt.

The next morning we did not have any fresh bread for breakfast, and the look on Tommy's face was priceless. Brady lifted me up so I could sit on the counter and Tommy and I proceeded to make bread. The floor was a mess afterward, and Tommy had flour on his hands and face, but we would have fresh bread the next day, and Tommy declared it would be the best.

I'd been home for a week and getting stronger every day. Brady and I still hadn't talked, and I wondered if he was avoiding the conversation. It was after eleven, and Brady and I were on our way to the clinic. It was a follow-up appointment that Brady had made for me. I hadn't even known or thought to do that. When we got to the clinic, Brady wheeled me in, and we did not have to wait long to see the doctor.

The Doctor checked my ankle and shoulder, and then he tended to my cuts. I still had large areas of bruising, but they were starting to yellow up as they healed. He told Brady to get vitamin e for my scars, especially for my cheek. It wasn't bad, only a thin red line now, but the doctor didn't want it to become a permanent scar. My sling came off, and the doctor manipulated my shoulder carefully. He even said I could leave off the cumbersome clavicle collar too if I promised to not bang into anything. He checked my ankle last, and the doctor remarked that the swelling had gone down enough that I could now walk on it, but when I wasn't walking on it I should elevate it. He also told me I should ice it, then put heat on it every night. He showed Brady how to massage my foot to break up the blood that had pooled into an angry purple bruise. Brady was listening to what the doctor said with such a serious expression on his face that it made me feel cared for. Before the doctor left the room, he gave my knee a gentle pat and told me to take it easy. I saw Brady roll his eyes and it made me smile because he really did know me well. Less than forty- five minutes later I walked out of the clinic on my own.

On the way home we stopped at the store and picked up some items including vitamin e. Brady decided we needed to celebrate, so he drove us to the diner for lunch.

After we ordered Brady was fiddling with his silverware and I knew we were about to have the conversation I'd been waiting for.

"Are you ready to talk now Brady?" I prodded him with a little grin. He looked back at me uneasily.

"Yeah, I need you to know what happened."

"Okay, so tell me." I was acting like it wasn't a big deal as to why he had basically stomped on my heart after I had foolishly given it to him, but I was determined to put up a brave front.

Brady told me about Chelsea, and he described how very close they had been; that they were inseparable in college and how she had become a member of his family. He even said that he had thought they would one day get married. My hands were gripped tightly together while he talked. I couldn't believe how much it hurt to hear him talk so reverently about another woman.

"So after college, I went to Parris Island, for basic training, then I was sent to Afghanistan. That had always been the plan. We both understood we would be separated. She was a nurse, and I was going over to fight for our country, and get valuable experience so that when I came back, I could get a good job and marry her. We kept in touch via emails and FaceTime, and I thought we were fine." Brady was looking out of the diner window, and I could tell that just talking about it was difficult for him.

"Near the end of my tour, she became a little distant. She hadn't been easy to reach and the few times that we FaceTimed were short. I received fewer emails from her too." Brady shook his head, and I could tell he was reliving the emotions he had felt back then.

"Honestly, I just chalked it up to her being busy at the hospital. I was battle weary and so tired of looking over my shoulder, and I couldn't wait to get home. I'd seen so many horrific things; all I wanted was to get home to my loving girlfriend, and my family." Brady took a deep breath.

"Unfortunately, when I got home, I found out she was with another guy. I was blown away; I was so angry."

I could tell it was taking a lot out of him to tell me all this, but believe me; it was taking a lot out of me just listening to him.

"When I found her living with that guy I lost it. She had destroyed me, Belle. I re-upped the next day, because I didn't want to be in the same state as her, and I knew I couldn't handle seeing her with the other guy. I was so stupid."

Brady paused and took a sip of his water.

"I thought I'd be better off fighting in a war than seeing her. What kind of an idiot does that? My mom, dad, even Kip tried to talk me out of it, but I didn't listen. I was sent back to Afghanistan almost immediately, per my request, and a few months into my tour I was on a dirt road with my platoon and bam the guy walking next to me stepped on an IED. I had been distracted, and I should have seen the change in the ground elevation. My buddy died, and I lost my leg."

I reached across the table and gave his hand a squeeze. He squeezed me back, letting me know he appreciated that small gesture of support, but I knew he wasn't done talking. I also knew he still had to get to the part about why he had been so mean to me, and I hoped to heck I could handle what he was going to say.

"After I got out of the VA hospital I just stayed in my house. I saw Kip once in a while, but I just didn't want to see anyone else. I couldn't stand to think that everyone was going to be thinking of me as handicapped. I basically holed up in my house and drove my parents nuts." He took another sip of water.

"Then I met you Belle, and I found that I liked being with you. I liked my job at your farm, and I was falling for you Belle. I was falling so fast and so hard."

He was using past tense, and I started to tear up. I was thinking 'Oh boy here it comes, the 'you're nice, but you're not Chelsea part of the speech.' I wasn't quite ready for that. I mean I understood that I wasn't normal, I was old fashioned and led a simple life. I wasn't like other girls with all their pretty clothes and perfect makeup. Sadly, hearing Brady say it out loud was going to sting worse that I thought it would.

I was going to start crying, and I didn't want Brady to see that so I jumped up as quickly as my healing body would allow.

I mumbled that I needed to use the restroom.

As I started to walk away, Brady grabbed my hand and pulled me back down into the booth next to him. I couldn't help when a tear leaked out, but I quickly wiped it.

I don't understand why I was so hurt waiting to hear him say out loud that he still loved Chelsea. He had said that he didn't have a girlfriend anymore, but he must have thought it best to totally come clean with me. I didn't blame him, how could I. I was a rube, a country bumpkin, and simple farm girl. There was no way I could compete with the girls he'd grown up with. Chelsea was a knockout, a nurse. She was normal.

"Belle, look at me." His fingers lifted my chin, and my lips quivered.

I inhaled a deep breath. "I'm sorry I'm emotional. I get it, Brady. I do. I guess just hearing you say it out loud." I couldn't finish my sentence.

"Say what?"

"You know. 'I really 'liked' you. I 'was' falling for you." I emphasized liked and was with hand air quotes.

"Belle, listen to me. Sheesh. I'm screwing this up." For some reason, he pulled me closer to him and put his arm around me holding me in place. Sweet Brady was trying so hard to let me down easy, The waitress brought our food at that exact moment, and Brady pushed our plates back so he could lean closer to me.

I watched as an assortment of expressions rolled across his handsome face. I was struck by how emotionally strong he had to be to endure what he had been through. I needed to be more like him.

"I'm sorry Brady. I'm sorry for everything you've been through."

"Don't be sorry for me Belle, just be you. You're the only person who sees me for me. You don't look at me like I'm handicapped."

I started to say he wasn't handicapped and he shushed me with a finger to my lips.

"I know. I'm not handicapped." He then gave me a gentle smile.

"Let me finish."

I'd thought he had and my stomach rolled knowing I would have to listen to more.

"So when Chelsea started calling me a few weeks ago I never accepted her calls. I didn't want to talk to her. Then one day Tommy called and said that Chelsea was at the house and she wouldn't leave unless I spoke to her. That was the day you asked me to stay for dinner and I couldn't. I went home to meet with Chelsea, and we ended up talking for a good while. We'd always been so comfortable with each other. She apologized for cheating on me, and she seemed so sincere. After that night she and I started talking again on a regular basis. Brady felt me tense up. "I know I should have told you. I'm sorry, bad decision. The thing is Belle, that when I was with her, I'd remember something that I wanted to tell you. When she and I went out, all I did was think about you. After a few days, I realized that I didn't want to be with her. I wanted to be with you. I was so conflicted. Being with her was how it was supposed to have been, so I allowed her to recreate it. I felt so guilty about being with her, after you and I, well you know." Brady rubbed my arm with his hand.

"I didn't want to hurt you, so I pushed you away. I can't imagine how that felt."

Now I had tears running down my face, and I covered my face with my hands and wept. Brady had his hands on my shoulders and felt them being torn from me.

"What the hell Brady?" I knew that voice. Adam. Adam had me out of that booth so fast I couldn't even react.

"Put her down," Brady said I could hear the anger in his voice.

Adam placed me on a chair behind him and when he turned back to the table where Brady stood seething.

Page, our waitress came hurrying over. "If you're going to fight, take it to the parking lot."

I could see the other patrons all watching us, and I was embarrassed to be the center of such ugly attention.

"I'm just talking to her Adam. I'm not hurting her."

"She looks like she's hurting to me." Adam was livid.

Adam tuned back to me and leaned down. He put his hand behind my neck and whispered in my ear. "Say the word Belle, and he's toast."

"Toast?" I asked quietly.

Adam rested his cheek against mine in a very possessive and protective display.

"It's an expression. I'll beat the crap out of him."

"Oh, I figured that's what you meant," I whispered back. I sighed and put my hand on his shoulder.

"Adam, Brady and I were having a long overdue talk. I was crying because I was emotional."

"See," Brady said with his large arms crossed angrily over his chest.

Adam stood up. "All I see is a woman in tears. You may not have hurt her, but she is hurting. I'm taking her home."

Brady stepped to Adam and Adam took a step towards Brady. I stood up and wedged myself between the two of them.

"Guys stop, please."

"What's going on?" Jeannie asked as she hurried over to us.

"Everything is fine," I said not in the least bit confident that it was. I turned to Brady. "Brady, can I have a few minutes alone with Adam please?"

Brady did not look happy. "What about lunch?"

"Can we take it home?" Brady nodded and motioned for Page, the waitress.

I walked with Adam to the parking lot.

"You were crying, Belle." He said hurriedly when we got to his truck.

"Because what we were talking about was painful to hear."

"You and Brady are together?"

"We were, for a very short time, and then we weren't. It's complicated. That's what he was explaining to me."

"You were crying," he repeated. His voice was barely above a whisper.

"I know."

Adam had his hands on my arms and looked me square in my eyes. "I like you, Belle. Give me a chance."

I looked away from him feeling uncomfortable and saw Brady walking out of the diner with Jeannie.

"Adam I like you too, but."

"But you like Brady more?"

I shrugged. "You saved my life. I like being with you, but first I need to heal, and Brady and I need to finish our talk. I think he and I will end up being friends. I couldn't keep the sadness from my voice."

Adam held up his hand. "Say no more. When you're ready we can explore our friendship further, until then, friends it is." His voice was scratchy, and I could tell he was upset.

"Thank you, Adam."

He nodded and shoved his hands in his pockets. I didn't want to hurt Adam. I didn't want to hurt me either. What if Brady was like this all the time? One minute acting as he liked me then the next minute acting cold. Did I want to risk missing out on a chance to get to know Adam? Then there's Kip, sheesh, he would have a cow if I didn't make a go of it with Brady, and I started dating Adam.

As Jeannie and Brady approached us, I saw that Brady's eyes were clouded with worry. He had no idea what I was thinking. We had not finished our talk. I owed him that. Heck, I owed me that.

I looked at Jeannie. "Jeannie, are you on your lunch break?"

Jeannie was looking wide-eyed at Adam, and I swear she was blushing.

"Oh I'm sorry, let me introduce you two. Adam Fitzpatrick this is Jeannie Swift. Jeannie this is Adam Fitzpatrick. Adam and his dad were the ones that found and rescued me."

"Well thank you, Adam Fitzpatrick," Jeannie said giving Adam a very bright smile.

Adam was still looking at me with a pained expression on his face.

Brady held up the bag of food. "Ready?"

"Yes. Adam, will you come visit again?" I asked him softly.

"Yes, we still have business to discuss."

"Oh, right."

Brady and I turned and headed for his truck. When we left Jeannie and Adam were talking.

23
Brady

Adam liked her; it was so obvious. I completely bumbled trying to explain myself to Belle, and I honestly had no idea what she was thinking inside that gorgeous, smart head of hers.

She was sitting quietly in the passenger seat, and outwardly she appeared calm and collected, but she was holding her hands tightly together on her lap, and her knuckles were white. My girl was hurting, and I hated that I was the cause of it.

"Belle, talk to me, please."

I kept glancing over at her, and because I was driving, I couldn't see her face. I needed to see her face, especially her expressive eyes.

I pulled over to the side of the road and took off my seatbelt. Then I got out of the car walked to her door and opened it. Anxiously I unbuckled her seatbelt.

"Look at me, Belle."

Belle gradually turned towards me. My truck was big, but because of my height Belle and I were face to face, I hated that she was trying to look everywhere except at me.

I had one hand on the door and the other on the roof of my truck. "I'm so sorry that I hurt you. I care for you, Belle."

"But you care for Chelsea," her voice waivered with uncertainty.

I looked down at the gravel road because the pain I had caused her was visible in her ice blue eyes.

"I thought I did. I was confused." I ran my hand through my hair exasperated. "It was easy being with her again; I didn't want to hurt you."

"It's okay," Belle said stiffly. "I get it."

"You get what?" What the hell was she thinking?

"I get that you want to be with Chelsea. You love her."

"No, no, that's not what I'm trying to tell you. I'm messing this up," I paused and got my thoughts together. "Belle, I want us to be together, you and me."

She stared at me like I'd grown another head. "Do you think you will ever be able to forgive me?" Belle didn't answer right away, and honestly, I deserved every long, agonizing second she took to think about her answer.

She finally looked me in the eye. "You don't love Chelsea?"

I shook my head.

"You did hurt me, Brady. You know better than anyone how closed off I've been from people my entire life. You were teaching me to be with people. You were showing me the world I'd been missing."

"I know," I whispered.

"What you and I shared. I thought that was special."

"It was."

"I wasn't." She answered heatedly. "If it meant something to you, you wouldn't have been with another woman. You wouldn't have even thought about being with someone else." I started to interrupt, but she held up her hand.

"I understand that you two have history. She hurt you. A hurt you'll always remember because of what happened to you in Afghanistan, and I'm sorry about that, I really am." She paused, and I waited for her to tell me to go to hell. I deserved it. "But?"

"But I'm leery." She said as she studied me, her face was somber. "Perhaps you don't know what you want. Maybe it's not over with Chelsea, and I'm just a passing whimsy."

I had to smile with her old-fashioned terminology. "I'm over her Belle."

She shook her head back and forth. "I don't know what to think Brady?"

"I won't hurt you again Belle."

"How can you be so sure? What if another girl turns your head? What if I'm intended to be with Kip or Adam, and by giving you another chance I ruin a chance for me to find happiness?"

I hung my head. There was absolutely nothing I could say to that. I looked back into her sad blue eyes.

"If being with Kip or Adam makes you happy Belle then I guess I'll have to be content just being your friend, and I will always be your friend, Belle, because I know, without a doubt, that I want, no, I need you in my life. All I want is for you to be happy. That's how I know I care about you Belle. I only want what's best for you." Tears leaked from

her eyes and before I knew it, she had thrown
herself into my arms.

She sobbed on my shoulder, and I held her tightly
against my chest. I didn't know why she was crying.
I loved that I was holding her in my arms but hated
that she was unhappy.

"I'm sorry Belle, whatever I said to make you cry
I'm sorry." I hushed into her ear.

I felt her hand reach between us and she wiped her
eyes and then pushed back so she could talk to me.

"Brady you didn't say anything wrong. You said
everything right." Her lips turned upwards, and for
the first time in weeks, I felt optimistic.

"So we're good?"

"Define good?" She said with a nervous giggle.

"I'm going to continue to take care of the farm,
and every day I'm going to show you that I care for
you, only you."

Belle

My heart had turned to absolute mush listening to
Brady. I knew I would be in for a serious hurt if he
pushed me away again, but I also knew if I didn't
give him and me a chance, another chance, that I
would always wonder.

I lingered in his welcoming arms gathering my
emotions. My Gram would be appalled at how
much I had cried in the last month. Granted losing
Momma and Josh were cry worthy events, but I
had never been this emotional before. Maybe I was
more like Momma than I thought.

"Are you okay?" Brady asked gently.

"Yes, sorry about that."

"You're allowed to cry, Belle."

I wiped my teary eyes and faced Brady.

"So now what? How does this work?" I asked gesturing between us.

"What do you mean?"

"Brady, I'm walking now. You don't have to stay on the farm anymore."

"I know, but you're not completely healed yet. Plus, nothing weird has happened while I've been here. You're finally sleeping, right?"

That question made me smile because it was so true and he knew it. I'd been sleeping great since Brady had been staying with me.

"If I stay on the farm I can work longer. I have a few projects I want to take on if you agree that is." He added quickly.

"Like what?"

"Well, I want to rebuild the chicken coop. I drew up plans that I'll show you. I want to put up motion sensor lights around the house and barn. The driveway needs to be grated. Your grain bins need replacing, and I'd like to add more pigs."

"That will be a lot of work, but Brady, the pigs. I don't generate enough leftovers to sustain the pigs I have. Even if you were to stay here with me, there isn't enough table waste to feed two pigs."

"Yes, but the diner does."

"What?"

"I spoke with Mrs. Angelina, and she will give us the diners leftovers. We have to supply the diner with a regulation refuse receptacle for the food scraps, and we have to pick it up a couple of times a week, but it's a win-win. She won't have to pay for an extra garbage haul, and we get all their the food leftovers.

I grinned so widely my cheek hurt. "Brady that's the shrewdest idea I've ever heard," I told him enthusiastically.

He blushed, and I gently pushed a lock of his dark hair from his forehead. "You really are an intelligent man," I told him softly.

Brady took my face in his large hands and leaned in. "I want to kiss you, Belle, please tell me I can kiss you."

I answered him by pulling him closer. Please don't let him hurt me I prayed as our lips touched. The kiss was so tender that I trembled, and there they were, fireworks. My heart hammered, and my insides zinged wildly. He ended the sweet kiss, and the look in his eyes was one I knew I would never forget.

"I care about you so much Belle. You are easily the best thing that has ever happened to me."

I melted hearing his heartfelt declaration. He pulled me to him again, and this kiss was more eager, more, passionate, more Brady. The proverbial fireworks shot off again. How could kissing make me dizzy? I was spinning. Maybe this was what my Gigi had called swoon-worthy. She said when she had met my Great Grandfather he was swoon-worthy.

Brady pulled back after a few heated seconds, and I could see that his pupils had dilated and that his breathing was as erratic as mine. He turned my knees so I was facing front again in the truck and he buckled me back into my seatbelt.

During the ride back home we talk about the numerous plans Brady had for the farm. I loved that he wanted to make the improvements. We talked about ways I could contribute without taxing my shoulder and ankle.

When we arrived back at the farm, Brady bounded out of the truck, quickly opening my door for me before helping me down. As I stood on the ground in front of him, he pulled me into a gentle embrace, and I put my arms around his back and settled my cheek on his chest. His chin rested on my head, and I couldn't help but feel like we were two pieces of a puzzle that fit together.

"Belle?"

"Umm?" I didn't pull away from his chest I was too comfortable.

"Please don't date Adam." Brady's voice was strained and low.

"I won't Brady." I paused, but before I could speak Brady answered my unspoken question.

"I don't need to date anyone Belle. I have all I want right here in my arms."

"Brady?" I hesitated. I had to know even though it sickened me.

"Did you and Chelsea, when you reconnected, did you, you know? Make love?"

"No." He answered quietly. I believed him. "I didn't even kiss her Belle; I swear."

"Okay," I said as I snuggled in closer.

Brady walked inside with me, and we ate the lunch that we had brought home. Then he told me he was going to work in the garden. I insisted I could weed too so I changed into more appropriate attire, and Brady plopped my big straw hat on my head before we walked out to the garden hand in hand. An hour later my shirt was plastered to my skin. Brady had taken his off, and I had snuck a good many peeks at his glorious body. He stood up and mopped his brow with his tee shirt and then he helped me to my feet.

"How about a swim?"

"Yes!"

"Will you be able to make the walk?" He asked me seriously.

"I think so, plus the cold water will be good for me."

A half hour later we were heading to the swimming hole. On the walk there I moved slowly since my ankle was still stiff and sore. I was thrilled to be mobile though so I couldn't complain. I noticed that Brady was limping more than usual. He always had a slight hitch to his gait, but it seemed more pronounced. I had noticed it when he was fixing the shed, but Adam was nearby, and I didn't want to ask Brady about it in front of him.

When we got to the swimming hole, I took off the beach cover that Brady had given me and Brady laughed seeing that I was wearing the makeshift swimwear that Kip had fashioned for me.

"We have got to get you a suit girl." He laughed playfully.

"Why? I think this is perfect." I giggled.

Brady sat on the grassy ledge above the water so that his back was to me. He slipped off his one boot and pushed down his jeans. He wore a pair of swim trunks underneath. He then unfastened his prosthetic, took that off before pulling off his jeans.

I realized that he still wasn't comfortable displaying his leg to me, and that made me sad. Brady stood up and athletically hopped closer to the water.

"Last one in is a rotten egg!" I yelled from behind him.

I jumped down the bank, and as I started to pass him he grabbed onto my arm, playfully holding me back and we ended up falling into the cold water together.

I was laughing as I adjusted my concocted bathing suit that had slipped sideways. Brady had a huge smile on his face. The man was handsome as sin when he smiled. I pushed myself into deeper waters, and Brady followed. He caught me around my waist and pulled me against his hard chest. He stood in the chest-deep water, my legs naturally wrapped around his athletic hips.

Brady moved a piece of wet hair from my face and then dragged the back of his fingers down my cheek, my jaw, and my throat. The water was freezing, but I was warm as could be. My arms were around his neck; my fingers threaded lazily through his short dark hair.

My body responded to our embrace, and Brady glanced at my chest and looked back at me with a mischievous smile.

"Cold Belle?"

"Maybe?" I coyly responded. Wow, was I flirting?

"Maybe, huh?" Brady pulled me against him and brought his lips crashing down on mine.

I stroked his back, his arms, and his neck as our kiss heated up. Holy smokes this man could ignite a wet match. With one of his hands under my behind and his other hand on my neck, Brady dominated me completely, and I loved it. When we pulled apart, I had to believe it was simply so we could both take a breath. Then just as quickly as we had pulled apart, we dove back in for another kiss. After a few very intense minutes Brady rested his forehead on mine.

"I love kissing you, Belle." His voice was thick with emotion.

"I love kissing you too," I answered softly.

"Fireworks?" He asked with a hint of insecurity lacing his deep voice.

"Big fireworks," I admitted with a crooked grin. His face exploded into a huge smile, and my heart filled with joy seeing how happy he was.

We clung to each other until we heard a branch cracking in the woods across the swimming area. Our heads swiveled quickly in that direction.

"I forgot my gun again," I whispered.

Brady nodded towards the flat rock that jutted out of the water, and we swam to it. Brady put me upon it and keeping his arm around me as he scanned the nearby bushes.

"It could have been a deer." He said, but I knew he didn't think it was a deer any more than I did.

We remained quiet and when we were convinced there was nothing ominous stalking us we went back to playing in the water.

An hour later we were sunning on the grassy bank. We lay on our backs, holding hands and watched the puffy white clouds drift across the crystal blue Vermont sky. I couldn't have been happier.

We decided to head back, and when Brady sat up and reached for his prosthetic, I noticed how raw his stump looked.

"Brady, your leg."

"It's nothing."

"You have been doing too much. It looks awful."

"Thanks." He said sarcastically.

I pulled his shoulder back, so he faced me and pulled him down on top of me.

I took his face in my hands. "Brady McDaniel you know good and well what I'm saying. Don't be like that with me."

He sighed, "I know, sorry. It's not because of working the farm though."

He took my hands in his and kissed each palm lightly, before letting them go. I put my hands back on his shoulders. His hands bracketed my face. His chest was flush against mine, and I parted my legs to allow his hips to settle between my thighs. It was intimate, and his beautiful eyes darkened.

"Talk to me, Brady," I said to him softly.

He hesitated slightly.

"The only person who knows this is my Dad." He confided in me.

"Okay."

"I've applied for a job that requires a physical test. I've been working out. I have to toughen my leg up."

"What kind of job?"

"It's in law enforcement. I'm hoping to become a Deputy, and I want to specialize in Search and Rescue."

I couldn't contain my smile. "That's wonderful."

"It's a start. I've been running every morning. I'm using a blade prosthetic that I got at the VA hospital. The fit is different, so I have some blisters. I'm also experimenting with different prosthetics to see which ones will best suit different terrains. The Search and Rescue training requires me to climb rock faces, swim, repel, ski, and track through woods. I have to be in top physical condition."

"Why didn't you tell me earlier. I would have rubbed your leg."

He kissed me sweetly and smiled. "I only started a few days ago, but I was trying to keep it a secret."

"Why?"

"If I don't pass the tests." His voice trailed off.

"Brady I know how dedicated you are. I'm sure you'll pass, but if you don't then that means your destine for something else."

"Such an optimist." He teased.

"Your experience alone will make you an incredible asset. Even if you don't participate in the actual search, you could coordinate the efforts."

Brady chuckled. "My dad said the same thing." He leaned down placing his hands behind my head, threading his fingers through my still damp hair and kissed me. His soft lips molded into mine and his tongue licked mine, softly coaxing them open. I couldn't hold back a throaty moan of desire. Brady moved his hips, and I felt his thick length rub me intimately.

Brady put his arm under my knee and held it up in the crook of his elbow opening my private area wider as he rubbed his full length against me. He was so hard, and the friction was heady.

"Oh God Belle." Brady husked out. His other hand gripped my rear intimately as he stroked rapidly against me. His fingers slipped underneath my cutoff jeans, and we both groaned loudly as he found my wetness. He rocked into me faster, and his face found refuge in my neck as he licked and sucked my skin erotically.

I was close. I matched Brady's pace unabashedly finding my release so quickly that I yelled out his name. Hot waves of pleasure undulated from my body, even my eyelids tingled. Brady groaned, and his strong chest quivered as he pressed his steely length against me. Warm wet liquid seeped through his bathing trunks to mix with my own wetness. He moaned my name into my neck, and I clutched him tightly moving my hips in little circles to coax every delicious climatic spasm from him.

He lay on top of me using his forearms to lift some of his weight from me, but our bodies were fused together so perfectly that I was comfortable. We were breathing heavily as we held each other enjoying the post orgasm bliss.

Brady rolled off me grabbing my hand and holding it to his chest. He had an adorable smile on his face. I turned so I could lay my head on his shoulder, and he accommodated me by wrapping his arm around my shoulders and holding me to him. He placed a kiss on my forehead and the peace I felt laying in his arms was nothing I'd ever felt before.

A few quiet minutes passed, and I was so completely relaxed that I was falling asleep, but Brady tapped me gently.

"I need to go back in the water Belle."

I realized he wanted to clean up, so I sat up allowing him to do the same. I watched from the sun-warmed bank as he deftly hopped off the grassy ledge into the cold water.

Brady

We headed back to the farm hand in hand. I was head over heels for Belle. Just looking at her made my chest tighten. Thinking about how close I came to losing her gutted me. I still wanted to take it slow. We may have just had an intensely physical encounter, but there was so much more I wanted to experience with her. She was a virgin, and I wanted her to initiate when we would make love. I didn't want to push her into anything she didn't feel comfortable doing.

The water had felt great on my tender limb, but the second I placed my leg back into the plastic sleeve the stinging of the raw wounds had me limping again.

"When we get back I'd like to rub some ointment on your leg if that's alright?" Belle asked as we trudged along.

I hated feeling so damaged.

"Brady?"

"Yeah, okay."

Belle stopped walking, and I saw her cock her head as if she was listening to something. Experience made me listen instead of talking. She looked at me, and I nodded letting her know I too had just heard movement in the woods behind us. I turned slowly keeping Belle between me, and whatever was in the woods. Another rustling sound drew our intention, and I took off running in that direction, leaving Belle, where she stood on the trail.

I crashed through the dense underbrush; my leg was screaming in pain. I could hear whatever I was chasing running away from me. I instantly picked up that this was not an animal.

The sounds of branches and leaves being stepped on were coming in sequences of two, not three or four like an animal would make. I couldn't see the trespasser through the dense woods, and I quickly reasoned that if the person were inadvertently trespassing, they would not have run. It was most likely a hunter poaching on Belle's property. I slowed my chase and retraced my steps back to where I'd left Belle.

When I reached her, I realized I had made a grave mistake leaving her unprotected. Her face was pale, and she was trembling. When I was within arm's length, she reached for me, and I held her against me. She wasn't crying; I knew she just needed to be held.

"It was a person wasn't it?"

"Yes."

"Were they watching us?"

"I think it was probably a poacher. It was only one person. What are you thinking?"

Belle shrugged.

"Tell me, Belle."

"I guess I'm just paranoid because of all the things that have happened at the house."

I kissed her lips then her forehead. "We'll figure it out. I won't let anything happen to you."

"Brady you're not going to be with me all the time."

I frowned knowing that she was right. I took her hand in mine, and we continued walking along the trail.

When we got back to the farm, Belle went to shower, and I changed out of my swim trunks so I could put the animals away for the night. When I went back inside Belle was in the kitchen.

"Brady how about hamburgers for dinner?"

"Sounds good. I'll start the grill."

I walked out back to the stone patio. Belle's grill was the old charcoal kind. It was built from stone and had flat stone surfaces near the grilling surface and a chimney behind the griddle to vent the large pits area. There was a spit above the grilling area too, with a hand crank. I took charcoal out from the tightly closed tin bin near the grill and arranged the charcoal pieces before igniting them.

Belle came outside carrying a tray. She placed a plate with two burgers and two pieces of cheese along with a wooden handled spatula on one of the flat ledges. She carried everything else to the picnic table. I watched as she set the table with a salad and silverware. She went back inside and came out with a pitcher of lemonade. She poured a glass and walked it to me. I took the glass from her and thanked her with a kiss that had her melting into me. When we came up for air, she giggled.

"Wow, what brought that on?" She said snuggling into my embrace.

"That was my thank you for my lemonade."

"I'll have to bring you lemonade more often." She laughed pushing away from me. I pulled her back to me and kissed her again. I kissed her breathless. I pulled away just slightly and took her chin in my fingers, so she was looking into my eyes.

"Belle, I'd kiss you all day if I could. You have no idea what you do to me." My voice was husky, and I hoped I was conveying to her just how much I cared.

She pressed a gentle kiss to my lips. "You're sweet."

"I'm serious," I told her. She hesitated. I think she saw how sincere I was, and I didn't like the small worry line that appeared on her forehead.

I kissed the frown line. I knew it would take time for her to fully trust me again.

We grilled the burgers and enjoyed a peaceful dinner on the stone patio. We remained outside talking about everything from the weather, to childhood stories until the mosquitoes chased us inside.

After we washed the dishes, Belle turned to me, and I knew I wasn't going to like what she was going to say.

"Brady, thank you so much for taking care of me, for sleeping here, but I don't feel it's appropriate for you to sleep here now that I'm mobile."

"I had a feeling you were going to say that."

Although I had prepared myself my heart felt as if it was being squeezed in a vice.

I gathered my bag that I had in the mudroom off the kitchen and walked to Belle who was waiting for me at the front door.

"Thank you, Brady." My sweet Belle said taking my hand.

We walked outside to my truck, and I hefted my bag into the bed. Belle froze, and I saw a look of concern on her face.

"Brady I never rubbed your leg down."

I gave her a quick kiss on the lips and jumped into my cab. "It's okay. I'll take a rain check."

"I'll see you tomorrow?" She asked, and I didn't miss the apprehension registering in her voice.
"I'll be here bright and early," I assured her. She smiled faintly. "Are you going to be okay?" I asked.
"I hope the ghost stays away." She joked half-heartedly.
"Do you want me to stay? I'll sleep in the barn." I was dead serious.
"No." She laughed. "I'll be fine. I'm pretty tired. I'm going to read and go to bed early."
"Call my cell if you need me, okay?"
"Okay, thanks."
As I drove away, I kept looking at her in my rearview. She was standing in her driveway with her slim arms crossed in front of her. I lost sight of her when I rounded the curve in her drive.
When I got home, my Mom gave me an impromptu hug, and I knew that my Dad had shared with her that I was applying for the deputy job. Tommy and my dad were watching television. The house smelled like fresh baked cookies. I grabbed one from the cooling rack before my Mom could swat my hand away.
"How's Belle?" My dad asked.
"She's good. She's walking on her own. I know she's still sore though."
"I would imagine so; she took a beating." He reminded me; I didn't need to be reminded. Seeing her bruises had been disturbing.
"I'm making her cookie's." My Mom interjected as she flew around the kitchen.
"She'll like that Mom, thanks."

I settled on a chair near the couch and munched on the cookie. "You okay?" My dad asked.

"Yeah, I don't like that she's alone out there. I'm worried about her."

My dad shot my Mom a quick look, and I saw her smile before turning her back to pull another batch of cookies out of the oven.

"She wouldn't let you stay?"

"No, I told her I'd sleep in the barn, but she pretty much insisted I come home. She's old-fashioned like that."

"She's good and proper." My Mom piped in.

Dad chuckled. "She is a throwback all right."

"Yeah." I agreed. My dad chuckled again and slapped my knee as he stood up.

"You got a letter today." He tossed a long white envelope onto my lap.

I opened the official-looking envelope. It was from the town's administrator.

I read it and then reread it. When I looked up from it both my parents and Tommy were looking at me anxiously.

"I'm approved to take the civil exam and physical tests for the Deputy Certification, and I have a meeting tomorrow in Springfield to discuss the process. Dad, it says here that Lansing and your department is sponsoring the training I need?"

"The town council voted unanimously to sponsor you, Brady. They want you to work here. The training for the job is intense and expensive. You have to have a department sponsor you to even get into the program, and the town council decided to not only sponsor you but to pay for it as well. It's a gesture of goodwill. We sponsor you. You pass the tests, become a deputy, and work for us."

"They're willing to do this knowing that I'm an amputee?"

"Son, the council knows what kind of a man they'll be getting. You'll make a great deputy."

"It's unbelievable." I shook my head in disbelief. My Mom came over and sat down by me. "Brady I'm so proud of you."

"Thanks, Mom."

"Does Belle know you want to be a deputy?" Tommy asked. I looked at him a little surprised. "She does. Why?"

"Just making sure you don't F - it up with her again." He laughed.

"Language." My dad said swatting the back of his head. I tossed a couch cushion at him and stood up.

"Well, I have an early day. I'm heading to bed." I kissed my Mom goodnight and went into my room. I looked at the clock and saw that it was after 9:00 PM. I wanted to call Belle, to tell her about my letter, but I didn't want to wake her if she was asleep.

24

Belle

I settled into bed and picked up a book that lay on my nightstand. I had decided not to read Steven King anymore I was scared enough with all the crazy things I'd been experiencing. The house was eerily quiet and knowing that Brady wasn't on the couch right outside my door had me hyper-aware of any noise. I opened my window, but not as wide as usual considering it was summer. I couldn't concentrate on my book, the mystery I'd gotten from the library, so I turned off my light and lay back.

The sounds of nocturnal animals leaves softly rustling, and the sweet, fragrant scent of pine drifted through my open window. The familiar sounds and smells of a Vermont summers night began to lull me to sleep. I loved Vermont. Then I sleepily giggled. I only knew Vermont.

I awoke to the unwelcomed sound of footsteps in the room above mine, my Momma's room. This time instead of jumping out of bed and grabbing my gun I lay in bed and listened. I was frightened beyond words, but I also wanted to make sure I wasn't dreaming. I needed to be able to explain exactly what I heard to Brady. I didn't want him to think I was nuts. Was someone in my house or was it a ghost? Could a ghost start a fire?

The footsteps grew louder. It was as if the ghost wanted me to react. Finally, I got out of bed, took my gun from its rack, and headed up the steps stomping my feet as I climbed. My heart was pounding so hard that it drummed in my ears. "That's right!" I yelled. "Here I come. Maybe this time you'll stay around so I can see you!"

I walked to Momma's door and nudged it open with my foot. There was no one in the room. The windows were closed, but one of the travel brochures from her drawer was lying on her mattress. I froze upon seeing it, and the air whooshed out of my lungs. I turned completely around with my gun raised, looking down the sight, trembling. No one was in the room; it was empty and undisturbed except for the brochure.

I opened Momma's closet slowly. That's where I had put the items that I had found in her room that I planned to look over when I had some time, especially her journal. The box was right on the shelf where I'd left it. I shut the door and backed out of the room.

When I reached the doorway, I stopped. "Momma if this is you, please stop. You're scaring me. Are you telling me you want me to travel? I don't understand. Please, Momma. Please go to heaven." I closed the door and headed back to my room listening for any more sounds. I placed my gun back in her place and burst into tears.

It had to be Momma's ghost. She was trying to tell me something, but it was scaring me to pieces. I was weeping when I climbed back into my bed.

I woke up to the rooster crowing, and I rubbed my swollen eyes. I heard Brady's truck roll in, and I quickly jumped into the shower hoping to wash away the fatigue and unease plaguing me. I was debating on what to tell him if anything. We had just gotten ourselves to a good place, and I did not want to pull him into my craziness. I had lain awake for a long time last night thinking about Momma's ghost. I was convinced that she wanted me to take a trip, travel and maybe she was telling me she wanted me to sell the farm. I couldn't be positive, and I was so tired that when I finally drifted off to sleep all my thoughts colliding with each other making for an awful nightmare.

When I got out of the shower I checked my face, and I was relieved to see that I looked okay, maybe a little tired, but not like a crazy loon, like I was feeling.

I made coffee and brought a cup out to Brady who was in the barn.

"Hi, Beautiful." He said the second I walked in. He reached me in three long strides and swept me up in a grand embrace followed by a searing kiss. The coffee sloshed over the sides, and I squealed delightedly as I tried to balance the coffee cup. "Brady your coffee." I giggled.

He kissed my cheek while keeping an arm around me. Then he took the cup from me taking a large sip. "Mmm, you make the best coffee, Belle. Thanks."

"You're welcome."

Brady placed the coffee on an exposed side beam and continued with the morning chores. He was

ushering the sheep into their corral, so I walked
Henny and Bessie outside.

"Hey, that's my job," he said with a bright smile.

"Brady I like to do this too." I laughed.

He walked to his coffee and took another sip. "I
know. I'm only teasing."

"I'll make eggs. Come inside when you're done,
okay?"

"Be there in a few minutes."

I could feel his eyes on me as I walked back to the
house. He couldn't see my face, but I had a huge
grin plastered on it.

When Brady came in, I had just finished plating his
breakfast of eggs, fried ham, orange juice, and my
bread, of course.

"Wow, a feast. Thank you."

We sat down, and I watched as he dug in. He was
talking, and I didn't hear a thing he was saying. I
was watching how animated he was and how his
handsome face was lite up. He took a breath from
talking only to chew his food. I stared at his lips
and remembered how they felt on mine. How he
had buried his face in my neck as he pushed against
me.

"Belle? Belle?"

I had completely zoned out. "Belle, what are you
thinking about?"

I blushed furiously. I sure as heck wasn't going to
tell him what I'd just been thinking. I stammered
and then stood up quickly with my plate taking it to
the sink.

Brady stood up and pulled me down on his lap.

"Oh no, you don't, woman. You didn't eat a thing. What were you thinking about?"

"Brady," I said squirming self-consciously.

"Come on tell me. Are you okay? Did you have a good night?"

I remembered Momma's ghost, and I averted his eyes.

His body tensed. "Crap, what happened?"

He knew me too well.

"The ghost visited again."

Brady's arms tightened around me, and the alarmed look in his eyes was exactly what I had been trying to avoid.

"Tell me what happened."

"I heard footsteps. I went upstairs, and there was a brochure on Momma's bed."

"A brochure?"

"A travel brochure. Momma had travel brochures in her personal things. She wanted us to travel after she sold the farm."

"Babe, you're Mommas in heaven. You know that right?"

I nodded. "But I think she's trying to send me a message."

"Do you want to sell the farm?"

"No. I don't think so, but I've never known any place else. I've never been any place else. I feel like I'm deciding without having all the information I need."

"That makes sense."

"It does?"

"Sure. This farm has been your world. You're just starting to experience what life is like beyond your property and this town." He paused and rubbed my back. "Just please don't make a quick decision. You have had so much change in your life lately. First, let yourself heal from losing your Mom and then I'm sure you'll be able to make a good decision."

I wrapped my arms around Brady's neck. "You're so smart," I said kissing him after each word.

He chuckled and stood up with me still in his arms. Whoa, he was strong. He placed me on my feet and then took his plate to the sink.

"Belle, I don't believe in ghosts and if you're hearing footsteps that has me worried."

"I know me too. I swear I'm not imagining them, Brady."

"I believe you, that's why I'm so concerned. Should we call my Dad?"

"I'd rather not, okay?"

"Okay. I have to go to Springfield to meet with someone about the job I told you about."

"Really? That's great."

"Would you like to come with me?"

I thought about visiting the fun town again, but I was tired from lack of sleep and Brady had a meeting and would not have been with me, so I decided against it.

"I think I'll stay here."

"You sure?"

"Yes, thanks."

Before Brady left, he did a thorough check of the upstairs. I showed him the brochure still lying on the bed, and he looked really concerned.

"What are you thinking?" I asked him as we walked back downstairs.

"I'm thinking I don't like you being out here on your own. I'm going to ask my dad to drive by while I'm gone."

"You don't have to."

He cut me off by giving me a hard and thoroughly wonderful kiss.

"I won't say anything, even though it goes against my better judgment, but I am telling my dad to drive by."

After he left, I cleaned up the breakfast dishes and put together a meal in the crockpot for dinner. I didn't know if Brady would stay. The last time I had assumed that he would stay for dinner, he hadn't, and that still stung, but I felt we were beyond that.

I called Dr. Lachlan and was delighted to hear that William could come home. He was going to be in a splint, but he needed his mom, so the doctor was releasing him.

I hopped into my truck and headed to the vet's office. As I drove down the windy mountain road that separated my place from town, I slowly began to pump the brakes, like I had been told to do when going down the steep incline. The second time that I pressed lightly on the brake pedal alarm rifled through me as the pedal depressed, without any resistance, to the floor. I stomped on the

unresponsive pedal again and again, but it kept
hitting the floorboard. My truck was gaining speed
as I raced down the precipitous mountain road.
I held on to the wheel tightly, panic seizing me as I
tried to steer the out of control truck down the
gravel road. I debated jumping from the cab, but I
was going so fast it would be suicide. My entire
body seized with fear. My fingers clutched the
wheel as a fresh wave of terror stole my breath. A
car passed me, and I narrowly missed sideswiping
it. The driver honked at me angrily.

My truck was swerving dangerously, and I was
going so fast that the landscape outside my window
passed in a blur. I was panicked that I might crash
into car another and God-forbid hurt them. I
couldn't live with myself if that were to happen. I
was still slamming my foot on the pedal, praying
the brakes would somehow start working. I had to
do something.

There was a drainage ditch running along the side
of the road to my right and beyond the ditch were
woods. If I steered into the drainage ditch, I didn't
know if I'd jump over the ditch and crash into the
woods, or if my tires would stick in the ditch, and
eventually slow me down enough that I could
purposely crash safely. It was the only option I had
before I reached a more populated area.

I braced myself and steered towards the side of the
road. I didn't anticipate the ditch being as deep as
it was. My front right tire slammed into the ditch,
and the steering wheel jerked out of my hands; I
screamed in terror. My back tire followed the front

tire and my seatbelt roughly dug into my chest and neck as my body was momentarily flung to the side over the middle console. My arms grasped the dashboard just as the trucks front end smashed into something that sent the truck into a front-end headstand. My airbag exploded smashing into my face forcefully. My seatbelt held me fast, even though I was upside down and I yelped in pain as it tightened on my collarbone and chest. I heard metal scraping and glass breaking as my truck jumped the ditch and smashed into the trees. My last coherent thoughts were, "I'm going to be with my family again and that Brady was going to be mad I didn't go with him."

A bright light was shining in my eyes, and I heard my name being called, but it was muffled. Red and blue lights were bouncing off my rearview into my eyes making me squint. I tried lifting my arm, but it was pinned under the steering wheel, which was pressed tightly against my chest.
"Belle, geez, Belle please answer me."
The voice finally registered as Kip's, and I tried to answer him, but it came out as a moan.
"Belle, can you hear me?"
I must have moved my head, and I heard him say "Thank God."
"She's alive. Get that can opener over here now."
I blacked out again, and this time when I regained consciousness, it was to the excruciating sound of metal ripping pulled apart. Still dazed I listened to the sounds of Kip and the men around him trying

to rescue me from my truck. I was suspended
partly upside down, my steering wheel was pressed
uncomfortably against my chest, the airbag now
soft and threatening to suffocate me. My one free
arm was lying across the middle console. I wiggled
my feet and was relieved I could feel them, and
nothing felt broken. Even though I couldn't move
my one arm, I could move my fingers. My clavicle
was killing me, and I hoped I hadn't broken it
again. My seatbelt was cutting into me, but I knew
wearing it had most assuredly saved my life.
I heard Sheriff McDaniel yelling, and then a loud
thud sounded sending a vibration through the
truck. Cool air washed over me as the door to the
truck was pried from its frame. I pushed the airbag
away from my face so I could see. The windshield
was cracked with an intricate spider webbed
pattern, so much so that I couldn't see out of it.
"Belle, Can you hear me?"
"Yes." My voice didn't even sound like me. It was
low and scratchy.
"Good girl. Listen I have to let the EMT guys look
at you before I get you out, okay?"
I didn't answer I was feeling sick and I was afraid if
I opened my mouth I would vomit.
A man climbed in and carefully perched over me
using a little flashlight to look into my eyes and all
over my body. The smell of gas permeated my
senses so thickly that I retched, and mumble a
sorry.
"I smell gas." I heard someone say. "It's catching
fire." Someone else yelled.

"Joe, get out of there now!" Sheriff McDaniel yelled. The Paramedic scrambled out of the smashed in cab of my truck. The man hesitated; I could tell he was concerned about leaving me. "Joe, now!"

Joe backed out of the confined space, and a searing blast of heat heated my feet as orange flames crept up my dashboard.

I was woozy and thought I had just been left alone to die until I felt my seatbelt slacken, and strong arms pulled me roughly from the smoke and heat. Kip.

Kip had me in his arms, and he was sprinting. He had only taken a few paces from my truck when it exploded loudly, launching both of us into the air. Kip pressed my face into his chest and cocooned me with his massive body as we rolled on the dirt road. We lay on the road for a few seconds catching our breaths. Kip carefully unwrapped himself from me, and I saw dark smoke rising from what was left of my truck. Firefighters ran to hose it down; Joe the paramedic and Sheriff Mac Daniels were running towards us.

Kip made me lay still while he assessed me for injuries and I obliged since I was too sore to move anyways. Sheriff McDaniel knelt next to me, and he and Kip shared a look.

"Belle, what happened?" Sheriff McDaniel's asked.

"The brakes." I gulped in a breath. "The brakes didn't work."

The Sheriff ran his hands over his face, and Kip looked horrified. I knew I was lucky to be alive, again.

Tears clouded my vision. Why was all this happening to me?

"Honey are you in pain?" The Sheriff asked.

I shook my head. "Brady?" I managed to choke out. I needed Brady.

His dad answered. "I called him. He's on his way."

Joe piped in. "Tell him to meet her at the clinic we're rolling."

I was lifted onto a board, and my neck was secured with a brace, and then I was strapped down. It was scary. I imagined what my mother might have experienced in her last moments of living. The Sheriff had said that she died immediately, but I didn't know if he was just spare me. She may have been strapped to a board like I was as they tried to save her life. Tears dripped down my cheeks.

Kip and the Sheriff helped carry the wooden palate I was strapped to, to the ambulance. The door closed and I heard the haunting sound of the siren cutting through the usually quite countryside.

I was wheeled into the same clinic I had just recently been released from, and Margaret met me in the hallway.

"Girl, you like it here or what?' She tried joking with me. I smiled at her weakly.

"Missed you too," I joked back.

I was taken into a curtained room, and Doctor Travers walked through the fabric opening.

Margaret was already washing my face. It must have been covered in blood because the gauze pads came away red.

"Belle, talk to me. Do you know what day it is?"

"Thursday," I answered. I knew he was checking if I was concussed. "What happened? Where are you hurting?"

As I told him what happened, he took my pulse, checked my eyes, and tapped me everywhere. Margaret handed him steri-strips, and he affixed them near my hairline. That was a good sign that I didn't need stitches. There was a commotion outside the curtained room, and Brady burst in.

"Brady wait outside." The doctor told him sternly. His eyes were wild with fear.

"I'm okay Brady," I told him with a wobbly voice. I wasn't, but he looked so distressed I wanted to calm him down.

Just hearing my voice pacified him. Just seeing him calmed me. The doctor must have recognized this because he allowed Brady to stand next to me. Brady took my hand in his, and I held it like it was a lifeline.

When the doctor finished his examination he stood up and made a few notes on an iPad.

"Belle, I don't think anything is broken. You're going to be sore. You have a large bruise on your rib cage. Does it hurt to breathe? Any stabbing pain?"

I took a deep breath, and although it hurt a little bit, I knew I had not broken any ribs or punctured my lungs. "No," I said.

Brady's eyes searched my face. I could tell he was a mess, but so was I so. Tears ran down my cheek, and Brady wiped them away.

"You have a cut on your forehead, that will bruise, but I don't think it needs stitches. You'll need to ice it tonight. You'll need to ice your ribs too. How's your shoulder?

I rolled it and smiled weakly. "Good."

"That's good. Let's sit you up and see how you do." He and Brady helped me to sit up. I was a tad wobbly, but my body had taken another huge hit. I sat on the edge of the bed, and the Doctor once again checked my pupils and manipulated my neck, arms, and then my ankles. He ran his fingers over my back and used the stethoscope to listen to my breathing, this time placing the cold round piece on my bare back.

Brady held my hand the entire time. It felt awkward like I was a nuisance. He wasn't making me feel that way. He wasn't even talking, but I couldn't shake the feeling that I was becoming a burden.

"Can she go home Doc?" Brady asked.

The Doctor took the stethoscope from his ears and sighed.

"Yes, she needs to rest though. Her body has been traumatized, and she needs to sleep."

I wanted to sleep too. I was exhausted and overwhelmed.

"I want her to take Advil like clockwork for a day. If she experiences anything suspicious bring her right back here. Will you be staying with her?"

Brady didn't even look at me, but I was too weary even to care.

"Yes," he replied immediately.

"Okay then." The Doctor looked at me. "Belle, you're going to be sore for a few days. Let Brady take care of you and get some rest."

Brady had an odd look in his eye and once I again I had that off feeling that I was imposing on him. Margaret returned with a wheelchair, and she wheeled me out while Brady brought his truck to the front. The whole situation was surreal. The Sheriff's car pulled up as Brady stopped in front of us.

"Belle, are you going home already?" The Sheriff asked when he reached me. Brady was standing next to his dad.

"Yes, I'm going to stay with her again." I didn't miss the 'again' he had attached to the end of that sentence.

"Can I follow you home? I need to ask you some questions."

"Okay." I wasn't thinking about what the Sheriff was going to be asking me I was thinking how I could convince Brady that I was well enough to be on my own. The problem was I didn't want to be on my own. I was scared silly.

Brady helped me from my chair. He was ominously quiet, and I had the oddest feeling that my world was about to implode. Brady gently assisted me into his truck and buckled me in. When he walked around the back of his truck, I saw in the side-view mirror that he stopped to talk to his father. His dad put his hand on Brady's shoulder and patted it. Brady walked away from his dad getting into the truck with me.

We headed back to the farm.

"What happened?" Brady asked.

I was upset, and hurting and now Brady was acting distant again. I was not going down this road again.

"First why don't you tell me why you're acting so angry with me?"

Brady glanced at me, and his lips tightened. He slapped the steering wheel.

"I'm not angry Belle, I'm concerned."

"No Brady. I know concerned. You're mad."

He paused, and I saw him look at his dad's Sheriff car following behind us.

"I can't stay with you."

"I don't need you to stay with me."

"You need someone to stay with you, Belle. You hear ghosts; you've had two bad accidents."

I crossed my hands over my chest defensively. "I don't need someone to stay with me." I huffed.

"Belle, I want to stay with you, but I can't."

"I didn't ask you to babysit me, Brady."

"Geez woman, will you listen to me, please. I want to, but I can't."

"You are making no sense." I retorted heatedly.

"I have to leave town."

"What?"

"I found out this morning. Remember I told you about the job?"

"Yes."

"I got a letter yesterday that I am being sponsored by the town of Lansing to go through training to be a Deputy in Lansing. I was also given the go-ahead to join a Search and Rescue training that takes place at the same time. Not everyone gets sponsored; it's a big deal. I went to Springfield today to discuss when everything would take place, and I was told that I have to report tomorrow. I'll be gone for a month."

He looked to me, and I could tell he was upset. "Belle, I have to go. It's a great opportunity. Not everyone gets sponsored, and I know my dad pulled in favors for this. I thought I'd start training in a few months, but there's an opening in the training group that starts tomorrow. It's been recommended that I attend."

I softened my tone. "Okay. I get it. You're leaving, you don't want to, but that doesn't explain why you're so angry at me."

"Cripes, Belle, I'm not. I'm worried about you. I don't want to leave you alone. I'm going to miss you like crazy. I'm worried about the farm. I'm seriously torn on whether to go or not."

"Oh, you're going Brady McDaniel," I replied heatedly.

He glanced at me warily, and I said it again. "You're going."

We pulled to a stop in front of my house and Brady walked around to my door quickly.

"Can we talk about this later?" He whispered as his dad pulled in behind us.

"Maybe," I said walking to the porch and settling on a chair.

The Sheriff settled in a chair next to me, and Brady disappeared inside the house.

"He's going to training," I told his dad.

His dad chuckled. "He told you."

"If he misses this opportunity I will be livid with him. You're his dad; you need to make sure he goes."

"Belle, he's worried about you."

"I can take care of myself." Brady chose that moment to walk back outside. He had a glass of water and two pills in his hands.

"Yeah, and look how well that's working out for you." He interjected sarcastically.

"Now son." The Sheriff replied quickly.

"Dad, I'll be too worried about her. Maybe I can apply next year."

"You will not!" I said stamping my foot belligerently.

"Damn it, Belle."

"Don't you swear at me Brady McDaniel!"

"Stop it, both of you!" The Sheriff's voice was harsh, and it quieted us immediately.

"Business first. Belle, I need to know what happened?"

I started to retell him what had happened when we heard a truck coming down the drive. It was Adam's truck.

"Shit," Brady swore under his breath, and his father shot him a look that I wouldn't want to be on the receiving end of.

Adam and his father walked towards us, and Adam knelt down next to me. "Are you okay?"

"I'm fine. How did you know?"

"Jeannie called me."

I cocked my head realizing that he and Jeannie must have exchanged numbers. I smiled, and he winked at me knowing that I had put two and two together. He and Jeannie must have gotten on very well. That was awesome.

"Belle, what happened?" Mr. Fitzpatrick asked.

I realized that I was going to have to tell the story a dozen times if I didn't take control of the situation

"Can everyone sit down, please? I'll tell you all together, so I don't have to retell it." The Sheriff didn't look pleased.

"Sheriff if you have any questions I'll answer them alone if you like, but seriously can I just tell everyone what happened at the same time, please?" Brady had to put his hand over his mouth to stifle a chuckle.

"Okay, Belle. Tell us what happened. From the beginning and," he said looking at the other three men, "no one interrupts or asks a question except for me. Got it?" The Sheriff said gruffly.

Everyone agreed, and they all sat down. I took another sip of water before speaking.

"I was on my way to pick up William." I turned to Brady. "Oh my gosh William."

"I'll get him later."

"Thank you. Anyway, I got in my truck and was heading down Turner Mountain Road. You know how steep it is, and my Momma always said to pump the brakes cause it's so steep, so I did. I pumped the brakes, and they just gave out. I had my foot pressed all the way to the floor. The truck was barreling down the road, and I was trying to keep it on the road. Then a car went past me, and I almost hit it. The driver honked at me. He was mad. I realized that I could hurt someone and I didn't want to do that, so I steered into the ditch hoping to get the truck to stop. I hit something in the ditch, and the truck flipped. That's all."

I let what I had said sink in, and I watched the four men as my story sunk in.

"Belle, has anyone been around your truck?" The Sheriff asked.

"No."

"Did you stop anywhere before you headed down the mountain?"

"No, I was on my way to get William. I didn't stop anywhere."

"What are you suggesting Sheriff?" Mr. Fitzpatrick asked.

"No questions remember?"

"If Belle needs a lawyer. I damn well will ask questions." Mr. Fitzpatrick answered hotly.

"The Sheriff sighed. "She doesn't need a lawyer.

"Where's my truck?" I asked interrupting the silent war waging between the two men.

"It's been towed to Springfield."

"Why Springfield?" Adam asked.

"No questions." The Sheriff admonished wearily.

I knew I'd ask him that question too, but I'd wait until we were alone.

The Sheriff stood up. "Brady walk me to my car please." Brady stood up. I could tell he didn't like leaving me alone with Adam and his father.

"So you and Jeannie?" I asked when Brady was out of earshot.

He smiled. "We've been on a couple of dates."

"That's great. She's so kind, and you're, well, you're my saving angel. This is awesome!"

"We're keeping it low key."

"Okay, my lips are sealed, but why?"

"She wants to tell Kip. I guess they are very close."

"They are."

"She wants to tell him in person, and she hasn't had a chance."

"See, she's kind."

"She is. Don't tell Brady. Jeannie says they are best friends."

"I won't, but I hate keeping secrets from him."

Mr. Fitzpatrick coughed reminding us that he was there.

"Belle, we were planning on stopping by today anyway. We had hoped to talk business."

Brady walked back onto the porch and sat down. "What did I miss?" Brady said eyeing Adam.

"They wanted to talk business," I told him.

"Do you want me to leave?"

I hesitated. "No, please stay," I told Brady.

"Mr. Fitzpatrick I'm not interested in selling at this time. Is there a time element attached to this deal you are brokering?"

Adam's dad shot him a look that expressed that he was not pleased.

"Adam hasn't talked to me about anything if that's what you're thinking," I told him.

"I was actually hoping my son would have talked to you." He said emphasizing the words would have

"Oh," I said grimacing. I had been attempting to keep Adam out of hot water with his dad, and instead, I threw him in it.

"Dad, I told you I hadn't had a chance to talk to her."

Mr. Fitzpatrick looked really mad, scary mad. He stood up and motioned for Adam to do the same. "I'll be in town for another day or two. My offer is good for five weeks from today. After that, it's off the table."

Mr. Fitzpatrick walked away, and Adam kissed my cheek and said he'd call me tomorrow. Brady was scowling.

When we were alone, I turned to Brady. "Brady, Adam and I are just friends, and you are going tomorrow."

25

Brady

I was so conflicted. It was a great opportunity, one that others would practically kill for. The training was paid for, and to be trained you had to be sponsored, and I was being sponsored. I just could not bear to leave Belle on the farm all alone. She'd had two accidents that could have killed her, and she heard ghosts. I'd never be able to concentrate wondering how she was.

I looked at my beautiful girl. She had a bruise forming under the small white bandage, and she was still in her shirt that was covered in dry blood. She was covered in dirt too. Why was she covered in dirt?
"Why are you covered in dirt? Did you climb out of the truck into the ditch?"
Belle looked away from me, and I knew that I hadn't heard the entire story.
"Belle?"
"Well, I was trapped in my truck, and they used a machine to cut me out, and then it caught on fire, and Kip grabbed me, and we were running, well he was running and carrying me, and the truck exploded, and knocked us to the ground," I hurriedly explained in one breath.
"You have got to be kidding me!" I yelled. I saw her cringe and felt bad.

"Belle, why didn't you tell me that? Does my dad know?"

"First of all, I didn't tell you because we were discussing your future. And yes, your dad was there."

"I'm not going; no way."

"Oh yes, you are."

"Belle."

"Brady."

I shook my head and stood up heading for the barn. I needed to cool down, and I needed to think.

Belle

After I watched Brady walk away, I went inside and fell asleep on the couch. I woke up three hours later feeling achy, but well rested. I could hear Brady fumbling around in the kitchen. He saw me sit up.

"Oh good, you're up. I need to run into town, and my Mom wants us to stop by for dinner. Do you feel up for that?"

"Sure. What are you doing in the kitchen?"

"I'm looking for a treat for William."

"You went and got William?"

"No. Adam did."

"Adam?"

"Yes. I didn't want to leave you alone, and you were sleeping so soundly that I called him and he picked him up.

Brady came over to the couch and sat next to me.
He took my hand in his.

"I don't want to argue with you, Belle."

I put my head on his shoulder.

"Me either."

"I may have an idea that we can both agree on."

"Oh?"

"I'll explain at my parent's house."

"Okay," I answered skeptically. "Are we going
there so everyone can gang up on me? I'm not
going to change my mind about you going, you
know?"

He kissed my head. "No Baby. My Mom just wants
to feed you." He said with a laugh.

"I have to run into town. Adam's going to stay here
with you, okay?"

"Okay."

Brady left, and Adam and I first walked to the barn
so I could see William. My poor little lamb was
hobbling next to his mother, but I swear they both
looked happy. Adam and I walked back outside; it
was a gorgeous day. We sat on the front porch
talking and waiting for Brady to return. I was
thrilled to hear how well he and Jeannie were
getting on. According to Adam, they'd had a few
dates and Adam was all smiles when he talked
about her. I asked if I could tell Brady yet and
Adam said Jeannie still had not talked to Kip, so
that was a big no.

When Brady returned, Adam went to meet him,
and I watched as the two men shook hands. Brady

walked Adam to his truck; they were deep in conversation. I wondered what that was all about?

Two hours later Brady and I were on our way into town. I had showered and seen William happily reunited with his mom, and after my nap, I was feeling surprisingly good for someone who had been in an accident just that morning. Although I tried to act nonplussed, I was besieged with thoughts that Brady would be away for a month, and this was my last night with him. That did not feel so good. I knew Brady was up to something. I couldn't assess his mood though. He seemed okay, but there was an underlining current of unhappiness.

We stopped in front of Mr. Bee's office, and he hopped out telling me he'd be right back. I watched Donna jump from her chair the second Brady walked in, but I could tell Brady was deflecting her flirtatious advances by his body language, and how quickly he walked away from her. It made me think about Brady being away for a month. How many women would he be around? Surely the men and women that were training would have days off. They would most likely blow off a little steam at some of the local bars. I was beginning to feel like pushing Brady to go maybe wasn't the brightest idea. Then I realized how selfish I was being. Brady returned to the truck, and I was shocked to see that Adam was with him. Adam climbed into the back.

"Hey, Belle."

"What's going on?" I asked looking back and forth between the two men.

"We will tell you at dinner," Brady said looking at Adam in his rearview.

"Brady I'm getting a little anxious about this dinner."

"Don't worry Belle. I promise it's all good." Adam said rubbing my shoulder from the back seat.

Brady saw Adam touch me and I could see his jaw tighten. What the heck was going on here? Brady was letting Adam console me?

When we got to his parent's house, Brady ushered me inside. We walked through the living room, into the kitchen, and outside onto a large wooden deck where his Mom and Dad were waiting for us.

After the hugs and welcomes, the men were immediately handed beers, and Mrs. McDaniel handed me a lemonade and vodka concoction. I couldn't even taste the vodka, so I knew to sip the drink slowly. Something was going on, and I wasn't sure if I was going to like it or not.

The men were discussing the Red Sox versus Yankees series that was coming up. I listened to them knowing very little about the sport. Sheriff McDaniel was standing next to a silver and black grill watching over steaks while Mrs. McDaniel set the picnic table with colorful plates. On another table were side- dishes of cold salads and corn on the cob wrapped in tin foil that had already been grilled. I offered to help, but Mrs. McDaniel's shooed me away with a little hand wave.

Brady looked at Adam, and I saw Adam nod back to him. Brady turned to me, and a shiver ran up my spine. "Belle, we have an idea. One that we hope you'll agree too."

He was sitting next to me, and I turned towards him slightly and whispered. "You're scaring me, Brady. What's going on?"

Brady put a small folder on my lap. I looked at him, and he motioned for me to open it. When I did, I saw that it contained travel brochures for Boston, New York City, Steam Boat Springs, Colorado, and California's Disney Land.

My heart was pounding in my chest. I didn't understand. Why would he be giving me travel brochures? When I lifted the brochures out of the folder, I saw there were plane tickets and travel itineraries attached to each brochure.

"I don't understand." My voice cracked.

"Belle, I need to do this training."

"I know Brady. I want you to go."

"Honey." I blushed he just called me 'Honey' in front of his parents and Adam. "I want to make sure that you are safe while I'm gone."

"I'll be careful Brady. I promise." My voice was barely above a whisper.

He grinned, but the smile didn't reach his eyes. "I know you can take care of yourself, but I'd still worry about you."

"But." I tried to interrupt, but he shook his head effectively shushing me.

"I want you to take a trip, a little vacation actually. While I'm gone, we want you to travel." He gestured to Adam and his parents indicating that they agreed with him. " We want you to see America and enjoy yourself."

My heart was beating so quickly that I thought I might pass out. I couldn't leave my farm. I didn't know anything about traveling. I'd get lost. I'd...

"Belle, stop thinking whatever you're thinking and hear me out."

I nodded, but I was on the verge of an anxiety attack.

"You and Adam."

"Adam?"

"Adam," Brady repeated. "Are going to travel to all these places. Adam will be your guide and keep you safe. I will be able to train without worrying, and you'll get to have fun, and travel like your Mom wanted."

"You want me to go to all these places with Adam?" I was floored.

"Yes. You know I'd love to be the one to take you traveling for the first time. I wish I could, but I can't."

Tears burst from my eyes, and I sobbed into my hands. No one spoke, and I felt so foolish. Brady was sending me on a trip with someone that he thought liked me. He was putting my safety and well-being ahead of his jealousy. He had no idea that Adam and Jeannie were together. I couldn't even tell him. He had to be thinking there was a risk of me falling for Adam while we were away together. I knew at that very moment that I loved Brady McDaniel with all my heart.

Brady put his arm around me, and I cried into his chest. "Belle, I'm sorry. I thought you'd be happy. Please don't be upset."

I pulled myself together. I could see that his parents looked concerned and Adam was puzzled as to why I had started crying.

"I'm not upset." I was finally able to voice. "It's just that this is so Brady of you," I said looking at him.

"Brady of me?" He asked puzzled.

"Selfless," I said.

It was Brady's turn to blush. "I just want you, safe Belle. We want you safe." He said indicating Adam and his parents again.

"Brady, this would be a great adventure, and I appreciate that you set all this up, but I have a farm to maintain."

Brady nodded to Adam. Adam moved to sit on the ottoman in front of me. "I have hired an older couple that use to work on our ranch in Burlington. They are retired, but I know for a fact that they have been bored silly. They would love to come to your farm and take care of the animals, house, and garden and keep it running while we are away. If you'll agree, of course." He added quickly."

"But the cost?"

Brady put his hand on my knee. "It's all taken care of. You just have to agree."

I looked at the McDaniel's, Adam, and Brady; everyone was anxiously waiting for me to answer. "I don't know what to say?"

"Say yes, Belle." Adam urged me.

I looked at Brady. I wanted to ask him more questions when we were alone.

"We can talk more about it tonight." He said reading my mind. "We all care for you Belle, and we want to make sure you stay safe."

Sheriff McDaniel was plating the steaks, and he turned towards us. "Belle, maybe this will help you decide. Your misadventures; these accidents you've had. Well you know they have not been accidents, right? Your brakes not working today were not an accident either. The brake line had been cut, and the CSU in Springfield found accelerant had been splashed inside your trucks engine. It really will be for the best if you took a few weeks away from here while we figure out who wants to hurt you."

"My brakes were cut?"

"Dad, when did you find out?"

"I got the call right before you got here. If you hadn't put together this impromptu trip for Belle, I would have suggested something like it."

Brady had taken my hand in his. "Belle, please go on this trip with Adam."

His eyes were troubled, and I hated that I was causing him so much worry. I didn't want to cost him the chance at a job I knew he would love either. I had to say yes.

"Okay Brady, for you." I could hear the collective sighs of relief.

He kissed my cheek and whispered. "This is for us."

My heart ached for him. He was sending me off on a trip with someone he was clearly jealous of just to keep me safe.

Sheriff McDaniel placed the platter of steaks down on the table, and Mrs. McDaniel handed us plates so we could serve ourselves from the side table. Brady was quiet during dinner. I knew he was relieved that I was leaving town, but I speculated that he was also uneasy about me being with Adam for all that time. I wanted to tell Adam that he had to tell Brady that he was with Jeannie.

Unfortunately, I was never able to get Adam alone. There was no way I'd break Adams confidence and tell Brady on my own. Adam and Jeannie were correct that Brady would tell Kip, and none of us wanted Kip to be hurt.

We dropped Adam off after dinner at his Bed and Breakfast. As he was getting out of the back, I had to ask.

"Adam I can't think your dad is pleased with you taking this trip with me."

Adam chuckled, "Actually, he loves it. He thinks I'm going to woo you while we are gone and convince you to sell."

I saw Brady's subtle reaction to the word woo, his grip tightened on the steering wheel. Adam said he would come for me tomorrow at noon. I thought about all the packing I had to do. Mrs. McDaniel had loaned me her two suitcases. I didn't even know what to pack. I'd have to rely on Brady for that.

While we drove home, I decided that tonight I was going to make sure Brady knew how much I cared for him. I didn't know if I'd tell him that I loved him. I wanted to, but what if he wasn't ready to hear it? What if it scared him away from me? I didn't know how long people waited before they said those three sacred words. I just knew I had to make sure Brady knew that Adam was not a threat to him.

26

Belle

When we got home, we walked to the barn to check on the animals. William was curled up next to Mimi, and that sight was warming. We walked back to the house hand in hand.

Brady put the suitcases on the floor in my room. He moved to leave. "Brady?"

He turned back to me, and the sadness in his eyes almost brought me to tears.

"We need to talk." I motioned for him to sit on the bed, but he remained standing.

"We should talk in the living room, Belle." He said quietly looking around the room.

"No Brady. We need to have this talk in here." I lifted my tee shirt over my head and watched as Brady's jaw drop.

I unhooked my bra and tossed it on the floor with my tee shirt, unbuttoned my denim shorts, and pulled off my underwear along with my shorts. I stood in front of Brady completely naked.

Brady was staring at me like I'd lost my mind and I wondered if I had made a grave error. Maybe removing all my clothes was way over the top? My little inside voice responded sarcastically, 'You think?' I was acting like a loose woman; I was going to lose him.

"What are you doing Belle?" Brady whispered.

I took a deep breath. "I'm showing you that you have nothing to worry about when I'm away with Adam. I want to make love with you Brady

McDaniel." I sounded way more confident than I felt. My knees were shaking.

To my great relief, Brady reacted instantaneously. I was crushed against his chest, and his lips found mine.

"Are you sure Belle?" Brady said huskily between delicious, moist kisses to my neck. I didn't even have a chance to answer him. "Please tell me you're sure." He repeated. His hands skimmed my waist and settled on my hips possessively.

"I want this Brady." I managed to say. He had me breathless.

He picked me up and laid me down on my bed. His eyes left mine to rove my body. If his face hadn't been so expressive, I might have felt self-conscious under his scrutiny, but his eyes were literally worshipping me.

Brady stood up and whipped off his tee shirt. His chest and back were magnificent. His arms rippled as he continued getting out of his clothes. His muscles bunched and released and now my mouth hung open. His lower abdomen was well defined and looked rock hard and below that, an impressive bulge pressed against his fly. His eyes remained on mine, and he slowly unbuckled his belt, unbuttoned his jeans, and then pushed them down to his ankles. He then sat on the edge of the bed and looked down at his prosthetic. I saw the uncertainty cross over his face.

My sweet man was still self-conscious. I sat up and scooted off the bed to kneel in front of him. I saw his breath hitch, and I focused on taking off his prosthetic instead of the large, very hard appendage that was inches from my face.

I unlaced his boots and took the one not attached to the prosthetic off. I then took off the prosthetic and placed it on the floor. I tenderly ran my hands over his legs, and I looked up to see Brady watching me with a heated expression. His hands reached out to bracket my cheeks, and I leaned against one of them. When I tore my eyes from his, I couldn't help but look at his steely maleness. I'd never seen one in the flesh before, and instead of feeling awkward or embarrassed I felt empowered that I had that effect on him.

I slowly reached for him, and Brady closed his eyes anticipating my touch. I slid my hand up and down, exploring his length and he moaned appreciatively. A small drop of pre-cum leaked from his dome-shaped head and I swiped at it with my finger. I don't know why I did what I did next, but I will never, ever, forget the expression on Brady's face when I lifted that finger to my mouth and sucked the white liquid bead off of it.

His eyes were smoldering as he watched me, and my female parts were tingling and so very hot. Moisture was pooling between my legs, and I shifted my position hoping to alleviate the building pressure.

Brady took my hand in his and repositioned it so that I gripped him. Then he guided my hand so that it was moving up and down his length. I held on to his thigh as I loved him with my hand and then I moved closer and placed a kiss on his satiny pink head.

Brady's hand's thread through my long hair and his throaty moan told me he liked my mouth on his hardness. I used my tongue to caress him and then I took his peach shaped head in my mouth and sucked on it as my hand continued to stroke his base.

I heard Brady hiss, and the ecstasy I saw on his face was emboldening. I continued to pleasure him with my mouth. I had no idea if I was doing it correctly. There was a chapter about oral sex in my book, but I hadn't gotten to it yet. I just knew my man liked it.

Brady rocked into my mouth; I loved how turned on he was. Then all of a sudden he stopped moving. He lifted me off my knees, and he pulled me onto the bed alongside him.

He gave me a searing kiss, and I savored how his bare chest felt against mine. My nipples were hypersensitive and diamond hard, and his muscular chest was pressing against them only made them harder.

Our bodies seemed to mold together. I could have kissed him for hours, but we both had other ideas. Brady broke our kiss and forged a sensuous trail down my neck and my upper chest until he reached my breasts. He lavished them with kisses and sensual caresses. He was taking his time loving every inch of me, and I was out of my mind with desire.

Brady looked up at me, and I realized neither of us had said a word since we had started kissing. Everything was being said with our touches. He continued to kiss his way down my torso, and when he got to my stomach, he rearranged his body so that he was between my legs.

His hands roamed my hips and thighs as his mouth wickedly made its way to my heated juncture. Brady paused for a second and watched my face as he slid his finger through my wet folds and then he sucked that finger into his mouth. That simple, sexy act had my nether region on fire, and hot liquid flowed from me. My fingers trailed through his hair as he dropped his mouth to my female lips. His tongue slid through my wetness and my hips bucked on their own accord. I instinctively tried to close my legs, but Brady gently held them open with his strong hands while his mouth found my sensitive pearl.

I moaned loudly as he continued to work me into a frenzy. I felt the swirling pull of an orgasm start in my spine, and when Brady pressed a finger into my heated core, I convulsed as an electric-like current of sheer pleasure shot through my body. A tsunami of hot bliss tore through me, and I shook from head to toe.

Brady continued to suckle me as I bucked against his mouth. Another smaller but equally intense orgasm tore through me, and I whimpered from the onslaught of sensation. He continued to devour me until I had to push him away. He refused to budge until he was satisfied that he had rung every trembling bit of gratification from me.

Brady climbed back up my body, stopping only to kiss my breasts before moving to my mouth. I could taste my saltiness on his tongue, and it was carnal and erotic.

His thick hard member was leaking pre-cum, and he settled himself between my thighs, rubbing his steely length through my very wet, warm female lips.

I had just experienced the most intense orgasm imaginable, yet what he was doing to me now had me craving more.

"I want you, Belle. I want to be your first. I want to feel you come apart with me inside of you."

I ran my hand over his cheek. "I want you to be my first Brady. I want to feel you inside me. I need to feel you inside of me, please." I murmured, practically begging for his love.

Brady reached for his wallet, which he had placed on the nightstand and withdrew an aluminum square packet. I knew what it was, and I was appreciative that he had thought to protect us, but I couldn't help the overwhelming jealousy that ran through me. My thoughts were that he carried one with him; therefore he must have had sex often.

"What's the matter?" He said holding the packet in his hands. "It's a condom."

"I know what it is," I mumbled.

"What's the matter? Have you changed your mind?"

"No," I said looking away from him.

He took my chin in his fingers, so I was looking into his eyes.

"Tell me."

"It's silly."

"Let me decide that." He said kissing my lips gently.

"You carry a condom with you. That means that you must have sex often. I hate that. I have this ache inside of me just thinking of you with other girls. I know that's silly."

"No, it's not." He said grinning happily. "It's awesome."

"Awesome?"

"It means you care for me, Belle. You don't want me to be with another woman, and honestly, I'd hurt anyone that wanted to be with you."

"I've never been with anyone else though, and you have."

"Not in a long time Darling."

"I care for you Brady, and I want to be good for you."

"You are. We're good together."

"Tell me what you like. Show me. I need to know how to love you properly."

He kissed me again. "We will guide each other. I want to be good for you too. I'm putting this on," he said holding up the square packet. "Because even though I think someday I'd love to have children with you, now is not the time."

I wrapped my arms around his neck and pulled him down for a passionate kiss. Once again he said just what I needed to hear. I loved this man!

Brady rolled the condom over his maleness, aligned his head up with my entrance, and surged forward. Gently he pressed into me and even though I was wet with desire it was tight and slightly uncomfortable.

"I'm sorry Baby." He grunted, as he pressed inside me further. "I know this hurts."

"Don't stop Brady. Please don't stop." Even though it was uncomfortable; it was a pleasurable hurt. One I knew would be well worth the discomfort. Brady reached my hymen, and he dropped his head against my chest. He was sweating, and I knew he was trying so hard not to hurt me.

"I want you, Brady. All of you." Brady obliged and pushed in. I felt the pinch; it only hurt for a second. He kissed my neck as he held still while I got used to his girth. When he began moving again, he worked himself in further, and as the pain subsided, a pleasurable sensation replaced it.

I moaned, and this time when Brady pressed in, I meet his thrust. "It feels so good." I moaned. Brady drove deeply into me, and I knew when he was fully seated because he groaned so sexily that I moved my hips stroking his rod from within, hoping to prod that moan from him again.

"Oh God, Belle."

Gripping his athletic hips with my knees, I pressed upwards and rotated my hips in a tight circle. Brady moaned with a low sexy timbre and dropped his forehead to mine.

"Belle." His voice was vibrating with passion.

I had my arms wrapped around him, and I held onto his back as he struck up a cadence with his hips that had me writhing beneath him.

He grabbed my hands and held them above my head against my pillows. My breasts and sensitive nipples rubbed against his chest, and his cock massaged a place inside me that had me lifting my hips to meet his deep lunges.

I was on the precept of what I knew would be a cataclysmic orgasm. A searing jolt of orgasmic pleasure ran through me. Warm liquid dripped from me drenching our still joined bodies. My eyelids sizzled, and my eyes literally rolled backward.

"Brady!" I yelled gripping his back. My insides seized around him gloving his length within me. Brady trembled.

I knew he was close because he pressed himself fully into me, holding himself there. He groaned, and I felt his body tighten then quake as he found his release.

We lay panting in each other's arms as we waited for our breathing to return to normal. The sheets were wet beneath us, and I felt wonderfully complete.

Brady rolled to his side taking me with him. He was still inside of me. My cheek rested on his bicep, and he kissed my forehead. "That was amazing." He whispered. "Are you okay?"

I nodded and kissed him tenderly. "I am way better than okay."

"I mean are you sore? Do you hurt? I'm such a jerk, you were in an accident today and."

"Brady stop."

"But you must be sore?"

"This is a really good sore," I said kissing his cheek. The grin he had on his face was one I would always remember.

Brady sat up and moved to the edge of the bed. He took off the condom, tied it, and hopped to the bathroom. When he returned, we held each other enjoying what I knew was termed post-coital bliss. I didn't know if there was more current verbiage to describe it, but I knew that's what it was, and it was heavenly.

I moved from under the covers and opened my window and then joined Brady.

"Do you always sleep with the window open?"

"Yes, I always have. Even in the winter, I like it opened a crack."

Brady held me against him. "Maybe you should keep the windows locked until we find out who has you in their crosshairs?"

"I still can't believe someone wants to hurt me. I don't even know anyone. The only person who I can even think of that may be mad at me is Dirk."

"Dirk barely remembers you decking him. He was plastered."

"Really?'

"Yeah and he would never do any of those things to you. He may be an ass, but going after you serves no purpose."

"Who could it be?"

"Well, who has something to gain from you leaving here or God forbid if you die?"

"No one."

"Who inherits your farm if something happens to you?"

"Mr. Bee says he would sell it... Oh. Are you thinking the Fitzpatrick's?"

"Not Adam. He wouldn't hurt you. I don't know if I trust his dad though."

"Wow, that's a scary thought."

"You just be careful Belle. Adam will protect you with his life, but you be careful."

"I will. I promise." I snuggled into him. "I know I should be excited about taking this trip, but I have such a heavy heart right now." I confided to him.

"You're going to have a great time."

"If I were with you I'd have a better time."

"Thank you for saying that."

"Brady what you're doing for me is unbelievable." He huffed and kissed my cheek. "Not really. I'm a little selfish. Knowing that you're safe I'll be able to train without worrying, and that will give me a better shot of passing my tests."

"I meant having Adam go with me."

His body tensed alarming me. "I have a confession. I have another reason for wanting you to go on this trip."

"Tell me?"

He sighed deeply and stroked my arm with his hand. "You just said that you didn't like that I've been with other women, but I think it's a good thing."

"I'm all ears Mr. McDaniel," I replied pretending to be displeased.

He chuckled and tapped my nose. "I care about you Belle, like no one else ever before. I know this because I have something to compare what I feel for you against. That's why I'm so confident about how I feel about you."

"I guess that makes sense."

"Now you, my sweet Belle. You have nothing to compare your feelings for me against, so I am concerned, because you may discover that you have stronger feelings for someone else."

"Are you talking about Adam?"

"Anyone, Adam, Kip, someone you meet on your trip. It's one of the reasons I want you to travel Belle. I'm hoping you will come back here and still want to be with me. I also hope that you'll figure out what you want while you're away."

"What do you mean?"

"Like whether you want to stay on your farm or sell it? I am hoping you experience enough on this trip that when you come back, you will know what you want. That you'll be able to give Adam and his dad an answer about your farm without any regrets."

He paused, "I also realize that I could be sending you on a path that may not include me in your future and that scares me."

I couldn't believe how selfless he was. "You're worried?"

"I am, but Belle, if you come back still caring about me, then you'll know that what we have is special."

"I already know that," I whispered.

When the conversation had turned serious, we had moved so that we were facing each other. He kissed my knuckles. "I don't want to lose you, but you being safe is my priority. If you fall for Adam, or someone else while you're away, well then I guess you were never mine, to begin with." His voice was sullen as his green eyes stayed on mine. "My Momma use to say that. 'If you love something set it free. If it comes back to you, it's yours forever. If it doesn't, it was never yours, to begin with.'"

"I never heard that before, but that's exactly what I am thinking."

"I don't want to be set free," I said quietly. Brady pushed in closer, and I rested my head on his shoulder while he stroked my back.

"I won't give up on you Belle. Adam cares for you, and that's why I know he'll take such good care of you."

"We're friends Brady, that's all." I couldn't elaborate, but it was true, and I wasn't breaking my word.

"He will take more if he can. A lot can happen in four weeks."

"I know. Don't think that I haven't thought about you and other woman."

"What are you talking about? I'll be training."

"Yes, but you'll have down time. Brady, I may be naive, but I'm not dumb. I know you'll go to bars and you'll have days and nights off. There will be plenty of women around."

"Sweetheart, I won't even notice them."

"Sure," I said feeling juvenile voicing my concerns. Tears leaked out of the corner of my eyes. "I'm going to miss you," I told him quietly. "I'm going to miss you too."

We didn't sleep much that night. Brady was an amazing lover, and I hoped I pleased him as much as he pleased me. My body felt like loose Jell-O from all the orgasms he had delivered. When the rooster crowed, I tiptoed from the bed to start the coffee. I didn't want to wake him, so I slipped on his tee shirt that was on the floor and used the mudroom bathroom. His shirt smelled like him, a woodsy, leathery scent, and I wondered if it was from his soap or if he used cologne. There were still so many things I didn't know about the man. I knew the important things though. He was kind and brave, but lacking confidence because of his injury.

He had seen awful things in Afghanistan, and he had lost good friends. I knew that haunted him, yet he never complained. He had a wonderful sense of humor, and he was good looking with a strong, muscular body.

I hurried to make breakfast because Brady had said he would help me pack before he went home to pack himself, and we were pressed for time. When Brady came out from my bedroom, he was wearing his jeans and no shirt. He was fresh from a shower, and I almost burnt my hand staring at how yummy he looked. I had the coffee ready along with a large breakfast. He didn't even move to the table he came straight for me and wrapped me in his powerful arms. I buried my head in his neck and held him. What was supposed to be a wonderful month of travel was going to be the longest month of my life.

"You look great in my shirt." He said after kissing my neck tenderly.

"You look great without it." I giggled.

Brady gave me a kiss that had me whimpering. Before I knew what he was doing, he had lifted me away from the oven, after checking that the burners were off, and carried me into the living room. His shirt had hiked over my hips, and I could feel his hardness in his jeans pressing against me.

He placed me on the back of the couch, and as he kissed me stupid, he was somehow able to remove his shirt from me. Brady held on to me as I perched on the couches back, and with one hand he undid his belt and jeans and let them drop to the floor along with his boxers.

Brady latched on to one of my nipples and drew the hard bud into his mouth. When he kissed his way back to my mouth, I was a hot mess.

"This one's for me, Baby. It's going to be fast, okay?"

I nodded unable to keep a coherent thought in my head. Brady touched every sensitive place he could reach before lining himself up and driving into me. I was so wet he slid in completely; my tight core gloved his hard shaft. We moaned simultaneously with the heady sensation.

With his forehead resting against mine Brady rhythmically pumped his thick hard length into me. I could see that he was watching where we were joined, and I watched as well, which only made it more stimulating. His cock would pull almost entirely out of me, glistening with my essence and then he'd press back in. It was so erotic that my female bits tingled and I felt an orgasm start to bloom deep inside of me.

Brady began to kiss me again and as his pace quickened. I was holding on to his biceps with my legs wrapped around his hips. He leaned back and watched my face as he began to rapidly hammer into me. He was hitting an erogenous zone inside me that was quickly sending me over the edge. I felt Brady's body tightened and he hurriedly slipped his fingers between our conjoined bodies and strummed my clitoris immediately hurling me into a long, mind-blowing, body quaking orgasm. Brady let out a throaty groan of pleasure as we imploded together.

Still joined I rested my head against his chest as he held me tightly.

"That was unexpected," I panted still catching my breath.

Brady chuckled. "One look at you wearing my tee and I couldn't help myself."

"Ummm, I'll have to borrow your shirts more often." I giggled.

I was wrapped firmly in Brady's arms as he gave me a kiss that had me longing for more. When we came up for air, the expression Brady had on his face melted my heart.

"It will go fast, Brady," I said referring to our month long hiatus from each other.

"I hope so. I want to pass these tests, Belle. I felt like I was walking around in a nightmare until I met you. You brought me back to life. You made me want a future. Now I've been given this awesome opportunity, and all I keep thinking about is being away from you."

I paused as I gathered my thoughts. I wanted to tell him that I loved him, but I squirreled that impulse away.

"You know I'll be thinking about you all the time, right?" I told him.

Instead of answering me Brady kissed me again. He wanted to believe me, but all he knew was that he was sending me off on a great adventure with another man who he thought had feelings for me. I pulled out of the kiss and brushed his bangs off his face tenderly. "I'm yours, Brady. All Yours. After last night you should know that." I was searching his eyes for a glimmer of hope. It never appeared. He thought he was losing me.

As we ate our now cold breakfast, I tried to appear happy even though my heart was aching for Brady. I too was sad that I was going to be away from him for a month, and I was a tad anxious that he might fall out of likes with me. I was, however, very confident that my feelings for Brady would only get stronger. Unfortunately, my handsome, sweet man was thinking that he was sending me into the arms of another man.

After breakfast I showered while Brady did the animals, then Brady helped me to pack. He laughed when I packed his tee shirt.

"I want to sleep in in it. It smells like you." I told him as I folded it into the case.

I didn't have many clothes, but I was informed that I was to 'shop till I dropped,' as Brady put it. He had pre-arranged everything with Mr. Bee. Adam was bringing me a credit card, and extra cash that he had picked up the night before.

When my bags were packed Brady carried them to the porch, and I reluctantly walked him to his truck. Adam had already called and said he was on his way with Mr. and Mrs. Gordon, the couple that would be overseeing the farm if I approved of them.

We held each other mixing in kisses, well wishes, and miss you's. I gave him a small jar of the salve that I had applied to his leg the first day I met him. I also gave him the little compass I had purchased that first trip to Springfield. Brady unquestionably loved it and said he'd keep it with him the whole time. Brady gave me a small paper print out of a picture that he had taken of us after I had gotten my license.

"Thank you, Brady. I love this."

"And thank you for the salve."

"You better use it, mister," I said hoping my voice wouldn't give away how emotional I was feeling.

"I will. I promise."

"Will I get to talk to you at all?"

"I'm afraid not very often. The training facility was built purposely out of cell phone range."

"What about on your days off?"

"I have Adams cell number. I'll call that when I get a chance."

That didn't sound promising. I hid my anxiety by giving him another kiss.

After a final hug, he got in his truck, and I tearfully watched him head down my driveway. When all I could see was the dust trail left by his truck on my drive, I folded my hands, bowed my head, and prayed that he did well in his training and that he stayed safe.

As Brady's car disappeared a Deputies car pulled in my drive and parked. I walked to the car.

"Is everything all right?" I asked.

"Yes, I'm just going to hang here until Mr. Fitzpatrick arrives, bosses orders."

I wondered if the boss was the Sheriff or if the Sheriff's son was behind the protective detail.

Less than a half hour later a truck followed by a car pulled in the front loop. I didn't recognize either of them. Adam hopped out of the car, and an elderly couple stepped down from the cab of the truck. As I walked to meet them the Deputy car pulled a K turn and left.

"Hi," I said reaching my guests.

"Belle, this is Mr. and Mrs. Gordon."

I shook their hands. Mrs. Gordon held on to mine. "Please call me Bev, and this is Jeb."

"Okay, thank you."

"This is a nice little spread," Jeb said turning in a full circle. His smile put me at ease.

"It's been in my family for generations."

Adam was busy gathering the suitcases out of the bed of the truck. "Belle where do you want them to sleep?" He asked with his arms full. I was slightly taken back; I thought I would get to feel them out before committing to letting them stay and run my beloved farm.

"Oh goodness. I hadn't even thought about it." I said nervously. I thought about the bed that Brady and I had spent a wonderful night romping in. Did I want them in there?

"Sweetie lets worry about that later. Why don't you show us your farm?" Bev said.

"Okay." I took a deep breath. "Let's start at the barn."

I gave them a tour of the barn and corrals explaining the animal's schedules and any other pertinent information. Jeb was looking at me with a small smile on his face.

"You know all of this don't you?' I asked a little embarrassed that I was explaining how to take care of my animals to a pro.

"It's still good to hear how you do things. I think keeping them on their normal and time schedule helps them to calm when their main caregiver isn't home."

I instantly became a Jeb fan. With one sentence he had put me at ease about leaving my animals.

Bev must have interpreted my grinning face correctly.

"We love animals, Belle. We understand that it is very hard for you to leave them, and trust me; we are going to shower them with love while you're away if you allow us to stay, that is."

"Thank you. I think you'll be perfect staying here." Adam was pleased as could be and told Jeb that if they had any questions at all, they could call him on his cell. That reminded me of how out of touch I would be with Brady.

I introduced them to Bessie and Henny giving both animals loving pats, and when I showed them the sheep, I made sure to point Mimi and William out to them. I explained that William was still a little weak from his fall. I saw Adam give Jeb a sideways glance and I wondered if Adam had shared what had happened.

The tour continued as I showed them the garden. Bev was ecstatic seeing all the vegetables and flowers.

"This is wonderful Belle. I know how much work it to keep a garden of this size producing."

"It will be fun getting our hands dirty again," Jeb replied enthusiastically.

I showed them the gardening tools and where the outside water hook up and hose was.

"Belle is there a watering system?"

"No, I just lug the hose over and give them a good drink."

Next, I showed them the shed that Adam and Brady had just fixed. Jeb took some time looking at the mowing tractor.

"So you mow with this?"

"Yes, but it has other attachments too." I showed him the plow, and the chains in case they needed to move something heavy.

"It's in good shape for its age."

"My Gram took care of it. Then after she passed my Momma was pretty good with it. I haven't been as steadfast with the maintenance, and I'm sure it's showing signs of neglect."

"Nonsense," Jeb said. "It's in tip-top shape."

We walked into the house and Bev's eyes lit up. "It's beautiful. I love the natural wood, and it's decorated perfectly."

"Thank you."

Bev moved to the kitchen area. "Jeb look here, a six burner gas stove. I'm in heaven."

Jeb chuckled. "My wife is a wonderful cook."

Adam had been walking with us, and while Bev and Jeb took stock of the kitchen and pantry, he pulled me aside.

"So where do you want them to sleep?"

"I don't know."

"Your room has the biggest bed."

I stammered. "I don't know."

Adam gave me a curious look then he grinned. "You don't want them in your room because you and Brady?" I didn't let him finish his sentence.

"Adam, shush." I was mortified and even more annoyed that he seemed to be judging me.

"I'm sorry, it's none of my business."

"No, it's not," I told him feeling awkward.

Adam sighed. I knew he had not liked my slight rebuke, but he recovered quickly.

"I've never been upstairs, how big are those beds?"

"Mine is a double. My Momma's is a queen."

"So, let's put them in there."

"Okay, can you give me a few minutes to arrange things?"

"We need to leave in a half hour."

"That's all I need."

I hurried first into my bedroom and took the sheets off the bed and put them in the hamper. My heart squeezed recalling what Brady and I had shared in the bed on those sheets. I then remade the bed with fresh sheets. Next, I made up Momma's bed. I put clean towels on the dresser and took a quick look around. Satisfied that everything looked presentable, I went into Momma's closet. I wanted to bring Momma's leather journal with me so I could read it while on my vacation. When I opened the box, it was empty. Adam must have walked in, and I had not even heard him.

"What's the matter?"

I jumped because I hadn't heard him.

"Cripes! Adam." I gasped.

After putting the Gordon's suitcases on the bed, he walked to where I stood and looked inside the metal box and then to me.

"It's empty."

"I know."

"Belle, you're white as a ghost."

"I had put my Momma's journal in here, and there were some legal papers too. They're gone."

"Maybe you moved them?"

"No, they were in here."

"Belle, you've had a few knocks on the head along with a pretty stressful month. Maybe you just don't remember moving them?"

"No, I don't think so." I was racking my brain. "No, I never moved them. I wanted to read the journal and look at the papers, so I put them back in this box, and put it in here."

I was thoroughly alarmed, and I could tell Adam thought I had simply misplaced them.

"Adam, they were in here," I told him, miffed that he didn't believe me.

He placed his hand on mine and shut the box's lid. "We have to get going, Belle. You can explain to Bev what the journal and papers look like and they can keep their eyes open for them."

I didn't have much choice, and Adam wanted to get to Boston before it got dark.

We walked downstairs to find Bev and Jeb waiting for us in the living room.

"Belle, any last minute instructions?"

"No, nothing I can think of. Anything you need just charge to my accounts in town. If you have any questions, please call Mr. Bee; his number is by the phone. Dr. Lachlan is the vet I use. Her number is by the phone also. I appreciate you taking care of my place."

Bev took my arm in hers as we walked outside. "You have a great time Belle. I hear you haven't traveled much?"

"Not at all actually."

"Don't you worry about a thing, taking care of your place will be fun for us. You enjoy yourself." Adam hugged Bev goodbye and shook Jeb's hand. "Call me if you need us." He told them. I sat in the passenger side of the car gazing around my little farm with a mix of sentimentality and anxiousness. Adam got in the car and patted the top of my hand. "Relax Belle. They're good people. Jeb is the best guy I know with animals, and Bev will probably get twice the amount of vegetables out of your garden than usual, she's like a plant whisperer."

I nodded unable to respond because of the lump that had formed in my throat.

27

Brady

I hated leaving her. I thought back to the last time I had left someone I'd loved, and my stomach rolled with uneasiness. I was happy that Belle had agreed to leave town. I was concerned for her safety and after what my dad had revealed last night I knew I would have never been able to leave if she hadn't gone.

Sending her with Adam was a double-edged sword. I knew he liked her, heck everyone liked her, and he was a stand-up guy, a guy worthy of Belle. The time we had spent together working on her farm had us connecting in a number of ways. The main one being that we were both Veterans.

I had been surprised when he had asked me what my intentions were with Belle. I was taken back, and then I realized he was just looking out for her, and I couldn't fault him for that. He was holding something back from me, and I had no idea what it was, but I couldn't shake the feeling that it somehow involved Belle.

When I cultivated my plan to send Belle on vacation, I reached out to Mr. Bee first. With Mr. Bee on board, I next spoke with Adam.

He was surprised, but I was serious about wanting her to remain safe. I knew Kip was unable to leave his job for that amount of time, and with me away Adam was the next best person to take care of her. He, of course, asked why I wanted her to take the trip. He offered to stay on the farm with her and guard her there. I didn't want to get into all the reasons I wanted her to take the trip. I would tell them to Belle, but I just didn't want to share them with Adam, yet.

He was honest with me and said he would use the time with her to convince her to sell the farm, and although I hated the thought of her selling it, I respected his honesty. I was also relieved he didn't say that he wanted to win her over emotionally. I thought he might; I had to trust that what Belle and I had would be strong enough to endure his advances.

We discussed the logistics of the trip. I was determined to pay for everything, but Adam said he would write his part of the trip off as a business expense. We also decided to tell Belle at my parent's house, together.

Now, as I drove further away from her, my fears regarding the entire plan assaulted me. My reasons for her taking the trip were valid, even sensible. Unfortunately, my heart was taking a serious beating. I loved her, and although she had given me a great gift last night, and I knew she cared for me; there were so many variables in play that I couldn't count on her feelings for me remaining the same.

She might sell the farm and move away? She could fall in love with Adam? Maybe, she would meet another man, and decide that she wanted to date him? I tamped down the queasy feeling that rolled in my stomach. I had a mission to accomplish. It was imperative that I be the best person in the training camp. My dad had said that I had to finish in the top three in the physical tests. He also said I had to nail the written part of the test, and he advised me to study for it beyond what the required course reading was. All my fears would be for naught if I had nothing to offer Belle.

I needed this for me too. I had been barely living, and now, because of how I felt about Belle because she showed me how resilient she was after she lost her mother, Josh, and almost her life; twice, I was determined to be strong too.

I needed the job Lansing was offering. It was one that I would enjoy doing, one that would provide for me, and someday for my family. If I passed, no, when I passed these tests and became a Deputy, then, and only then, would I be able to tell Belle that I loved her, that I wanted her in my life forever, because then I would have something to offer her.

I packed my duffle once again thinking about the last time two times I packed it before. The first time Chelsea had sat on my bed and cried, she had begged me not to go. The second time I was a broken man, pissed at the world and Chelsea for betraying me.

My Mom, Dad, and Tommy were waiting for me in the living room. Tommy was unusually quiet. My Mom was a little teary-eyed, and she handed me a box filled with her home-baked treats, before hugging me goodbye. I wasn't going halfway across the world to fight in a war, but I knew my family would miss me. I also knew that they were worried about me, and my damaged body handling the rigorous trials that lay ahead. Tommy wished me good luck and gave me a bro hug.

My Dad walked me outside carrying the treats my Mom had made. He placed them in the passenger seat as I dumped my duffle in the truck bed.

"I'm proud of you Brady." He said placing his hand on my shoulder.

"Thanks, Dad. I'm a little nervous."

"Brady you're one of the strongest most determined people I know. I realize that you have to deal with an issue that the others won't, but your Mom and I know you can do this."

"My new blade is pretty bad ass," I said with a chuckle.

"You're smart, strong, and the best marksman I know. Your mobility will be tested, but don't underestimate your worth."

"Thanks, dad."

I got in the truck and looked at my dad standing next to my door. He was the most honest man I knew, and if he thought I could do this, then I could.

"Dad, I'm really worried about Belle. Will you keep me updated?"

"Of course."

"If you find out who's behind her accidents please call Adam too."

"I will. I'm frankly very relieved that she will be out of town. These attacks on her have escalated, and no one seems to have a motive. Well except for the Fitzpatrick's."

"Adam wouldn't hurt her dad. I think he's in love with her too."

"Too?"

I grinned. "Yeah."

"She's a great girl Brady. Are you sure sending her off with Adam was the best move?"

"It was the only move Dad. She comes first."

"You're a good man, son."

"Can I ask that you pay a couple of visits to her farm, just to check on things? Introduce yourselves to the Gordon's; they are the couple that Adam lined up to take care of the place."

"I'll do that tomorrow."

"Thanks, Dad. I'll call when I can."

"Good luck son."

28

Belle

It was a three and a half hour drive to Boston. On our drive, I told Adam that I wished Jeannie would tell Kip about them because I wanted Brady to know. I hoped that would provide him some solace and he would be able to concentrate on his training. Adam said he was going to talk to Jeannie tonight and he would relay to her what I said.

I was fidgety having to sit in the car for so long. Adam kept me occupied by telling me what we would be doing in Boston. Then he taught me how to play the License Plate game. The game required finding the letters of the alphabet, in order on license plates. I became totally engrossed in the game until we reached the city limits. Then I forgot all about it. When we passed into the city limits, I was flabbergasted at the size of the buildings, the traffic, and the sheer number of people that I was seeing. Adam chuckled seeing my astonished expression.

We pulled into a Marriott, and I felt like a country bumpkin. I stared at everything and everyone. Adam kept me close to him, but besides placing his hand protectively on the small of my back, he was a gentleman. As we followed a young man who was wheeling our luggage on a gurney type vehicle, I noticed how nicely dressed the persons who passed me were. I realized I was going to have to do some shopping. On our way to our adjoining rooms, a few men gave me the once-over. They weren't even trying to hide their perusals.

Adam noticed me stiffen when a pair of men blatantly looked me over.

"You're a beautiful woman Belle. They are just appreciating you," he whispered.

"I don't think I like being looked at like a prized pig," I whispered back.

Adam burst out laughing. "I have to remember to tell Brady that one."

Hearing Brady's name tugged on my insides. I wished he were with me. Was it only this morning that he had made love to me? It seemed like ages ago.

Adam showed me how to work the plastic card that let me into my room. Inside my room, he pointed out the door that separated our two rooms. He said he would keep his door unlocked in case I needed him. Adam left my room telling me that he was going to change and make reservations for dinner. He would call for me at 6:00.

I walked around the perfectly decorated room with the queen-sized bed. The bellhop had placed my luggage on a thigh-high stand, and I opened my case and took out the red dress. This would have to do for tonight. I hung the dress in the closet and stood to look out the window. A knock sounded on the door of my room that led to Adam's. I unlocked it to find Adam talking on his cell. When I opened the door, he handed me the phone and walked into his room.

"Hello?"

"Hey, baby."

I whimpered hearing Brady call me baby.

"Belle, are you okay?"

"Yes." I hesitated. "I like when you called me baby," I told him softly.

Now he paused. "I miss you already Belle."

"I miss you too."

"So what do you think of Boston?"

"It's so big. The buildings are so tall, and there are so many people, so many more than when we went to Springfield." I heard Brady chuckle.

"It's a nice city. If you think Boston's big wait until you get to New York."

"Where are you now?" I asked.

"I'm at the training base camp waiting for a bus with about thirty other recruits. It's my last chance for a while to call you. I just wanted to hear your voice."

"Thanks for calling. You're going to do great Brady. I know you will."

"I hope so. There are more recruits than I anticipated."

"So what happens next?"

"The first three days we are in classes during the morning, and we will have training in the afternoons and evenings. Then we take the written exam on the fourth day. When the tests are graded, only the persons scoring in the top half will remain for the rest of the training. So on Thursday night half of these guys will be gone."

"Then what?"

"From what I understand the rest of us will then start specialized training. We will be placed into small groups and be trained in everything that a Deputy needs to know. We even have a physical conditioning coach. I also heard that the firearms expert has won multiple awards and that we are expected to put in extra time at the shooting range because one of our final tests involves firearms and it's an important one."

"Sounds exciting," I said hearing the enthusiasm in his voice. "Will you be able to let us know how you're doing?"

"If I get a chance I'll call." Then he laughed nervously. " I guess if I meet you in Boston, you'll know I didn't do well on the written exam. If I see you in Steamboat Springs, that means I didn't make the second cut, which is a speed and agility test."

"Don't even joke that way, Brady. Think positively. Are those your only tests?"

"There is the firearms test, and then the final test is a practical, which is a test administered in the field."

"In the field?" I asked not understanding the jargon.

"The instructors simulate a real-life situation, and we have to successfully solve the case."

"Is that the last one?"

"That's it. If I pass the tests and remain in the top of my class, I will pass, and then Lansing can hire me as a Deputy."

"It's wonderful that you already know that you'll have a job when you pass."

"I've been talking to a few other recruits, and I'm hearing that the Governor wants to put together a specialized state wide Search and Rescue team. It would be unbelievable if I could be a Deputy, with Search and Rescue qualifications, and then be considered for the State S and R team. I'm getting a little ahead of myself." I heard him chuckle.

"They'd be lucky to have you."

"Thanks. Well, I better get going they are starting to load the bus."

"Brady." I started to choke up. "I miss you."

"Belle." His voice was low, and I knew he was feeling the same emotional pull that I was. He started to say something when I heard a whistle from his end. "Belle, I have to go. I miss you too. Have fun. Take pictures. I'll call when I can."

Adam and I had a quiet dinner at a very swanky restaurant that overlooked the bay. I was mesmerized seeing the city lights bouncing off the wavy water, and I loved watching the boats of all sizes that passed by us. Adam ordered for me, and when a lobster was placed in front of me, I gaped at the red, ugly creature. I used my fork to tap the hard shell and only when Adam burst out laughing did I look up from my plate.

"You've never had lobster before have you?"

"No, but I've seen pictures, and my Gigi said it was her favorite food, but I've never had one before."

Adam reached across the table and used his fork to point at the white meat in the tail

"That's the tail meat. Use that little fork to pull it out of its shell and dip it in the butter." He pointed his fork at the tin cup filled with warm butter.

He watched me as I struggled to pull out the meat without making a mess. When it came loose, I found that I had disengaged one complete side of the tail from its striped shell. I cut it into bite-sized pieces before I dipped one piece into the butter and put it in my mouth.

"Oh my goodness," I said after I swallowed. That is delicious. I took another bite, and Adam used his cell phone to take a picture of me enjoying my lobster.

He got a funny look on his face when he looked at his phone.

"What?" I asked seeing his odd expression.

"Nothing, it's just the picture." he didn't finish his thought.

He handed me the phone, and I stared at the picture of me. Is that really what I looked like?

I was wearing my red dress, and the color looked great on me. My cleavage was showing, but not too much; it was actually more alluring than exploitive. My long blond hair hung over one shoulder, my skin had a warm, healthy glow to it, and my eyes were luminescing in the restaurant's dim lights. It was the look on my face, as I closed my lips over the forkful of lobster that gave me pause. The look on my face was provocative.

Adam pressed a few buttons on his phone and then put his phone away.

"What did you do?" I asked Adam seeing him put the phone down.

"I sent the picture to Brady."

"Do you think he will like it?"

"Belle, he's going to love it."

"I guess I have to take your word for that. It looked a little." I paused.

"Sexy as hell." Adam finished.

"I don't want Brady to think."

Adam interrupted me. "Stop Belle. He wants you to have fun, experience new things. He will like that you tasted lobster for the first time."

"I guess you're right. It's just I feel guilty for having fun without him."

"Well, you better get over that right now girl, because we have four more weeks and there is no way I'm going to deal with a mopey Mattie for a month."

I laughed out loud. "A mopey Maddie. My Gigi used to say that!" He instantly made me feel better.

We spent five days in Boston, and I saw my first baseball game, ate more lobster, and watched a parade celebrating the 4th of July. Adam also drove us to the Cape, and I swam in the ocean for the first time. Well, swim isn't the best word to describe what I did. At first, I was so afraid of the unrelenting waves that I only went in up to my knees. Adam encouraged me to go out further, and I immediately wiped out so badly that my new bikini bottoms rolled down my ass, but luckily no one saw. Adam said he didn't anyway. After he

taught me how to duck under the waves, I started
to have a blast.

We spent the night in a nearby motel because I
wanted to stay for another day. The second day
Adam rented boogie boards and showed me how
to ride them. My skin was browning up, and Adam
took a bunch of pictures of me. I have to admit my
eyes were bluer than ever against my sun-bronzed
skin.

We left the Cape and drove straight to the airport. I
had never been on a plane, and my stomach was a
wreck. Adam promised me we were safe, but I was
still pretty scared. When we were buckled into our
seats, Adam handed me a stick of gum explaining
that chewing gum helped alleviate the pressure in
the ears when taking off. I was on a plane and
chewing gum; two first for me. I sat in the window
seat, and as the plane taxied down the runway, I
grabbed Adam's hand and held it tightly. I was
white knuckled.

When we reached our cruising altitude and were
above the clouds, I began to relax. I couldn't
believe I was in the air flying to Steam Boat
Springs, Colorado. Adam and I talked about
Boston and then what I would find in Colorado.
We also talked about him and Jeannie.

He told me that he and Jeannie had gone out to
lunch when Brady and I had left them in the diner's
parking lot. He said they had really hit it off. He
asked her to dinner and before she accepted she
wanted to know what the deal was between him

and me. Adam said he was honest with her. He said he told her that if I had given him any encouragement, he wouldn't have asked her on the date. He told me that he told Jeannie that he liked me, but he realized that Brady and I had some deep connection that wasn't going away anytime soon. He and Jeannie spent more time together, and they found that they had a lot in common and enjoyed each other's company. He admitted to me that he missed her and that he thought they might have something special. I couldn't help but wish that Brady had heard that.

When we landed in Denver, I could not take my eyes off the beautiful mountains. We caught a smaller plane that flew us closer to Steam Boat Springs, and then Adam rented a jeep. We stayed at the most adorable motel called The Rabbit Ears. Its backdrop was a magnificent mountain, and it was situated near the Yappa River right in the quaint downtown.

The first night we were there was a Friday and Adam, and I went to the rodeo. I loved it and made Adam stay until the end even though we were both tired.

The next day we shopped, and I bought jeans, a skirt, another pair of cowboy boots, two very girly tee shirts, and a pair of sunglasses. I bought Brady an exquisite knife, and when I showed it to Adam, he reminded me I wouldn't be able to bring that on the plane, so we walked to the post office, and I mailed it to his home in Lansing.

I loved Colorado. It was Vermont on steroids. Adam took me tubing down the Yappa. We went fly-fishing; horseback riding, and we rode a chairlift to the top of the mountain where we ate in the restaurant. Every night I got into bed; exhausted from my day's adventure and after praying that Brady was doing well, I fell fast asleep.

The last night we were in Steam Boat Springs Brady called. I didn't even know he was on the phone. Adam and I were sitting on a blanket at an outdoor concert in town. I was having fun listening to country music from the local band. Adam's phone rang and after a few seconds he indicated that he'd be right back and he left me alone on the blanket. When he returned he handed me the phone. I could tell by his facial expression that something was wrong.

"Hello?"

"You're having fun I see."

"Brady!" I jumped up from the blanket and walked to a quieter spot for privacy.

"How are you?"

"I'm fine." His answer was clipped.

"What's wrong?"

"Nothing. You're having a good time?"

"Yes. I can't wait to tell you everything we've done."

"I've gotten all the pictures." His voice sounded tight.

"Did you see the one after I wiped out in the wave?" I laughed nervously; something was wrong.

"Yeah, I saw it."

"Brady, what's the matter? Are you passing your tests?"

"I am."

"Okay, then what's the matter?"

"Nothing." But I could tell there was something wrong.

"Talk to me. I've missed you."

"I bet," he said sounding off.

I heard some commotion on his end, and I heard a female voice say. "Come on Brady we have to go."

"Brady responded by saying, "Coming."

"Belle, I have to go."

"Brady, I." But he had hung up.

I slowly walked back to the blanket and Adam was looking uncomfortable.

"What's going on?" I asked him as I handed him back his phone.

"I don't know. I think he thinks you and I are becoming a couple."

"Why would he think that?"

"I don't know. I've sent him a ton of pictures."

"Maybe the pictures you sent look like we were together. Did you tell him we weren't? Did you tell him about Jeannie?"

Adam shook his head. "I wanted to tell him, but he wouldn't let me."

He wasn't telling me everything, and I was really upset that I hadn't gotten Brady to tell me what he was upset about. I had been having such a great time, but if Brady thought I was with Adam, it would ruin everything.

"Adam call him back or do that text thing. Tell him about Jeannie."

"Later." Adam didn't sound too happy either. Adam stood up and gathered our blanket. The concert wasn't over, but we were done.

We walked back to the Rabbit Ears, and Adam stopped at the nearby grocery store and bought a six-pack. We sat on the picnic tables that overlooked the wide river and drank in silence. After I finished my second beer and was feeling slightly brave, I confronted Adam.

"Spill it, Adam. I know you're hiding something."

"No, I don't think it's anything."

"Why don't you let me decide?"

Adam took a long pull from his beer.

"I'll think about it, Belle. I'm mad that he thinks we are together. I don't want Jeannie thinking anything either you know."

"Call her."

"She's been at a conference in Chicago. I haven't talked to her in a week."

"Call her now."

Adam took out his phone and pushed a few buttons. I watched as he listened to the ringing. I knew exactly when Jeannie answered because his entire face lite up.

I got up from the table, tapped his beer with my empty bottle, smiled at him, and went to my room to give him some privacy.

As I lay in my bed, I couldn't get Brady's bewildering attitude off my mind. I should have reminded Adam to tell Jeannie to tell Kip about them. I was hurt that Brady had acted so mean, but I was also mad that he wasted precious time that we could have spent catching up by being short with me. I had no idea when he would call again. The next morning Adam was all smiles, and I was a slug, because I had tossed and turned all night. We boarded the small plane to go back to Denver, and from Denver, we flew to Los Angeles.

Adam told me he had a great talk with Jeannie and that she was going to be talking to Kip in the next few days. He was working, but his first night off they were going out for drinks, and she would explain things to him then. I was relieved and hoped that the next time I talked to Brady Adam could tell him how little of a threat he was.

I wasn't a fan of LA. It was smoggy, and there were too many people. Everyone was glitzy, and I felt like a fish out of water. We visited Disney on day one, and I did enjoy the rides, but the lines were ridiculous. We took a tour of a movie studio and saw the sidewalk, in front of a Chinese restaurant, where the movie stars put their hands in cement. I knew my Momma would have loved that.

Adam made me shop, and I hated it. Everything was overpriced. I did purchase a sundress and sandals. I hoped to wear them for Brady when we got back home. I hadn't heard from him again and even though it had only been four days I was starting to worry.

It was our last night in LA, and I was happy to leave the bustle of the city. I even told Adam if he wanted to skip New York I wouldn't mind. I had enjoyed Boston and Colorado was magnificent, but LA confirmed that I was a country girl. I wish Brady would call so I could tell him that.

We were staying in a hotel suite. We had a shared common room and with separate bedrooms. I had just finished packing, and as I stepped into the common room, I heard Adam's phone playing a tune indicating that someone was calling him.

"Adam your phones playing music." I looked at the phone's screen and saw that it said, Brady. "Adam, it's Brady," I said excitedly.

"Adam came rushing out from his room, pressed the green button and swiped it, answering the call. "Brady, you're on speaker. How's it going?"

No one answered, but we could hear people talking. It sounded like he was in a bar.

"Brady, man you there?"

He still didn't answer. Then we heard a muffled female voice. "We are so good together."

The next few words the woman said were inaudible, but we could make out the word girlfriend.

I looked at Adam and gulped nervously. He tried to end the call, and I blocked his hand. The female spoke again.

"Brady, what we did last night, that was special."

We then heard a subdued but muffled voice, we both knew it was Brady.

"It was an interesting night." We heard him chuckle; then there were no voices but another unmistakable sound. Adam looked at me, and I knew he was thinking the same thing as me, that

Brady and the girl were kissing. He reached to turn the phone off, and this time I let him.

I stared at the phone and felt the tears well up in my eyes.

"Did he want me to hear that?"

"No, he must have dialed me inadvertently. We call it butt dial. Belle, there has to be an explanation. I know he cares for you."

I nodded and wiped my eyes. "Well, I guess his little experiment worked both ways."

"What do you mean?"

"He said that going away would give me a chance to see if I truly cared him. I guess it also served for him to discover if he cared for me; I guess he doesn't."

Adam looked sick, and I felt bad for him.

"I'm not going to fall apart Adam. Ever since Steam Boat Springs, I knew something was the matter."

Adam opened his mouth, shut it, and opened it again. "So about Steam Boat Springs. What I neglected to tell you was that when he and I were talking, there was a girl near him that kept interrupting our conversation. They seemed pretty chummy. When I asked him about her, he said she was a friend, just like you and I were friends."

"Oh." That's all I could say. I was numb. "Listen I'm pretty tired. I'm going to go to bed."

"We can go have a drink, Belle. It's only seven."

"No, I'll pass you go ahead."

"Belle, please come out with me."

I answered him by shaking my head no and quietly shut my door. I sat on my bed and refused to give in to the tears that threatened to wash down my face.

I was a fool. I'd been a fool regarding Brady since I'd met him. He'd made my head spin with his good looks and charm. Now some other woman had his attention. It sounded serious. She had said it had been special. It hurt thinking that he was making love with her, his girlfriend, the way he had made love with me. I now understood the meaning of a broken heart. I swear my heart felt as if it had been cut open. I undressed and got under the covers wishing I were home. I missed my house, my animals, and my simple life.

I realized how smart my grandparents had been secluding us. They had been protecting me from the hardships of the outside world. People could be mean. I knew that was a vast generalization. I thought about the people I had met. Kip, Jeannie, and Adam were nice, but Dirk was not. Brady had shown his true colors; again, he was a jerk. I was even stupider for falling for him, again. Ugh! I did like Brady's parents though. Mr. and Mrs. Bee were sweet too. I wasn't sure about Sam Fitzpatrick though.

I heard Adam come in and when he knocked on my door, I pretended to be asleep. I just didn't want to talk about Brady and I sure as heck did not want his pity. I had brought this on myself.

The next morning we took a taxi to the airport and as we talked about LA and everything we had done Adam's phone played again.

"Hello?"

I could only hear what Adam was saying.

"Oh God."

Pause

"Is she okay?"

Pause.

"We'll be home as soon as possible." He ended the call.

"What's the matter?"

"Bev's had an accident. She's in a coma."

"Oh no."

"We're going home, okay?" Adam said quickly pushing dome buttons on his phone.

"Absolutely," I told him.

A few minutes later Adam looked up from his phone. "We are booked on a flight that leaves in an hour."

He knocked on the taxi's screen. "Are we close to the airport?"

"Two minutes away." The driver told us.

We flew into Albany because it was closer than Boston. Adam rented a car and called Jeb as we left the car rental lot. When he got off the phone, he told me what he knew.

"She's still in a coma. Jeb found her in the basement. She must have passed out and hit her head on the floor."

"Poor Bev."

"Jeb's has been taking care of your animals, but he is relieved that we are coming home because he doesn't like leaving her in the hospital alone."

"That's understandable."

Adam called his dad next, and I knew he was asking if he had talked me into selling my property. Adam deflected the questions and told his dad about Bev. When he hung up, Adam told me his Dad was on his way back to Lansing too. I figured he too was close with the older couple and wanted to give them support.

It took seven hours to get home, and I was exhausted, happy, and sad all at the same time. Adam dropped me off at home and said he was going to the hospital, but he would be back.

I dragged my suitcases inside, changed, and then immediately went to the barn.

The barn looked great, and it was super tidy. It looked better than I'd ever seen it. My Gram would have been so pleased. The animals were all happy and healthy. The chickens were in a new larger coop with better nesting platforms. The pigs were huge, so I knew they were eating well. William wasn't hobbling at all, and he had gotten so big. Henny looked wonderful and greeted me with nuzzles, and I swear Bessie was smiling.

I walked behind the house and was amazed at how the garden had grown. The flowers were brilliant, and the vegetables were abundant. I was going to have to spend some time in the garden tomorrow if I wanted to keep Bev's hard work from being wasted.

When I went back inside, I saw that the house was immaculate. Bev and Jeb had surpassed any expectation I had had. I heard a car pulling in, and I walked to the door to find the Sheriff walking up my porch steps.

"Hi, Belle. Sorry, you had to cut your trip short."

"Did Adam call you?" I asked wondering how he had known.

"Yes, I knew about Bev's accident, and after he dropped you off, he called me."

"Any luck finding out who's been out to get me?"

"No. Nothing's happened since you left."

"That's so odd." I gestured for the Sheriff to have a seat and he did.

"Can I ask how your trip was?"

"It was fun. Eye-opening." I couldn't garner any enthusiasm, and I was wondering if Brady had told his dad that he and I were not dating anymore.

"You don't sound like you had a good time?"

"So how's Brady's training going?" I changed the subject. His father gave me a peculiar look.

"I was going to ask you how he was."

I stuttered. "I haven't talked to him."

"Really?" His father seemed concerned.

I immediately felt exhausted, and I was afraid I was going to get stupidly emotional in front of Brady's father, so I attempted to hasten his visit.

"Anyway, thanks for stopping by. Adam said he'd be back later."

"Is he going to stay here?" Why did that feel like a reproach?

"No, I'm sure he will want to be with Jeannie tonight."

"Jeannie?"

"Yes, he and Jeannie have been dating."

The Sheriff smiled. "She's a nice girl."

"Yes, I like her," I told him.

The Sheriff left, but before he did, he reminded me to stay alert and to call him if there were any signs of trouble. I waved goodbye and watched his car leave my drive.

Adam called my house phone and asked if I was okay. I told him I was and I asked about Bev. He told me she was still in a coma, but stable, and the doctors were trying to figure out what made her pass out in the first place. I told him to give Jeb my best and to tell him the place looks great. He once again asked if I was really okay, and again I told him I was. I explained that I was going to put the animals in the barn because it was supposed to storm and then I was going to take a bath and go to bed.

He told me that he was going to see Jeannie and that he would come back to the farm later. I said that wasn't necessary and I thought about how the Sheriff had asked if Adam was going to be staying with me. Once again I told Adam that I was fine and that he should stay with Jeannie tonight. He paused, and I knew he was thinking about it.

"Adam, I'm fine, really. Bring Jeannie for breakfast, okay?"

"Okay, but if you get scared or you even hear a twig break you call me."

I laughed. "I will. Adam. Thanks for taking me on my trip. It was great."

"It would have been Belle if Brady hadn't f-ed it all up."

I chuckled sadly. "It's okay Adam. The trip was worth it. I know I'm a country girl, and that I love my farm. I guess I'm just not made to be loved."

"Belle that's pretty severe."

"It's the truth."

"It's not, but we'll talk about it tomorrow."

"Sure."

"No kidding Belle, I know a bucketful of eligible men that would think you are fabulous, and they will treat you with the respect you deserve."

I giggled. "Uh, no thanks."

"Haven't you ever heard the old saying that when you fall off a horse, you need to get right back on again?"

"Yes, I've heard that. I don't think that applies here."

"Okay, what about the one that you have to kiss a lot of toads before you find your Prince?"

I laughed out loud.

"Adam that's funny. You made that up!"

"No, it's a real saying. I swear." We were both laughing now.

We said goodnight. I was honestly happy that he was going to see Jeannie tonight.

I went back to the barn and saw the leaves on the trees turn their undersides up, going silver. Yup, it was going to storm. I brought in the animals and fed them. I put the pigs in their outside hut and made sure they had food and water.

Satisfied that my animals were hunkered down for the night, I went inside and made myself a peanut butter sandwich and drank a glass of milk before going into my room.

I unpacked my bags and put them by the front door so Adam could give them back to Mrs. McDaniel. I knew I was being a coward, but I couldn't bring myself to return them myself. I didn't have a car anyways.

I brushed my teeth and ran myself a bath. I sunk down into the warm bath water. My hair was piled on top of my head because I had washed it that morning, and I didn't want to get it wet. I'm not sure how long I sat in the tub for. The water had cooled and my fingertips were shriveled. I got out of the cooled water and threw on Brady's tee shirt. I was obviously a glutton for punishment; I should have burned the damn shirt, but I put it over my head, and Brady's comforting scent surrounded me. I wondered if his new girlfriend slept in his shirts.

It was a warm night and even though it was going to rain I opened the window in my room and got into bed. I closed my eyes and listened to the quiet of my farm. It was like a balm to my pained emotions. There was no way I would be selling my place, my home. I would go to college, get a job and live here for the rest of my life. Alone. That's when the tears fell.

I must have slept through the rooster's crow
because it was near 8:00 AM when I rolled over
and looked at the clock. With my swollen eyes still
shut I smiled. I was surprised that I had slept so
soundly. I stretched and climbed out of bed to use
the bathroom. When I went back into my
bedroom, I saw that the rain was splattering inside
my open window, so I shut it. It was going to be a
dreary day. Perfect, it matched my mood I thought
morosely. I went to the kitchen to make coffee,
and my phone rang. When I answered it, I found it
was Mr. Bee.

"Good Morning Belle."

"Good Morning Mr. Bee."

"I heard you were home. I saw Adam last night."

"Yes, we came back as soon as we heard about
Mrs. Gordon."

"Yes, we are all concerned about her. Belle, I'd love
to hear about your trip, but I also have something
to tell you. It's rather important, can you see me
today?"

"Sure Mr. Bee, but I don't have a car. Can Adam
drop me off after breakfast?"

"That would be fine. I'll see you then." I placed the
phone back in its holder

That's when I heard them. Footsteps. The
footsteps were coming my Momma's room right
above me.

This time I wasn't cautious. I ran up the steps. If
this was Momma, she was going to get a piece of
my mind. I opened the door to the room and pain

exploded on the side of my head sending me into
blackness.

Adam

Jeb was a mess. Bev was in a coma, but thank goodness she was stable. It was unclear why she had blacked out causing her to fall and hit her head in the first place. Belle was putting up a brave front, but she was miserable. I'd been calling Brady every chance I got. I left him a ton of messages. I was going to tell him what a scumbag I thought he was.

I headed to Jeannie's apartment. I couldn't wait to see her. I had only been with her a few times before I had left with Belle. The week, she had attended the conference we had talked and texted all the time. I had tried not to text or call Jeannie with Belle around. It wasn't that I was hiding it anything from Belle; it was just that I didn't want Belle to think that she was keeping me from being with Jeannie. I knew Belle; she would have felt like she was a burden if she knew how close Jeannie and I had gotten.

I'd had fun with Belle and honestly seeing her experience things for the first time was a kick. I tried taking pictures so Brady would see them too, but it backfired, and he got the wrong idea. I was still plenty pissed at him.

Brady

My training had been brutal, but worth it. I was
stronger than I'd ever been. With my new
prosthetic blade, I was just as fast too. My
marksmanship had always been good, but I was
even better now, steadier. I improved under the
tutelage of the Master Sargent. I had aced the
written test. The speed and agility tests had been
tougher. I finished third in the distance running
test, second in the speed test, but eighth in agility
test. My damn blade had gotten caught in a tire,
and I had fallen. I got up quickly and finished, but I
knew my time was shot to hell. I was still pleased
with what I had accomplished.

That night we had all gone into town. All I could
think about was calling Belle. I knew she'd be
proud of me. When we reached the town's limit, I
powered my phone up. It immediately pinged as
texts and pictures began to download. All the
pictures were of Belle, or Belle with and Adam.
Under one of them, he wrote' look at our girl.'
They looked like a couple. There was another
picture of Belle blowing a kiss to Adam. She was
smiling in every damn one of them. The selfies she
and Adam took broke my heart. They were leaning
into each other and looked truly happy. I realized
that Adam had sent them so that I would know
that Belle had chosen him and that they were
together now. Another one of his texts had said he

had to tell me something and he didn't want me to be mad at him. Was he serious? He steals my girl, and he wants me to remain friends with him. F - that.

There were only eight recruits left; two of them were women. One of them was pretty obvious, about wanting to hook up with me. She had been sitting next to me in the van and when she saw the pictures I was looking at she remarked what a great looking couple Belle and Adam were. Shit.

That night I got drunk, really drunk, and Vanessa was doing everything she could, hoping we would end up together. She didn't leave my side the entire night. When I was stupid enough from the alcohol, I called Adam. I wanted to hear what he had to say. I was too drunk to leave the table that Vanessa and I were sitting at. The entire time I was on the phone, Vanessa had talked suggestively to me. I knew damn well she was doing it on purpose, in case I was talking to my girl. I had told her I had a girlfriend the first day we met, hoping to keep our work relationship in check. Luckily when Adam handed the phone to Belle, the other girl recruit made Vanessa go to the ladies room with her. I know I was a dick to Adam and I was even worse when I talked to Belle. I didn't care. They had broken me. My attempt to hear them out had turned into me being a jackass.

That night I foolishly made out with Vanessa. We stumbled out of the bar pawing each other, and I backed her up against the siding hoping to produce enough desire to momentarily forget Belle. Vanessa wanted us to get a room, but I couldn't. I hated kissing her. I was just doing it because I knew that Belle and Adam were probably kissing and probably doing more. The thought made me sick to my stomach. I walked away from Vanessa leaving her breathless and wanting. I was a total jerk to everyone that night.

The next day I apologized to Vanessa. I told her I liked her as a friend, but it wasn't going to be more than that. I'd lost Belle, but I needed to excel in my training; I was still going to turn my life around; for me.

I trained harder than ever, and I knew I was getting noticed. I was easily the best shot out of the eight remaining trainees, and some days I even scored higher than the rifle range master, which I was pretty proud of.

The next week flew by. I was aching inside. At night I'd close my eyes, and all I'd picture is one of the happy Belle - Adam selfies. My days were crammed with learning the protocols of Vermont law enforcement and training for search and rescue. I was working as hard as my body would physically allow so that when I fell into bed at night, I would pass out.

We had one week left in training, plus the practical, which would be sprung on us, but Vanessa had heard from one of our instructors that we were ahead of schedule.

That night we were woken up and sent on a mission. At first, we thought it was practical, but we learned it was an actual search and rescue mission.

We were looking for a father and son who had gone missing from their campsite in upstate Vermont. We were loaded into vans and drove upstate that night. When we arrived, we were put into teams of two, given walkie-talkies, and a map. Each partner group had a section of the National Forest that they were to search. Vanessa and I were partnered together. I wondered how she had pulled that off.

When dawn broke, thirty responders took off to scout the forest. Vanessa and I had been given a portion of the National Forest that contained a cliff that needed searching, because of the many ledges and small caverns on it. I knew we would have to repel down to search it thoroughly. We would climb up the backside of the mountain to get to the cliff and do a slow repel down.

We had forty-pound packs on, and walking was difficult. We reached our designated search grid. Vanessa and I had gone off trail a few times to be thorough.

Vanessa started to fall behind me about five hours in. She wasn't a big girl, and her pack was heavy. She wasn't complaining, but she was holding me back. My leg was on fire, and I could feel that my stump was rubbing in the plastic cup. I was sure it was close to bleeding. My skin had toughened up over the last three weeks, but I guess not enough. We rested on a rock, and I took off my pack and found Belle's ointment. Then without looking at

Vanessa, I took off my blade and rubbed the ointment on my swollen stump.

"Geez." I heard Vanessa say. I looked up, and she was gawking at me.

"I'm sorry I didn't mean to stare."

I didn't answer her. I reattached my blade and sucked down some water before standing up.

"Brady, I heard you were an amputee, and I've been ridiculously impressed, but it looks so painful right now."

"It's fine. Come on we have to get going." I helped her up, and I thought she held onto my hand a little too long.

We reached the toughest part of the climb, the one that would lead us to the rock face. This was the part I was worried about. I hadn't tested my new blade on an incline this steep. Vanessa was sweating profusely, and her face was as red as her hair that was tucked under the ball caps we wore.

"We have to get up there and down the rock face before we lose daylight," I told her.

"Brady I'm exhausted. I don't know if I can keep up."

"You have to. We are not allowed to leave our partners, and that father and son could be hurt. Get moving."

I turned my back on her and started up the steep embankment. I had to carefully find a foothold that my rubber tipped blade would hold on to. I could hear Vanessa behind me climbing. My fingers screamed as I dug them into the small grooves I

found to hold onto, and I could feel blood
dripping down my pant leg.
It took an hour but I made it to the top I looked
behind me, to see Vanessa was barely moving.
"Come on Vanessa. Make tracks."
"Brady go on, I'll catch up."
"No way."
"My packs too heavy. I'm going to drop it."
"Don't even think about it," I yelled down to her.
I dropped my pack and tied myself to a tree.
Ignoring the burning pain in my leg, I repelled
down to her. She was twenty yards down from the
top. I took her pack off of her and then together
we climbed up to the top. When we reached the
summit, we allowed ourselves a few minutes to
regroup.
Vanessa lay on her back and just tried to catch her
breath. I had to take off my prosthesis and wipe
the blood out that had collected inside the cup.
Vanessa started to say something, and I gave her a
look that shut her down.
We tied our ropes to separate trees and repelled
down the rock face. Halfway down we heard
crying. I swung to the side and saw them. The boy
wasn't moving, and the father was on such a small
ledge that I was afraid if he moved he would fall.
"Thank God you're here." The father sobbed.
"Vanessa, call in our coordinates."
I checked the boy's pulse and found one, but the
kid was not responding to any stimuli, so I knew he
was hurt bad. His arm and leg were broken, and he
had taken a hard hit to his head. There was a gash

on his forehead that was about three inches long, and it had bled profusely.

"He's alive right?"

"He has a strong pulse," I told his dad giving him a positive to hold on to. "Are you hurt?'"

"I'm fine. Andy though, is he going to live?" The father was starting to move too much, and I could see that the little ledge that he was on was not going to hold for much longer.

"Mr. Langdon, we need to get you off this ledge."

"How? How? I don't think..."

The man was in a full-blown panic attack, and I had to get him to focus and secured to the line. "Listen, listen to me." I had to shake him pretty hard before he concentrated on what I was saying. "I'm going to put this harness around you, and then we are going to put one on your boy."

I looked at Vanessa and saw that she was trying to swing over to us. Unfortunately, there was a large rock that jutted out between us that she couldn't swing past preventing her from reaching us.

"Vanessa drop down."

"I'm trying to get to you."

"I said drop down. I'm sending the father down. You'll be able to guide him better from below."

Vanessa repelled down, so she was below us.

Mr. Langdon was shaking, and I was concerned that he was going into shock. I braced my foot and blade on the rock face wall. I used my other arm to help Mr. Langdon get into a harness. I looped his harness into a claw and attached the rope to a loop in the front of my harness. I was going to have to lower him down using my arms.

As I started to lower the man he kept muttering, "Please just save my son."

I used my legs to support me as I lowered the shaken man to Vanessa. When he got to her, I wait to hear off belay - which meant she had him. Finally, I heard her call up, and I pulled the rope back up to me.

My arms were shaking from the strain of lowering the 180-pound man. I was sweating, and my hands were slipping so I quickly put on gloves that I had in my pocket.

I attached the rope to the young boy's harness. He was still out cold. I was going to have to bring us both down the rock face using my legs and only one arm. I hooked the boy to me and strapped his chest to mine so that he wasn't flopping forward. I still held on to him. His legs dangled and kicked against mine.

I very slowly began to lower us to the ground, which was fifty yards away, plus it was getting dark. When we reached the ground Vanessa and the father was prepared for us. They took the boy from me, as I unhooked my harness

There was no time to rest. I took out my med kit and silver thermal blanket and played medic to the boy. His fractures were not compound, but when he regained consciousness, he was going to be in pain. I butterfly bandaged his wound while his father hovered over me. Vanessa was talking on the walkie. I could hear everything.

There was a trail a half-mile from where we were. We needed to get there, and the rangers that were in the vicinity would meet us with a four-wheeler. We needed to go now before it got too dark or we would be spending the night in the forest.

I slugged some water, put my pack on, and lifted the boy into my arms. The father had heard our transmission and stood up with Vanessa's silver thermal still wrapped around his shoulders.

Vanessa put her pack on, and we bushwhacked using a compass. The compass Belle had given me. My leg was killing me, and I knew it was torn up. I wasn't stopping though. I was limping badly, and the father even asked if I was hurt.

My arms were tired from the strain of the repel and carrying the boy. There was no way Vanessa could carry him, and the father hadn't even offered. I took some solace in the fact that I must have appeared capable.

Finally, we heard the whine of a small engine, and a few seconds later we stepped out on a trail. We walked down the darkening path and soon saw the green four-wheeler heading towards us.

Two Rangers and a medic were on the ATV. It was then I realized Vanessa and I weren't getting a ride home.

"Are you sending someone back for us?" Vanessa asked. I already knew the answer.

"You guys did great. First light." He then tossed us two canteens of water and two sandwiches before heading back down the mountain.

Vanessa looked like she was going to cry, so I put my arm around her shoulder trying to comfort her. Big mistake.

She leaned into me and tried to pull me down for a kiss. I stepped back from her.

"Vanessa stop."

"I thought. I thought you were." She was stammering

"I was just trying to comfort you. Come on let's make camp and eat."

I rigged a tarp up, and it was then we realized we didn't have our thermals. Mine was on the boy, and the father had Vanessa's.

I took out the garbage bag that I had lining my pack and sat on it. Vanessa didn't have one, so I moved over so she could sit on mine with me. Our backs were resting against a tree.

"Well we either use the tarp to keep us warm or keep the tarp above us, keeping the dew off us, and we snuggle."

Vanessa was not giving up. I didn't even answer her.

I ate my sandwich and then found a private place to take care of business and doctor my leg without Vanessa looking on. When I got back to our little camp, Vanessa was sitting in the same spot looking at me with her big brown eyes. I knew she was tired and probably a little unnerved. She was a country girl, but camping with comforts is a lot different than camping with out.

I cut the tarp down and wrapped Vanessa in it.

"How will you stay warm?"

"I'll be fine."

I sat back down, and Vanessa pulled the tarp around herself remaining against my side. I would have built a fire, but we under a fire watch and there were no fires allowed because of dry conditions. It got darker and colder, and the sounds of the forest surrounded us. I took out my gun and held it on my lap.

Vanessa was shaking from the cold. "Brady please share this with me. I'm freezing."

I had to admit I was freezing too, but I didn't want her to read anything into it.

"Vanessa if we share this tarp and use our bodies to stay warm it's a survival thing. Do not read anything into it."

"I won't, I promise. Please just hold me."

We wrapped the tarp around us keeping our packs under our head, and she backed into the warmth of my chest. Her rear was against my groin, and I knew she was trying to get a rise out of me, literally, but I wasn't interested, and I was too damn tired. It wasn't that she wasn't good looking, she was very cute, but I didn't want her. For the second time in my life, I loved someone who didn't want me.

I woke up stiff, sore and with morning wood. Vanessa thought she was the cause of my hardness because she turned to face me and pressed into me. I rolled away from her and got up to go to the bathroom. When I returned, she had rolled the tarp up and was sitting on her pack.

"Sorry, I thought, you know, maybe you had changed your mind."

I sighed. "No, just morning wood."

She giggled, blushed furiously, and she looked so cute that I had to laugh with her.

The four-wheeler came back for us, and we were driven to where the rest our group was waiting for us. We were congratulated, debriefed, fed, and taken to showers. Then we headed back to our training camp.

Everyone was asking Vanessa, and I questions about the rescue. Vanessa was talking non-stop. I just shut my eyes and tried to nap. I was wiped out, and I hoped we would be given the night off. When we got back to camp. The lead instructor told us we had the day off and that we didn't have to report back until noon of the next day. I went straight to my bunk and fell asleep. When I woke up the camp was quiet. When I went outside the instructor told me everyone was in town. He was on his way in to have a bite to eat, so he offered me a ride. He invited me to eat with him, and I accepted. He was a Veteran too, and we swapped stories. He confided to me that I had impressed a lot of people while training and with the rescue yesterday. I had to admit I needed to hear that. I was emotionally beat thinking about losing Belle, and my body was worn out physically. I was hoping it wasn't all a waste of time. The poor time on the agility test still hung over my head.

I left my instructor to seek out the rest of my crew. I had a whole night to relax. I was going to get drunk, again. When I found them at the bar, the only bar in town, Vanessa was shit-faced. She sat on my lap, and I couldn't move her off of me fast enough. She had her arms wrapped around me, and she kept whispering to me how wonderful the night we had spent together was. How special it had been. She was making it sound like we had had sex and I sure as hell didn't want anyone else thinking that.

After prying her from my lap, I avoided her as much as I could but the alcohol soon had me goofy, so when she caught up to me again I didn't have the energy or good sense to push her away. I just laughed at her silly flirting. She buried her face in my neck and then she passed out.

"Well shit," I said. My buddies were laughing.

"Come on guys help me."

"Want us to help you to a hotel room?"

"Damn, come on Addie help a fellow out." Addie was the other girl in our group.

Addie took pity on me and helped uncoil Vanessa from my neck before walking her to the rest room. I walked outside and saw the instructor I had eaten dinner with getting into one of the vans. I jogged over to him.

"Can I have a ride back?"

"You done already?"

"Yeah, I'm beat."

He nodded, and I hopped into the passenger seat. I forgot that I had my phone in my shirt pocket and I pulled it out after I felt it vibrate. There was a text from Adam.

you ass

What? He steals my girl, and he's calling me an ass.
I looked to see if I'd missed any calls and to my
surprise, I saw that I had called Adams phone.
When I checked the time, I realized that I must
have butt dialed him, in this case mistakenly
pocket-dialed him, about an hour earlier.
I didn't understand his text to me. Why the hell
would he call me an ass? I wanted to call him, but
we had already driven out of cell phone range.

The next day I slept in for the first time in three
weeks. I read through one of the manuals. Used the
ointment Belle gave me on my leg and relaxed on a
chair in front of my bunk area. I thought, one more
week of this. I just had to handle one more week.
At noon we went to the firing range and then we
did hand to hand with another instructor. We ate
dinner then we took a test on medical procedures
and CPR. It was after 9:00 PM when we finished,
and I was bushed.
The CO met me as I walked towards my cabin.
"McDaniel we need to have a chat."
"Sir."
"You've passed son. We aren't sending you on the
practical in the field. You and Smith have already
proven you know what to do."
I was speechless. We had heard the practical was
going to be given to us in the next few days.
"What do I do now Sir?" I asked.
"Well, son if you want to go home I'm heading to
base camp now. You can go home tonight."

"Tonight. Hell yeah!"

I ran to my bunk and loaded my duffle. The guys wished me well. When I got into the van Vanessa was already there.

"Isn't this great Brady? We get to go home. We passed!"

I was ecstatic, and my first thought was that I couldn't wait to tell Belle and then I remembered that she was in New York City, with Adam.

31

Brady

I drove home thinking about sleeping in my bed
and eating one of my Mom's meals. They were
going to be so proud of me. Hell, I was proud of
me. I passed! That meant I could become a Deputy
and apply for the State Search and Rescue job that
everyone was buzzed about.

When I got home, it was after midnight. I quietly
went to my room I didn't want to wake everyone.
There was a package sitting on my bed, and I saw it
was postmarked from Colorado. My address was
written in Belle's handwriting. I opened the small
box up and found a knife in a leather holder. A
little note sat at the bottom of the box.

I hope you like this.
Thinking of you.
Belle

Yeah, she was thinking of me all right; she had
metaphorically stuck a knife in my back. I tossed
the knife down on my dresser and stripped down
to my boxers. I fell asleep as soon as my head hit
the pillow.

"Brady's home!" I heard Tommy yell. I groaned
when I saw that it was only 7:00 AM.
He came into my room. "What are you doing home
man? Did you get flushed?"

My Dad was standing behind him looking worried.
I threw my pillow at him, and he deftly caught it
and threw it back. "No, I passed."

"Mom, Brady passed!" Tommy yelled.

I heard my Mom whoop happily making me smile.
"You're home a week early." My Dad said after
Tommy left.

"Yeah, long story. I did it, Dad."

"I had no doubt." He said, busting out a large
smile. "Get up and tell us all about it over
breakfast."

He closed my door, and I got up and threw some
clothes on.

My Mom prepared a feast, and I told my family
about camp and the training. They were equally
impressed with the successful search and rescue
mission. Even Tommy didn't have any sarcastic
remarks.

My Mom cleared the breakfast dishes, Tommy had
disappeared to get ready for work, and dad and I
enjoyed another cup of coffee.

"How's your leg?" My Mom asked cautiously. I
didn't blame her. In the past, I had barked at any
one who would have had asked that.

"It's pretty beat up. I have ointment that Belle gave
me." Even saying her name had a lump gathering
in my throat. I needed to get over that.

I saw my Mom give my Dad a look. I knew that
look.

"What's going on?" I asked peering over the rim of
my mug before taking a sip.

"She's home." My Dad said watching me.

"Home? She's not due home for a week."

"There was an accident on the farm a few days ago. The woman taking care of the place fell, and is in a coma."

I rubbed the back of my neck. I had goose bumps. "Is she going to be all right?"

"Doctor thinks so." My Dad continued to look at me. "Does Belle know you passed?" He asked.

I shook my head and took another sip of coffee. "No. I haven't talked to her in a week."

"Oh?" My Mom asked sitting down. My father took her hand in his, and I saw the slight squeeze he gave it. Tommy walked back into the kitchen to grab his lunch from the fridge.

I nonchalantly as possible told my parents. "Belle's with Adam."

Tommy looked at me oddly, and my Mom and Dad looked at each other.

"Yes." My dad said carefully. "She was with Adam on the trip you asked him to take her on."

I sighed and shook my head. "No, I mean she and Adam are together. They're a couple."

Tommy laughed. "Brady, they aren't a couple, and if they are Jeannie is going to kick his ass."

"Language," my Mom said automatically.

I looked at my Dad. "Son, I don't know why you think that. I just saw Belle yesterday. She told me that Adam and Jeannie are dating."

Tommy shook his head. "Yup, they have been for a while. They just kept it a secret until Jeannie could tell Kip."

"What?" I felt my stomach flip, and I put my mug down.

"Why would you think they were together?" My Mom asked.

I dug out my cell phone and showed them the photos Adam had sent. My parents looked at them, and Tommy looked at them from over their shoulders.

"Looks like she's having fun." My Mom said quietly.

"Mom, look at them. They're together."

"I don't see it," Tommy interjected.

"Look at what Adam wrote underneath this one." I scrolled to a selfie where Adam had written; *our girl likes the ocean* under the photo.

The picture was of Belle blowing a kiss as she sat on the sand.

My Mom looked at me. "Did she know Adam was sending you pictures?"

"I think so."

"Brady, sweetheart. She's blowing you that kiss."

I took the phone back and looked at it. Dread built up inside of me and the coffee soured in my gut.

"But he wrote our girl?

"Perhaps he meant she's his as a friend and yours as more?" My Mom suggested.

"Or maybe he forgot the Y in our?" My Dad said with a frown.

"Shit," I swore softly.

"But Adam said he had to tell me something important, and he didn't want me to get mad."

Tommy shrugged his shoulders, "hmm, not sure, but probably that he was dating Jeannie and he wasn't able to tell you about it until Kip had been told."

I looked at my little brother. When the hell did he get so wise?

"Brady?" My Mom asked gently. "What did you do?"

"I was pretty mean to Belle on the phone last week." In my head, I was screaming, 'and you made out with another woman.' I felt sick.

"You're right. It could have been a typo or just a figure of speech, but it could also be that they were together." I said trying to justify how I'd been thinking.

"Dude, no way," Tommy said crossing his arms. "Adam and Jeannie are a couple. I saw them last night. They were pretty lovey-dovey."

I hung my head. "What did I do?" I mumbled. My Dad got up and got ready for work. I continued sitting at the table. I was numb.

"So anything else been going on around here?" I asked trying to get my mind off the nauseous feeling I had.

Tommy volunteered more news. "Dad said Belle's Dad contacted Mr. Bee."

Dad walked back into the kitchen.

"Yup, two weeks ago. He wants Mr. Bee to introduce him to Belle."

"Dad, maybe he's the one that's been trying to hurt Belle. He's related to her by blood, that's how the property is handed down."

"I already checked him out, Brady. He just recently returned from a business trip in Denmark. He's married and lives out of state. He wasn't in the country when all these accidents happened to Belle."

"Does Belle know yet?"

"No, that's for Mr. Bee to tell her."

I carried my plate to the sink. I needed to talk to Belle. Maybe I should first talk to Adam. As I debated what to do our house phone rang. I only heard my dad's side of the conversation.

"Hello?"

Pause.

"Slow down, say that again."

Pause.

"Okay, I'm on my way."

My Dad hung up and looked at me. "That was Adam. He and Jeannie went to have breakfast with Belle this morning, and she's not there."

"Oh no," my Mom gasped.

"Maybe she's in the barn, or on a walk, or swimming?" I interjected hurriedly.

"They didn't look at the swimming hole, but she's not around the farm. She couldn't go into town; she doesn't have a car. They called Kip, and he hasn't heard from her. Mr. Bee talked to her this morning."

"I'm coming."

My dad looked at my mom and shrugged his shoulders. "Okay, let's go." I followed him out the door.

On the way there my dad said to remain in the background. He didn't want any drama. He was hoping she was just out for a walk, but because of her other accidents, he wasn't taking any chances. When we got there. Adam and Jeannie were standing on the front porch holding hands. They both looked concerned. When I got out of the car, Adam gave Jeannie a look, and he dropped her hand and headed towards me. My dad got between us.

"This is not the time boys. Adam talk to me."

Adam gave me a cold stare and then looked back to my dad. "I told Belle that Jeannie and I would come out for breakfast. When we got here, she's nowhere to be found. Mr. Bee talked to her a little bit ago. Kip hasn't heard from her, and her animals are still in the barn. I don't like it."

I didn't either. It was drizzling, but Belle would still have let the animals outside.

We walked inside to get out of the rain. "Did you look all over the house?" I asked.

Adam looked at me like he was ready to take my head off. He didn't acknowledge me with an answer.

"Adam, did you look all over the house?" I asked again.

"Yeah, I didn't see her. Her beds not made so she slept in it, and she brewed coffee."

My dad started to move through the house one room at a time, and I followed him. We looked in the basement, and I saw the dried blood on the cement floor near the wooden hutch.

I looked at my dad, and he acknowledged what I saw with just a head nod. That must have been where Mrs. Gordon had fallen.

Next, we looked in her bedroom. It was clear that Belle had slept in her bed. Her scent was everywhere, striking me as if punches to my gut. I noticed that her jeans were on her dresser along with a bra, underwear, and socks. Her old barn boots were underneath.

"Dad, those are the clothes she would have worn to do the animals."

My dad radioed in for another deputy. I could tell by his expression that he was worried.

I knew Belle would never take a walk or go anywhere without taking care of her animals first. Being in her bedroom brought forth the images of how we had spent our last night together. I rubbed my hands over my face. What had I done? I pushed the awful realization that I had lost her again aside. First, we needed to find her. My instincts were telling me she was in trouble. I walked back out of her room, and I was shocked back to reality when Adam grabbed my arm.

"What the hell Brady? Why are you here? Haven't you caused her enough grief?"

"Adam I'll admit that I was not that nice to her when we talked last, but I thought you and her were together."

"What?"

"What?" Jeannie echoed.

"The pictures you sent. And then the text under this one." I pulled out my phone and scrolled to it.

"You idiot! I forgot the stupid Y."

"What about you texting me that you had to tell me something important to tell me and you didn't want me to get mad."

"I wanted to tell you about Jeannie!"

We stared at each other, Adam was a second from trying to punch me, and I was going to let him. I friggin deserved it. Jeannie got between us.

"That doesn't explain your butt dial two nights ago." He spit out, he was fuming, and Jeannie held him back with her palms.

"Butt dial? What are you talking about? I was still training."

"Well you clearly weren't training," He used his fingers to make air quotes when he sneered the word training, "Belle and I heard you and a woman talking about the special night she and you had spent together, and how good you were together."

That sounded familiar. Why did it sound familiar? Holy smokes! I knew what conversation they had heard. My phone had been in my shirt pocket. Vanessa must have touched the call button when she was on my lap. Adam had been the last person I had called, so my phone had dialed his.

Oh, My God. They heard that!

Jeannie met my eyes. "Uncool Brady." She admonished me.

"Nothing happened," I told them defensively. 'Not that night anyway' I said to myself. This was bad, very bad.

"Yeah, right," Adam said walking away from me.

I looked at Jeannie. "I swear nothing happened that night."

"Brady, I've known you forever. Something happened."

I shook my head. "Belle must hate me."

"Can you blame her?" Jeannie said turning to follow after Adam. "Just leave her alone Brady. She has friends. We'll take care of her. Adam already has a buddy who wants to meet her."

I saw red. They were already fixing her up with other guys? I hung my head. They were right. I blew it. She deserved someone better than me.

My Dad put his hand on my shoulder. I didn't know how much he had heard, but he was not interested in my stupid drama now. He was worried about Belle.

"Did you look upstairs Adam?"

"Yes. Nothing. She's gone."

My father started climbing the steps. I knew he would want to check every place himself. I followed behind him.

"Brady, get your head together. You've been trained for this. I need you. Belle needs you."

"Does she dad?" I said pathetically.

"Damn it, boy. She needs the man that can find her. You know she isn't on any hike. Not in this weather, not without taking care of her animals. Put aside what you're thinking and feeling and help me find her."

My dad was correct. I had been trained in this. I would do everything I could to find her. I just hoped that she was still alive when we did. That thought sickened me.

First, we looked in Belle's bedroom. "Anything look different?" He asked me then Adam. We both shook our heads.

We walked into her Momma's room next. The Gordon's had been sleeping in it, and their clothes and personal items were neatly spread about the room.

"What about in here? Anything?"

Adam opened a box that was on a dresser.

"Her books still missing, but that happened before we left."

"What book?"

"Belle found a box that had a journal her Mom kept, plus some legal papers and family photos. Belle had them in that box." Adam pointed to the box on the dresser. "Before we left she came up here to get the journal. She wanted to read it while we were away. It was gone."

"Crap." My dad said out loud.

We looked around, but with the Gordon's things in there we really couldn't see if anything was out of place. We were just about to leave the room when I noticed something. A small smear of dried blood was on the closets white painted doorframe.

"Dad, wait."

I knelt next to the small smear.

"Is that blood?" Jeannie asked nervously.

"Okay, you and Adam go wait on the porch," Dad said to Jeannie.

Adam hustled Jeannie out of the door. I knew Dad was preserving a possible crime scene.

My Dad pulled out latex gloves and opened the closet door. There were clothes hanging up, shoes on the floor; there was nothing unusual there. We were about to close the door when I felt something.

Dad had already backed away from the closet, but I parted the clothes and put my hand inside the closet, moving it over the back wood paneled wall. A very slight stirring of cool air washed across my fingertips. I moved my hands around more. Yes, I was certain air coming from the back of the closet. I grabbed the clothes, hangers and all and threw them to the ground behind me.

"Brady, what the hell?"

"Dad, there something back here."

I ran my fingers over the grooved wood. I felt wetness, and I stepped from darkened closet to see blood on my fingers.

"Shit," I said softly showing my dad my bloody fingertip.

I wiped my fingers on my jeans, and my dad pushed in behind me as I scrutinized the closet.

"There's a slight breeze dad. Do you feel it?"

My dad silently nodded. I could read his face; he thought we were about to find Belle, dead.

I pressed my hands against the back wall, and I felt a slight give. My fingers touched upon a fake wooden groove and when I moved it a door in the back of the closet swung open.

"Holy smokes!" My dad said.

I used my phone for light and looked in the
doorway. There was a ladder inside the opening,
and there were metal rungs descending downward.
I peered over the ledge and just saw darkness.
I turned to shimmy into the opening, and my dad
grabbed my shoulder.
"Brady wait."
"I got this dad. Give me your gun. Dad reached
into his ankle holster and gave me his second
weapon. I didn't even know he carried a second
gun. I lowered myself, so I was standing on the
first rung.
"There's more blood dad," I said shining my light
around the tight space.
"Be careful," Dad told me as I disappeared beneath
the closets flooring. I was happy that I had put on
my blade instead of my shoe prosthetic. With the
new blade, I had traction because of the rubber
that had been mounted on the tip of the blade, and
on a small area underneath. I quickly made my way
down the rungs. I was pretty sure I had passed to
the side of the large stone fireplace in Belle's living
room. I yelled that bit of info up to my dad.
When I reached solid ground I looked around.
"Dad I'm on the ground." I yelled up the shaft.
"What do you see?"
"The floors dirt." I shined my phone around and
saw a small tunnel and a metal handle opposite the
tunnel. "I think I'm in the basement. There's a
tunnel dad. It appears to be leading away from the
house. There's a handle. I'm opening it now."

I pushed on the handle, and a door opened slightly but stopped as it hit against something solid.

"Dad I think I'm in the cellar, come down here, but use the steps."

I heard when my dad reached the cellar.

"Brady?"

"Yeah, I hear you. Dad, I'm going to open the door.

The door swung open. It was directly behind Belle's wooden hutch. The cabinet was on wheels, and even though it was heavy, it was easily moved. When I stepped out and shut the door, I saw that the hutch concealed any marks the wheels would have left on the dirt floor.

I opened the hatchway again. "Dad there's a tunnel that leads away from the house. I'm going to follow it."

"Hold up son."

I waited impatiently as my dad radioed his deputy to keep Adam and Jeannie on the porch and for him to keep his eyes open.

"Brady, I'm not sure about this."

"Dad the tunnel runs north-west, towards Belle's shed. I'll go about 200 paces. If the tunnel runs further than that, I'll come back, and we'll regroup."

"Okay." He answered, but I could tell he was worried. "Dad really, I got this. Let's find her."

I took off running down the small tunnel. I had to run hunched over and every few steps I saw drops of blood either on the packed dirt wall or the ground. There were support beams every ten feet, and I wondered when it had been built. The tunnel was starting to slope upwards, and I moved faster hoping I was reaching the end. I knew Belle had no idea it existed. Belle, I hope she was okay.

My heart was pounding, but it wasn't from exertion it was because I was so afraid for her. I reached one hundred paces, and I could see that the tunnel continued. I held my phone ahead of me looking for blood, praying not to find a body, Belle's body, so I ran as best I could crouch over. The tunnel ended abruptly. I estimated that I was about one hundred and fifty yards away from Belle's house. My cell phone light exposed another ladder that was affixed to beams. I pointed my phone up the ladder and saw that there was a square lid fitted above the ladder. I climbed up and pushed on the closure. It moved easily, and I pushed it off to the side and pulled myself out. I was in the woods behind the shed.

I looked around the area I was standing in and saw more blood. The top of the shafts lid was cleverly camouflaged and sat in the center of a dense thicket. There was a small trail leading down out of the thicket, and I could see it had been used recently.

I walked the perimeter quickly looking for any signs of Belle but didn't see any. I ran back towards the house, and the look of relief on my dad's face when he saw me was evident.

My dad headed towards me, and Adam and Jeannie flew off the porch, even though the deputy tried to

hold them there. My dad gestured to his Deputy
that it was okay, so he followed behind them.
"Did you find her?" Adam asked. The man was
worried. I realized he probably felt responsible
because he had left her alone.
"No, but there's blood. She was taken away using
the tunnel. It ends behind the shed in the woods."
"A tunnel?" Adam asked shock registered on his
face.
"Oh God." Jeannie cringed, and Adam pulled her
against him to comfort her. Seeing them together
only intensified the horrible assumption I had
made. I had messed up the best thing that had ever
happened to me.
"Did you see any tire tracks?" My dad asked.
"No, but we have to expand the search, just in case
I missed them."
I led everyone to the tunnels entrance. My dad
knelt down and surveyed the cover and the matted
down grass.
 "Looks like it was one person. I only see one set of
prints."
"Then where's Belle?" Jeannie asked frantically.
"He's carrying her." My dad and I said at the same
time.
We spread out, and after five minutes the deputy
found four-wheeler tracks. They were barely
noticeable, and my dad commended his deputy for
spotting them.
"She's gone?" Adam inserted anxiously.
I turned to Adam. "I think she's still on the
property, at least I hope so."

"Brady." My dad said putting his hand on my arm. "Son, you can't possibly know that."

I interrupted him. "Listen to me. Adam, you said Mr. Bee talked to her this morning correct?"

"Yes, we called him when we couldn't find her. He said he said he called her first thing this morning."

"And what time did you two get here?"

Jeannie and Adam looked at each other. "About ten minutes after 8:00."

"Dad, Mr. Bee would have called Belle from his office, probably at 8:00 or close to that. He always opened his office at 8:00 AM, on the dot. You can set your watch to it."

My dad nodded grinning ever so slightly at me. "Go on."

I looked at Adam.

"Did you see anyone, any cars, truck, or four-wheeler on your way here?"

"No, no one," Adam said. "I'm sure."

I looked back at my dad.

"Adam and Jeannie were here at 8:10. They would have passed whoever took Belle if whoever took her had used the main road."

Belle's driveway was a mile long, and the County road ended at her drive. There were no other roads or driveways near hers.

"Dad, she's being held here, on her property."

"But why?" Jeannie asked.

I shook my head. "I have no idea, but one thing I do know, if they wanted her dead, we would have found her body. Belle's alive."

32

Belle

I forced myself from the painless refuge
unconsciousness provided grappling for lucid
thoughts. Snippets of reality poked through the
fog. My head throbbed with a pulse of its own, and
my cheeks and lips felt unnaturally tight.
 I tried to open my eyes, but all I saw was
blackness. My first coherent thought was that
something was covering them.
Why?
I lay still mostly because I was in such intense pain
that I was afraid if I moved I might cause the pain
to worsen. I smelled dirt, damp dirt, and as my
other senses kicked in, I realized I was lying on my
side, and my back was against something cold and
hard.
Where was I?
I listened but heard no sounds except the severe
pulsing in my head. My wrists were aggressively
tied behind my back, and my ankles were bound
together so tightly that my anklebones scrapped
against each other. I cautiously drew my knees up
to my chest hoping to garner some warmth from
my legs. I was able to move them, but it hurt to do
so. My tee shirt, well Brady's tee shirt, clung to me
like a cold, wet rag. The coppery taste of blood
pooled in my mouth and my weak attempt to spit it
out culminated in thick liquid clinging to my lips
and chin.

What had happened? Whatever it was had severely injured my face; that much I did know. I was dazed, nauseous and in the worse pain, I'd ever felt. I gently moved my arms as best I could to see if they were hurt. It evoked memories of when I had done that after the ravine incident.

I was too woozy to assess for other injuries because whatever had happened to my head and face was severe. I wasn't sure if I was bleeding anywhere and I had to remain laying on my left side because the pain on the right side of my face was excruciating.

As panic began to set in, I tried to focus on my breathing. I was shivering so hard that the vibrations from shaking were killing my face and head. I wished I could see, but there was no way I could rub my face against the ground to remove my blindfold without hurting myself further.

I painstakingly curled into a tight ball trying to garner some warmth. Where ever I was damp and dark. Oh God, had I been buried alive?

As much as it pained me to do so, I rolled to my left and then to my right. I lifted my bound feet upwards and was relieved that they met no walls. Okay, so I wasn't in a close-fitting spot; like a casket, but I felt like I was underground. It was eerily quiet, and that frightened me more than knowing that I was seriously injured. No sound; no people; no one coming for me.

Brady

Dad had called in neighboring towns for help, and I paced the length of the porch impatiently waiting for them to arrive. Finally, everyone that was going to be coming was standing around Belle's dining room table. There were sixteen of us in total. My dad and me, Kip, Austin and Joe, three-quarters of our fire department, Adam, Dad's two deputy's, four deputies from two neighboring towns, three Forest Rangers, and Vanessa. I couldn't believe it when she climbed out of the car with the three Forest Rangers. She said her brother was a Forest Ranger on the other side of Green Mountain and he had received the call for Searchers. He had told her about the missing woman, and she offered to help.

I was out of my mind with fear for Belle. I prayed she was safe. I knew she was bleeding and that worried me. If Vanessa could help, then so be it, I just hoped she didn't try any crap. I could feel her eyes on me, but I was focused on only one thing, bringing Belle home safely.

I was well aware that Belle would probably not even talk to me if, no, when, we did find her, but right now all I wanted was for her to be found, alive.

Dad spread a map on the table, and we formulated a plan. We surmised that if Belle's kidnapper wanted her dead, she'd be dead. Whoever had her could have killed her in her house or even the tunnel. My gut told me, and luckily everyone agreed, that whoever took Belle needed her alive. That left two viable options, presuming he wanted to keep her alive. Either he had hidden Belle somewhere on her land, which included the mountain, or he was trying to escape with Belle and was going to try to connect with a rural road. Going over the mountain would not be easy. There were no roads, and the woods were thick with trees. The other side of Green Mountain was all State land and just as untouched as Belle's side of the mountain. Time was going to be a factor in this search, and everyone knew it.

Dad and the Forest Rangers divided up the mountain into search grids. Vanessa's brother also alerted his team of Forest Rangers still on the other side of Green Mountain to be on the lookout for a four-wheeler. Dad had arranged for roadblocks to be set up on the only two roads anywhere near Belle's property.

The final task was partnering up and taking areas. Vanessa was walking to me. I knew she wanted to be my partner, but thankfully Kip reached me first. He and I chose one of the more rugged areas to search. It contained a tall rock face almost halfway up the mountain. We would be trekking a mile into the forest and then make a steep climb up the mountain.

Years ago Kip and I had hiked that very area of the mountain, but we had taken a different route than the one we would take today. We had come across a really cool waterfall. The fast-moving mountain water cascaded over the rock face causing a small natural rock enclosed pool to form, perfect for swimming. Large boulders provided ledges to jump into the water from, and afterward, we had laid on them because they were warm from the sun. The water squeezed between two large boulders to continue running down the mountain. I knew Belle's swimming hole was an extension of the same stream.

It had started raining, and the dismal gray sky held a chill. I prayed Belle was dry and warm. I looked at the barn and hoped she had done the animals, if not they were going to have a lousy day too. Everyone grabbed their packs. My Mom had brought mine, which contained my new blade. She also brought a bunch of bologna and cheese sandwiches for the search crew. I thanked Mom for my pack and asked her to see if someone could check on Belle's animals, she said she would, and that made me feel a little better. I stood by as she kissed my dad goodbye. An image of Belle doing the same for me in thirty years skipped across my brain. My gut pinched; she was going to make someone a great wife. Realizing that she wouldn't be mine made me ache.

Sixteen searchers, eight teams, all with walkie-talkie's left the house and fanned out in different directions to look for Belle.

Kip and I headed out jogging through the dense forest. The weather was dismal, and even though the soaking rain didn't completely penetrate the foliage and thick pine boughs, the damp cold temperature did.

I couldn't imagine what Belle was going through. As we pushed through the forest, my thoughts were overrun with my memories with Belle. I wished I could take her to the waterfall we had discovered. I'd often thought about revisiting the magical place, but this was not how I expected to do so. Belle probably didn't even know it was on her property. She would have loved the clandestine natural spot.

A lump formed in my throat, I loved her, and I had hurt her, again. I was a fool. I prayed she would be found unharmed just so that she could ream me out, which I totally deserved. I knew my stupid actions had destroyed any chance I had with her. That didn't matter; I just wanted to find her; please, I silently begged God, please let her be found alive.

I shook off the pity-party, I had to get a grip on my feelings, or I might miss something. Belle was resilient, but her body had endured so much lately. The thought of her being harmed had me running faster.

We ran through thickets and around boulders and trees keeping as close as possible to a direct line to the rock face. I didn't think that whoever had taken Belle had gone the way we were going because there was no way a four-wheeler could traverse the crowded tree terrain, but I knew for a fact, that it was the quickest route to the waterfall and that was where we needed to start our search.

Kip and I hadn't spoken since I'd left for training camp. As we ran, I wondered if he was upset about Jeannie and Adam. He and Jeannie had always been close, and I knew they had occasionally hooked up.

Kip broke our silent run by telling me how impressed he was with my agility. I explained that the blade I was wearing had been altered specifically for this type of terrain and that I'd been training on it. It definitely made a difference. He asked about my training, and I told him that I'd passed and that I would be a Deputy in Lansing. He was happy for me for had the good sense not to be too jovial; we were on a life and death mission. We could celebrate after Belle was found, alive.

Kip asked if I'd talked to Belle since I'd gotten home. I paused before answering. As much as I hated to tell him what a jerk I'd been, I did. I told my best friend everything, as we continued to move through the woods.

Kip listened and didn't judge, but I knew he wanted to say something.

"You can say it, Kip. Tell me how stupid I am. It's nothing I'm not telling myself."

He glanced at me sideways. "It's not good Brady. She liked you; a lot."

"I know." I didn't tell Kip that we had slept together, I already felt like the worst human ever.

"Honestly Brady, I bet if you just talk to her. Explain that you thought she and Adam were dating, she might understand."

"You think she would?"

"She might. She's pretty levelheaded. I mean it's not like you cheated on her."

My silence had Kip's head whipping to me. "Oh man, tell me you didn't?"

"I kissed someone. We made out. It was a mistake, a big one. I was trying to get Belle out of my head. I thought she was with Adam."

"Still Brady that might be a deal breaker."

"I know," I answered glumly as I thrashed through the brush with a stick I'd picked up.

"Who did you kiss? Someone you met at a bar?"

"No." I paused. "You know the redhead who is helping us search?"

"No way? She's cute."

"Yup. She was a trainee too. She was with me when we found that father and son."

"She's really cute." I made note that that was the second time he referenced how cute Vanessa was.

"Well when you f-up, you f-up in a big way." Kip panted.

"Yeah." I sighed heavily. I knew I was screwed. Belle would never talk to me again. I grimly thought that first, we needed to find her alive, and then she could go about not talking to me.

"So are you okay with Adam and Jeannie being together?" I asked in a clipped voice. Our run was taking a toll on both of us.

"Actually I am. I care for Jeannie, so I'm glad she's happy. Adam's a good guy."

"I thought you might be upset."

"Nope and they were pretty classy about the whole thing. They didn't tell anyone they were dating until Jeannie had a chance to tell me in person. It took a couple of weeks, but we finally managed to meet up, and that's when she told me."

"That's pretty cool of them. I wish I'd known."

"I heard Belle was annoyed that it took so long. She wanted to tell you about them so you wouldn't be jealous of her and Adam. She swore to Adam that she wouldn't say anything to you, and she kept her word, but she wasn't happy about it."

"If I had known about them I wouldn't be in the mess I am with her right now," I answered sharply.

"Yeah, Jeannie said the same thing and Adam's beating himself up about everything. He feels responsible for you two breaking up, and on top of that, he left her alone last night. He's feeling pretty guilty."

"Why couldn't they let me know?"

Kip chuckled. "Because you're my best friend and you would have told me."

I thought about that for about a second. "Yeah, I probably would have."

Kip and I were sweating as we emerged from under the thick canopy of trees in the forest. The dark clouds above were heavy with moisture, and I knew the rain was not going to be stopping anytime soon. As I looked up the mountain, I could not see that the top because it was eerily fogged over.

We found a tiny dirt trail that was headed upwards, towards the rock face and waterfall. It was well hidden, but animals must have used it recently, despite its sharp incline, because we spotted it as soon as we had emerged from the forest.

As we advanced up the precipitous trail, we hoped to hear from the other teams. If a team found ATV tracks or any other signs of Belle, we would contact each other, then concentrate our search where they were, using the same search parameters. The problem was, right now, we were searching the whole darn mountainside and her front property. I kept checking the walkie-talkie, making sure it was on and functioning.

Kip and I were halfway to the waterfall when I heard the cackle of the walkie-talkie. We stopped to listen.

"This is team Cat." Each team was given a letter as a way to identify themselves to the rest of the group. It was protocol to begin a transmission by using a word beginning with that letter when they spoke over the walkie-talkie.

"Go ahead Cat." I heard my dad respond.

"We're at Latitude 43.227853 Longitude -72.938713 Altitude 850 meters and there are fresh wheel tracks on the trail leading to the cliff."

"Ten-four Cat. We will converge."

I took out a map and pointed to where the C team was. Kip and I knew exactly where they were. The trail they were talking about was the one that Kip and I had used in high school and was wide enough for a four-wheeler to climb. It ran up the mountain to the waterfall where Kip and I were headed.

"We'll be the first to reach that area," Kip said looking at me anxiously.

I didn't even respond. With a renewed sense of urgency, I started climbing faster. The trail was so vertically inclined that we were using our hands to climb as well as our feet. My leg was sore, but not as sore as when I was searching for the father and

son. Kip easily matched my pace, and I was
thankful that I was partnered with him.

As we reached the small plateau that held the
naturally formed swimming area, I pulled Kip
down behind some brush. We were both breathing
heavily, and we took a few moments to catch our
breath. We vigilantly scrutinized the area. The
water rushing over the ridge above plunged into
the pool making enough noise that we knew it
would cover any inadvertent sounds we might
make.

I pushed the button on the walkie-talkie and
whispered. "This is Dog. We are at the waterfall.
We are going black, respond with clicks."

My dad pressed his button twice without talking to
acknowledge me. I turned off the walkie-talkie, and
Kip nodded, agreeing with my decision. We didn't
need an inadvertent transmission to announce our
presence. We had no idea if Belle, or whoever had
taken her was even here, but this was a very likely
spot. The fact that the four-wheeler had been
heading up here and that there were a bunch of
hidey-holes in the layered boulders behind the
waterfall, made this a perfect hideaway. I prayed we
would find her. Alive

I whispered to Kip as we continued to look around
the area. "We have to be smart. He could be
watching. He may have a partner or rigged an
alarm."

Kip nodded. "What do you want to do?"

"First we fan out. You go left; I'll go right. Watch
your footing and for any trip wires." I had a sudden

back flash to Afghanistan and had to take a
steadying breath.

Kip was staring at me, and I shook off the awful
images invading my brain.

"You okay?" he asked me quietly.

I nodded and gently slapped his upper arm.

"Yeah, we'll converge at the rock face. We'll be on
either side of the waterfall. Then we'll search the
hidey-holes. If you see anything use hand signals
only, ok?"

"Roger that."

We took off in separate directions to circle the
swimming area. I was keeping low and was glad to
see Kip was staying down too. I was hyper-focused
and felt myself go into the zone, as I called it.
When I scouted, I was so in tune with everything
around me that I could hear a bug ten feet away.
My skin was sensitive, picking up even the slightest
disturbance in the air. My hearing and sight became
overly perceptive, and my breathing slowed. I
inhaled a deep breath. I was trained for this. I was
good at this.

I reached the edge of the rock wall. To my left was
the tall rock face and waterfall and to my right was
an incline of thick brush that was impossible to
climb up without a rope. The waterfall, which was
only about two feet wide, was ten feet away from
me. Kip was on the other side of the waterfall
about the same distance as I was from the falls.
Looking behind the falling water, I saw that Kip
was indicating that he was going to look in a small
cave that he'd spotted. I anxiously watched as he

ducked down and leaned in. He stepped backward and shook his head.

I studied the two-story wall of solid rock and noticed an opening about twelve feet up right behind the falling water.

I pointed at it, and Kip gave me the thumbs up. I indicated that I was climbing up, and he should remain on the ground, and I could tell he didn't look happy about that, but he finally nodded.

I took off my pack and laid the walkie-talkie on top of it before starting to climb. The rocks were wet, and I didn't have as good of footing as I did on the trail. The tip of my blade was proving it's worth, especially when I found small crevices that I could place it in. I was pretty psyched that I was climbing as quickly as I was. I only slipped once and saved myself from a fall by hanging on by the tips of my fingers, before I found a foothold and righted myself. I looked down at Kip. He was watching me as he inched his large frame under the falls to spot for me. If I fell, my best friend would take the brunt of my fall. The ledge he was traversing was so thin that he had to sidestep on his tiptoes with his thick chest was pressed tightly against the wet rock.

I continued to free climb, and when I reached the small opening, I listened for any indicating sounds before I cautiously peered inside. It was too dark for me to see anything, but I could tell it was a good - sized cave. I took another second to listen then I hand gestured to Kip that I was going in and he gave me a thumbs up.

There was no way someone could have carried Belle up the rock face to this cave, but there could be another way in. I guardedly stepped through the small opening and crouched low keeping my back to the wall. I still couldn't see well, so I waited until my eyes adjusted to the darkness. I felt cool air wash over me indicating there was definitely another opening somewhere in the cave. As my eyes began to distinguish shapes, I realized the cave was even larger than I first thought and that I was in only a small portion of it. I could see that the cave curved, and there was a dim light coming from beyond the bend, casting a shadow.

I couldn't tell if the light was from a lantern or flashlight or if there was an opening in the ceiling of the cave allowing light to filter in. There was no sun out today, but any light would create shadows inside the darkened area.

I hugged the wall and crept to the bend. I paused and regulated my breathing. I was well aware that I could be walking into a wild animals den, so I was ready for anything. Silently I unsnapped the leather piece holding my gun in place as I crept towards the opening. The cave's ceiling was now high enough that I could stand upright, but it wasn't very wide. I moved then I listened, moved closer still, and then I'd stop and listen again. When I reached the entrance to the opening, I leaned back against the wall to listen again. This time I heard what sounded like the rustling of paper.

I cleared my gun from its holster and cautiously stepped through the opening to find myself in another little tunnel. The walls were narrow, but I could easily see that five yards away from where I stood the tunnel opened into a large cavern. The glow was coming from that area, and my gut told me a lantern was giving off the light that was allowing me to see.

I slowly edged my way towards the larger area and cautiously peered inside. I inhaled sharply seeing a man, about my age, sitting against the far wall reading a leather book. A small campers lantern sat beside him. He had a pack next to him, and he was eating an apple with a knife. With practiced stealth, I surveyed him and the area. The first thing I noticed was that the man wore combat boots and fatigues. He sliced the apple with precision telling me that he was adept with the weapon. There was no sign of Belle, but behind him, there was another passageway.

I crept inside the dimly lit cavern and hoped the element of surprise would serve me well, but unfortunately, that didn't happen. I heard a moan come from the area beyond the cavern. Belle! The man's head lifted from the book, and that's when he saw me. He rolled to the side, and I watched as he pulled a Glock from behind his pack and expertly pointed it in my direction. He fired off two shots before kicking the lantern over, distinguishing the only viable light source.

I dove to the side just to the left of the tunnels opening and pulled my gun out. The man was firing off cover shots, and I aimed at the short bursts of light coming from his gun. My first two shots hit rock, and I heard them ricochet wildly. The man realized that his gunfire was showing me where he was so he stopped shooting. The room became eerily quiet. Sweat rolled down my already damp back. I hoped Kip had heard the gunshots. I could hear movement, and I fired in that direction and then rolled to avoid him shooting at my position. His bullets pinged where I had been, and I knew I should radically change my location. I stood and ran towards the far wall. I had estimated that it was three yards away, so I went down at two yards, and army crawled until I felt rock wall with my hand. The unmistakable sound of Velcro being pulled apart permeated the stillness. He was opening his pack, and that couldn't be good for me. I crept until I located the tunnel where I'd heard the moans come from and quickly crawled through it.

Whimpers of pain were emanating from within the dark, dank room. I could smell the coppery scent of blood. Carefully I made my way towards the woeful moans of distress. I heard a gurgle sob, and that's when I could make out a form. I inched closer and saw Belle laying on her side curled in a fetal position. She was shivering so hard that her entire body was quaking. I leaned in close to her and saw the damage to her face. The bastard had not even bandaged her bashed in face. My gut lurched seeing the awful condition she was in. I was about to place my hand on her arm when a shot sounded, and a horrific pain ripped through my shoulder. I grunted and rolled away from Belle.

Another shot was fired, and pain exploded into my thigh stopping me from rolling. I shot blindly around the room using my left hand since my right arm was immobile. I must have hit him because I heard a grunt of pain. Once again I rolled despite the horrific pain in my back and leg.

My blood chilled when I heard the man laughing. He must be crazy I thought. I had no time to contemplate my next move because a large body slammed on top of mine. As the man straddled me, I saw that he was wearing night vision goggles. Shit!

My bullet had grazed his cheek and blood was pouring from the wound landing on my face. In one hand he held his Glock and in the other the knife. My combat training kicked in, and my adrenalin spiked allowing me to fight him despite my injuries.

"I like the knife so much better for a kill." He sneered, staring down at me confidently. My one arm was raised protectively waiting to see which of his hands was going to bring my death.

The crazy fool put his gun in the back of his pants waistband and started slicing at my arm. He was trying to stick the knife in my chest, and I was holding him off using all my strength. I frantically attempted to twist away from him. I was bigger than he was and hoped I could throw him off me. He realized that I was not going to be an easy kill, so he turned and drove the knife into my already damaged thigh. I screamed in pain.

His sinister laughter echoed in the cave, as I felt the energy ebb from me. The man pulled the knife from my thigh and plunged it into my stomach. I lay still, my body preparing for death. I watched as if seeing a slow-motion horror film as the man got off of me and plucked his gun from his waistband. He stepped towards Belle. I had never been in so much agony; my vision tunneled, I knew I was dying.

"You are too much trouble alive." I heard him say as he pointed his gun at her.

My only thought was to save Belle. Somehow I got to my knees and launched myself to cover Belle's body with my own. I heard a shot go off and my body bucked as it took yet another hit. Images flashed through my brain featuring a slideshow of my life, and as I lay shuddering on top of Belle. My last thought was that Belle was wearing my tee shirt.

33

Kip

As soon as Brady crawled through the opening and was out of sight, I inched my way to his pack and picked up the walkie-talkie.

"This is Dog," I whispered. "Brady's gone into a cave behind the falls." I heard two clicks telling me that my transmission had been received. I stared at the hole waiting to hear or see him. I checked my watch; minutes ticked by and my anxiety level rose. I thought about climbing up after him, but I honestly didn't think I'd fit through the small hole that he had disappeared into.

I had looked at my watch again and decided that if I didn't hear from him in five minutes that I would scale the cliff and if I couldn't squeeze into the large fissure I'd at least be able to look inside.

That's when I heard the shots. I quickly turned on the walkie-talkie and radioed in, "shots fired."

My stomach lurched, and fear sent an electric surge of adrenaline through my body.

Brady's dad came over the airwaves saying they were 5 minutes out, but team Cat said they were on top of the ridge above me. I looked up and saw the redhead signaling to me. The walkie-talkie crackled and I heard a male say. "This is Cat we have a four-wheeler up here." I didn't even listen to the rest of the transmission. I tossed the walkie-talkie down and headed up the rock face.

As I climbed the walkie-talkie below me crackled again. "This is Cat there is an entrance to a cave above the falls ten paces from the birch tree nearest the stream. We're going in."
I climbed even faster.

Vanessa

My brother and I had heard the gunshots, and when we saw the caves entrance, we booked it inside. I knew Brady was in there and although I hoped he hadn't been on the receiving end of the gunfire, I couldn't be sure.

We moved as quickly as we could. The enclosed passageway was about four feet high, so we ran hunched over. We used our flashlights to guide us even though we knew that would give our position away.

Another round of gunfire came from within the cave. These sounded closer than the last burst we had heard. Deranged laughter echoed off the caves walls. My brother and I both had our guns drawn as we ran single file into the dark chamber.

I was in the lead because my smaller stature had enabled me to maneuver through the tiny tunnel faster than my brother. A man's back was to me, and I took in the horrific scene in microseconds. Brady had thrown himself over a woman, and the man had shot him. He was about to shoot him again, but I quickly fired off three blasts that hit him in his head and back. The man with the gun collapsed, his gun still gripped in his hand. He landed at the woman's feet.

My brother Abe and I moved quickly to the three bodies. I could smell the blood. My heart hammered in my chest, not because I had just killed a man, but because Brady, looked dead.

I ran to Brady as my brother checked the man to make sure he was dead.

"Dead," he confirmed.

He quickly stood keeping his gun and flashlight leveled, sweeping the dark area.

I rolled Brady off the woman and checked his pulse. He was alive, but his pulse was thready at best. I quickly glanced at the woman. I knew she was alive because although she was unconscious, she was shivering.

"They're both alive, but hurt bad," I spoke aloud. I heard Abe radio for help.

Abe turned towards the sound of moving feet coming towards us. The huge man that had partnered with Brady emerged from an opening opposite the way we had come in; his gun was drawn. It took him a second to see the horror before us. He reached me in three strides and sunk to his knees next to me. His clothes were torn and he had scrapes on his hands and face. I knew he was Kip, Brady's best friend.

"Are they alive?" he asked frantically.

My brother was leaning over Brady assessing his injuries. Not only was Abe a Forest Ranger but he was also an EMT.

"Yes, but Brady's bad. We need a chopper or he's not going to make." Abe was applying pressure to Brady's wounds. He told me to shine my light on Belle.

We immediately saw the damage to her face. "Shit," my brother swore.

Kip took the walkie-talkie from the ground and radioed that we needed a chopper. We heard Brady's dad say that it was already on its way, but it needed a spotter, and they were still a minute away. I could see that Kip was not leaving Brady's side and my brother had the medical training, so I ran outside and pulled two flares from my pack. I lite one of them and pointed it straight up.

Brady's dad and his partner along with two other teams arrived simultaneously. As I held the flare, I pointed to the caves entrance. Brady's dad raced inside along with another man. I told the rest of the group what I knew. Finally, I could hear the chopper. I tossed down the one flare that was dwindling and cracked the other one, holding it high above my head. The chopper hovered above us; there was no way it was going to be able to set down.

My brothers work partner Jeff used hand signals to request a basket. I ran back inside to tell them that the chopper was there.

Movement from the caves entrance drew my eyes from the chopper. The men must have decided to forgo stabilizing Brady and Belle by waiting for a stretcher. The tunnel was too narrow to carry them properly anyway. Brady's large friend cradled him in his arms. Brady was a big man himself, but Kip was larger and obviously very strong. He ran with Brady's body to the already lowered basket and carefully laid him inside of it. It was hard not to notice how much blood was coating Kip's clothes. Jeff strapped Brady in and signaled for them to reel it up. Another man carried Belle the same way that Kip had carried Brady. He was noticeable grief-stricken looking at her. I wondered if he was her boyfriend. When Brady was secured inside the chopper, another basket dropped, and Belle was strapped inside of that one. As soon as Belle's wire stretcher had cleared the helicopter door the chopper rose and veered off. We stood silently watching until it was out of sight.

Jeff saw the hopeless expressions on the faces of Brady's father, Brady's friend Kip, and the other man, who I heard Kip call Adam. Jeff told the group that the man who was in the helicopter was one of the best emergency paramedics in Vermont. He continued by saying that the man had served two tours in Iraq and saved countless lives. I know he was hopeful that Brady's Dad and friend's would take some comfort in knowing that; I didn't. I'd seen how badly Brady had been injured. I was numb knowing he might bleed out before the chopper even reached the hospital.

I heard four wheelers approaching and watched as four more members of our search group drove up the dirt trail that my brother and I had found. Brady's dad told everyone to grab a ride. As upset as Brady's dad was he still had the presence of mind to instruct his two deputies to take pictures inside the cave and to bring down any evidence and the body. He also told them to drive the other four-wheeler down, but to use gloves.

It was still raining, and we were wet, cold, and pensive as our caravan made its way back to Belle's property. When we arrived, the Sheriff thanked us before quickly jumping in his car with Kip and Adam and speeding down the driveway.

No one was offended; we understood that his son was badly injured. We were standing on Belle's porch rehashing the day when the other two four-wheelers arrived. The one four wheeler had the body of the man I shot, rolled up in a tarp, and secured to the back seat. The Deputy drove that four-wheeler into the nearby shed and shut the door. He went to his car and used his radio. The second deputy took a garbage bag from his ATV and put it in the trunk of his car before walking over to us.

He too thanked us for our help, and he promised to keep us informed. He then turned to my brother and me and asked if we would come to the station to give a full accounting of what happened.

We agreed to meet them there. I wanted to go to the hospital but didn't feel it was appropriate. We said goodbye to the remaining members of the search team, and then we followed the deputy to the station. I was so worried about Brady that I was physically sick to my stomach. My brother saw how pale I was and luckily he pulled over as I emptied the contents of my stomach along the side of the road.

He rubbed my shoulder when I sat back up and told me that the first kill was always the hardest. He thought I was upset about killing the man. He had no idea that I couldn't have given a rat's ass about that dirt bag. I was sick thinking that Brady might not survive his devastating injuries.

34

Belle

A pinch on my arm pulled me from
unconsciousness, and a warm blanket was placed
over me. A loud continuous whoop-whoop sound
pierced my already throbbing head, and I groaned.
I realized the blindfold was off me, but something
was still covering part of my face. My hands and
feet had been untied. I struggled to open my eyes;
my head felt as if it was going to implode from the
pain. A deep voice told me to relax. Nausea boiled
inside me, and even though the blanket was warm,
I shivered violently because I was so cold. I was in
agony, disorientated, and very afraid.
I managed to open one eye, and I realized I was in
a helicopter. A man wearing a green jumpsuit, and
a helmet with a microphone piece attached to it
quickly checked underneath whatever was covering
half of my face. He then turned away from me and
went back to work on someone lying in another
wire basket, like the one I was in.
Bloody gauze bandages littered the floor nearby.
The man that was leaning over the basket worked
frantically on the other person. A small mobile
heart monitor was on the floor beeping, a plasma
bag was emptying into the injured person, and I
could see that the bag was draining quickly; that
couldn't be good.

The man in the jumpsuit moved slightly to get something out of his medical kit, and that's when I saw that the injured man was Brady.

"No, no, no, no." I started pleading out loud. My face was so swollen that my words were inaudible.

"Step on it Matt or we're going to lose him." The medic yelled into his microphone.

I was crying as I watched the man desperately trying to save Brady's life. I had no idea what had happened, or why he was hurt, but I knew it had to be because of me.

I reached for Brady's hand, but I was strapped in the basket and couldn't move. The heart monitor attached to Brady blasted a loud uninterrupted signal.

"Fuck." I heard him utter.

I watched the medic's back as he continued to furiously administer care. Brady's heart had just stopped, and I was terrified for him.

The medic took out small paddles and spoke tersely to the pilot. "Matt he's flat-lining."

I watched as he shocked Brady's heart with the defibrillator. It took two tries, but the reassuring sound of Brady's heart beating again had me sobbing with relief. I felt the chopper start to descend and the medic quickly checked that I was still secure in my basket. As soon as we landed the helicopters doors, one on either side were thrown open. Our baskets were placed on gurneys, and both Brady and I were wheeled away.

A week had passed, and I had endured three operations since I'd been brought in. I had suffered a broken cheekbone, a cracked eye socket, a detached retina, which they luckily had reattached, a split upper lip, and I'd lost a molar. I had a severe concussion and wasn't allowed out of bed. I honestly couldn't have left it anyway. I was dizzy most of the time and I a grueling headache that kept me continually nauseous.

My week consisted of being operated on, sleeping, and when I did wake up; I was in such pain that the nurses quickly dosed me back into la-la land.

The second week I started to regain my faculties. I remained catheterized, but they had taken the feeding tube out of my nose. I was now on a liquid only diet. I didn't care. I had no interest in eating. The nurses told me that I had had a few visitors, but I don't remember any of them. I still wasn't allowed out of bed, but because I wasn't being operated on every other day I was slowly being weaned off of the heavy pain medicines that had kept me in a state of loopy unconsciousness.

I had a significant memory lapse, which the doctor assured me was normal for someone who had suffered the trauma that I had. I remembered running upstairs because I'd heard footsteps, and then I remember seeing Brady on the helicopter. That was it. I had no idea what had happened between those two horrible moments.

When I was lucid, I asked how Brady was. I was so afraid I would be told he had died. My nurse would not answer me, and I became so agitated that she called the doctor who finally disclosed to me that Brady was alive. He refused to tell me more than that telling me I needed to concentrate on getting myself better.

The first visitor that I was conscious for was an official one, Brady's dad. He looked haggard as he pulled a chair up to my bed. I asked how Brady was and I watched the larger than life man gather his emotions before answering me. He told me that Brady was in ICU and had not regained consciousness. Sheriff McDaniel said they were hopeful. The way he said hopeful sounded anything but. He asked me how I was feeling and I told him I was starting to feel better. My mind was reeling knowing that Brady was still unconscious. Two weeks was a long time to be in ICU.

The Sheriff paused before asking a few questions.

"Belle, what do you remember being abducted?"

I explained that I heard footsteps upstairs and that I had run up the steps, but I didn't remember what happened after that.

My head was starting to ache again. "Can you tell me? Do you know?" I asked anxious to understand what had happened.

"You were hit with a shovel Belle. We found it."

That explained the injuries to my face. I cringed.

"Did you know about the tunnel under your house?"

"A tunnel? No, where is it?"

"There is a shaft in your Mom's room, in her closet, and it goes to the basement. There is a concealed door behind your hutch that also accesses the tunnel. We believe the same person that attacked you attacked Mrs. Gordon. She told me she was hit from behind, but she did not see who hit her."

"She's awake now?"

"Yes, she's going to be fine."

"Where does the tunnel lead too?"

"From your basement, it runs under your shed, and there is an exit about forty yards into the woods. It's very well hidden."

I digested what the Sheriff had just revealed to me. I couldn't believe that there was a tunnel in my house that I didn't know about. Maybe it was built to help slaves escape? But if that were the case it didn't make sense that neither my grandma's nor my Momma never told me about it.

"So when I heard footsteps, I really did hear footsteps? The fire? The rose smell, it was all real?"

"Yes."

I couldn't help it, but just knowing that I hadn't been going crazy had me sobbing. The nurse came into the room and asked if I was all right. I told her I was. She wanted to give me more medicine, but I refused it.

"Tell me what happened Sheriff. Why did someone do this? How did Brady get hurt?"

The Sheriff explained everything that he knew. I could tell he was finding it difficult to talk about it, especially when he got to the part about Brady. He didn't know what had transpired when Brady had found me. Sheriff McDaniel's said they would wait for Brady to wake to fill in the blanks. The Sheriff

then described how a woman, who had been part
of the search team that had been assembled to find
me, saw Brady throw himself on top of me right
before my abductor tried to shoot me. Brady took
the bullet intended for me in his back, and the
woman killed the man that had shot Brady.

I gasped upon hearing the details. Brady was in
ICU and could very possibly die because he had
thrown his body over mine. He put his life in
mortal danger for me. Guilt pummeled through
me, and hard sobs racked my frame.

"I'm so sorry," I responded as I sobbed
uncontrollably.

My head exploded in pain as I bawled. I grabbed
the pink plastic bowl from the nightstand and
threw up the meager contents of my stomach. The
Sheriff buzzed for the nurse, and she came quickly.
She gave the Sheriff a nasty look after she helped
me. I was still weeping, but I tried sucking in deep
breaths to calm myself.

"That's probably enough Sheriff, don't you think?"
The nurse said after disposing of the contents of
the bowl.

"No, no, I need to know." I choked out.

The nurse did not look happy. "I'm getting the
doctor." She huffed indignantly and left us alone
again.

"I'm sorry Belle I know this is difficult to hear. I
have a few more questions though, okay?"

"Yes." I blubbered. He handed me a tissue, and I
thanked him and used it to wipe my nose. He
waited patiently while I composed myself.

"Do you remember anything else?" he asked.

"No, just seeing Brady in the helicopter. That's all."

"Okay." He said tapping a pen on his boot. They looked like the same boots that Brady wore, and I had to look away from the Sheriff, or I knew I'd start crying again.

"Belle, do you know who this is?" The Sheriff showed me a picture of a man. I did not recognize him, so I shook my head no. The man looked very pale, like my mother had when I'd seen her in the morgue.

"Is he dead?"

"Yes. What about her?"

This time I recognized the person. "That's Miss Donna, Mr. Bee's secretary."

"Yes. Now how about this person?"

I stared at the picture in front of me. Something was niggling my memory. "There's something familiar about him, but I don't think I've ever met him. Have I?"

The Sheriff shook his head. "No, I don't believe so."

"What's going on? Tell me, please. Who are these men? What does Miss Donna have to do with this?"

The Sheriff settled back in his chair. I could see that he was debating on whether to tell me.

"I'm going to have to know eventually, Sheriff." I hoped that my voice conveyed to him that I would be strong enough to what he had to tell me.

He nodded and took a deep breath.

"Belle this man here is the one that abducted you and shot Brady. His name is Brandon Romella. Does that ring any bells?"

I shook my head no.

"His sister is Donna Romella."

I gasped. "Mr. Bee's secretary?"

"Their mother is married to this man." The Sheriff showed me the picture of the blond-haired older man again.

"This man's name is Elias Janson."

Elias, the man whose picture my Momma had. I felt nauseous.

My hand instantly flew to my mouth, and I found it hard to catch my breath. Tears squeezed out my swollen eyes to trickle down my puffy cheeks. Somehow I knew; I just knew. "Is he my father?" I whispered.

"Yes."

I told the Sheriff about the picture I had found in the box in my Momma's room. I kept staring at the picture that the Sheriff had handed me. It was easy to see the age progression now. As much as I knew I had looked like my Momma, there were small facial similarities that I shared with this man. My eyebrows were the same shape as his, and we had the same smile.

I looked at the Sheriff. "Tell me everything."

"Belle, what do you know about the Will and the Green Mountain property?"

"The Will?"

He nodded.

"Well, I only know what Mr. Bee told me. I inherited everything from my Momma."

"Have you ever read the Will?"

I shook my head. "No, not thoroughly. Mr. Bee told me what it said. Mr. Bee gave me a copy of it along with some other papers. I put the them in my Momma's box, but they were taken along with the journal and the photo of...of." I couldn't bring myself to say 'my father.'

The Sheriff wearily rested his elbows on his knees as he leaned closer to me. The poor man was exhausted. Our talk was wearing on him too.

"It is stipulated in the Will that your property, the mountain, can only be passed down through a blood relation."

"Oh, yes, Mr. Bee did say that. I'm sorry my memory is still foggy."

"Belle, your father did know about that stipulation."

"Oh, no." I knew where this conversation was going and it sickened me.

"Your father was aware that you were being offered quite a bit of money for your property. We are still unclear about this next part, but we believe, at first, he was just trying to scare you off the farm. We think he was working for someone to coerce you into selling your property. We don't think they knew to what extent though."

"The Fitzpatrick's?"

"No, not them or their client."

"Oh good." I was relieved that Adam and his dad were not involved.

"So, your father read the Will."

"I still don't understand." My head was spinning with all the convoluted details.

"Belle, your father was behind the events that he hoped would scare you into selling the farm. Brandon stole the journal and Will and told your father what was in it. According to Donna, after he knew about the Will he decided to kill you and claim the inheritance, your mountain for himself. He was your blood relation, so he would have had a legal claim to it."

"Oh no," my hand covered my mouth I was appalled.

"How do Miss Donna and her brother fit into this? How does she know him?"

"Your father left the country soon after he and your Momma divorced. He went back to Denmark. According to records, he returned to the United States a year ago. He married a woman, apparently to stay in the country. We believe that she and your father had history. The woman he is married to, Mary Ann Romella Janson, has two grown children; this man," The Sheriff raised the picture of Brandon Romella, then he raised Donna's picture, "and the person you know as Miss Donna."

The Sheriff paused and poured himself a cup of water and then offered me some, which I declined. After he took a sip, he went on.

"Elias, your father, convinced his two step-children to help him scare you off the property."

"How did they help him?"

"Your father knew about the tunnel. He told his step-kids about it. They helped him by setting the fire in your house, spraying rose perfume, walking around at night. We think this man, Brandon Romella, was the one to throw the tree limb on you, and tamper with your car brakes. He may have been the one to hurt Josh too."

"Why though? Why would he do all that?"

"Belle, your mountain is worth a great deal of money. People do all kinds of horrible things for money. Donna said your father promised them a lot of money in return for their help."

"Do you think he killed Momma?"

"We're looking into that, but I don't know if we'll ever know. Your father is a smart man. He's covered his tracks well."

"How?"

"Well, when you had your accidents he was not even in the country, and when you were abducted he had an alibi; he was sitting in Mr. Bee's office. We've only been able to connect him to these events because Donna has cut a deal with the Prosecutors office. Evidently, she only supplied your father with information that she smuggled out from Mr. Bee's office, and she also supplied the rose perfume."

"It's all so, so much. How did he know about the tunnel?"

"He built it."

"Really?"

"When your Mom and he were married your grandma's decided to build the upstairs so they would have privacy. Elias is an architect, and when he drew up the plans, unbeknownst to your Mom or grandma's, he also added in the tunnel."

"Why would he do that?"

"It seems that your father was in love with another woman, but her parents refused to allow them to marry. We believe it may be the woman he married a year ago. Elias made your Mom fall in love with him so he could marry her, stay in the country and be near the woman he truly loved. He built the tunnel so he could sneak out and visit her."

"Why did he leave the country the first time?"

"I'm not sure, but I think your grandma's found out about the other woman, and they called in some favors to get your Mom a quick divorce and then to have him deported."

My cheeks dampened again as tears fell. My father was evil. My poor mother, that's why she never wanted to talk about him, the man was a snake.

"He's in jail Belle. He won't hurt you again."

I didn't care about me. He had hurt Brady. My awful father had orchestrated a plan to chase me out of my home, and when he discovered he could inherit my property, he tried to kill me so he could have all the money himself. Brady was hurt because of my greedy father and me.

"Why didn't he just kill me? He should have just killed me." I murmured disconsolately.

"Belle, because he would be inheriting so much he needed to have a strong alibi when you were killed. He established that by being with Mr. Bee when you were abducted. We believe Brandon was

instructed to keep you alive for a few days while
your father remained in plain sight of everyone in
town, and then Brandon was going to kill you."
I'd just heard that I was supposed to have been
killed and I didn't even care. Brady had been
seriously injured because of me.
"I'm so, so sorry Sheriff. Oh God." I buried my
swollen face in my hands. "It's all my fault. Brady's
hurt, and it's all my fault." Uncontrollable sobs
wracked my body. I kept repeating, "I'm sorry, I'm
so sorry." The Sheriff must have called the nurse
because before I even registered what was
happening a needle was pressed into my arm and I
blacked out.

The next week I was beginning to feel physically
better, but emotionally I had shut down. Adam and
Jeannie had tried to visit me, but I had asked that
no visitors be allowed into my room. I was
mortified with what my father had done. I sat in
my sterile white bed, agonizing over the fact that
my father was a greedy monster and Brady might
pay with his life. I hated that I was alive, and Brady
was still fighting for his life because of his
selflessness.
A Psychiatrist came in to talk to me, but I remained
aloof and quiet. I hated myself. One day I heard
the nurses talking, and I learned that Brady had
regained consciousness and was beginning to
improve. I was so thankful that I broke out into a
torrent of tears and the nurse called the doctor
thinking that I had finally gone coo-coo. I was too

overwhelmed with emotion to relay that they were happy tears.

I was sure his family and girlfriend were probably relieved. Thinking of him and his wonderful family only made me cry harder. I pictured his girlfriend being in the room with him, holding his hand, and taking care of him. I hoped she was nice. He deserved someone nice.

He may have wronged me, and he'd hurt me, but that did not even compare to the pain and misery I had brought on to him and his family.

One afternoon Mr. Bee talked his way into my room by saying that he was my Guardian and the nursing staff believed him. He sat in the chair near my bed and just talked. He apologized to me for hiring Miss Donna. He went on to tell me that Bev and Jeb were at my house, caring for my animals. I had known this because Jeb had penned a letter that he gave to a nurse to give me when I had first woken up. Jeb had written to me about the farm and my animals and that he and Bev had everything under control. He added for me to hurry up and get well and that they would stay on the farm for as long as I wanted. They too loved my farm. After I had read the letter, I had cried myself asleep.

Mr. Bee proceeded to tell me all of the town's gossip. He carefully left out anything related to my family or Brady. I never spoke the entire time he was there. I was broken.

35

Belle

Finally, I was being released. Mr. Bee picked me up
and drove me home. I was under strict orders to
not do anything strenuous at all. I should have
been jubilant, but I was miserable.
I still hadn't spoken, and after a few days at home,
I knew Bev and Jeb were worried about me. I
wasn't eating, and I had dropped enough weight
that my shorts fell off my hips if I didn't belt them.
One afternoon I was sitting on my back porch
looking out over the very mountain that had been
the crux of so much pain. Despite that depressing
thought, I couldn't hate it. I loved the mountain. I
loved my farm. It was a part of me, and I knew I'd
never leave it.
The Sheriff had given Mr. Bee my Momma's
leather journal, and he had brought it to me. I had
been reading snippets of it whenever I felt strong
enough to do so. The journal lay on my lap
unopened when I heard a car pull up. I remained in
my chair; I knew Bev or Jeb would shoo away any
visitors.
I heard the sliding doors behind me open, and I
turned my head to see Kip walk through them.
I turned away from him. Why was he here? Then I
thought maybe something had happened to Brady.
My head whipped back to him. "Brady?"
Kip smiled gently, "He's fine. Well not fine, but
he's going to be fine."

I fought back the tears that threatened to drip by pushing my palms into my eye socket. I pressed too hard on the one that had cracked and grimaced.

"You got hit pretty hard," Kip said looking at my still bruised face.

I shrugged.

"Belle, talk to me. Mr. and Mrs. Gordon are really concerned about you. You won't see anyone; you're losing weight, the Gordon's tell me you rarely speak; were worried."

I turned from him and wiped a lone tear away. Kip moved to kneel near me. He took a strand of my hair that was veiling my face and threaded it behind my ear. "Come on. I thought we were friends?"

I sniffed and wiped a tear from my face. Then I looked up at Kip. He was smiling so tenderly at me. I didn't understand how could he even look at me?

I spoke so softly that Kip had to lean in to hear me. "I almost got Brady killed. How can you stand to even be near me? I don't even want to be near me."

Kip took my chin and with his fingertip brought my eyes back to his.

"Darlin, you had nothing to do with what happened to Brady."

I stared at him in disbelief. "Kip, if it weren't for me and my, awful, awful father Brady wouldn't be laying in the hospital."

Kip shook his head. "This was not your fault."

I shrugged.

"Belle, listen to me. No one, no one at all thinks it was your fault."

I looked down at the stone patio. "Brady?"

"Especially Brady."

"Have you talked to him?"

Kip stood up and sat in the chair next to me. He took my hand in his. "I see him every day."

"Is he okay? I mean, really okay?" My voice shook with emotion.

"He's going to make a full recovery. He's already driving the nurses crazy."

That made me smile. "His parents?"

"What about them?"

"Do they hate me?"

"Belle, what is your head wrapped around? No, of course, they don't hate you."

I sighed deeply.

"You going to be okay?" He asked softly.

"Maybe. I'm relieved to hear that Brady is going to be all right. He saved my life."

Kip grinned. "I know."

"Will you thank him for me?"

He didn't answer me. "Will you take care of yourself? Try to get out of this funk you're in and get back to being Belle?"

"I'll try."

"That's my girl. We'll go swimming as soon as you're able."

Thinking of swimming, of course, made me think of Brady. Another tear trickled down my cheek.

"You still care for him." It was more of a statement than a question.

"He saved my life."

"He's going to make a full recovery Belle."

I nodded I was feeling too emotional to try to talk.

"Okay then. I'll be back to visit. You take care of yourself."

Once again I nodded.

Kip headed to the door and stopped to look back. "Belle, go visit him."

I hung my head and shook it back and forth.

Another week passed, and I made myself take walks, and I worked with Jeb by feeding the animals and collecting the eggs each morning. I taught Bev how to make bread, and she taught me how to make lasagna. I still had an ache inside of me that would not go away. I never slept through the night, and the weight continued to slide off of me.

One thing I did do was to explore the tunnel. I was amazed at how well constructed it was. Jeb put deadbolts on the entranceways that were in the closet and basement of the house, and we put a lock on the opening that was in the woods.

Mr. Bee visited to tell me that my father had hired a lawyer, but Donna's testimony was rock solid, and the police had found the papers that she had copied for him in his apartment, so that tied him to everything.

Adam and Jeannie visited, and I was happy to see how well they were getting on. They only stayed a

few minutes because they were on their way to
Adam's families home. Before they left Adam
asked for a few moment alone to discuss business.
He once again pitched the offer to buy my place,
and I promptly refused it. Adam smiled and said he
knew I would, and I was relieved that he wasn't
mad. I bet his father was not going to have the
same reaction. I asked Adam if his client knew
what my dad was doing and he said no, that there
had been an anonymous buyer who wanted my
property. Mr. Bee didn't even know who it was.
Adam said he believed that they had hired my
father. I was relieved when I heard that. I still
didn't know why my property was in such demand.
He also said that the other buyer probably did not
even known the tactics my father had used to get
me to sell.

I'd been having bad dreams. I think I was
remembering being in the cave. The dream always
ended with me hearing a gunshot and feeling a
body fall on me. Bev handed me a cup of coffee,
and I thanked her. I had shared with her how I
made coffee, and evidently, Jeb loved it, so it was
always made by the time I ventured into the
kitchen each morning.
"Sweetie, how about some eggs today?" Bev asked
putting my usual piece of buttered toast in front of
me.
"No thank you," I told her repeating what I'd said
to her for the last two weeks when she'd tried to
feed me.

"Belle, you're wasting away. You're going to get sick if you don't start to eat."

I hung my head she wouldn't understand.

"Belle, I'm heading over to the hospital in Springfield today. I made cookies for the nurses that took care of me. Why don't you come with me?"

"The hospital?"

"Yes, dear. Come with me. Maybe there is someone you'd like to visit while I'm delivering the cookies." She gave me a gentle smile.

I grinned at her sweet deviousness. "I don't know."

"What's the worst that could happen?" She said giving me a wink.

I thought about it as I munched on my toast. The worst thing that could happen was that Brady would toss me out and make me feel worse than I already did, or what if his parents yelled at me. No, seeing him with his girlfriend might be worse than both those things. Bev broke through my nightmarish thoughts.

"Come on Belle. Take a shower. We're leaving at ten."

I decided that I would go, despite all the awful scenarios that I imaged happening. I would go and apologize. I could only hope that he would accept it.

Bev drove, and we chatted amicably during the drive. Well, she chatted, I listened. She was a fascinating woman. She had a college degree but chose to work alongside her husband on the farms

they had managed. They loved working for the
Fitzpatrick's, but their place was huge and became
too much for the two of them, so they retired. She
explained that they had become bored and were
excited when Adam had asked them to help on my
place.

We pulled up to the hospital, and I almost
chickened out. Bev didn't push me, but she had
that look on her face that said she'd be
disappointed if I didn't at least try so I got out of
the car and followed her inside.

Bev took the elevator to the third floor, and I went
to the desk and asked what room Brady was in. I
took the elevator to the fourth floor. My palms
were sweating, and I was at risk of hyperventilating.
I turned down one corridor and realized I must
have taken a wrong turn. I stopped and asked a
tall, pretty nurse that was carrying a clipboard
where room 421 was. The nurse's face morphed
into what appeared to be anger.

"What's your name?"

"What's my name?" I repeated thrown by the tone
of her voice.

"Yes, what's your name?" She replied like I was
daft.

"Belle Janson."

The nurses looked at her clipboard and then back
to me.

"You'll need to leave; Mr. McDaniel's doesn't want
to see you. He has put you on his no visitation list."
Her voice was laced with malice, and I wondered if

she somehow knew that I was the awful person responsible for Brady being in the hospital.

The air left my lungs, and if I hadn't been holding the rail on the wall, I might have fallen. I composed myself and straightened up. The nurse continued to stare daggers at me. I was officially a pariah.

I got back on the elevator and waited for Bev down in the lobby. I didn't want to upset her so when she asked how everything went; I told her it was good. The dear woman smiled, so pleased with herself, meanwhile I was reeling. Brady hated me. He blamed me for what happened to him. How could he not?

As we rode back to my farm, Bev prattled on about the wonderful nurses that had taken care of her. I sarcastically thought she must not have had the pleasure of meeting the mean nurse I had just encountered.

I sighed and stared out the window. I was so selfish. This was life. My Gram and Gigi had been dealt tough hands, and they had handled it. My poor Momma hadn't had an easy time of it either, and she had been the happiest of all of us. I had to get myself together.

Brady had been seriously hurt protecting me. I should be grateful to be alive, and that he was on the mend, but I wasn't. I felt guiltier than ever. It bothered me that Kip had told me to visit Brady. Why would he tell me to visit Brady if I wasn't even allowed in the room?

Four days later I was sitting out back on the patio reading the journal. As I took in what had transpired between my Momma and my father so many years ago, my heart ached for my Momma. She had been head over heels for my father. My Momma had written that she had met an exchange student named Elias Janson and that he was the best-looking man she had ever seen. She had first seen him when she had gone into town with her mother, my Gram. My Momma watched him from afar as he hung out on the picnic tables in front of the diner with all the other college kids. He was older than her and very popular.

One day when she had gone into town alone to pick up groceries, he walked across the street to help her load her bags into the family truck. My Momma was stunned and wrote that she stammered and felt like an idiot while they were making small talk, but Elias was charming and handsome, and he had made her feel special.

After that fateful day, Elias began to wait for Momma every week in the same spot. He would always help with the groceries, and then they would spend a few minutes talking. One day he came to out the farm and asked my Gram if he could date Momma, My grandmas were impressed with his manners and allowed them to date. Momma was surprised when he asked her out for the first time. He invited her to attend a dance at his college. She was surprised because she had heard from the cashier in the market that he was dating a girl in Massey, an extremely beautiful and very wealthy girl. When Momma asked Elias about her, he told her that they had broken up.

So Momma and Elias began dating and the day after he graduated college they were married.

I shut the book feeling depressed. I didn't want to read any further knowing what had happened next. I knew I would eventually read more, but I just couldn't read anymore right then. I was sad for my Momma, and I had a better understanding as to why my Grandma's and my Momma had kept me so secluded. They had been protecting me.

Thinking about my family made me remember that I hadn't been to their graves for a while, so I decided to visit the family cemetery the next day.

With the journal on my lap, I turned my face to the sun enjoying its gentle warmth.

I must have fallen asleep because the sound of the sliding door opening woke me. I looked to see Kip stepping onto the patio.

"Hi, did I wake you?"

"I was just enjoying the sun," I told him.

He knelt down next to me. "Your face looks better, but I don't think you're eating." He said with a small frown.

"Kip, I'm trying," I said slightly exasperated. I didn't need a lecture. I just wanted to be left alone. He had already pushed me to go to the hospital and look how well that turned out.

"I went to the hospital four days ago like you suggested," I told him, watching his reaction.

"You did?"

"Yes, and a nurse told me I wasn't allowed to visit Brady because he had put my name on a no visit list."

Kip was staring at me in disbelief. "Belle there is no way he put you on any list. I know for a fact that he would have really liked it if you had visited him."

Kip appeared to be telling the truth. I wondered if Brady's parents had put me on the list. That would explain why Kip hadn't known. They had been protecting their son from the woman who almost got him killed. Then again, maybe Brady just hadn't told Kip.

I sighed deeply and placed the journal on the table next to my chair.

"Yeah, well maybe he isn't telling you everything," I said with a bit of attitude.

"Trust me, he is."

"Anyway, thank you for visiting," I said dismissively. I was being so mean, but I couldn't help myself.

"Belle, you have to snap out of it. Mrs. Gordon says she's going to call your doctor if you don't start eating soon."

"I'm eating," I mumbled, annoyed that he hadn't gotten the hint to leave.

"How are you feeling otherwise?"

I shrugged my shoulders. "Fine."

"You don't look fine."

"Gee thanks, Kip. Can we not do this?" I said wearily. I was still smarting from my visit to the hospital that he had initiated. That visit had pretty much been my breaking point, validating my family's lifestyle; I was born to be a recluse. Why couldn't Kip just leave me be?

"We are doing this Belle." He countered.

I was irritated. No one understood the guilt I harbored. Even though I knew Brady was better, I still worried that his injuries might hamper him getting a job.

I attempted to change the subject and get Kip's mind off of me.

"So how are things? Is Brady still doing well?" I had to ask. I still cared. I'd always care. That revelation haunted me hourly.

He chuckled good-naturedly even though I was being a bitch.

"He's doing very well actually."

I hesitated. "Did you tell him that I was sorry?"

"You can do that yourself." Kip stood and pointed at the sliding door behind me. Brady was standing in the doorframe.

I jumped out of my chair but didn't know what to do next. He was thinner than the last time I'd seen him, much thinner. He had a day's growth on his usually clean-shaven face, and his hair was longer. His green eyes were assessing me like I was assessing him. There was a movement to his left, and that's when I saw a stunning redhead standing behind him. She had her hand resting possessively on his back. Oh God, he brought his girlfriend with him.

Standing in front of my chair my legs wobbled; thankfully Kip placed his hand under my elbow to steady me. I watched as the redhead helped Brady step through the doorway. He was moving slowly; his one forearm had pink scars, some larger than others, marring his skin. He walked with a limp, but it was on his other leg. What had happened to him? I still didn't know details.

"Hi." He said softly looking at me with an uncertain expression on his face.

"Hi," I answered uneasily. Why was he visiting me when he had not wanted me to visit him in the hospital?

He took a step towards me. "You still have bruises." He gestured to my face.

I sat down because I was seriously unsteady, just seeing Brady took my breath away. His girlfriend helped him to sit in the chair next to me. The woman was obnoxiously pretty. She was smiling at him, and I envied her. I was a horrible person.

"They're going away," I answered rearranging my hair, so it covered that side of my face.

I looked at his girlfriend who was still watching Brady intently. I was tense and keenly aware of how unattractive and unsophisticated I was compared to her.

"I'm Vanessa," she said with a happy singsong voice. She stepped towards me, and I started to stand up to shake her hand, but she quickly gestured for me to remain seated. Proving that she was not only attractive, but she was nice too. Lucky Brady, I thought sarcastically.

Vanessa stooped down and gently shook my hand. I was instantly assaulted with a plethora of contradictory emotions. I was jealous of the smiling beauty now standing in front of me, yet glad that Brady had someone worthy of him. I was mad at Kip for bringing them to my house, yet I was happy to see Brady in person. My heart throbbed with the love that I felt for him. I knew I'd always love him. 'Thou shall not covet,' ran through my brain. Oh, God, I'm trying not to, I silently prayed.

I looked to Kip for help to diffuse how awkward this situation was, but he was just standing next to Vanessa with a ridiculous grin on his face.

I looked back to Brady to find that he was observing me as if he was waiting for me to say something. I decided to get the visit over with as quick as possible. I still wanted to apologize to him so that was what I would do, even if it had to be done with others looking on.

I turned in my chair, so I faced him, and my soul ached; I missed him. "I'm so sorry you were hurt, Brady," I whispered. I turned to Vanessa apologizing to her as well. "I'm so sorry, Vanessa."

I saw Brady giving Kip a questioning look.

"Vanessa trained with Brady," Kip said looking at me and then back to Brady.

I nodded. "I figured," I said softly. I was willing myself to stay strong. I could get through this. The most important thing was that Brady was alive and happy. He deserved happy.

"Belle." Brady was frowning. "What do you mean you figured?"

I blushed feeling incredibly embarrassed. I couldn't look at him, so I looked down at my hands that were folded on my lap.

"Belle?" His voice brought my eyes back to him. I held together my shredded emotions. I could do this.

"She's the girl you were with when I was away. She's your girlfriend." I barely got the words out of my mouth. I don't know where the air in my lungs had gone.

"Oh boy," Kip said. "Come on Vanessa lets go for a walk." I watched uneasily as they walked around the side of the house towards the barn leaving us alone.

"Belle, Vanessa is not my girlfriend."

What? Had I heard that correctly? "She's not your girlfriend, but?"

Brady grimaced. "No," he interrupted, "there is no girlfriend."

He seemed upset. Maybe they had broken up because he had saved me. Now I felt even worse.

"But?" I repeated.

"You think I have a girlfriend because of what you heard on the phone, right?"

I nodded. I was trying to regulate my breathing. My chest ached.

"I know what you and Adam heard on the phone that night. I'm so sorry about that. Can I explain?"

I nodded wondering why he thought he needed to explain things to me. It would kill me to hear about his involvement with other women. Maybe that was the point.

"Adam was sending me pictures every day of you having a great time, and sometimes there were ones of the two of you together."

"Yes, I knew Adam was sending them to you. We thought you'd like them." I finished weakly.

Brady frowned. "I only saw them when I was in town when I got service. When I did go into town, I was bombarded with them. You looked so happy, really, really happy. There was one picture of you at the beach, and Adam had texted under it 'Look at our girl.' The next picture was one with his arm around you. I thought he was subtly showing me that you were with him, that you two had become a couple. A few days later he texted me that he had something important to tell me and he hoped I wouldn't be mad."

"Oh, Brady," I said softly.

He held his hand up to stop me from speaking further. He had more to say.

"I was a wreck Belle, and so jealous."

My 'oh-no' senses were kicking in. I knew I wasn't going to like what he was going to say next.

"You were with a girl," I whispered. "I know." It hurt even to say it out loud.

"When you were in Colorado, and we spoke, I was mean to you on purpose because I was convinced that you and Adam were hooking up. I thought I had lost you. That night I drank too much, I know that's a terrible excuse, and I kissed Vanessa. I thought if I kissed someone it might help me forget you. It didn't. It only made me feel worse."

I bit my lower lip to keep it from trembling as jealousy pounded through my body.

"Belle, say something."

My voice quivered. "I'm sorry you thought I was with Adam. I'm sorry I couldn't tell you about him and Jeannie, maybe if you'd known that things might have been different. But what I'm most sorry about is that you didn't think that what we shared the night before we left meant something." I angrily wiped at the wetness stirring in my eyes.

"Oh God Belle, it did. It meant everything to me."

"Then how could you think that I would just stop caring about you, and be with Adam? That's not what love is Brady."

"Love?"

"Yes, I loved you," I admitted reticently. "I would never have betrayed you. Never."

"I'm sorry Belle. The pictures, the texts, I was stupid."

I was feeling brave, so I asked knowing his answer might destroy me. "The woman that I heard on the phone. The one that said you and her spent the night together. Was that Vanessa too?"

"Yes, I spent the night with her. Let me explain, please."

I gulped nervously. Did I really want to hear this?

"She and I were on a mission together. We saved a father and son who were lost in the woods. The ATV that came to pick them up could only transport them. We had to spend one night in the woods. We didn't do anything."

"Oh." I was confused.

"We completed a mission, and it was a good night. We worked well together. That's what you overheard."

"It sounded like." I couldn't even finish my thought.

"I know how it must have sounded. Adam told me. He almost took my head off."

"He was as upset as I was."

"Yeah, I got that." He answered caustically.

"So you thought I was with Adam, so you were with Vanessa?"

"Yeah."

"That's why you came to see me today? To tell me that?"

"Yes, no," Brady responded seemingly flustered. I could tell that he had more to say, but he was struggling with it.

The silence between us was uncomfortable.

"Training went well?" I asked hoping to end the discomfort we were obviously both experiencing.

"It went great." He said looking relieved. "I passed. As soon as I'm able to, I'll start work here in Lansing."

"That's wonderful. I knew you could do it." I said softly. I meant it too. Brady could do anything he set his mind too.

He looked at me uneasily. "You've lost weight." I shrugged.

"Are you sick?"

"No, I'm fine." I paused. "I was on the helicopter with you when we were flown to the hospital."

"I heard that."

"Your heart stopped."

"I heard that too." he chuckled.

"It wasn't funny. It was horrifying." I said remembering with a shudder the disturbing sound of him flatlining.

"I'm sorry. I'm sure it was awful. Honestly, I'm just relieved you were not hurt worse than you were." His voice had gentled.

"Me?" I snapped." You were almost killed! Why Brady?" I had to know.

"Why what?"

"Why did you take that bullet for me?"

Brady cocked his head, and I could see he was debating on whether to tell me his answer.

He took my hand in his and looked at me with unmasked insecurity. The familiar fit of his hand surrounding mine made me draw in a deep breath.

"I would do anything to keep you, safe Belle."

Tears pricked my eyes. "But?" I said knowing he had more to say more

"No buts. I sent you on that vacation with Adam to keep you safe, and so you would experience someplace other than here. I knew Adam could protect you, and yes, I knew there was a risk of losing you to him. But honestly, I didn't think anything would happen between you two, especially after our night together."

"It didn't, nothing happened. I was never interested in Adam like that, even if he hadn't been dating Jeannie. I had already given myself to you. Head, heart, and soul."

"I know. I know." Brady sounded so disheartened.
"I was a dick to you on the phone because I
thought you were with him. It was stupid, really
stupid, and I did an equally foolish thing by kissing
Vanessa, but Belle, I never stopped loving you."
I inhaled sharply hearing him say those words.
"Brady." I croaked tearfully. Seconds ticked by I
couldn't speak.
"I love you." He repeated nervously.
He loved me? I was afraid to say anything. There
was no way he could love me after all the pain he
had endured because of me.
"You can't." I managed to mutter.
"When I heard you had been kidnapped. I just
wanted to find you. I prayed for you to be all right.
I knew that I had misread the pictures and texts,
and I knew you probably hated me, but that didn't
matter. I felt like the biggest jerk and wanted to
find you just so you could yell at me. Kip and I
were the first to reach you. When I saw that man
aim his gun at you, I didn't even think about it.
You were all that mattered. Saving you was all I
cared about."
"But you almost died," I said tearfully.
"But I didn't, and you didn't. "
He paused and took a deep breath. "Can you
forgive me for being a fool when you were away?"
"I almost got you killed," I answered with a
quivering voice. "You should hate me."
Brady frowned. "You think I should hate you?"
"Yes." I looked into his green eyes. "I hate me," I
replied glumly.

Brady tugged on my hand urging me to stand, which I did, and he gently pulled me down on his lap. I saw him wince in pain.

"Brady?"

"I'm fine. Trust me I need this, and I hope you do too."

His one hand rested on my hip, and his other hand spanned my battered cheek making me look at him. My heart pitty-pattered to life for the first time in over a month.

"I don't hate you. I love you, Belle."

I couldn't believe what I was hearing. Tears filled my eyes.

"Belle?' Brady squeezed my hip bringing my attention back to him. "Can you forgive me for not trusting you, for kissing Vanessa?"

"Yes," I replied softly. "Can you forgive me for almost killing you, for bringing so much trouble into your life? Ever since you've met me, I've been nothing but trouble for you."

"You did nothing wrong, Belle. And for the record, meeting you made me want to live again, so thank you." He pulled my forehead down, so it rested on his. "Did I ruin any chance I have with you?"

I stared at the handsome man. "You want to date me? After all this?"

"No Belle."

"No?" I whispered as my heart squeezed tightly and I lifted my head from his.

"No." he smiled tenderly and took my face in his hands holding me still, so our eyes were locked on each other.

"I want to love you forever if you'll let me."

I wiped away the tears trickling down my face and prayed that I wasn't dreaming. I felt the dark void in my soul dissipate.

Kip and Vanessa chose that moment to walk back around the house. They were holding hands.

Brady chuckled seeing my astonished expression upon seeing them. "Yeah, they started dating last week."

Kip looked so smitten, and Vanessa was talking non-stop. It made me smile.

Brady kissed my lips gently. "You're mine Belle; please tell me you feel the same."

"I do. I never stopped loving you," I paused and stroked his neck with my fingers. "Thank you for saving me, Brady."

"It was my pleasure," he grinned.

"Pleasure?" My thumb rubbed his cheek.

"Well maybe not pleasure," he admitted chuckling.

Kip and Vanessa stopped in front of us.

"So, you two good?"

Brady looked at me. "Are we good?"

"We are." My smile was so wide my cheek hurt.

Brady placed another tender kiss on my lips.

"We have to get going," Kip said to Brady. "Your Mom's probably pacing the driveway."

I carefully got off of Brady's lap. Kip reached out his hand, and Brady took it, and Kip assisted him to stand up.

I walked them through the house to the front door. Mrs. Gordon was busy in the kitchen, and I introduced her to Brady and Vanessa. I could smell the cookies that she was baking. I realized she too was a throwback, preferring to bake rather than buy.

I stood on the porch and said goodbye to Kip and Vanessa. As soon as they stepped from the porch, Kip placed his arm gently over Vanessa's shoulders. I was glad that Kip was happy, but I still had some jealous feelings regarding her and Brady.

Brady noticed my expression and took my hands in his.

"I'm sorry I kissed her Belle."

"I know." I acknowledge. "So much has happened to you, to me, to us."

Brady chuckled softly. "It won't always be this crazy Belle. " He gave me a sweet kiss.

"I have to go home. I came right here from the hospital, and my Mom and Dad are waiting for me."

"Of course," I told him wishing I didn't feel bereft that he was leaving.

Brady kissed me again, and I clung to him feeling whole for the first time in a month.

His handsome face lite up. "Can you come with me?"

"Now?"

"Yes." He held my hands with his. "Belle since I've regained consciousness all I've wanted was to talk to you. I prayed that you would forgive me. I've missed you."

"I've missed you too."

"I want to hear about your trip."

"I want to hear about your training." I frowned.
"Well, maybe not all of it."

Brady chuckled knowing that I was thinking about him and Vanessa.

"You know I almost signed myself out of the hospital last week to come see you. The only reason I didn't was that Kip said he would come by."

"Oh, so that's why he visited."

"He cares for you too Belle. He was concerned. You weren't letting anyone visit. He told me you had lost weight."

"I couldn't face anyone. I hate that you were hurt because of me."

"I was not hurt because of you." He said sternly. "Will you come with me, please?"

I thought about how I looked and what I was wearing. "I need to shower and change Brady."

Brady tapped my nose with his finger and a smile and walked back inside. He returned a few moments later and was grinning happily.

"Mrs. Gordon will drive you to my house as soon as you're ready."

"I don't know Brady; your parents may not want to see me?" I was thinking about the no visit list I'd been placed on, and I didn't want to cause his family any more distress.

Brady used his one arm to pull me into his arms. "I won't leave here if you won't come over and then my parents won't see me at all." He said giving me a determined grin.

"Okay," I told him nervously. "I'll come, but if you get home and, well, you need to rescind the invitation please call, okay?"

He laughed, "That's not going to happen." He placed a sweet kiss on my lips, and I shivered feeling the stirrings of sensual affections resurface.

36

Vanessa

Kip and I were sitting in Kip's truck watching Brady say goodbye to Belle. She was so different from what I had expected. She was quiet and shy, and a knock out beauty. She hadn't had any makeup on, and her eyes popped. Her skin was flawless, and I'd kill for her sexy plump lips. She was very thin, but according to Kip, she had dropped a lot of weight since being kidnapped. Belle's long blond hair was uncolored and natural. Kip had shared with me that he had had one date with her, but it had ended with them becoming friends. Brady cared for her and Kip said that she cared for him.

I felt awful that I had persistently hit on him when we were training. I hoped I hadn't caused any problems between them. I wasn't privy to their whole story, but seeing them together I knew they were in love. They were practically vibrating being near each other.

Kip took my hand in his.

"You okay?" He asked me.

"Yes, why wouldn't I be?"

"I know you liked him, Vanessa."

"I did, but he was pretty clear that he liked someone else, and just look at them, Kip. They are like magnet and steel."

Kip chuckled. "They are."

I brought Kip's large hand to my lips and kissed his knuckles. "Besides I kind of like his best friend." The look the big man gave me was smoking hot. We'd been dating for a week, and we had done nothing more than kiss. I was so ready for us to take that next step.

"He better hurry up," Kip said looking back to Brady.

"His Mom didn't know you were stopping here?"

"No, Brady wanted me to bring him home from the hospital because he wanted to stop here. He didn't want his parents to know."

"Why? Don't they like Belle?"

"I'm sure they do. They just don't know how much they like each other. Brady's been a wreck thinking that Belle hated him. He thought she and Adam had hooked up when he was away; they weren't. He messed up, no offense."

I giggled, "none taken, I think."

"Anyway, he heard that Adam was going to fix her up with one of his friends and he lost it. When he came too, I practically had to restrain him to keep in in the hospital."

"So why couldn't he tell his parents he wanted to talk to Belle?"

"His parents have been through a lot with him. His old girlfriend was practically part of the family, and she totally dumped on him. I think they always thought that they would get back together. Then he lost his foot, and he had a hard time bouncing back from that. Belle was the one who pulled him out of that funk. I think Brady didn't want to worry them."

"I still don't understand."

"Brady almost died, shit he did die. He chose her life over his own. His parents can't be too happy about that. They almost lost him. Since he started recovering, all he has been worried about was Belle. His parents don't know because he didn't want them to worry about him any more than they already were."

"They think Belle would hurt him?"

"I think they want their son to heal both physically and emotionally. I'm not sure if they know what happened between them. If they did they should also understand that Belle was, hurt by Brady, twice. It's been a messy situation. They just want their son to be happy."

"Well, they are going to be happy then because Brady has the biggest smile on his face," I said watching Brady walk towards us.

"Yeah, my man is feeling good." Kip paused. "You know she went to visit him last week, and someone told her she was not allowed to."

"Really?"

"She said her name was on a no visit list."

"Do you think it was his parents because we know it wasn't Brady?"

"I honestly don't know, but I need to tell him."

I smiled at Kip thinking what a great friend he was. "So, tonight, would you like to come to my place for supper?"

"That would be nice. Will your brother be home?"
My brother and I shared a house.
"Nope, he's on duty all night."
Kip's grin widened. It was going to be an epic
evening. Everyone was going to be happy I
thought with a cheesy grin on my face.

Brady

I hated leaving Belle. I watched her standing on the
porch as we drove away with mixed emotions. I
was feeling better than ever that she loved me, but
driving away, after getting back together with her
just seemed wrong.
Thank goodness Kip had been able to drive me
home. My mom had wanted my dad to get me, but
I told them I needed some Kip time. My dad
chuckled and told my mom that I'd be fine.
My Mom had been acting off all week. I knew she
had been out of her mind with worry and I felt
terrible about that, but I was determined to talk to
Belle. I needed to apologize to her in person. I
didn't want to deal with my parents and my
screwed up love life. I just wanted to talk to Belle
and not have to answer a barrage of questions from
my wonderful family. I never expected Belle to
forgive me. I had no idea she felt responsible for
me being hurt.
I was feeling tired, and I shut my eyes listening to
Vanessa chatter on about something, I think she
was asking what Kip wanted for dinner. That girl

sure could talk. Thank goodness Kip was a good listener.

I was jolted awake when I felt the truck roll to a stop. I opened my eyes to find we were in my driveway. There were balloons tied to the lamppost, and my Mom ran out the door followed by my Dad and Tommy.

I opened the back cab door, and Kip turned around to say something to me, but my family was so excited to have me home that they quickly helped me out of the truck.

I had seen all of them the day before, but I was still hugged and kissed as if I'd been away for years. I loved my family. I felt bad that I'd put them through so much anguish.

My Mom asked my friends if they wanted to come inside and Kip told her that they had previous plans. I grinned at my best friend. I think I knew exactly what plans they had.

"Brady, I wanted to tell you something," Kip said to me.

"We'll talk to tomorrow," I replied happily as my family continued to usher me into the house.

"Thanks for the ride," I yelled over my shoulder.

Tommy carried my small bag inside, and I slowly followed behind him as we entered the house. My brother ran upstairs to put my bag in my room, and I sat down on the couch. My Dad sat down in his chair, and my Mom disappeared into the kitchen.

"How are you feeling?" My dad asked.

"I feel great actually. A little tired." I watched as Tommy bounded back down the stairs and sat next to me. Dad was grinning. I knew he was happy to have me home.

"Do you have a rehab schedule set up?" He asked.

"Yup, twice a day."

"Two times a day, isn't that pushing it?"

"Dad I need to regain my strength."

My dad chuckled. "Just don't overdo it."

"I won't. I can't wait to eat some solid foods."

The knife to my gut had nicked my stomach, and I had been on a strict liquid diet up until a few days ago.

"I'm on soft foods right now, eggs, yogurt stuff like that."

Mom came out of the kitchen and placed a beer in front of my dad and a protein drink in front of me.

"Thanks, Mom." She went back into the kitchen.

"Where are you going?" I asked her.

"I'll be right back. I have a surprise for you."

I chuckled. My Mom had probably whipped up some super healthy soft meal for me. I knew she was well aware of my dietary restrictions.

Tommy was telling me about pre-season football. He had filled out since the beginning of the summer and I was not surprised when he told me how much he could lift. He was going to be bigger than me in a few years.

"So Dad I stopped at Belle's before I came home today."

Tommy and my Dad stilled, and I thought that was odd.

"Were you aware that she blames herself for what happened to me?"

My Dad sighed. "She apologized to me when I saw her in the hospital, and Kip said she was having a hard time."

"Dad she has been beating herself up."

"I was under the impression that you two were not together anymore." My Dad said nervously.

"That was all on me; you know that." I reminded him. I looked at Tommy. He didn't seem surprised. He probably knew all about my f-up. Gossip in a small town was inevitable.

"So did you two have a good talk?" My Dad asked cautiously.

"Yes, I apologized, and thankfully she accepted it." My Dad nodded. I continued, "And for the record, she apologized to me too because I'd gotten hurt."

"That wasn't her fault," Tommy interjected.

"Exactly," I said.

"As long as you're happy Brady. " My dad said before taking a long pull from his beer.

"I am. I invited her over."

"When?"

"Now. She wanted to shower first. She should be here shortly."

My dad had a strange expression on his face.

"What's the matter?" I asked. "Please tell me you don't blame her for what happened?"

"No, not at all, it's just."

My dad never finished his sentence. My Mom walked back into the living room, and Chelsea was trailing behind her.

My Mom was smiling, and I looked at my dad who appeared worried.

"Chelsea, what are you doing here?"

My Mom came up to me and put her hand on my shoulder. "Honey, Chelsea has been so concerned about you. We've been talking almost every day. She told us how you two were talking again. Just like old times." My mother added happily.

I looked at Chelsea who continued to smile as if she hadn't told my Mom a colossal lie. Chelsea was a nurse at the hospital I'd been in, but I hadn't seen her the entire time I was there.

"Mom, I."

The doorbell rang, and Tommy hopped up to answer it. I knew that it was Belle. I stood up as quickly as my healing body allowed to greet her and to put distance between Chelsea and myself, but Chelsea grabbed me by my waist and pressed into my chest, embracing me tightly.

Tommy opened the door, and Belle stood on my front porch holding a Tupperware container. Her bashful smile faded when she saw Chelsea in my arms. She took a faltering step backward.

"Belle, wait."

I tried to get Chelsea to release me, but she was like a friggin octopus. "Chelsea let go of me. Tommy, stop Belle!" Belle had already turned and walked off the porch.

I glared at Chelsea. "What the hell Chelsea?" I shoved away from her and made it to the door in time to grab Belle's hand before she reached the bottom step. The Gordon's were still in our driveway I then gave Belle the most ardent kiss I could deliver. My heart was pounding, and I could feel hers beating against my chest. When I released her from the kiss, her sweet lips were puffy, and she had the most adorable expression on her cute face.

"I love you; please come back inside," I whispered into her ear.

She smiled meekly and waved to the Gordon's so they would know Belle was in good hands.

When I walked us inside, I knew she was nervous so held her tightly to me. Belle belonged with me, and I had to make sure she knew it.

I looked at my family knowing they had to be confused by Chelsea's deception and Belle's arrival. My mother's jaw hung open. My dad's face was unreadable, and Tommy had a goofy smile on his face. Chelsea was so livid that her face was mottled with red, angry splotches.

"Brady, please don't do this! I know you're just trying to make me jealous. We're good together. Your Mom knows that. We're going to end up together eventually. I'm just hurrying that along."

I gave Belle a reassuring squeeze. "Mom, Chelsea and I never talked when I was in the hospital," I said scowling at her. "I love Belle. I think I fell in love with her the first day that I met her." I looked at Belle and saw that she was surprised by my public declaration. A tiny smile appeared on her lips, and she hugged me using both arms. She peered up at me, and my world tilted when I saw the beautiful smile on her face. "She loves me too," I announced quietly never taking my eyes from her. I turned to my family who had gone silent.

My Mom was gaping at Chelsea.

"Chelsea, I think you need to leave." My Mom said using her no-nonsense Mom voice.

Chelsea turned to my Mom. "But I love him, and you want us to be together too, you told me that."

"I want my son to be happy." My Mom looked at Belle and me. "And I can see that he is; with Belle. I can't believe you lied to me. Please leave."

Belle's small frame had become rigid, and I watched as her expression morphed into one of anger.

"You're the nurse!" Belle exclaimed leaving my arms and blocking Chelsea's path to the door. Chelsea paled then put her hands defensively on her hips and sneered at Belle.

Belle looked past Chelsea to me. "Brady, I went to see you in the hospital four days ago, and she told me I couldn't because you had put me on a no visit list."

"He'll never love you the way he loved me." Chelsea hissed before shoving past Belle and storming out of the door.

Tommy shut the door and had the biggest grin on his face. My baby brother was enjoying the commotion.

I stepped to Belle and put my hands on her shoulders.

"No visit list?" Brady asked perplexed.

Belle appeared to be embarrassed, and her voice softened. "She said I couldn't see you because I was on a no visit list. Kip told me that you hadn't put me on any list; I just wasn't sure." Belle paused.

"I wondered if your parents had put me on it," Belle whispered the last sentence.

I stared at my family and immediately knew that they had no idea about any list.

My Mom was upset, and my Dad put his arm around her. "No Belle, we never said you couldn't visit Brady. There is no such thing as a no-visit list." My dad told her gently.

My Mom was still shaken. "Brady, I'm so sorry. Chelsea has been speaking with me every day for the last two weeks. She said that you and she were talking again. I was led to believe you were a couple."

"No Mom, we never spoke, and even if we had, I would never have dated her again. She manipulated you, Mom."

"Why didn't you tell us how you felt about Belle?" She asked gently.

"I wanted to, but I really messed up with her." I gazed at the beautiful woman in my arms, and my voice softened. "I wanted to talk to her, I needed to apologize, but I wasn't sure how I'd be received. I didn't want you to have to deal with any more drama."

My Dad looked at my Mom, and I knew they were communicating silently.

I rubbed Belle's arm. "You came to see me?" I asked quietly.

Belle nodded.

"And Chelsea told you that you weren't allowed too?"

"Yes."

"Man, she's a wacko," Tommy said.

"I'm sorry about that Belle. It would have meant everything to me if you had visited."

I turned to my parents. "I'm sorry Chelsea lied to you, I wish you would have said something to me."

"She said you two were keeping it under wraps until you were discharged," my Mom said. "I'm sorry Belle if I had known I would have never invited her here."

Belle remained possessively tucked into my side, and I rubbed her arm affectionately.

"I invited Belle for dinner; I hope that's okay?"

My Mom stepped to us. "Of course it is!"

I smiled at my Mom trying to make Belle feel welcomed after the craziness that she had walked in on. I felt the tension drain from Belle's body, and I kissed her temple affectionately.

Belle

We sat down to eat, and I saw that Brady's dinner was different than ours. I didn't want to ask why because I knew it had something to do with his injuries. I still didn't know the exact injuries that he had suffered, but right then was not the time to ask.

I enjoyed the easiness of the family conversations, and it reminded me of when my family would sit down to dinner at the end of a long day. So much had changed in the last few months. Summer was ebbing away and thinking of fall made me think of college, and then I thought about my farm. With Brady starting work he wouldn't be able to be my farm hand any longer. The Gordon's had been unbelievable, and I knew I would miss them when they left.

After dinner, we sat in the living area and ate the cookies Mrs. Gordon had sent as dessert. Tommy regaled us with all the local high school gossip, like who was dating whom, and who had gotten their license and his hopes to be the starting linebacker, whatever the heck that was.

Sheriff McDaniel's turned on the television because evidently his favorite show was starting and he never missed it. I was sitting next to Brady, and he held my hand possessively in his, my head rested on his shoulder, and his cheek rested on top of mine. Before too long I could hear Brady's soft snores, and I realized he had fallen asleep. I looked at the Sheriff sheepishly. I didn't quite know what to do. He smiled gently, and I saw that he was going to wake Brady up, but I gestured to leave him sleeping.

"I can take you home Belle. I have my license." Tommy whispered.

"Thank you, Tommy, I'd appreciate that. The Gordon's are seeing a movie in Massey, and they won't be home until much later."

I carefully dislodged myself from Brady's warmth and said my thank yous and good night.

Mrs. McDaniel hugged me and said once again that she was sorry about Chelsea. Sheriff McDaniel was standing next to her waiting to walk me to the car.

I took a deep breath I still felt like I owed them an apology; they had been through hell. "Sheriff, Mrs. McDaniel I want to apologize to you both for Brady getting hurt. If it hadn't been for me."
The Sheriff held up his hand to stop me from saying anything else.
"Belle, what happened to Brady was because of one greedy man. Brady was instrumental in finding you. He was out of his mind with worry. What he did was selfless, but it's who he is too. He loves you, and if you and he are going to make a go of this, I think you both need to forgive yourselves. You have no reason to apologize to anyone. Let's all move forward and enjoy what lies ahead."
I smiled widely at the Sheriff. "Thank you. I swear that was something my Gigi would have said."
The Sheriff walked me outside and opened the car door for me. Tommy was already waiting inside with the engine running.
"Right home after you drop her off son." The Sheriff said.
"Yes, Sir," Tommy answered obediently.
Tommy was a good driver and when I discovered that his birthday had been last week I made a mental note to bake him a loaf of bread as a thank you.
Tommy was such a little gentleman when we got to the farm. He walked me to my front door and asked if he wanted me to check out the house before I went inside. I told him that was very sweet, but with my father locked up and the

Gordon's living with me I wasn't expecting any
trouble.
I bade him goodnight and went inside heading
right to my bedroom.

37

Belle

I changed into a pair of flannel shorts and a soft
tee shirt and took my Momma's journal out on the
back patio. I turned on the outside lights so I could
read. I decided to skip to the back of the book.
By the time I finished reading, I had tears
streaming down my face. Momma had cared deeply
for Sam Fitzpatrick. He had been kind and a
gentleman and had brought fun back into her life.
He had taken her dancing and to her first Mall. I
learned she was working up the nerve to tell me
about selling the farm, and she couldn't wait to
introduce me to Sam.

Momma had wanted to sell the farm but not
because he had pressured her, but because she
wanted to travel with me. She had wanted me to
see places and do things that she hadn't
experienced. Momma had also written that she
hoped that I would find a good man to love. After
I read that I looked up into the stunning Vermont
star-filled sky and said, "I did Momma, and you
would love him."

The one thing I read that bothered me was that the
last few weeks of Momma's life she felt as though
someone was watching her. I shivered thinking I
knew exactly how she felt.

I closed the book, and just as I turned the patio
lights out, I heard a commotion in the barn. Henny
was outside I could see her from where I sat, so

were the sheep and pigs. The chickens were in their coop, but they were cackling up a storm when they should have been sleeping. I hoped a fox or weasel hadn't snuck into the barn. I couldn't see Bessie, and that made me anxious. Both animals were well into their late stages of life, so I was always worried about them. I put the book on the kitchen counter and got the flashlight from the drawer and my Henry from over the fireplace.

I wasn't afraid of anything except that something may have happened to Bessie or that my poor chickens were being assaulted.

I tried to make a lot of noise as I walked to the barn to scare off any thieving critters. When I reached the barn doors, I thankfully heard Bessie moo, but the chickens were still squawking loudly.

Brady

My Mom gently shook my shoulder waking me up, and I opened my eyes to find the television on, but Belle was gone. My father walked inside as my Mom stood next to me.

"Where's Belle?" I asked sleepily.

"Tommy drove her home," my Mom replied.

"I'm a lousy host falling asleep like that." I chastised myself.

"Honey you were tired. Belle knew that."

"Was she okay?"

"Of course." My Mom looked at my dad, and my dad nodded ever so slightly. My parents were so in sync that they could communicate without words. It made me smile.

"Your girl apologized to us for getting you hurt."

"Yeah, I told you, she's carrying around a tremendous amount of guilt."

"I told her she was not to blame and that you both needed to forgive yourselves so you could move forward."

I grinned cheekily. "That's pretty good advice dad. How did Belle take it?"

"She said it's something her Gigi would have said."

I chuckled. "Well, I'll call her to properly say good night."

My parents said goodnight to me as I headed up to my room. I was bushed, but the horrible empty feeling that had been inside me was now replaced with happy contentment. It was all because of Belle. The only thing I needed to do now was to get myself 100 percent better so I could start my job, nest egg some money and ask Belle to marry me. I did not like being away from her for even a minute, not at all.

As I got ready to turn in I saw the knife from Belle sitting on my dresser. I took it and sat down on my bed.

I discovered it was not just any knife; it was incredible. It's something I would have bought for myself had I seen it. An Old Timer Premium Trapper Folding Knife with Saw, Gut hook, and Clip Point Blade. I loved it.

I ran my fingers over the handle before placing it on my nightstand. I wanted to call Belle to thank her, but knew she probably wasn't home yet, so I lay on my bed thinking about her and all we had endured. I fell asleep with a smile on my face because the girl of my dreams loved me. She loved me. I was the luckiest man alive.

I woke up hearing my parents talking in their bedroom, and when I looked at the clock, I saw that it was a little after 9:00 PM. Their bedroom door opened and I watched as my dad walked pass my door dressed in his uniform.
"Dad?"
He stopped and poked his head in my room. "Go back to sleep Brady."
"What's going on?"
He looked pensive, and it unnerved me.
"Donna Romella was just discovered dead in her apartment."
I sat up. "Donna?" It dawned on me who he was talking about.
"I have to go. I got the call as a courtesy from the Prosecuting attorney in the case against Belle's father. I want to go to Massey, see the crime scene, and talk to the Sheriff myself."
"You want me to come with you?"
My dad grinned. "When you're sworn in son, I'll be making you come with me. Get some sleep."
I lay back down and tucked my arms behind my head. I wondered if Belle was still awake. The Gordon's were still out I was sure of that. Their movie wasn't even supposed to start until 7:30 PM. I wanted to thank her for the knife, and honestly,

I'd missed her so much I just wanted to hear her voice. I got up and hopped to the desk where I had left my cell phone. I hopped back to bed and sat down before calling her.

The phone rang and rang, and after ten rings I hung up. My Spidey senses were kicking in, but I didn't want to jump to any wrong conclusions. I'd done that one too many times already. She was probably just sleeping, or maybe she was sitting on her patio and couldn't hear the phone. If she was sleeping it was pretty darn selfish of me to wake her up, but still. I pressed in her number again, and once again it rang ten times. I just didn't like the coincidence that Donna had been killed and I couldn't reach Belle. I could probably use that as an excuse to visit her though.

Maybe I'd just drive down her driveway and see if she was awake. If she was, I could stop in and say hi. Who was I kidding? I wanted to hold her and kiss and tell her I loved her again, and then I would say goodnight properly and leave her be.

I was grinning as I dressed.

I left a note on the kitchen table letting my parents know I was visiting Belle. I chuckled, my parents weren't idiots, and they would know exactly why I was going to see my girl.

I took off in my truck feeling giddy that I was going to be seeing Belle shortly.

Belle

I pushed open the heavy barn door and swung my flashlight left to right keeping my Henry in my right hand in case I needed it to scare away a predator. Bessie's eyes gleamed red in the bean of the light. She appeared to be agitated but otherwise okay. I headed towards the newly constructed chicken coop. Jeb had built it while I was away. There was now an area inside the barn for the chickens to roam when the weather was poor, then there was the actual coop where we would shut the chickens in at night, and then there was a hatch type door that when opened, the chickens had access to the outside. It was ingenious, and I knew the idea had been Brady's because he had left the plans that he had drawn in the barn. I opened the door that led to the inside chicken area and discovered that the chickens had flown the coop, literally. They were everywhere. We always put the chickens inside their little protective coop every night. They slept better because they felt safe.

It took me a good twenty minutes to get the agitated birds back inside their coop. I figured that Jeb must not have latched the coop shut and it had accidentally opened. I chuckled seeing the discombobulated hens and knew I'd be getting no eggs from them tomorrow.

I took a quick look at the sheep, pigs, and Henny before heading out of the barn. The clean, crisp Vermont air was turning cooler as the telltale signs of fall began to emerge.

As I stepped out of the barn, I heard the rumble of an engine and then headlights bouncing along my dirt drive. As the truck got closer, I saw that it was Brady's truck. I had two simultaneous reactions. One was that he had rethought his feelings for me and wanted to set me straight, or that he wanted to see me as much as I needed to see him. I quickly dismissed the first awful scenario; Brady loved me. When he alighted from the truck his handsome face told me all I needed to know. I jogged to him, and as he rounded the front of his truck, I jumped into his arms.

He caught me with ease, but I did hear him grunt. "I'm sorry," I said between delivering kisses to his stubbly cheek.

He chuckled, "No worries. Please feel free to greet me like that all the time.

Brady turned me, so my back was to the truck and proceeded to kiss me into a puddle of happiness. "What are you doing outside?" Brady asked between sweet nuzzles to my neck.

"The chickens were squawking up a storm I went to check on them."

I felt Brady tense just ever so slightly.

"What are you doing here?" I said breathlessly enjoying his arms around me.

"I wanted to say goodnight." He whispered before taking my lips.

The kiss was bone melting, and I whimpered under the intense onslaught of sensual sensations washing over me.

"Brady." I moaned into his mouth. My hands were threaded through his soft dark hair as I returned his ardor.

Brady grasped my hip gently and released my mouth.

"We should go inside." He said holding me close. Then he paused. "Were the chickens okay?"

"Yes, Jeb must not have closed the coop door tightly. They were awake and running around all confused, thinking it was morning."

"Dad said Jeb used the design I had drawn up."

"It's fantastic Brady. I can't wait for you to see it."

Brady pulled me under his arm, and we walked to the house.

When we got inside Brady turned me around, so my back was against the just closed door. Our mouths fused as he pressed against me and drew my hands above my head forcing my chest against his. I could feel his passion hard against my stomach, and I rubbed promiscuously against it. Brady pulled back slightly resting his forehead against mine.

"I figure we have about one hour before The Gordon's get back." He murmured in a husky voice.

My eyes met his, and I grinned. He pulled away from me, took my hand, and led me to my bedroom. We stood facing each other both breathing heavily as we started to undress slowly. Neither of us took our eyes off each other.

Brady pulled his shirt over his head, and I did the same thing. We both froze looking at each other's torso.

Brady had two pucker scars on his chest. One was near his shoulder the other was just under his ribcage. The worst scar though was the thick ugly red one that was on his stomach. I gasped seeing his wounds.

Brady was staring at me, and the look on his face was concern and shock. He jaw hung open and I saw tears in his eyes.

I burst into tears seeing his injuries. He immediately stepped to me and pulled me into his arms.

"Belle, you're so thin. I knew you had lost weight, Kip told me, but you lost so much."

"Me? Brady, are you kidding! Look at you. I had no idea how much you were hurt. I can't stand that you got hurt." I was sobbing against his chest as he held me.

"Belle please don't cry. I'm fine now. I'll be as good as new in a few weeks."

"But Brady?" I whimpered weakly.

"But nothing, Belle. What about you? How much weight have you lost?"

I shrugged wiping away the remnants of my tears.

"Sweetheart are you sick?" He asked me with so much concern in his voice that I almost started crying again.

"No. I lost some weight because of my injuries, but I just haven't felt like eating."

Brady ran his hand over my rib cage. "What were your injuries? Kip wouldn't tell me anything."

"Will you tell me what happened to you if I tell you what happened to me?"

Brady paused, but then he drew his shirt back over his head and helped me with mine.

"I think we need to sit down for this conversation."
He said gently.

We walked back to the living room and sat next to each other on the couch.

Brady began. "So I know you were abducted and taken through the tunnel, but that's all I know."

"There isn't much more to tell. I heard footsteps, and when I ran upstairs, I was hit really hard on the side of my face. Your dad told me I was hit with a shovel."

"You don't remember anything else?"

"When I came too, I was blindfolded, and my arms, and legs were bound. It was so cold, and I knew there was dirt underneath me." I shivered remembering the awfulness.

"I wasn't having very lucid thoughts because of the pain, but I thought I had been buried alive." Brady rubbed my arm. "The next thing I remembered was being in the helicopter." I rested my head against his shoulder, and Brady put his cheek on my head and waited for me to go on."

I saw the medic working on someone, and when he shifted his position, I saw you. Brady that was so awful. Then your heart stopped, and I was crying and even though my head was strapped down I was could see him use the electric paddles on you. It took two tries to get your heart restarted." I told softly.

"I'm sorry you had to see that."

I laughed half-heartedly. "You can't apologize for something you couldn't control."

Now Brady laughed, and I took my head off his shoulder to see that he was grinning. Then I realized that what I had just said to Brady applied to me as well and he was letting me know it. "Oh." I giggled.

"Yes baby, oh." He said kissing my head.

"So tell me what happened to you."

"You sure you want to hear this?"

"Yes."

"I don't want you to feel responsible for what happened."

"Okay."

"I'm serious Belle. I'll share what happened, but you can't think any of this was your fault. Promise me."

"It isn't that easy Brady," I whined.

"Sweetheart, I love you. I will always want to protect you. You were a victim too. I think you forget that."

A warm mushy feeling blanketed me. Brady was a true hero; my hero. He loved me.

"Thank you, Brady. Thank you for saving me, for loving me, for saying what you just said."

He kissed me sweetly, and I felt so blessed at that moment.

"Okay, ready?" He asked.

"Yes, as ready as I'll ever be." I shuddered.

"So I returned home early from training. I had passed all the tests and saved a father and son during a real search and rescue. They counted that as my field practical. I was feeling good about that, but I was wrecked about losing you to Adam."

"Which was ridiculous," I interjected lightly.

"Yeah. So that first morning I was home I was enlightened to the fact that Adam and Jeannie were dating. I showed my Mom the pictures and the texts that Adam sent, and she told me that I had misread what he had sent. I was feeling like a total loser. I never stopped caring for you Belle. I realized that I had messed up big time and that you probably hated me, so it wasn't a good morning. Anyway, Adam called dad, and that's when we found out you were missing. We organized a Search and Rescue, and since I was specifically trained for this, I wanted to help."

Brady had his arm around me, and I had my hand on his thigh, and my head rested on his shoulder. I knew telling the story couldn't have been easy for him.

"We divided up the mountain and Kip and I were paired up. I found a cave halfway up a rock face, and when I went in, I heard you moaning and discovered a man in there. You weren't in the area that the man was in and when I tried to sneak up on him he saw me. We exchanged gunfire and I managed to work my way to the part of the cave that you were in. I found you, but the man had put on night vision goggles, and he shot my shoulder and then my leg. Then he jumped on me. We struggled, and he stabbed my leg and then my stomach." Brady shook his head, and I saw the painful memory etched on his handsome face.

"I was going to pass out. I saw spots. He thought he had killed me. I heard him say he was going to kill you and I somehow got on my knees and launched myself to cover your body. His shot hit my back."

"Oh, Brady."

"You promised." He said quickly.

I nodded, but there was an emotional lump in my throat.

"I don't remember anything after that; oh wait I do." He got the most adorable smile on his face. "You were wearing my tee shirt."

I started laughing. "It's not even funny, but that's what you remember?"

"Yup, could have been my last living thought." he grinned. "I told you I liked how you looked in my tee shirt."

"Not funny Brady McDaniel."

"Kind of is, now. Anyway, Vanessa and her brother had found the other entrance to the cave, and they heard shots. Luckily they were able to get to us just in time. Vanessa shot him. She saved both of us."

"I didn't know that. I didn't know anything except your dad had said you had taken a bullet for me." We sat next to each other, each thinking back to that horrific day. Headlights filtered through the living room window.

"The Gordon's are home," I said lazily.

"Guess I should probably head home then," Brady said glumly.

I didn't want him to go, but it would have been too inappropriate for him to stay the night with the Gordon's sleeping upstairs.

"We'll carve out some time for us," I said standing up. Brady followed me to the door.

We walked outside and met the Gordon's on the porch. The men shook hands cordially.

I introduced Brady to Jeb.

"It's nice to meet you," Jeb said to Brady.

"You too Sir."

I asked about the movie, and they both said it was good. I had never been to a movie.

"Why don't we go see it tomorrow Belle?" Brady said with a grin.

"Really?"

"Yes, I'll pick you up at. 4:00, we will catch the early show."

"I'd love that," I told him.

The Gordon's were smiling at us, and we said goodnight to them, and I walked Brady to his truck.

"Are you going to tell Jeb about the chickens?"

"No, I'm sure it was a rare over sight."

We kissed goodnight, and I could tell Brady didn't want to leave any more than I wanted him too.

That night I slept better than I had in weeks. Brady called me in the morning, and we talked for a while. It made me think about Momma and how she used to talk on the phone with a hushed voice. I wondered if I had a silly grin on my face as she had.

After I got off the phone, I helped with the animals and baked bread with Bev. She and I were going to put up the blueberry jam, and we discussed when we should pick the sweet berries that were in season. Bev very tactfully asked me how things were with Brady and myself. I explained that we were in a good place. I told her that we had talked and I even confided to her that he had said he loved me and that I loved him. She was all smiles. This is how it would have been if my Momma was alive. As if a light bulb clicked in my head I made a decision. I asked Bev to drive me into town so I could meet with Mr. Bee.

When 4:00 PM arrived, I was waiting for Brady. I dressed in the red dress that Adam had said I looked really good in. I wanted to look good for Brady. The material clung to my body, and I noticed my curves were not as round as when I'd worn it last. I hoped I still looked nice though. A few more days of eating the way I had eaten today and I'd be back to normal.
Brady greeted me with a huge smile and his eyes roved up and down my body. "You look spectacular." He said kissing me on my cheek.
"Thank you. Am I too dressed up?"
"Maybe a little, but I'm not letting you change. You are hot, and I'll be the envy of every guy there."
On the way to Massey, I wanted to share with Brady the thought I'd had today that had inspired me to visit Mr. Bee. As we drove down the driveway, Brady took my hand in his.
"Tell me." He said with a laugh. He knew me so well.
That made me laugh too. "Okay well, the trip you sent me on reaffirmed what I probably already

knew." I paused. "I love Vermont, and I don't want to sell my farm or the mountain."

"Go on." He encouraged me.

"I want to know what you think of me asking Bev and Jeb to remain on the farm with me?"

"Really?"

"Yes. I thought about it today. I can't run it by myself."

"I'm glad that you want to stay here." He said with a mischievous grin. "I just wonder about them living in your house." He paused. "There may be times that you will want your privacy."

I chuckled softly. "Well, this is another thing I'd like your opinion on. I want to build them their own place. I know just where to put it too."

"That's a great idea. I don't mean to be crass, but can you afford it?"

"Yes, I talked to Mr. Bee today, and we even looked into it. I would buy a prefab log home and have it placed a half-mile up my drive. There's a clearing there with a great view. I wouldn't even see it from my house, so we'd both have privacy."

"Have you discussed this with them yet?"

"No, as a matter of fact, they are in Springfield today and won't be back until really late. Jeb is meeting with a farmer that may want to hire him."

"So logistically how would this work?"

"They would live on the farm free of charge, and I would give them a salary. Jeb would continue to do what he is doing now. I would have to talk with Bev about what her role might be. I'm hoping to get her to take care of the garden. That will free me up to take college courses."

"I really think that is a super idea. Aren't you the smart one."

"So you think it's a good idea then?"

"Yes, brilliant actually. You keep your farm, and I keep you near me." He said with a sweet husky voice.

The movie was fun, and I could not get over how big the screen was. It was in what Brady had called surround sound and the first time I heard it I almost covered my ears because it was so loud. Brady bought me popcorn and even though I'd had popcorn before nothing compared to the salt and buttery, fluffy pieces that I gorged on there. Brady kept his arm around me as we watched the romantic comedy, and I couldn't help but notice all the looks he got from the woman in the theatre. I giggled to myself knowing that I would have been gawking at him myself if I weren't the lucky one with him.

By the time we got back to the farm, I could tell Brady was exhausted. He had said he'd had two rehabilitation sessions and had met with the Mayor of Lansing to discuss his job before coming to get me.

The Gordon's weren't home yet, and as much as I didn't want Brady to leave, I knew it would be totally selfish of me to talk him into staying with me until they got home. He, of course, walked me to my door and he asked me if I wanted him to stay. I told him a little white lie and said that I always wanted him to stay. However I was super tired, that was the lie. I explained that Bev and I were leaving early in the morning to pick blueberries, which was true. We shared a long kiss goodnight, and after Brady saw me safely inside, I watched my man drive off.

38

Brady

I was beat, but happier than I could ever
remember. Once again I hated leaving Belle, and I
knew I was going to have to remedy that soon. We
belonged together. She was the one for me, in the
'forever, I do,' way. First I wanted to start my job,
only then could I take the next step. The one thing
I was certain about was that we were going to have
a record short engagement period. I wanted her in
my life, and my bed every day, as soon as possible.
I was thinking about different ways to propose. I
already owned a diamond that needed to be put in
a setting. My grandma had left Tommy and me
stud earrings that were 1 and a 1/2-karat. We each
had one diamond to make into an engagement ring.
The diamonds were flawless.
Tomorrow I would drive into Springfield after my
morning rehab session and visit the jewelry store
that my grandfather had gone to and my dad as
well.
Car headlights were coming towards me, and I
turned down my high beams as they did too. I
didn't recognize the car, but I was in happy,
thinking about marrying Belle, la-la land, so I didn't
think anything about it until I was 5 minutes
further down the road. Then, I slammed on my
brakes, and K turned my truck speeding back to
Belle's home.

Belle

I wanted to wait up for the Gordon's and pitch my idea to them. I knew they had met with someone today about another job and I hoped they had not already accepted it. I changed into a pair of jeans and a tee shirt, made a cup of coffee, and sat out on the front porch to wait for them. It was so peaceful, and I was totally relaxed as I listened to my animals, the frogs in the pond, and the rustling of the leaves.

I thought I heard a car engine off in the distance, but after a few moments, I didn't hear it anymore. The mountains that surrounded my farm often projected echoes from the country roads. It was another thing I loved about living where I did. The mountains were a natural amplifier. I could hear a bear's mating call a mile away if the wind were blowing the right way.

The calm of the night was once again abruptly disrupted by the sounds of agitated hens. I sighed, they had probably gotten out again. Maybe the coop needed a new latch? The moon was almost full, and the stars were brilliant so I didn't need a flashlight.

Inside the barn, I headed straight for the chicken coop area. I opened the door, looking at the floor in case a hen was near it, I didn't want any to escape. When I stepped through the door, I quickly pulled it shut behind me. There was less light in the coop area than I thought and I cursed myself for not bringing the flashlight.

I shuffled through the large area carefully stepping over the hens and propped the swinging hatchway open. Then I began shooing the hens back inside.

I heard the click of a gun being cocked and I froze.

"Turn around slowly." A woman's voice came from the corner of the chicken area near the new entrance, which led to the outside.

I turned very slowly to find a woman standing in the corner aiming a handgun at me. She was in her forties, and there was something familiar about her, but I couldn't put my finger on it.

"You've ruined my life, just like your mother did," the woman sneered.

"Who are you?" I kept my voice as calm as possible, but inside I was quaking.

The woman clearly had her own agenda, and it didn't include answering my question.

"Let's go." She gestured for me walk ahead of her. As we exited the barn, I was looking for anything in the enclosed chicken area that I could grab as a potential weapon, but there was nothing. She pushed the gun barrel into my back directing me towards the woods. We were only a few yards from the barn when she stopped me.

"That's far enough."

I stopped and turned to face her. The moons golden light filtered through the birch trees and when I turned to face her, I saw that there was a hole dug into the ground next to where I stood. A shovel was leaning against a nearby tree. The hole was oblong shaped and about two feet deep, the size of a shallow grave.

"Who are you?" I repeated nervously. My mouth was so dry from fear that I could barely talk.

"You look like her." The woman said eyeing me with disdain.

I had never seen this woman before. "Who?"

"Your slut of a mother." She spat out.

I was shocked at how hateful the woman sounded. Her short red hair was a mess, and her eyes were wild. The fear spreading through me chilled me to my bones and I shivered.

"My mother?" I choked out.

"My Elias was deported because of your mother." Her voice was harsh and barely negligible.

This had to be the woman my father was cheating on my Momma with. It baffled me why she would still be holding a grudge.

"She ruined my life. I thought I'd never be happy again, but my Elias came back to me."

I was inching towards the shovel, but she saw me and fired off a shot near my feet, freezing me in place.

"Now you're doing the same. My Brandon is dead, and Elias is in jail, but he'll be free soon. I made sure of that."

I was trying to process what she was saying. I hoped she would continue talking, and maybe the Gordon's would come home.

"My Elias never loved your mother. He only wanted to stay in the country. My parents said he wasn't good enough for me, but he was."

The woman was crying now and the hand she held the gun with was shaking badly. I was afraid it would go off.

"I had to kill my own baby for him."

I heard what she said, but it didn't make sense. She had killed her baby?

"My poor Donna. I had no choice you know. She was going to tell the judge everything. Elias would have rotted in jail for the rest of our lives."

Donna?

"You're Donna's mother?" I was so horrified that my voice creaked. The final puzzle piece clicked into place.

"Your family is done ruining my life. Once I kill you, Elias will be cleared. He will inherit Green Mountain, and sell this God-forsaken place!" She was so unhinged that spit flew from her mouth as she spoke. She paused to catch her breath, wiping her mouth with her dirt-caked hand, leaving a smear of dark earth on her face.

"Then we can move to Denmark. We will finally be together." The last sentence she spoke in a soft dreamy voice. This woman was unhinged.

I saw movement off to the side of the woman, and Brady's head poked out from behind a tree. He was going to jump her, but as he stealthily stepped away from the safety of the tree, his shadow fell between us. The woman twirled to face him; her gun leveled at chest.

I launched myself between them. My torso knocked the barrel of the gun askew just as the gun fired. A sharp sting heated my side, and I yelped in pain as I fell. I heard Brady yell my name and then a gun fired from the opposite direction, and the woman cried out and fell to the ground screaming in pain.

It took less than a second for Brady to drop to his knees next to me. As I caught my breath, I watched as Sheriff McDaniel and one of his Deputies sprinting to us.

Brady's eyes were wildly assessing me. "Belle are you all right? What the hell? Why would you do that? Shit! Belle, you better be all right." Brady was beside himself, and as the Deputy made sure the woman was not a threat anymore, Brady's father knelt down next to Brady.

"Belle where were you hit?" He asked quickly.

"My side."

The Sheriff lifted my shirt, and I grimaced in pain. Then he did the oddest thing ever. He smiled.

"It only grazed you. The bullet grazed your side," the Sheriff said clapping Brady on his shoulder.

Brady looked at my wound and then back to my face. "You could have been killed!" He roared.

I was hurting, but I only felt a sharp stinging sensation, like when I use to skin my knee as a kid. I grinned up at Brady; he was steaming mad, and then his father started chuckling. Brady was looking at us like we had lost our minds.

"You're both nuts. Belle, you could have been killed." He repeated sounding vexed.

"But I wasn't."

"You could have..."

His father interrupted him. "Why don't you help your girl up son so we can get a bandage on her scrape." Sheriff McDaniel said giving me a wink. Brady helped me to my feet and gave me an embrace that conveyed to me that he was seriously shaken up.

"How did you know to come back, Brady?"
It took a few seconds for my question to sink in. He was unnerved. His voice was gravelly. "I passed a car on the road. I didn't recognize it. I couldn't see who was inside. There was no place else the driver could have been going."

"She is Donna and Brandon Romella's mother. She's in love with Elias. She killed Donna." I said looking over at the woman who was weeping uncontrollably.

"Did you know Donna was dead?" I asked the Sheriff.

"I did." The Sheriff said looking at Brady.

"We didn't want to worry you," Brady added indicating that he had also known.

"She killed her two days ago," the Sheriff added. "I got a call tonight from the Sheriff in Massey that Mary Ann Jansen, formerly Romella was missing. She was a person of interest in her daughter's murder."

"That's horrible. She killed her own daughter hoping to keep Elias out of jail. She wanted to kill me because she said I'd ruined her life and so Elias would inherit Green Mountain.

The Sheriff looked at the Deputy who had rolled Mary Ann Jansen onto her back after putting handcuffs on her. "How bad is she hit?" He asked his Deputy.

"You just winged her. Good shot."

As we walked out of the woods, Brady was quiet, and that worried me.

The Gordon's were pulling down the drive as we came from around the barn and Jeb jogged to us. He was instantly concerned, and Bev took me in her arms and gave me a motherly hug after the Sheriff explained to them what had happened.

The Deputy had already put Mrs. Romella in his car, and the Sheriff said for him to call the other Deputy and that they were to take Mrs. Romella to the clinic, but she was to be kept handcuffed the entire time.

We walked inside, and Bev had me sit at the dining room table. Brady, the Sheriff, and Jeb sat down too. I explained what had happened, and as I spoke, Bev put some ointment on my small wound and then applied a gauze bandage.

The Sheriff asked me to tell him what had happened and when I finished he closed his notebook that he had been making notes in. He had been there in time to know already what Brady had done. Satisfied that I was okay, he stood up and gave my shoulder a reassuring pat. He looked at his Brady, who was quiet and looking pensive. "Walk me out, son." He said standing from the chair.

Brady

I didn't know whether to shake her or kiss her stupid. She had just saved my life. I had only been two short feet from the outstretched hand of that woman holding the gun, and that bullet would have hit me dead center. I was tough, but I doubted my still healing body could have handled another traumatic injury.

When I had pulled back into Belle's drive, I spotted the unfamiliar car tucked off to the side halfway down the driveway. I parked near it and jogged towards Belle's home. My heart hammered in my chest. I knew Belle was in trouble. As I jogged down the drive, I kept to the trees lining the driveway. I heard the woman talking well before I saw them. Their voices had carried in the quiet of the night. I crept towards the voices, using the darkness of the woods to remain out of sight. When I saw the gun pointing at Belle, my heart froze.

I made my way towards them hoping to jump the woman. Everything happened so quickly. My shadow alerted her that I was there. She spun towards me and fired, but somehow Belle got between the bullet and me. I was sure she was dead. Instead, she rolled on her side, and when I knelt next to her, I was completely dumbfounded when she gave me a quirky smile followed by a grimace of pain.

I walked my dad outside.
"You okay son?"

"Did you see what she did?" I asked still reeling from what had happened.

"I did." My dad said with a small grin.

"She could have been killed."

My dad chuckled. "Dad, it's not funny."

"No, it's not funny, I agree."

"Then why aren't you more upset?"

"Son, that woman loves you just as much as you love her. What she did was selfless. It is also exactly what you did for her. Do you have any idea how rare that kind of love is?"

I was staring at my dad. What he was saying was sinking into my stupefied brain.

"She does love me," I said still dazed.

"As much as you love her." He added.

That made me smile.

"I'm staying here tonight," I told him quickly.

"If she lets you." My dad added with a smirk.

That made me chuckle, "Yes, if she lets me."

She did.

39

One Month Later - Epilogue

Brady

I was the luckiest man in the world. Belle was walking towards me holding Mr. Bee's arm, and she looked radiant. She was wearing a long white dress that was simple and fit her frame perfectly. Her long wavy hair was braided intricately and adorned with delicate white flowers. She was breathtaking. Her blue eyes never left mine as she approached me, and pride filled me knowing that the magnificent woman walking down the aisle was only a few minutes away from being my wife. Mr. Bee handed her to me, and I shook his hand then he gave Belle a fatherly kiss on the cheek. I took her hands in mine, and kissed her on her lips; I couldn't help it. Pastor John coughed indicating that it had not been the time to kiss her yet, and everyone chuckled. I didn't care I loved this woman.

"You are beautiful Belle," I told my blushing bride. It was so cliché, but so true.

"You are looking very handsome yourself," she whispered back.

We were standing on the back patio of Belle's farmhouse. Green Mountain was providing a spectacular backdrop. Fall was the most beautiful month in Vermont, and the vibrant foliage was on full display. Bev, my Mom, and Mrs. Bee had transformed the backyard into a magical setting complete with tiny white lights and fresh wildflowers.

Our guest list was small, my family, Mr. and Mrs. Bee, The Gordon's, my new work brothers, and our closest friends.

Pastor John presided over the ceremony, and when he announced that we were husband and wife our friends and family clapped and cheered.

"You can 'now' kiss your bride." He said with a chuckle emphasizing the word now.

I gave Belle a pretty spectacular kiss if I do say so myself. When we pulled apart her beautiful pale blue eyes locked on to mine, and I wanted to whisk her away.

We had not been intimate since that one night back in June. We had had a few romantic evenings, which had been fulfilling and highly sensual, but we hadn't made love. I knew she was as eager as I was to consummate our marriage.

The Gordon's had been living in her house up until a few days ago, and we both had been crazy busy. Except for the night after she had encountered Mrs. Romella, Belle insisted that I go home each night. Belle's old fashion way of thinking was one of the things I loved about my wife. I was, however, glad that she had bent the rules that one time before I had gone to training. The Gordon's were going to stay on the farm and help us run it. I loved the place, and Belle was beyond happy that I wanted to live there. The Gordon's had moved into their pre-fab log home a half mile down the drive two days ago, and Bev had become an incredible surrogate mother figure in Belle's life.

Belle had enrolled in the County College, and she was both eager and nervous to start. I had started my job in Lansing; I had also been asked to join the newly formed State Search and Rescue Division. What I was most excited about, however, was that I had also received an invite to train with the newly established Vermont State S.W.A.T. The Range Master from training had recommended me. I would attend training sessions for one weekend a month for four months. After the four months, I would be called in when needed.

Our wedding guests enjoyed a catered dinner, and we danced to a band that often played at The Rustic. I asked for them to play a lot of slow songs so I could hold Belle.

The evening had drawn to a close, and I could not wait to take my new wife to bed. We weren't going to take a honeymoon right away. I was only a week into my new job, and Belle didn't want to miss any classes.

After the final guests, who were my parents and Tommy of course, had said goodbye, Belle and I walked out back to make sure that it was clean and void of food scraps. Animals would not hesitate to come on the patio if it meant getting a good meal. I didn't want anything interrupting our first night together as man and wife.

Satisfied with the clean-up that the catering service had done, Belle unplugged the string of tiny decorative lights and the patio was blanketed in darkness.

The moon was bright, and a million brilliant stars twinkled above us putting on a show for my wife and I. The moon was huge and illuminating. Green Mountain stood majestically in the moons soft glow.

Belle was staring at it, and I put my arm around her. She relaxed into my side and placed her head on my chest.

"It's beautiful," I said looking at the mountain.

"It is."

"How can something so magnificent cause so much pain?" Her voice was soft and thoughtful.

"The mountain didn't cause the pain Belle, people did."

Her arm tightened around my waist.

"I love it here Brady."

"And I love you."

She giggled.

"Thank you for wanting to live on the farm."

"This mountain, this farm, it helped make you who you are. I'd never ask you to leave it. I love it too." I kissed her cheek. "Especially now that I don't have to leave it every night."

Belle giggled knowing exactly what I was referring too.

She took my hand and led me inside.

"Let's go make someone to pass Green Mountain on too." She said playfully tugging my hand leading

me inside. I loved this woman. I loved my life.
Four months ago I barely left my house, meeting
Belle had changed my life. I stopped walking and
pulled my wife tightly against me, threaded my
hands through her softly bound hair.
"I love you, Belle," I whispered.
"I love you too Brady."
Then I picked up my bride and I walked her into
our room that was in the house that was on the
farm that looked upon Green Mountain.

The End

Thank you for reading Die For You. This book
and its characters are fictional. If you have a
moment I would appreciate you posting a review.
To read more of my books go to
www.zannesweeney.com